Amazon "The Best Books of [illegible] oks We Like" * May 2010 Indie Next List "Great Reads" * *Historical Novels Review* Editors' Choice

Praise for

The Hand That First Held Mine

"Artful." — *Los Angeles Times*

"[A] wistful English love story . . . O'Farrell is an excellent storyteller who expertly evokes the sharp thrill of first love and the sleepless, besotted blur of new-motherhood." — *Bust*

"[O'Farrell's] mesmerizing, enormously satisfying fifth novel . . . revolves around two fiercely independent, unmarried mothers . . . In viscerally poetic prose, O'Farrell captures 'the utter loneliness' of motherhood and 'the constant undertow of maternal anxiety' . . . *The Hand That First Held Mine* evokes Shirley Hazzard's 1980 masterpiece, *The Transit of Venus.*"

— *Washington Post*

"Sea change has long been Maggie O'Farrell's forte — but never more evidently than in her affecting new novel . . . *The Hand That First Held Mine* is a woman's novel — full of moments, both intimate and universal, that will resonate particularly with all mothers. But the book has other gifts, also suitable for men, in its portrayal of change — especially sudden, deep, unprepared-for change — and the ways in which an instant can change a life forever." — *Buffalo News*

"O'Farrell creates a suspenseful atmosphere . . . When she finally reveals the connections between the two generations and lifts the opaque curtain, we enter a scene of surprising grace and hopefulness."

—*Boston Globe*

"Many contemporary female novelists have tackled this terrain, but few have reported back in such depth . . . O'Farrell's sharpness of perception, her talent for the telling detail and the ability to evoke both places and states of mind show that she could set her characters free to explore the world and create their own destinies. This suggests that it will be worth watching for her future work." — *Washington Times*

"O'Farrell has a singular knack for sensing the magnetic fields that push and pull people in love . . . A remarkably taut and unsentimental whole that embraces the unpredictable, both in love and in life."

—Amazon, Best Books of April 2010

"O'Farrell draws these seemingly disparate lives together deftly, with great feeling and perfect tension, making for a superb read."

—*Historical Novels Review*

"[O'Farrell's] writing is haunting, intriguing, almost an art form . . . It's hard to put this book down . . . Reading *The Hand That First Held Mine* is like riding a roller coaster: never knowing what's around the next bend, but anticipating a thrill; and when the ride is over, one wishes to buy a ticket for more of the same." —*New York Journal of Books*

"*The Hand That First Held Mine* by Maggie O'Farrell is one of those surprisingly riveting literary novels that will have you in tatters when you turn its final pages . . . O'Farrell can really write." —*Booklist*

"O'Farrell brings to mind Sue Miller but with a British and darker flavor; her sure hand for psychological suspense . . . continues to be most impressive." —*Library Journal*

"O'Farrell is . . . ridiculously pleasurable to read. And now, undeniably literary with a capital L." — *Guardian* (UK)

"Like Daphne du Maurier before her, Maggie O'Farrell writes books designed to stir up the female subconscious and bring our most primal fears to the surface. Although you may resent the ease with which O'Farrell pulls your emotional strings, this book will still leave your stomach in knots." — *Daily Mail* (UK)

"*The Hand That First Held Mine* is award-winning O'Farrell's keenly anticipated follow-up to her richly imagined, deeply disturbing *The Vanishing Act of Esme Lennox,* which had reviewers reaching for superlatives and making glowing comparisons with Rebecca West, Daphne du Maurier and Katherine Mansfield. Her skilfully constructed new novel will surely test their vocabularies to the limit." — *Herald* (Scotland)

"O'Farrell has a remarkable ability to convey the texture of human emotion with precision. In *The Hand That First Held Mine,* she also demonstrates a masterful gift for storytelling." — *Observer* (UK)

"O'Farrell's fifth novel firmly establishes her as the thinking woman's (and book clubs') favourite author. Her combination of exquisite, almost dream-like prose and highly-pitched emotionally-wrought domestic drama certainly creates a heady pull." — *Mirror* (UK)

"Love, secrets, and motherhood make this novel emotionally gripping."
— *Elle* (UK)

"An intense story of love, motherhood and childhood secrets . . . It's beautifully written and thought-provoking. O'Farrell fans will not be disappointed." — *Grazia* (UK)

"Another delight . . . A compelling portrait of motherhood."
— *Good Housekeeping* (UK)

"*From After You'd Gone* to *The Vanishing Act of Esme Lennox,* Maggie O'Farrell has written movingly about the female psyche and familial trauma. With *The Hand That First Held Mine,* she applies that skill to issues of early parenthood in a novel that plays to all her strengths."

—*Financial Times* (UK)

"Searingly unforgettable." —*Easy Living* (UK)

"O'Farrell's cinematically vivid novel is moody and powerful and plotted at a breakneck pace. This book, like life, will disarm you with its unannounced twists and tragedies and moments of unexpected beauty. She delivers to readers that rarest of experiences—total emotional investment. Hers is a brilliant feat of prose marksmanship—also, it made me cry on the subway."

—Heidi Julavits, author of *The Effect of Living Backwards* and *The Uses of Enchantment*

"O'Farrell deftly depicts the long-after shocks of death, betrayal, and life-changing love as her richly complicated characters play out an immensely satisfying plot. *The Hand That First Held Mine* is a dazzling and absorbing novel."

—Margot Livesey, author of *The House on Fortune Street*

"O'Farrell is an uncommonly perceptive writer, and *The Hand That First Held Mine* is an unforgettable story of family, ambition, and love. I couldn't stop thinking about it long after I read the final page."

—Lauren Grodstein, author of *A Friend of the Family*

The Hand That First Held Mine

By Maggie O'Farrell

After You'd Gone

My Lover's Lover

The Distance Between Us

The Vanishing Act of Esme Lennox

The Hand That First Held Mine

The Hand That First Held Mine

Maggie O'Farrell

Mariner Books
Houghton Mifflin Harcourt
Boston New York

for IZ
for SS
for WD

First Mariner Books edition 2011

First U.S. edition

www.hmhbooks.com

First published in Great Britain by Headline Review, an imprint of Headline Publishing Group, 2010

Library of Congress Cataloging-in-Publication Data
O'Farrell, Maggie, date.
The hand that first held mine : a novel / Maggie O'Farrell.
p. cm.
ISBN 978-0-547-33079-2
ISBN 978-0-547-42318-0 (pbk.)
1. Women painters—Fiction. 2. Motherhood—Fiction. 3. Family secrets—Fiction. 4. London (England)—Fiction. 5. Psychological fiction. I. Title.
PR6065.F36H36 2010
823'.914—dc22 2009042058

Printed in the United States of America

DOM 10 9 8 7 6 5 4 3 2 1

And we forget because we must.

—*Matthew Arnold*

Part One

Listen. The trees in this story are stirring, trembling, readjusting themselves. A breeze is coming in gusts off the sea, and it is almost as if the trees know, in their restlessness, in their head-tossing impatience, that something is about to happen.

The garden is empty, the patio deserted, save for some pots with geraniums and delphiniums shuddering in the wind. A bench stands on the lawn, two chairs facing politely away from it. A bicycle is propped up against the house but its pedals are stationary, the oiled chain motionless. A baby has been put out to sleep in a pram and it lies inside its stiff cocoon of blankets, eyes obligingly shut tight. A seagull hangs suspended in the sky above and even that is silent, beak closed, wings outstretched to catch the high thermal draughts.

The house is set apart from the rest of the village, behind dense hedge, on the crest of a cliff. This is the border between Devon and Cornwall, where the two counties crouch, eyeing each other. It is a much-disputed piece of land. It would not do to look too long at the soil here, soaked as it will be with the blood of Celts, Anglo-Saxons, Romans, filled out with the rubble of their bones.

However, this happens in a time of relative peace for Britain: late summer in the mid-1950s. A gravelled path curves towards the front door of the house. On the washing-line, petticoats and vests, socks and stays, nappies and handkerchiefs snap and writhe in the breeze. A radio can be heard from somewhere, one of the neighbouring houses perhaps, and the muffled thwack of an axe falling on wood.

The garden waits. The trees wait. The seagull, balancing in the sky above the washing, waits. And then, just as if this is a stage set and there is an audience, watching from a hushed dark, there are voices. Noises off. Somebody screams, another person shouts, something heavy hits the floor. The back door of the house is wrenched open. 'I can't bear it! I tell you, I can't!' the someone shrieks. The back door is slammed, resoundingly, and a person appears.

She is twenty-one, soon to be twenty-two. She is wearing a blue cotton dress with red buttons. A yellow scarf holds back her hair. She is marching across the patio and she is holding a book. In her bare feet, she stamps down the steps and across the lawn. She doesn't notice the seagull, which has turned in the air to look down on her, she doesn't notice the trees, which are tossing their branches to herald her arrival, she doesn't even notice the baby as she sweeps past the pram, heading for a tree stump at the bottom of the garden.

She sits herself down on this tree stump and, attempting to ignore the rage fanning through her veins, she balances the book on her lap and begins to read. *Death be not proud,* the words begin, *though some have called thee mighty and Dreadful.*

She bends with tense concentration over the page, sighing and flexing her shoulders. Then, without warning, she lets out a sudden growl and flings the book away from her. It hits the grass with a subdued thud, its pages fluttering closed. There it lies, surrounded by grass.

She gets to her feet. She doesn't do it as anybody else would, gradually moving from sitting to standing. She leaps, she starts, she bounds, she seems to stamp on the soil as she rises as if, like Rumpelstiltskin, she would crack it open.

Standing, she is at once confronted by the sight of a farmer in the lane, driving a flock of sheep, a switch in one hand, a dog darting about him. These sheep encapsulate what she hates about her home: their shredded, filthy backsides, their numb-faced stupidity, their witless bleating. She would like to drive them all into a threshing machine, over the cliff, anything, just to rid herself of the sight.

She turns away from the sheep, away from the house. She keeps only the sea in her sights. She has had a creeping fear of late that what she wants most – for her life to begin, to take on some meaning, to turn from blurred monochrome into glorious technicolour – may pass her by. That she might not recognise it if it comes her way, might fail to grasp for it.

She is closing her eyes to the sea, to the presence of the cast-aside book, when there is the sound of feet thudding through grass and a voice, saying, 'Sandra?'

She snaps upright as if she has received an electric shock. '*Alex*andra!' she corrects. This is her name, given to her at birth, but her mother later decided she didn't like it and shortened it to its final syllables.

'Alexandra,' the child repeats obediently. 'Mother says, "What are you doing and will you come in and—"'

'Away!' Alexandra screams. 'Go away!' And she returns crossly to her stump, to the book, to her analysis of Death and its needless pride.

At the exact same moment, half a mile away, Innes Kent – aged thirty-four, art dealer, journalist, critic, self-confessed hedonist – is kneeling on the dirt to examine the underside of his car. He has no idea what he is looking for but feels that he ought to look anyway. He is ever the optimist. The car is a silver and ice-blue MG; Innes loves it more than almost anything else in the world and it has just ground to a standstill at the side of this country lane. He straightens up.

And he does what he does in most situations that frustrate him: he lights a cigarette. He gives the wheel an experimental kick, then regrets it.

Innes has been in St Ives, visiting the studio of an artist whose work he'd been hoping to buy. He had found the artist rather drunk and the work far from completion. The whole excursion has been a raging disaster. And now this. He grinds his cigarette underfoot, then sets off down the lane. He can see a cluster of houses ahead, the curved wall of a harbour reaching out into the sea. Someone will know the whereabouts of a garage, if they have garages in this god-forsaken place.

Alexandra does not – cannot – know the proximity of Innes Kent. She doesn't know that he is coming, getting ever closer with every passing second, walking in his hand-made shoes along the roads that separate them, the distance between them shrinking with every well-shod step. Life as she will know it is about to begin but she is absorbed, finally, in her reading, in a long-dead man's struggle with mortality.

As Innes Kent turns into her road, Alexandra raises her head. She places the book on the ground again, this time more gently, and stretches, her arms held high. She twirls a strand of hair between finger and thumb, hooks a daisy between her toes and plucks it – she has always had gymnastic joints; it is something of which she is rather proud. She does this again and again until all eight gaps between her toes hold the frank yellow eye of a daisy.

Innes comes to a halt beside a gap in a thick hedge. He peers through. A pretty sort of country house with bushes, grass, flowers, that kind of thing – a garden, he supposes. Then he sees, close by, seated under a tree, a woman. Innes's interest never fails to be piqued by the proximity of a woman.

This specimen is without shoes, hair held off her neck in a yellow scarf. He raises himself on tiptoe to see better. The most exquisite column of a neck, he decides. If he were pressed to write a description of it, he would be forced to employ the word 'sculptural' and possibly even 'alabaster', which are not terms he would bandy about lightly. Innes's background is in art. Or perhaps 'foreground' would be a more accurate term. Art is not a background for Innes. It is what he breathes, what makes life continue; he looks and he doesn't see a tree, a car, a street, he sees a potential still-life, he sees an interplay of light and shade and colour, he sees a deliberate arrangement of chosen objects.

And what he sees when he looks at Alexandra in her yellow scarf and blue dress is a scene from a fresco. Innes believes he is beholding a perfect rural madonna, in profile, in a marvellously – he thinks – tight-fitting blue frock, with her baby slumbering a few feet away. He shuts one eye and regards the scene first with one eye, then the other. Really, it's a beautiful composition, with the tree overhead counterpointed by the flat stretch of grass and the uprightness of the woman and her neck. He would like to see it painted by one of the Italian masters, by Piero della Francesca or Andrea del Sarto perhaps. She can even pick flowers with her toes! What a creature!

Innes is smiling to himself, trying it out again with both eyes, when the scene is shattered by the madonna saying in a clear voice, 'Don't you know it's very bad manners to spy on people?'

He is so taken aback that for a moment he is speechless (not something to which he is accustomed) and he watches, fascinated, as the woman stands up from her tree stump. The della Francesca madonna morphs before his very eyes into a version of Marcel Duchamp's *Nude Descending a Staircase.* What a sight! The woman coming towards him down the raised lawn echoes Duchamp's effect exactly! Her anger seems to spike the very air!

Innes has been steeped in the Dadaists of late, so much so that two nights previously he had a dream entirely within one of their paintings. 'My second favourite dream', he rates it. (The first is too graphic to relate.)

'It is also,' the madonna is bearing down on him, jaw set, hands on hips, and he has to say he is rather glad of the hedge between them, 'illegal. I am perfectly within my rights to summon a policeman.'

'I'm sorry,' he manages to say. 'My car. It seems to have broken down. I'm looking for a garage.'

'Does this look like a garage to you?' Her voice is not, as he might have expected, smoothed with a Devonian burr but sharp and cut like a diamond.

'Um. No. It does not.'

'Well, then,' she is advancing ever closer to her side of the hedge, 'goodbye.'

As she says this, Alexandra gets her first proper look at the peeping Tom. He has hair quite a bit longer than she has ever seen on a man. His shirt has an unusually high collar and is daffodil yellow. His suit is light grey needle cord and has no collar at all; the tie he is wearing is the colour of duck eggs. Alexandra comes two steps closer. Daffodils, her mind reiterates, duck eggs.

'I wasn't spying,' the man is protesting, 'I assure you. I'm seeking aid. I find myself in a bit of a fix. My car has broken down. Would you happen to know of a garage near here? I don't mean to tear you away from your baby but I have to be back in London sharpish as I have a print deadline. Nightmare upon nightmare. Any assistance and I'm your grateful slave.'

She blinks. She has never heard anyone speak like this before. *Sharpish, fix, print deadline, nightmare upon nightmare, grateful slave.* She would like to ask him to say it all again. Then part of the speech filters through to her. 'It's not my baby,' she snaps. 'It's nothing to do with me. It's my mother's.'

'Ah.' The man inclines his head sideways. 'I'm not sure I would categorise that as *nothing* to do with you.'

'Wouldn't you?'

'No. It must at least be acknowledged as your sibling.'

There is a slight pause. Alexandra tries, without success, not to examine his clothes again. The shirt, that tie. Daffodils and eggs. 'You're from London, then?' she asks.

'I am.'

She sniffs. She adjusts the scarf across her forehead. She examines the bristles on the man's chin and wonders why he hasn't shaved. And, unfathomably, a half-formed plan of hers crystallises into a definite desire. 'I'm planning,' she says, 'on going to live in London myself.'

'Is that so?' The man starts to rummage animatedly in his pockets. He brings out an enamelled green cigarette case, removes two cigarettes and offers her one. She has to lean over the hedge to take it.

'Thank you,' she says. He lights it for her, cupping the match in his hands, then uses the same match on his own cigarette. Close up, she thinks, he smells of hair-oil, cologne and something else. But he moves back before she can identify it.

'Thanks,' she says again, indicating the cigarette, and inhales.

'And what,' the man says, as he shakes out the match and tosses it aside, 'may I ask, is holding you back?'

She thinks about this. 'Nothing,' she answers, and laughs. Because it's true. Nothing stands in her way. She nods towards the house. 'They don't know yet. And they'll be set against it. But they can't stop me.'

'That's the spirit,' he says, smoke curling from his mouth. 'So, you're running away to the capital?'

'Running,' Alexandra replies, drawing herself up to her full height, 'but not away. You can't run away from home if you've already left. I've been away at university.' She takes a draw on her cigarette, glan towards the house, then back at the man. 'Actually, I was sent down and—'

'From university?' the man cuts in, cigarette halfway to his mouth.

'Yes.'

'How very dramatic. For what crime?'

'For no crime at all,' she returns, rather more heatedly than necessary because the injustice of it still stings. 'I was walking out of an exam and I came out of a door reserved for men. I'm not allowed to graduate unless I apologise. They,' she nods again at the house, 'didn't even want me to go to university in the first place but now they're not speaking to me until I go back and apologise.'

The man is looking at her as if committing her to memory. The stitching on his shirt is in blue cotton, she notices, the cuffs and the collar. 'And are you going to apologise?'

She flicks ash from her cigarette and shakes her head. 'I don't see why I should. I didn't even know it was only for men. There was no sign. And I said to them, "Well, where's the door for women?" and they said there wasn't one. So why should I say sorry?'

'Quite. Never say sorry unless you are sorry.' They smoke for a moment, not looking at each other. 'So,' the man says, eventually, 'what are you going to do in London?'

'I'm going to work of course. Though I might not get a job,' she says, suddenly despondent. 'Someone told me that for secretarial work you need a typing speed of sixty words per minute and I'm currently up to about three.'

He smiles. 'And where will you be living?'

'You ask a lot of questions.'

'Force of habit.' He shrugs unapologetically. 'I'm a journalist, among other things. So. Your digs. Where will they be?'

'I don't know if I want to tell you.'

'Why ever not? I shan't tell a soul. I'm very good about secrets.'

She throws her cigarette butt into the green, unfurling leaves of the hedge. 'Well, a friend gave me the address of a house for single women in Kentish Town. She said—'

His face betrays only the slightest twitch of amusement. 'A house for single women?'

'Yes. What's funny about that?'

'Nothing. Absolutely nothing. It sounds . . .' he gestures '. . . marvellous. Kentish Town. We'll be practically neighbours. I'm in Haverstock Hill. You should come and visit, if they allow you out.'

Alexandra arches her brows, as if pretending to think about it. Part of her doesn't want to give in to this man. There is something about him that suggests he is used to getting his way. For some reason she thinks thwarting him would do him good. 'That might be possible, I really don't know. Perhaps—'

Unfortunately for everyone, Dorothy chooses that moment to make her entrance. Some signal on her maternal radar has informed her of a male predator in the vicinity of her eldest daughter. 'May I help you?' she calls, in a tone that contradicts the sentence.

Alexandra whirls around to see her mother advancing down the lawn, baby's bottle held out like a pistol. She watches as Dorothy takes in the man, all the way from his light grey shoes to his collarless suit. By the sour turn to her mouth, Alexandra can tell at once that she does not like what she sees.

The man gives Dorothy a dazzling smile and his teeth appear very white against his tanned skin. 'Thank you, but this lady,' he gestures towards Alexandra, 'was assisting me.'

'My *daughter*,' Dorothy stresses the word, 'is rather busy this morning. Sandra, I thought you would be keeping an eye on the baby. Now, what can we—'

'*Alexandra!*' Alexandra shouts at her mother. 'My name is Alexandra!'

She is aware that she is behaving like a cross child but she cannot bear this man to think her name is Sandra.

But her mother is adept at two things: ignoring her daughter's tantrums and extracting information from people. Dorothy listens to the story about the broken-down car and, within seconds, has dispatched the man off down the road with directions to a mechanic. He looks back once, raises his hand and waves.

Alexandra feels something close to rage, to grief, as she hears his footsteps recede down the lane towards the village. To have been so close to someone like him and then for him to be snatched away. She kicks the tree stump, then the baby's pram wheel. It is a particular brand of fury, peculiar to youth, that stifling, oppressive sensation of your elders outmanoeuvring you.

'What on earth is wrong with you?' Dorothy hisses, jiggling the pram handle because the baby has woken up, squawking and tussling. 'I come down here to find you flirting with some – some gypsy over the hedge. In broad daylight! For all to see. Where is your sense of decorum? What kind of an example are you setting for your brothers and sisters?'

'And, speaking of them,' Alexandra pauses before adding, *'all of them,* where's your sense of decorum?' She sets off up the garden. She cannot spend another second in her mother's company.

Dorothy stops jiggling the handle of the pram and stares after her, open-mouthed. 'What do you mean?' she shouts, forgetting momentarily the proximity of the neighbours. 'How dare you? How dare you address me in such a fashion? I'll be speaking to your father about this, I will, as soon as he—'

'Speak! Speak away!' Alexandra hurls over her shoulder as she sprints up the garden and crashes her way into the house surprising, as she does so, a patient of her father's who is waiting in the hallway.

As she reaches the bedroom she is forced to share with three of her younger siblings, she can still hear her mother's voice, screeching from the garden: 'Am I the only one in this house to demand standards? I don't know where you think you're going. You're supposed to be helping me today. You're meant to be minding the baby. And the silver needs doing and the china. Who do you think is going to do it? The ghosts?'

Elina jerks awake. She is puzzled by the darkness, by the way her heart is fluttering in her chest. She seems to be standing, leaning against a wall of surprising softness. Her feet feel a long way away from her. Her mouth is dry, her tongue stuck to her palate. She has no memory at all of what she is doing here, standing in the dark, dozing like this against a wall. Her mind is blank, like a ream of unmarked paper. She turns her head and suddenly, with a great heaving, everything swerves on its axis because she sees the window, she sees Ted next to her, she sees that she is not in fact standing. She is lying. On her back, hands clasped over her chest, a stone lady on a tomb.

The room is filled with the sound of breathing. A pipe somewhere in the house shudders, then falls silent. There is a slight scratching on the roof tiles above her, like the clawed foot of a bird.

It must have been the baby who woke her, shifting its curled position inside her, stirring perhaps after a long sleep, a leg kicking out, a hand flailing against skin. It's been happening a lot lately.

Elina swivels her head to look around the darkened room. The furniture, crouching blackly in the corners, the blind over the window that glows with same dirty orange as the streetlights. Ted beside her, hunched under the duvet. Books are piled up on Ted's bedside table, his mobile phone glows green in the gloom. On her bedside table there is a stack of something that looks in the dark like outsize handkerchiefs.

There is another noise that comes from somewhere near Elina's head, a sharp, sudden *heh-heh* sound, like someone clearing their throat.

She starts to turn over in bed, towards Ted, but she is struck with a searing pain in her stomach, as if her skin is splitting, as if someone is holding a blowtorch against her. It makes her gasp and she puts down her hands to check, to reassure herself with the feel of the drum-tight skin, the swell of the baby. But there's nothing there. Her hands encounter only space. No swollen bump. No baby. She clutches her stomach and feels deflated, loose skin.

Elina struggles upright – the scald of that pain again – letting out a strange, hoarse scream, and seizes Ted by the shoulder. 'Ted,' she says.

He groans, burying his face in the pillow.

She shakes him. 'Ted. Ted, the baby's gone – it's gone.'

He springs from the bed and stands in the middle of the room, in just a pair of shorts, his hair spiked, his face stricken. Then his shoulders slump. 'What are you talking about?' he says. 'He's right there.'

'Where?'

He points again. 'There. Look.'

Elina looks. There is indeed something on the floor beside her. In the half-darkness, it appears to be a bed that a dog might sleep in, an oval basket. Except this one has handles and inside it something is swaddled in white. 'Oh,' she says. She reaches for the light switch, clicks it on and the room is immediately flooded with yellow brightness. 'Oh,' she says again. She looks down at the empty skin of her stomach, then at the baby. She turns to Ted, who has flopped down again on the bed, muttering about how she'd scared the shit out of him.

'I had the baby?' she says.

Ted, caught in the act of plumping his pillow, stops. His face is uncertain, frightened. Don't be frightened, she wants to say, it's all right. But instead she says, 'I had it?' because she needs to establish this: she needs to ask, to vocalise it, to hear it asked.

'Elina . . . you're joking. Aren't you?' He lets out a nervous, low laugh. 'Don't, it's not funny. Maybe you . . . Maybe you've been dreaming. You must have been dreaming. Why don't you . . .' Ted trails into silence. He puts a hand on her shoulder and for a minute he doesn't seem to know what to say. He stares at her and she stares back. She allows the thought: There is a baby in the room with us. It's here. She wants to turn around and look at it again but Ted is clasping her shoulder now and clearing his throat. 'You had the baby,' he says slowly. 'It was . . . in hospital. Remember?'

'When?' she says. 'When did I have it?'

'Jesus, El, are you—' He stops himself, rubs a hand over his face, then says, in a more level voice, 'Four days ago. You had three days of labour and then . . . and then he came. You came out of hospital last night. You discharged yourself.'

There is a pause. Elina thinks about what Ted has said. She lays out the facts with which he has provided her, side by side, in her head. Hospital, baby, discharged, three days of labour. She considers the idea of three days and she considers the pain in her abdomen but decides not to mention it now.

'Elina?'

'What?'

He is peering into her face. He smooths the hair away from her brow, then rests his hands on her shoulders. 'You're probably . . . you must be terribly tired and . . . Why don't you go back to sleep?'

She doesn't answer. She struggles out from under his touch, across the mattress. She clutches at her abdomen as she does so, pressing her teeth into her lip. It feels, down there, as if something might very easily spill out unless she holds it in. She crouches above the baby, looking carefully down. He, Ted said. A boy, then. He is awake, eyes wide and alert. He looks up at her from his wicker basket, his face quizzical, enquiring. He is wrapped up like a gift in a white blanket, his hands covered with white mittens. Elina reaches out and pulls them off – tiny things they are, light as cirrus clouds. His hands flex, opening and closing on empty air.

'Ah,' he says. A strangely adult noise. Very firm, very considered.

Elina puts out her hand and touches the damp heat of his forehead, the rising and falling of his tiny, bird-like chest, the curve of his cheek, the curled flesh of the ear. His eyes blink as her fingers cross his vision, his lips opening and shutting like someone lost for words.

She slides her palms under him, lifts him up. He is her baby, after all; she is allowed. She puts him against her, his head below her shoulder, his feet in the crook of her arm. There is, she acknowledges, something familiar in the weight of him, the lie of him. He twists his head towards her, then away, towards her, away, then gazes fixedly at the strap of her T-shirt.

'You do remember, don't you?' Ted says again, from the bed.

Elina pulls her face into a smile. 'Of course,' she says.

When she returns to bed, a long time later – she has been staring at the baby, lifting off his hat, looking at his hair, the surprising deep-water blue of his eyes, putting her finger in his palm to feel the answering clench – Ted is asleep, his head resting on his arm. She is sure she won't sleep again: how can she when she's got so cold, when there is this pain, when she seems to have had a baby? She edges as close as she dares to Ted, whose body seems to fan heat towards her. Elina pushes her head down underneath the duvet, where it is dark and hot. She won't sleep again.

But she must have, because what feels like minutes later she comes round to a bedroom so bright and glaring she has to hold her hand over her face and Ted is dressed and saying he has to go and kissing her goodbye.

'Where are you going?' she says, struggling on to her elbow.

His face falls. 'To work,' he says. 'No choice,' he says. 'I'm sorry,' he says. 'The film,' he says. 'Behind on the assemblies,' he says. 'Take some leave at the end of the shoot,' he says. 'Hopefully,' he says.

This is followed by a short argument because Ted wants to call his mother to come and help. Elina can hear herself saying no, can feel herself shaking her head. He then says she can't be on her own, that he'll call her friend Suki, but the idea of anyone in the house is horrifying. Elina cannot think how she would talk to these people; she cannot imagine what she might say. No, she says, no and no again.

And she must be winning this argument because Ted is scratching his head, fiddling with his bag and kissing her goodbye, and then she hears him descend the stairs, the front door slam and the house is silent.

She longs more than anything to sink again into the oblivion of sleep, to press her cheek into the pillow, to bring down the portcullises of her lids over her eyes. She can feel the proximity of such sleep, she can taste it. But next to her is the noise of puffing, struggling, small mammalian pants.

She peers over the edge of the bed and there he is again. The baby. *'Hei,'* Elina says, surprising herself by talking Finnish.

The baby doesn't answer. He is intent on his own battle with something unseen: his arms flail in the air around him, he makes small, gruff, growling noises. And then, as if a switch has been flicked, he lets out a yell, a long, loud shout of anguish.

Elina draws back, as if she's been slapped. Then she sees that she has to get up. She has to address this situation. It is up to her. There is no one else. The baby takes a big breath and launches into another cry. Elina bends, wincing, and picks him up. She holds his rigid, angry body. What can be wrong with him? She tries to summon up the advice of the baby books she's read but can remember nothing. She walks to the window and back. 'There, there,' she tries. 'It's OK.'

But the baby screams, arching his back, his face all mouth, his skin a livid pink.

'It's OK,' she says again, and then she sees that he is twisting his head, stretching wide his mouth, like a front-crawl swimmer turning for air. Hungry. That means he's hungry – of course. Why didn't she think of that?

She sits down in the chair, just in time because her legs are feeling strangely shaky, and lifts her T-shirt, hesitating, trying to remember those mystifying diagrams of breastfeeding. Latching on. Positioning. Common feeding problems. But she needn't have worried. The baby seems to know exactly what to do. He goes for the breast like a dog offered a bone and begins to suck, avidly for a few seconds, then more slowly, then avidly again. Elina stares down at him, dumbstruck by his calm, his efficiency. They sit there for what feels to Elina like an unaccountably long time. Is this normal? To sit like this for half an hour, three-quarters of an hour, more than an hour? The morning goes on outside in the street: people walking up the street towards the Heath, people walking down the street towards the bus stop. The patches of sunlight edge across the carpet towards Elina's feet and the baby still feeds.

Elina thinks she may have fallen asleep in the chair because she comes to and her whole body is in sunlight and the baby lying on her lap, rather like a cat, staring this time at her wristwatch.

She tests herself, scans her mind. Has she remembered anything?

Has it come back to her while she was sleeping? The birth, the birth, the birth, she intones to herself, you must remember, you have to remember. But no. She can recall being pregnant. She can see the baby here, lying in her lap. But how it got there is a mystery.

She puts both hands to her face and rubs her skin, scuffing it with her palms, trying to rouse herself. 'So,' she says into the silence, her voice wavering slightly. Why is the house so silent, as silent as someone expecting an answer? 'Here we are.' She is, she notices, talking Finnish again. 'What would you like to do now?' she asks the baby, as if he is a guest with whom she has only the slightest acquaintance.

She raises herself up, slowly, slowly, clutching his body to her, and trails downstairs, feeling her way, never taking her eyes off the baby's face. Her son. He came out of her. She knows this because Ted says so and because there is something in the angle of the baby's forehead, the swirl of hair there, that brings to mind her father. She passes the open bathroom door as she drifts downstairs and she sees on the floor a changing mat with red stripes and she remembers, she actually remembers, buying this. She remembers being disgusted by the decoration on such things – arrays of mincing teddy bears, anthropomorphised fish with leering grins, ducks with long-lashed, kohled gazes. Around the mat are arranged some nappies, a packet of wipes, a cloth octopus, a jar of ointment. Who put these things there? Was it her? And when?

At the bottom of the stairs is a pram and this, too, she remembers. Their friend Simmy bought it for them. He arrived with it one evening, pushing it in front of him. This was before. When she was still pregnant. A strange contraption it is, with silver wheels, a concertinaed hood in navy blue, a smart, shiny brake for the wheels. There are sheets in the pram, she sees, and a blanket. She hovers next to it for a moment. Then she lowers the baby into it, just to see what will happen. The baby lies there matter-of-factly, as if used to such things. He kicks his legs. He gazes at the hood, he gazes past her, he gazes at the rivet holding the hood to the pram sides. He closes his eyes and falls asleep. Elina stands there, watching him for a while. Then she goes into the kitchen.

She arrives, somehow, at the doors to the garden. Two of them, large panes of reinforced glass. For security, Ted said, when she asked why the glass was so thick, so solid. She finds she is holding a mug, a folded newspaper. She bends to put them on the floor, and as she does so, something in her abdomen twangs and she gasps with the pain of it, dropping the mug and paper. She grips the door frame to stop herself falling, leaning her forehead into the glass, pressing her hand over the spot. She swears, in a variety of languages, over and over.

When she opens her eyes again, everything is still as it was. The kitchen behind her. The garden in front of her. It is very simple, she tells herself. You were pregnant and now you have a baby. But why doesn't she remember having it?

At the bottom of the garden is a wooden building, a room. Elina's studio, built for her by Ted. Or, at least, Ted paid two Polish men to build it for her. It is made of ash, bitumen, glass-wool insulation, stainless steel – she had asked them the words and they had had to look them up in a Polish dictionary to find the English word for her to compare, side by side, in her head with the Finnish. It had made them all laugh. One asked her if she missed Finland and she had said no, and then said yes, sometimes. But she hadn't lived there for a long time now. And did they miss Poland, she asked them. They had both nodded, silently. 'We go back,' one told her, 'in two years.'

Which means they must be back in Poland by now. Elina looks down the garden at the studio they built for her, the straight sides panelled in ash, the bitumen roof. It says in her passport, on her tax return, on forms she has to fill in that she is an artist. But she doesn't know what it means. She cannot recall when she was last in her studio, she cannot remember how you be an artist, what you do, how you spend your time. Her life in that small wooden building, all the hours she's spent in there, seem as distant as her time in kindergarten.

She could – it is possible – go down there today. She could take the key from where it hangs next to the fridge, pick her way over the wet grass, pushing the baby in his squeaking pram, open the door and go inside. She could look at what is pinned to the wall, at any canvases she's left leaning against the cupboards; she could try to reconnect with whatever it was she'd been doing before. She isn't meant to be working, she knows. But she could read in her studio, she could sit and look at the light coming in through the window in the roof. There is a chair in there – she reupholstered it herself in green wool, next to a window. It would be a good place to perhaps try and remember things.

She is thinking about this, biting her lip, considering, when she realises that there is a scent, an odour in her nose that has been there all morning. A slightly cloying musk. Like unaired clothes. Like wet paper. Like milk.

Elina turns. She sniffs the air. Nothing except the slight tang of laundry soap. She sniffs her pyjama top, then her hair, the skin of her wrist, the crook of her elbow, the hard heel of her palm.

It's her. She is astonished. A new smell. She doesn't smell like she used to, the way she has smelt all her life. It's her.

Ted yanks back his chair and slumps into it, tossing his bag to the sofa behind him. He switches on the screens and, while waiting for them to flicker to life, he scoots in the chair across the editing suite towards the in-tray. Phone messages, a couple of letters, a request for a reference, a scrawled note from a producer about an editing copy of a film Ted finished recently. He pushes his chair towards the phone and is about to pick it up when he stops.

He flips a pen between thumb and finger. He uncaps it, recaps it. He places both hands on the curved edge of the desk. He glances at the screens in front of him, one of which is displaying some kind of error message, something about a missing file. He looks away, at his shoes, one of which he sees is coming undone, at the phone, which has a red light flashing on and off, at the fathomless black faces of the speakers, at the pile of stuff sitting on the sofa. Fruit baskets, bunches of flowers sheathed in cellophane, a baby blanket tied up with a ribbon, a monstrous satin dog with an expression of vapid joy. On his desk, right beside his elbow, is a gold carrier-bag. It is the stiff, cardboard type, given out in only the most expensive shops, with a blue thread wound through the top. The editing-house receptionist gave it to him as he came through the door. 'Congratulations,' she'd said. 'A little boy!' And she'd hugged him and Ted had felt the zip on her trousers dig into the flesh of his hip, the cold metal of her bangles on the back of his neck.

'Thank you,' he'd said, when he took the bag, nodding at all the people who had gathered around – the office manager, the girl who fetched the coffee, an actress he vaguely recognised, a few other editors. 'That's really nice of you. It's really . . .' And then he'd had to stop because if he ventured any further into that sentence he would start to cry. He hasn't cried since he was a child, not once in his adolescence, not even when he'd had that accident, coming off a scooter in Greece. But he could feel the tears right there, like a wave rising up in his chest. Dear God, what was wrong with him?

Ted reaches again for the phone but withdraws his hand, using it instead to roughly massage his forehead. He allows himself the thought: What are you doing here? This is madness, he should be at home, he should be with Elina, with the baby, not here, fiddling about with the rushes of a project he has no interest in – how many more bungled-heist movies does the world need anyway? Why is he here?

It seems astonishing to him, as he surveys the desk, that everything looks so exactly the same. The DVDs lined up on the shelf, the sheaf of pens in their pot, the screens sitting side by side, the computer mouse with its trailing leash, his reinforced wrist rest (a futile attempt to ease his RSI), the postcard of one of Elina's paintings pinned to the wall.

He stares at the postcard, the red line that bisects the blue triangle, that towers over the black shape crouched in the corner. He'd seen the painting as it emerged on the canvas. He wasn't supposed to have seen it – she didn't like anyone to see her work before she deemed it finished – but he'd peered through the window of her studio when he'd known she wasn't looking. It was his way of keeping up with what went on inside her head. He'd seen it hang on the wall of her gallery, he'd watched the red dot go up beside it at the private view and the glow on her face as she saw this. And now it hung in the house of a music producer and Ted often wondered if he loved it as much as he should, if he looked at it as much as he should, if it was hung in the right way, in the right light.

Four days ago, she'd almost died.

The thought has a physical effect on him. One of disorientation and nausea, like seasickness or looking down from a high building. He has to lean his head in his hands and breathe deeply, and he feels the earlier tears crowding into his throat.

She'd almost died right there in front of them all. He'd felt death in the room, like a cloud gathering itself somewhere up near the ceiling, and its presence felt oddly familiar, as if he'd been somehow expecting it, as if part of him had known all along that this was how it might end. *Don't look,* the nurse said to him, *don't look.* And plucked at his sleeve. But how could he not? How could he turn away, like the nurse wanted him to, when it was Elina lying there, when it was his fault she was pregnant in the first place, it was him who'd done it, he was the one who'd whispered that time, in that hotel in Madrid, *let's not bother, just this once?* The nurse had taken his arm then. *Come away,* she'd said, more firmly. *You mustn't look.*

But he couldn't not look. He'd held on to the metal rail of a gurney, shaken off the nurse. People were running and shouting to each other, and in the middle of the room lay Elina and her top half looked so serene. White and immovable, her face expressionless, her eyes half closed, her hands folded on her chest, she was a medieval saint from a painting. Her bottom half – Ted had never seen anything like it. And at that moment, he seemed to stop seeing it. He seemed to stop seeing anything at all. Except a horizon that was possibly the sea, a lead-coloured sea that heaved up and heaved down, a featureless expanse of water. It was its endlessness that made him feel queasy, its reflective skin that mirrored the clouded sky. *Where is she?* he could hear a voice saying. *Where is she?*

Ted pushes his chair away from the desk with such force that it strikes the edge of the glass coffee-table behind him. He stands, he walks to the porthole in the door and back again. He sits down in his chair. He stands again. He strides to the window and lowers the blinds with a flick. He pushes the mouse one way, then the other. He picks up the phone, calls through to Reception and tells them to send the heist-movie director straight through when he arrives.

Elina keeps having these odd jumps. Lapses, she thinks of them. She must tell Ted about them. It's like the needle on the record player her family once had. She and her brother used to put on one of their parents' old Beatles LPs and take turns in stamping on the floor. The needle would leap from one song to another. The glee, the unpredictability of it! You could be in the middle of Lucy and her diamond sky when all of a sudden John was on about a show tonight on trampoline. And then on again to Paul and the rain coming in.

But there must be some kind of karmic punishment for inflicting damage on LPs because this seems to be happening in Elina's life. Maybe 'jumps' isn't the word. Maybe her life has sprung four thousand holes. Because one minute it was early morning and she was discovering the new smell and then suddenly she is lying on the living-room floor and the phone is ringing.

Elina eases herself to her feet. The baby is lying on a rug next to her, arms waving in the air, as if he is directing traffic. She can feel that her hair is sticking up on one side, a little like the punk effect she used to try for when she was a teenager. She squints at the phone for a moment before picking it up. She is so tired that the floor tilts if she moves too fast. She rests a palm on the sofa arm to steady herself, remembering that she has done this very same thing only recently, steadying herself before answering the phone, and she has the distinct impression that she has spoken to her mother at some point today but cannot recall what they talked about. Maybe this is her again.

'Hello?' she says.

'Hi.' Ted's voice is speaking into her ear. It comes from a place of noise. She can hear people shouting, people walking, a rustle, a bang. It is not the hushed, respectful silence of the editing suite. He must be on set. 'How are you?' his voice says from out of the din. 'Are you OK? How's it going?'

Elina has no idea how she is, how it is going. But she says, 'Fine.'

'What have you been up to?'

'Um.' Elina looks about the room and catches sight of the laundry basket, full of wet washing. 'I did some laundry. And I spoke to my mother.'

'Uh-huh. What else?'

'Nothing.'

'Oh.'

There is a pause. She considers telling him about the lapses, the holes. How would she begin? With the story about the record player? Or would she just say, Ted, I have these moments where life disappears into a hole and I can't remember what happens in them? I can't, for example, recall the small matter of having had a baby?

'I . . . er . . .' she begins, but Ted interrupts.

'Have you eaten anything?'

She thinks about this. Has she? She might have. 'I can't remember,' she says.

'You can't remember?' Ted repeats, and his voice is full of horror. Someone close to him is shouting loudly about the catering van. Elina tries to comb her hair flat with her fingers and, as she does so, she catches sight of a yellow leaflet beside the phone entitled *Coping With Blood Loss.* She picks it up. She holds it to her face and looks at the printed words.

'Elina?' Ted's voice startles her.

'Yes,' she says. She drops the leaflet. It swoops and slides under a chair. She'll get it later.

'You need to eat. The midwife said so. Have you eaten anything? Can you remember eating anything?'

'I can,' she says quickly, and lets out a little laugh. 'I mean I did. I mean I can't remember what I was going to have for lunch.'

But she still isn't getting it right. 'Lunch?' Ted says. 'El, it's three thirty.'

She is genuinely surprised. 'Is it?'

'Have you been asleep?'

She looks round the room again, at the place where she was lying on the rug before he rang. The thick pile of it is imprinted with the shape of a body, like a murder scene. 'Maybe. Yes. I probably was.'

'Have you taken your painkillers?'

'Um.' She casts her eyes around the room again. What would the right answer be here? 'Yes,' she says.

'Listen, I have to go.' There is a pause. 'I think I'm going to call my mum.'

'No,' Elina says quickly. 'It's OK. I'm OK, honestly.'

'Are you sure?'

'Yes.'

'You've got her number, haven't you? Just in case. I'll be back around six, I think. We're pretty much finished here.' His voice is placatory, wary. 'I'll cook us a nice dinner then. But eat something now, OK?'

'OK.'

'You promise?'

'I promise.'

She is sitting in a chair near the back door, looking at her studio again when the doorbell rings. Elina freezes, one hand pressed to the window. She waits. Ted's mother? Did he call her after all? She'll just stay here in the kitchen. Whoever it is will think no one's in and go away. She turns back to the garden. The doorbell shrills again, for longer this time. Elina ignores it. It goes again, for even longer.

Still at the window, Elina begins to imagine a scenario in which Ted's mother calls him to say that Elina isn't answering the door. And then Ted will worry that something has happened and he'll have to leave work and come home. Elina raises herself out of the chair, carefully, carefully, and, leaning her weight on the wall, goes through to the hall. The baby, she sees, is back in his pram, asleep.

When she opens the door, the person on the doorstep – not Ted's mother, but a woman with frazzled yellow hair, her large body squeezed into stretchy blue trousers – doesn't wait to be invited in. She doesn't even wait for Elina to speak. She pushes past her, muttering about the rain, marches down the hallway and sits on Elina's sofa, busying herself with papers and files and pen lids.

Elina follows and stands before her on the carpet, astonished. She wants to say, who are you, what are you doing here, who sent you, but something about the files and papers strikes her dumb. She waits to see what will happen next.

'So.' The woman sighs and shifts her blue bottom against the sofa. 'You're Natalie.'

It isn't a question and Elina has to think about this. Is she Natalie? She doesn't think so. 'No,' she says.

The woman frowns. She scratches her hair with the end of the pen. 'You're not Natalie?'

Elina gives a firm shake of the head.

The woman flips over a piece of paper, screwing up her eyes, and says, 'Oh.' It is a sound full of disappointment, of weariness, and Elina wants to say sorry, she wants to apologise for not being Natalie. She wants to say that maybe she could be.

'You're Elina,' the woman says, with another sigh.

'Yes.'

'And how are we today, Elina?'

Elina finds the interchangeable use of the plural in English confusing. She is one person, one only. How can she be a 'we'? 'Fine,' she replies, hoping this woman will leave.

But the woman has a list of other questions. She wants to know what Elina is eating and how often. She wants to know if Elina is going out, how much she is sleeping, whether she has joined a group, if she is planning to join a group, if she's taking her pills, if she is getting any help.

'Help?' Elina repeats.

The woman shoots her a sharp glance from under her yellow fringe. Then she looks around the room. Then she looks at Elina's pyjamas. 'Do you live alone?' she says.

'No. There's my boyfriend but . . .'

'But what?'

'He's at work. He didn't want to be. I mean, he was going to take time off. But he's got this shoot that's overrun and . . . well . . . you know.'

This causes much scribbling in the file. This woman with her files and questions is making Elina tired. If she weren't here, Elina could stretch herself out on the rug, lay her head on her arm and fall asleep.

'And how is everything healing up?' the woman asks, peering at something in her file.

'Healing up?'

'The scar.'

'What scar?'

The woman gives her another sharp look. 'The section scar.' An expression of doubt crosses her features for a split second. 'You did have a section, didn't you?'

'A section?' Elina circles the word warily. It means, she is sure, a part of something or a bit of something. A slice. She puts her hands to her abdomen and thinks about the searing, blowtorch pain there. 'A section,' she murmurs again.

The woman glances again at her notes. She lifts a page in her file, she lets it fall. 'It says here . . . let's see . . . non-progressive labour, complications and – yes – emergency surgery, blood loss.'

Elina stares at her. She would like to reach down, pick up the woman's bag by its straps and hurl it through the window. She imagines the tinkling clatter of smashing glass, the fragmenting of something so perfect, so clear, and the satisfying thud as the bag hits the pavement.

The woman is glaring back at her, her brows lowered, her mouth open slightly.

'I need you,' Elina says, forming each word very slowly, 'to leave. Please. I'm very busy. I have to . . . I have to be . . . somewhere. Would you mind? Maybe we could do this another day.' She is careful to be polite. She has no idea who this woman is but that is no reason to be rude. She walks the woman through the hall towards the door. 'Thank you so much,' she says, as she shuts the door. 'Goodbye.'

Alexandra shuts herself in her room for the rest of the day, pushing a chair under the door handle to keep out the siblings. They chitter and moan on the other side but she doesn't relent. She pores over a map of London. She gets down a suitcase from the wardrobe, shakes the dust out of its purple satin interior, flicks through her coat-hangers, deciding what she'll take for her new life and what she'll leave. The smaller siblings, enthralled by the drama of it all, start to pass notes and biscuits and, inexplicably, a hair ribbon under the gap.

'Maybe you should say sorry to the university,' one advises through the keyhole, 'and they might take you back.'

'But I'm not sorry!' Alexandra cries. 'I'm not sorry at all.'

'But you could just say it,' the reasonable child says. 'You don't have to mean it.'

But Alexandra roams the room. She eats some of the biscuits, she reads a chapter or two of a book, she puts up her hair, she takes it down, she redoes it in a chignon. She writes some furious, blotted pages in her diary. She does handstands against the mirror.

At dusk, when the family are downstairs having their supper, the self-imprisoned Alexandra is leaning out of the window, as far as she can without falling out, and trying to balance herself there, legs and arms aloft.

She has just found the fulcrum of her weight – almost, almost, her feet off the ground, her hands in the air, a suspended angel girl – when she hears the put-put-put of an engine down in the lane. She raises her head: the fulcrum is lost, her feet crash to the floor and she scrapes her waist on the sill. She peers into the dark.

There! Along the lane comes a car, light-coloured, open-topped, hurtling round the bend, hugging tight the curves, the sound of the engine rising and falling. The person at the wheel is unrecognisable, hair wild in the wind, shoulders hunched, but she is sure it is him. Alexandra raises herself on tiptoe and gives a single, solitary, unseen wave.

And as she does so, there is a screech of brakes and the car swerves. With the engine still running, the figure – tall, dressed in a pale suit – leaps from the car. Alexandra sees the flash of something white in his hand. He seems to pause for a moment. Is he looking at the house? Why, she wonders wildly, has she not turned on the light? He would have seen her, he might have seen her, standing at the upper window. She thinks about running to the wall to switch it on, but she daren't lose sight of him.

She sees him tuck the white thing into the hedge. She is sure of this. And then he is getting back into the car and a moment later he disappears around the bend.

Alexandra sprints down the stairs, through the kitchen where her family are eating and, stopping only to snatch a torch from a hook, bursts from the back door. Her feet are bare as she runs over the damp grass, the trees and bushes black cut-outs against the sky.

She moves quickly, knowing she might not have long if her mother follows her. In her haste she almost misses the note tucked into the hedge but her torch beam finds it.

Alexandra, it reads, in rather uneven black letters, *Here is my card. Look me up when you come to London. I'll take you to lunch. Yours, Innes Kent*

And then a curious postscript: *I share your dislike of the shortening of names but I must say that I'm not sure 'Alexandra' is entirely suitable for you. It seems to me that you require a name with rather more brio. I see you as a 'Lexie'. What do you think?*

She reads the note twice and the postscript three times. She folds it and puts it into the pocket of her blue dress. She sits down on the tree stump in the dark. She is Lexie. She is going to London. She will have lunches with men in duck-egg ties.

'Do you remember . . .' Elina says, and Ted keeps his eyes fixed on the TV because never were three words more designed to fill him with unease '. . . that place we went with the shower made . . .' she pauses because an enormous yawn overtakes her, her jaw cracking, her eyes watering '. . . made of . . .' her voice is drowsy, vague, as if at any moment it might wander out of the range of sense '. . . a hosepipe?'

'A hosepipe?' he repeats, baffled.

'Yeah. It had a . . . you know.' She collapses against him, yawning again, folding herself up like a deck chair. 'A what do you call it?'

'Er. No idea.'

'A soap-dish,' she muttered, with her eyes closed. 'Made of a can.'

Ted scans his mind. He doesn't think he's ever been anywhere with a hosepipe for a shower. Then he tries to think of places they've been away together. Rome? Or was that with Yvette? Rome: Elina or Yvette? Or was it the one before Yvette, that blonde girl? What was her name? Rome was with Yvette – he remembers her having a tantrum about sun cream in the Campo dei Fiori. He feels a flush of relief that he hadn't come out with the word Rome, that he'd stopped himself just in time. There was a place in Norfolk that he and Elina had gone to, a hotel in a lighthouse, but that had had a proper shower, surely?

'. . . goat outside,' she is murmuring, 'with a baby goat – how do you say it? – that was really white. Remember? You said it was the only clean thing we saw our whole time there.'

And suddenly he does remember. The image is right there, in his mind, called up as precisely as if on one of his screens at work. A tiny, thin-legged kid goat with startling white hair and fondant-pink lips. 'In India?' he says.

'Mmm.' She nods, her head moving up and down in his lap.

'Kerala,' he says, and thumps the sofa arm, delighted to be assailed with a series of recollections all at once: Elina outside a shop selling spices, them walking together through a eucalyptus forest, the new white kid goat they passed every morning, its mother tied to a stake, the treble of its bleat, that train journey they'd taken overnight and how he'd kept being woken by people clattering up and down the corridor, the buzz of the blue light. 'Kerala,' he says again, 'yes. There are some photos somewhere, aren't there? I'm sure I took some. I could go and get them.'

When there is no reply he looks down at her. She has dipped into sleep, her hand pressed between her cheek and his thigh, her lips slightly parted. He feels thwarted, disgruntled, the urge to reminisce about their trip to India awakened yet not played out. It's not often he's able to rise to such conversations and the one time he is she falls asleep. He registers the urge to say, 'Kerala,' loudly, or to shift himself a little more abruptly than necessary, just to see if she'll wake up to hear what he remembers about India, but is then ashamed. Of course he shouldn't wake her. What kind of a person is he, to think such things?

He lets his hand fall gently to her side, where it rests on the green wool of her cardigan. He reaches behind him for the blanket they keep on the sofa and drapes it around her. Then he watches the minute flicker of the pulse in her neck and imagines the vein, deep below the skin, dilating then shrinking, dilating then shrinking with the hot, thick blood sent shooting from the heart. The elastic, muscular stretch of it, every three-quarters of a second.

He looks at the delta of veins at her wrist, the thin violet patterns on her eyelids, the trace of blue that runs through her cheek, the web of vessels at the curve of her instep. He wonders for the first time if they used just one person's blood to revive her or whether it was the blood of lots of different people. And whether she is still her, if the very blood that pumps around her body doesn't belong to her. At what point do you become someone else?

He wishes he could forget what had happened, like he forgets so many other things. He wishes he could take a cloth to it and rub it out; he wishes he could pull a screen or a blind down over it; he wishes that every time he looked at her he didn't see the thinness of her skin, the unbearable fragility of her veins, how easy they would be to puncture. Most of all, he wishes it had never happened. He wishes she were still pregnant, sitting here beside him, that the baby was still in her, that they were both safe and she was still complete.

Ted swallows to banish this thought. He clears his throat, flexes his shoulders to ease some stiffness in his neck. He is beginning to see, at the corner of his vision, a flat, featureless sea again, feel the queasy swell of its motion. He picks up the remote control and changes channels, one, two, three, four times. A game show, an advert, a woman standing in a garden, a man with a gun, a shot of a lion crouching in long grass. Ted tosses the remote down again.

His memory has always been bad. Worse than bad. Whole chunks of his life are lost in a hazy miasma. Ted is certain, pretty much, that he remembers nothing before he was about nine, when he fell out of a tree in a friend's garden and broke his arm. He remembers the friend's father taking him to casualty, the cooling hotness of the plaster cast, the nurse teaching him the word 'gypsophila', and how embarrassed he'd been at the sight of his mother running through casualty, her coat flapping behind her, shrieking, 'Where is my son?' The rest, though, is a pleasantly dim hum, like the noise of a badly tuned radio.

His mother has a zeal for reminiscence: 'Remember that beach where you rode a donkey?' she will say. 'There was a three-legged dog. And you had an ice-cream that fell to the ground. Remember how you cried and cried? Remember how I took you back to the shop to buy another one? Remember?' He will nod but his memory of the incident is no more than images like holiday snaps, supplied by her, shuffled before his eyes by her so often that they have come to resemble or replace the memories themselves. She has a whole collection of stories like this about him and he knows them all: the time a hatbox fell from a wardrobe on to his head and he had a dreadful cut on his nose, which made her ashamed to take him out; the time he won a goldfish at a fair but dropped it in the car park and she held his face to her dress until it stopped flipping and flopping about in the dust; the time he asked a bald man what had happened to all his hair; the time he'd sung a song to his cousin because she'd fallen and scraped her shin. They are so familiar from her retelling that he knows them off by heart. But they don't seem in any way connected to him.

It occurs to Ted now and for the first time, as he sits on the sofa with the head of his resurrected girlfriend in his lap and his baby son lying asleep across the room, that this is possibly because none of these stories tally with his own blurred impressions of his childhood. His mother's version, a carousel of treats and donkeys and fairs and singing and summer holidays, is at odds with what he recalls. He remembers the extreme cold of their house, which was heated only on the lower floors by a recalcitrant oil-guzzling stove in the basement. On winter mornings the faded yellow of his bedroom curtains felt damp with ice. He remembers a great deal of time spent on his own. Him, the only child in a houseful of adults, sliding down the banisters, again and again, on interminable Sunday afternoons. Long, useless hours in the back garden, trying to coax next-door's cat down off the wall. He remembers a succession of au pairs, whose duties included walking him to school, taking him to the park, accompanying him on the Tube to the British Museum, making his after-school snack. He remembers one particular French girl – her name eludes him – presenting him, not with the usual jam sandwiches, but his own miniature *tarte Tatin*. He can still recall the way she turned it out of its pan, setting it upside-down on the plate, the crumbling, sweet warmth of the pastry, coupled with the caramelising pear, the sugar-tainted steam that rose off it. It had been so surprising that he had burst into tears and the French girl had hugged him to her angora jumper. But she hadn't lasted long and was replaced, if he remembers rightly, by a Dutch girl who fed him rye crackers.

When he hears about Elina's childhood, the camping in the woods, the trips out in boats to uninhabited islands, ice-skating on the archipelago on Christmas night, the sitting out on the roof tiles to watch the aurora borealis, he is astonished. More, he wants to say, tell me more, but doesn't because he feels he has nothing to offer in exchange. What could he tell her in return for a story about when, aged ten and eight, she and her brother decided to leave home and lived in a den they made in the forest for two days before their mother came to fetch them back? His au pair taking him to John Lewis to buy new shoes? Or what about Elina's account of the time she'd built a bonfire as big as the shed, which, when lit, burnt down the shed? Or when she sledged down a hill so steep, she slid all the way out on to an iced-over lake and sat there until she was numb with cold because the way the ice distorted sound was so fascinating she couldn't leave? He could tell her about his father taking him to the zoo and how he kept looking at his watch and suggesting lunch. Or about how, when he thinks of his childhood, he remembers most of all the feeling that life was going on elsewhere, without him. His father away for work. His mother attending to correspondence at her roll-top desk – 'Not now, darling, in a minute, Mummy's busy' – the au pairs coming and going to their English classes, the lady who came to polish the brass runners on the stairs and talked, compellingly, of her trouble 'down below'.

Ted looks down at Elina. He tucks the blanket around her more tightly. He looks across at the basket, which contains the sleeping, bundled form of his son. *His son.* He has yet to get used to the words. Ted wants sledging for this child, and dens and fairs and bonfires that accidentally cause infernos. He will take him to the zoo and he will not look at his watch once. He will learn to make *tarte Tatin* and he will make it for him once a week, or every day, if he wants it. This child will not be expected to go to his room for an hour after lunch for 'quiet time'. He will not be taken by teenagers who have only a passing acquaintance with English to buy school shoes or to look at Egyptian mummies in glass cases. He will not have to spend afternoons alone in a frosty garden. He will have central heating in his bedroom. He will not be taken to the barber once a month. He will be allowed – encouraged, even – to remove his shoes in communal sandpits. He will be able to decorate the Christmas tree himself, with whatever colour baubles he likes.

Ted drums his fingers on the sofa arm. He would like to get up. He would like to write these things down. He would like to stand over his sleeping son and say them to him, as a kind of pledge. But he can't disturb Elina. He picks up the remote control and changes the channel until he finds a football match he'd forgotten about.

*

In the dream – and it's one of those curious, halfway states when you're dreaming and you somehow know it – Elina is being made to hold a pillowcase. Someone has crammed it with fragile things. An alarm clock, a glass tumbler, an ashtray, a swirling snow scene of a wood, a girl and a wolf. The floor she is standing on is cold stone and the pillowcase too full. She cannot get a proper grip on it so she struggles to hold it, to contain all the things that are jostling and slipping. If they fall, they will smash. She must not let them drop.

A noise interrupts her. It is someone saying, 'ow.' A voice she knows. Ted's. Elina opens her eyes. The alarm clock, the snow scene, the tumbler, the stone floor disintegrate. She is lying squeezed between Ted and the end of the sofa, her head on Ted's thigh.

'Why did you say "ow"?' she asks the underside of his jaw. He is watching television, football by the sound of it – that odd drone and mumble, interpersed with hooting. He hasn't shaved for a while. Black bristles cover his chin, his throat. She puts out a finger to touch them, pushing them first one way then the other.

'You hit me,' he says, without taking his eyes off the screen.

'I did?' Elina struggles upright.

'You were asleep and you started flailing around and—' There is a surge of noise from the television, a crashing roar, a crescendo of hooting and, without warning, Ted emits an impassioned, garbled speech. Elina can't make out what the words are. Some are YES and some GOD and some are swearwords.

She watches him gesticulating, arguing with the television. Then, from over by the kitchen, there is another noise. A quiet, almost inaudible cheep, like a bird or a kitten. Elina's head snaps around. The baby. There it is again. A tiny 'eeuup' sound.

'Ted,' she says, 'don't. You'll wake the baby.'

The television is still booming but Ted is talking more quietly, about how he can't believe it. She listens hard but there is no more noise from the Moses basket. An arm appears over the side, arching slowly through the air, as if he's doing t'ai chi. But then he is still. 'What do you call those things with water and fake snow inside?' she asks.

Ted is sitting forward, his body tense. 'Hmm?'

'You know, children have them. You shake them and the snow swirls around.'

'I don't know what—' he begins, but something happens on screen and he hisses, 'No!' and hurls himself back into the cushions, in an attitude of profound grief.

Elina picks up something lying on the sofa next to her. It is a palette knife, with a malleable, soft blade, and she bends the blade this way and that between her fingers. Then she holds it close to her face, looking at it as a historian might examine an artefact from another age. The ingrained paint at the join where the blade meets the handle – she can see red, green, a fleck of yellow – the tiny crack in the pearly plastic of the grip, the trace of rust at the tip. 'Knife' is really the wrong word for it, she thinks. You couldn't cut anything with this. It wouldn't slice, it wouldn't pierce or gash or saw or any of those things that knives do, because real knives—

'What are you doing?'

Elina turns. Ted, she is surprised to see, is looking straight at her.

'Nothing,' she says, and lowers the palette knife to her lap.

'What is that?' he says, in the kind of tone that implies she might very easily reply *just a hand-grenade, darling.*

'Nothing,' she says again, and as she does so it comes to her what the palette knife is doing on the sofa, instead of in her studio. She'd been using it in here, mixing some plaster of Paris on the coffee-table, which is not something she would normally ever do. The house is for living, the studio is for working. But it had been hot and the short distance down the garden had seemed so long.

She becomes aware that Ted is still looking at her, this time with an expression close to horror.

'What?' she says.

He doesn't reply. He seems to be in some kind of trance, staring at her with a kind of guardedness, a nervous fascination.

'Why are you looking at me like that?' She sees that he is staring at her neck. She raises her hand to the spot and feels her pulse, leaping beneath her touch. 'What's the matter?'

'Huh?' he says, and appears to come back from wherever he was. 'What did you say?'

'I said, why are you staring at me like that?'

He looks away, fiddles with the remote control. 'Sorry,' he mumbles, then says, suddenly defensive, 'Like what?'

'Like I'm some kind of freak.'

He shifts in his seat. 'Don't be silly. I wasn't. Of course I wasn't.'

Elina pushes herself forward and struggles from the sofa. The noise of the football is suddenly too much. At one point she thinks she won't make it to standing, that she won't be able to straighten her legs, that they will buckle beneath her or that whatever it is that is inside her will fall out. But she grips the sofa arm and Ted lurches forward and seizes her wrist and together they hoist her up and she moves across the room, bent over a little at the waist.

She has been overcome by a desire to look at the baby. She needs to do this, she's noticed, at regular intervals. To check he's there, to check she hasn't dreamt it all, to check he's still breathing, to check he's quite as beautiful as she remembered him to be, quite as astonishingly perfect. She limps towards the Moses basket – it must be nearly time for another of those painkillers – and peers in. He is there, wrapped in a blanket, fists clenched beside his ears, his eyes screwed tight, his mouth shut in a firm pout, as if tackling this sleeping business with all the seriousness and concentration it deserves. She puts a hand to his chest and, even though she knows he's fine, she can see that he's fine, she feels a surge of relief flood through her. He's breathing, she tells herself, he's alive, he's still here.

She makes for the kitchen, holding on to the cooker for support, chiding herself. Why does she constantly fear that he's going to die? That he will slip away from her, out of this life. It's hysterical, she tells herself, as she scans the shelves for the teapot, and ridiculous.

The next morning the palette knife is on the floor next to the sofa. Elina gets down on her hands and knees to pick it up. And while she's there, she takes a look under the sagging weft of the sofa's underside. She sees other things: coins, a safety-pin, a reel of cotton, a hair-clip that could be an old one of hers. She considers getting a ruler or a wooden spoon and hooking out all these things – she would if she were properly interested in keeping a nice house. But she isn't. There are better things to do with your life. If only she could remember what they are.

She gets up and, as she does so, is aware of that sharp scorch of pain in the abdomen again. She wonders whether the time has come to ring Ted, to say, Ted, why is that scar there, what happened, tell me what happened because I can't remember.

But now would not be a good time. He'll be in his editing suite, his cave, as Elina thinks of it, removing and splicing the bad bits from films, making sure it all appears smooth and faultless, as if it was never any other way. And, anyway, it may all come back to her, she may remember on her own. He's been under so much pressure recently, since this film overran, since the baby came, walking about with that drawn, pale face he gets when he's either ill or stressed. She really shouldn't worry him.

She goes instead to the window. The weather has still not let up. It has rained and rained for days, the sky blurred and swollen, the garden sodden. Around her, the house ticks to the rhythm of water: on roof tiles, on gutters, down drains.

Before, when she was still pregnant, the weather had been sunny. For weeks and weeks. Elina would sit in the shade of her studio with her feet in a bucket of cold water. In the morning she would do her yoga exercises out there, when the grass was still cool with dew. She ate grapefruit, sometimes three a day, she did sketches of some ants, but lazily, without any real intent, she watched the skin of her stomach ripple, move, like water before a storm. She read books about natural births. She wrote lists of names in charcoal on her studio walls.

Elina stands at the window, watching the rain. The man from down the street is walking along the pavement towards the Heath, his dog behind him. She cannot fathom, cannot grasp what happened to that person, that Elina of the charcoal lists, the ant sketches, the natural births, the buckets of cool water in the shade. How did she become this – a woman in stained pyjamas, standing weeping at a window, a woman frequently possessed by an urge to run through the streets, shouting, will somebody please help me, please?

Elina Vilkuna, she says to herself, is your name. That is who you are. She feels she must confine herself to known things, to facts. Then perhaps everything else will fall into place. There is her and there is the baby and there is Ted. Or that's what everybody calls him – he has another, longer name but that one never gets used. Elina knows about Ted. She could recite his life to anyone who asked. She could sit an exam on Ted and pass with an A grade. He is her partner, boyfriend, other half, better half, lover, mate. When he leaves the house, he goes to his office. In Soho. He takes the Tube and sometimes he cycles. He is thirty-five, which is exactly four years older than her. He has hair the colour of conkers, size-ten feet, a liking for chicken Madras. One of his thumbs is flatter and longer than the other, the result of sucking it in childhood, he says. He has three fillings in his teeth, a white scar on his abdomen where his appendix was removed, a purplish mark on his left ankle from the sting of a jellyfish in the Indian Ocean years ago. He hates jazz, multiplex cinemas, swimming, dogs and cars – refuses to own one. He is allergic to horsehair and dried mango. These are the facts.

She finds she is sitting on the stairs, as if she is waiting for something or someone. It seems to be much later. Somewhere in the house she is aware of the phone ringing, the answerphone clicking on, and a friend of hers speaking into the silence. Elina will call her back. Later. Tomorrow. Some time. For now, her head is leaning against the wall, the baby is on her knee and beside her on the stair is a piece of blue cloth. Soft, fleecy material. Silver stars have been embroidered all over it.

Looking at these stars gives her an odd sensation. She is sure she has never seen them before and yet she can picture herself sewing them, the needle strung with silver, the sparkling thread led through and through the cloth. She knows the feel of the fleece, knows that a star near the hem is squashed slightly, and yet, and yet, she's never seen it before. Has she? As she looks she is sure that she did this embroidery in the hospital, in between—

She looks down to the hallway. Sunshine is glowing through the twin glass panels of the front door. She stands, picking up the baby and the starry cloth or blanket, or whatever it is, it's too small to be a blanket really, and descends the stairs. The light coming through the door is dazzling and she realises, with a leap in her chest, that it must have stopped raining.

She could, Elina realises, go out. What a thought. To go out into the streets, where the rain will be drying in patches from the roads and the leaves will have printed themselves on to the pavements. Out, where cars rev and turn, where dogs scratch themselves and sniff at the bases of lampposts, where people are walking, speaking, going about their lives. She, Elina, could walk to the end of the road. She could buy a paper, a pint of milk, a bar of chocolate, an orange, some pears.

She can imagine it so clearly, as if it's only a week or two since she was out there, in the outside. How long has it been? How long is it since—

The problem is there is so much to remember. She'll need, let's see, her wallet, her keys. What else? Elina sees a calico bag on the floor of the hall and she crams into it the blue-star blanket, then some nappies and wipes. Surely that will do?

There is something else, though. Something tugs at her, insistent, something she knows she has forgotten. Elina stands for a moment, thinking. She has the baby, she has the pram, she has the bag. She looks up the stairs, she looks at the lozenges of light set into the front door, she looks down at herself. She has the baby in one arm and the bag slung over her shoulder, across her body, across her pyjamas.

Clothes. She needs something to wear.

In the bedroom she surveys the heap of clothes on her chair. She picks them up with her spare hand and drops them to the floor. A pair of jeans with an enormous waistband, some dungarees, grey jogging pants, a sweatshirt with a trailing flower design. She finds something green tangled up with something red and she can't separate them with one hand so she gives them a shake, snaps them in the air, and a red scarf soars free, tossing out into the bedroom. Elina watches it as it falls in a graceful arc away from her, as it settles to the floor. She looks at it there, the red against the white carpet. She tilts her head one way, then the other, considering it. She looks back at the baby, who is making movements with his mouth, as if trying to communicate something to her. She doesn't look at the scarf again but she thinks of it, the way it shot out like that into the air.

She thinks that it somehow reminds her of something she has seen recently. And then she recalls what it is. Jets of blood. Beautiful, in their way. The pure, garnet brightness of them in the scrubbed white of the room. The way they would spin and resolve themselves into droplets as they travelled, before hurling themselves with definite, sure force against the fronts of the doctors, the nurses. The way they commanded such attention, the way they brought everyone running.

Elina drops the green smock and sits quickly on the chair. She is sure to keep a careful hold of the baby, of her son, and to keep looking at him, at nothing else, and she sees he is still mouthing secrets to her, as if he has all the answers to everything she needs to know.

Lexie stands at the window, cigarette in hand, looking down into the street. The old woman from the flat below is setting off on her daily walk. Dog lead in one hand, shopping-bag in the other, back bent into a comma under her coat, she inches, inches into the road, without looking left or right.

'She's going to get run over one day,' Lexie murmurs.

'Who?' Innes says, from across the room, lifting his head from the mattress.

Lexie points with the tip of her cigarette. 'Your neighbour. The one with a hunchback. And probably by you.'

She looks different from the girl who was reading on a tree stump. For one, she is naked, wearing only a candy-striped shirt of Innes's, open down the front. For two, her hair has been cut in sloping, silken curtains about her face.

Innes yawns, stretches, turns on to his stomach. 'Why would I want to run over my neighbour? And if you mean the old battleaxe from downstairs, it's not a hunchback it's a dowager's hump. Known in the medical trade as thoracic spinal osteoporosis. Caused by—'

'Oh, shush,' Lexie says. 'How do you know all these things anyway?'

Innes raises himself on to his elbow. 'A misspent youth,' he says. 'Years squandered on books instead of on the likes of you.'

She smiles and exhales a stream of smoke, watching as the woman and her dog reach the pavement. It is a stifling, close day in October. The sky is heavy, threatening electric clashes, but the woman is dressed, as she always is, in a thick tweed coat. 'Well,' Lexie says, 'you've made up for it since.'

'Speaking of which,' Innes twitches back a corner of the counterpane, 'come here. Bring me your cigarette and your body.'

She doesn't move. 'In that order?'

'In whichever order you damn well like. Come on!' He slaps the mattress.

Lexie takes another pull on her cigarette. She scuffs her bare foot against the arch of its twin. She takes a last glance into the street, which is empty, then sets off, running, towards the bed. Halfway across the room, she leaves the ground in a balletic leap. Innes is saying, 'Christ, woman,' the striped shirt is flying out behind her, like wings, the cigarette is trailing white ash, and all she knows is that she is about to make love for the second time that day. She has no idea that she will die young, that she does not have as much time as she thinks. For now she has just discovered the love of her life, and death couldn't be further from her mind.

She lands on the bed with a crash. Pillows and counterpane are tipped off, Innes seizes her by the wrist, the arm, the waist. 'We won't be needing this,' he says, as he pulls off the shirt, as he flings it to the floor, as he manoeuvres her back on to the bed, as he shoulders his way between the V of her legs. He pauses for a moment to pluck the cigarette from her fingers, takes a drag, then stubs it out in an ashtray on the bedside table.

'Right,' he says, as he turns to her again.

But this is anticipating. The film needs to be rewound a little. Watch. Innes sucks in a nimbus of smoke, lifts a cigarette stub from the ashtray, appears to envelop Lexie in a shirt and push her across the room, the pillows jump on to the bed, Lexie zooms backwards towards the window. Then they are back on the bed and they are both naked and, goodness, doesn't sex look oddly the same in reverse, except now they are lovingly putting on each other's clothes, one by one, then whisking out of the door, running down the stairs, and Innes is pulling his key out of his door. The film speeds up. There are Innes and Lexie in his car, scooting backwards along a road, Lexie with a scarf over her head. There they are forking food out of their mouths in a restaurant and putting it down on the plates; here they are in bed again and then their clothes fly towards them. Here is a woman in a red pillbox hat walking in reverse away from Lexie. Here is Lexie again, looking up at a building in Soho, then she is walking away from it with a jerky, reversed gait. Lexie is walking backwards up a long, dim staircase. The film is getting faster and faster. A train pulls out of a big, smoke-filled station, rattles backwards through countryside. At a small station, Lexie is seen to get out and put down her suitcase. And the film ends. We are back, neatly, to where we left off.

Lexie's mother gave her two pieces of advice when she left for London: 1. Get a secretarial job in a big, successful firm because that will 'put you in the path of the right sort of man'. 2. Never be in the same room as a man and a bed.

Her father said: don't waste your time with any more studying because it always makes women disagreeable.

Her younger siblings said: remember to visit the Queen.

Her aunt, who had spent some time in London in the 1920s, told her never to use the Underground (it was dirty and full of unsavoury types), never to go into coffee bars (they were full of germs), always to wear a girdle and carry an umbrella, and never to go to Soho.

Needless to say, she disregarded them all.

Lexie stood in the doorway, suitcase in hand. The bedsit was high among the eaves of a tall, thin terraced house; the ceiling, she saw, sloped towards itself at five different angles. The door, its frame, the skirting-boards, the boarded-up fireplace, the cupboard under the window were all painted yellow. Not a vibrant yellow – daffodil yellow, if you like – but a sickly, pale, dirty one. The yellow of old teeth, of pub ceilings. It was chipped off in places, revealing a gloomy brown underneath. This cheered Lexie in an odd way, the thought that someone had had to live there surrounded by an even worse colour.

She stepped further into the room and set down her case. The bed was narrow and sagging, the headboard listing to one side. It was covered with an eiderdown of fading purple curlicues. When Lexie turned it down she saw the mattress was grey, stained, sagged in the middle. She twitched it back again quickly. She took off her coat and looked around for a peg on which to hang it. No peg. She draped it over the chair, which had also been painted, some time ago, a pale yellow but a slightly different shade from the skirting-boards. What was her landlady's obsession with the colour?

The landlady, Mrs Collins, had met her at the door. A thin woman in a zipped housecoat and crescents of iridescent blue eyeshadow, her first question had been: 'You're not Italian, are you?'

Lexie, taken aback, had said no. Then she'd asked Mrs Collins what her objection was to Italians.

'Can't stand them,' Mrs Collins grumbled, as she disappeared into the front room, leaving Lexie in the hall, staring at the brown, peeling wallpaper, the telephone on the wall, a list of house rules, 'dirty so-and-sos. Here's your keys.' Mrs Collins reappeared in the hall and handed her two latchkeys. 'One for the front door, one for your room. The usual rules apply.' She gestured at the list on the pinboard. 'No men, no pets, always use an ashtray, keep your room clean, no more than two visitors at a time, in by eleven every night or the door will be bolted.' She leant in closer and scrutinised Lexie, breathing hard. 'You may look like a nice, clean girl but you're the sort that might turn. You've got that look about you.'

'Is that so?' Lexie said, depositing the keys in her bag and snapping it shut. She bent to pick up her case. 'At the top, you say?'

'Right at the top.' Mrs Collins nodded. 'On the left.'

Lexie took the keys from where she'd left them in the lock and put them on the mantelpiece. Then she lowered herself to the bed. She allowed herself to think, there, it's done, I'm here. She smoothed her hair, passed her hand over the purple curlicues. Then she turned into a kneeling position and, leaning on the window-sill, peered outside. Far below there was a rectangular patch of scrubby grass, boxed in on all sides by ivy-furred walls. She looked down the gardens. Some had rows of beans, lettuces, sprays of roses or jasmine; some still had the arched-spine shape of Anderson shelters hidden under lawn or soil or rockeries. One, further along, had a child's swing. She was pleased to see an enormous chestnut tree, leaves waving and dipping. And opposite was the back of a terrace similar to hers – that grey-brown London brick, zigzagged by guttering, the windows uneven, higgledy-piggledy, some open, one taped over with cardboard. She could see two women, who must have crawled out of a window, sunbathing on a flat bit of roof, their shoes kicked off, their hitched-up skirts inflating and deflating in the breeze. Below them, unseen by them, a child was running in decreasing circles, round and round his garden, a scarlet ribbon in his hand. A woman a few doors down was pegging out some washing on a line; her husband leant in the doorway, his arms folded.

Lexie felt lightheaded, insubstantial somehow. It was strange to look back into the gloom of her room, then out again at the scene beyond the window. For a prolonged heady moment, she and her room didn't feel real or animate. It was as if she was suspended in a bubble, peering out at Life, which was going along in its way, people laughing and talking and living and dying and falling in love and working and eating and meeting and parting, while she sat there, mute, motionless, watching.

She reached up to free the catch and force open the window. There. That was better. The veil between her and the world was lifted. She stuck her head out into the breeze, shook it vigorously, pulled the pins from her hair, freeing it so that it fell about her face. And the feel of it there, the zooming noise made by the boy running in circles, the faint sound of the sunbathing women's chatter, the graze of the window-sill against her elbows was good. Very good.

After a while, she turned back to the room. She moved the chair nearer the window. She shunted the bed against the wall. She straightened the mirror. She went clattering down the stairs to a surprised Mrs Collins to borrow a bucket, a scrubbing brush, some soda crystals and vinegar, a broom and dustpan. She swept, she dusted, she scrubbed the floor and the walls, the cupboard shelves, the gas-ring. She shook the eiderdown out of the window, beat the mattress, folded the clean sheets she'd stolen from home around it.

They smelt of lavender, of washing powder, of starch, a mixture that always summoned her mother to her mind – and always would, as she'd find out. Lexie pummelled the pillow into its case. She'd announced last night at the dinner table that she was leaving for London in the morning. It was all set up. She had digs, she had an appointment at the labour exchange on Monday morning, she'd withdrawn all her savings to last on until she started earning. Nothing they could do would stop her.

The expected uproar had ensued. Her father had pounded his fist on the table, her mother had shouted and then dissolved into tears. Her sister, with the baby in her arms, comforted their mother and told Lexie, with that drawn-in purse-strings mouth she had sometimes, that she was being 'characteristically irresponsible'. Two of her brothers had started to whoop and run circles around the table. The second youngest child, sensing a change for the worse in the atmosphere, began to wail from its high-chair.

She tossed the pillow on to the bed, then pulled the eiderdown in from the window. It was dark outside now; the windows of the terrace opposite were lit yellow boxes, suspended in inky space. In one, she saw a woman pulling a brush through her hair; in another a man was reading a newspaper, his glasses perched on his nose. Someone else was pulling a blind down, and a girl was leaning out into the night, just as Lexie had done earlier, loosening her hair into the just-moving air.

Lexie undressed, lay between the sheets, tried to close her nose to their smell. She listened to the noises of the house. Feet on the stairs, doors banging, a woman's laugh somewhere, then someone saying sssh. Mrs Collins's voice, querulous, complaining. A cat outside in a garden, emitting a series of yowls. A pipe knocking, then hissing in the walls. The banging and clatter of pans. Someone in the lavatory on the floor below, the surge and rush of the flush, then the slow trickle of the cistern filling. Lexie turned and turned in her starched sheets, smiling up at the cracks in the ceiling.

The next day she met a girl called Hannah from the ground floor who told her about a junk shop round the corner, and Lexie went there to buy some plates, cups and pans. 'Don't pay the first price,' Hannah warned. 'Always haggle.' She came back carrying a piece of hardboard, which Hannah helped her to drag up the stairs. On the third-floor landing, they had to stop to catch their breath and hoist up their stockings. 'What do you want this for?' Hannah panted.

Lexie propped the hardboard between the bed-end and the edge of the sink. She arranged the few books she'd brought from home on it, her fountain pen, a bottle of ink.

'What are you going to do on it?' Hannah said from the bed, where she was reclining, trying to blow smoke-rings.

'I don't know,' Lexie said, staring at it. 'I need to get a typewriter, practise my typing and . . . I don't know.' She couldn't say that she needed to carve something out for herself, something better than this, and that she didn't know how she was going to do it but that she thought having a desk might be a start. She ran her hand along its edge. 'I just wanted it,' she said.

'If you ask me,' Hannah said, grinding out her cigarette on the sill, 'pots and pans might have been more useful.'

Lexie smiled as she stretched up to take down the curtains. 'Perhaps.'

Another lapse. Elina is downstairs again, in the kitchen, and she is walking, up and down, back and forth, with her son over her shoulder and she's wearing her pyjamas with the baggy, flowered sweatshirt over them and the room is filled with noise. A driving, constant shrilling, and it is Elina's job to stop this noise. She knows this noise. It has begun to feel as if it is the only thing she knows: its pitch, its variations, its progressions. It starts as a *heh-heh*. There can be a few of these. Five, six, seven – anything up to as many as ten. After that begin the *ha-ngggs*: *ha-nggg, ha-nggg, ha-nggg*. It can stop there, if Elina gets it right, if she does a certain thing at an exact moment, but because she isn't sure what it is she must do or when, the noise can broaden and deepen out to the dread *uhHggg*: *uhHggg uhHggg uhHggg uhHggg*. After four of these, a gulp of silence, then on to the next four.

If she could just sleep, everything would be all right. Just a stretch of three hours, four maybe. She is so tired that if she turns her head there is a crackling sound, like someone crumpling paper. But she keeps moving. She moves around the kitchen, past the cooker, past the kettle, past the answerphone, which is telling her she has no fewer than thirteen messages, round by the fridge and back, an ache pulsing in her temples. It's roughly two seconds for every *uhHggg*, so that's eight seconds for each set of four and let's say another two seconds for the silent break, which makes ten seconds for the lot. Which makes twenty-four *uhHgggs* a minute. And how long has this been going on so far? Thirty-five minutes, which makes – how many? Elina's brain fails at the maths.

Later, in the silence that is always so taut, so fragile, Elina climbs the stairs alone. On the landing she hesitates. There are three doors to choose from: hers and Ted's room, the bathroom and the attic-room door, which is above her head in the ceiling.

She pulls down the squeaking silver ladder for the attic and climbs the rungs, rising into the room as if emerging from the sea. She looks at the way the light knifes in through the gaps in the blind, illuminating a dusty row of nail varnishes on the mantelpiece, the books lined up on the shelves, shut spines facing her, the vase containing a splayed arrangement of paint brushes, their bristles stiff, set into points. Her bare feet hiss on the carpet. From the desk under the window, Elina picks up a diary and leafs through it. Dinner, she reads, cinema, meeting, exhibition opening, haircut, appointment at gallery. She puts it down. This had been her room, her studio, back when she was Ted's lodger. A long time ago. Before the before. Before any of this. She opens a drawer and finds a necklace, a wand for mascara, a red lipstick, a half-used tube of ochre paint, a postcard of Helsinki harbour. The wardrobe door is stiff but Elina gives it a sharp tug with her dusty fingers and it opens.

In here is the only full-length mirror in the house. The door swings open, rectangles of light wheel across the room and Elina is suddenly face to face with a woman in a stained sweatshirt, the bleach growing out of her hair, her face waxy white.

She avoids her own eye in the mirror as she raises the sweatshirt and holds it under her chin. She puts her fingers in the elastic holding up her pyjama bottoms and turns it down, just enough, just for a second. Long enough to take in where the gash starts, at one hipbone, and where it ends at the other, its crooked, stumbling path through her flesh, the delicate violet of the bruising, the metal clips holding it all together.

She lets the hem of the sweatshirt drop. She remembers – what?

That she had been numb up to her armpits, like a floating head and shoulders, as if she were a marble bust. But it was a strange kind of numbness, where pain was absent but sensation was still present.

She could feel them, the two doctors, rummaging about inside her, like people who had lost something at the bottom of a suitcase. She knew it ought to hurt, it ought to hurt like hell, but it didn't. The anaesthetic washed coolly down and then up her spine, breaking like a wave on the back of her head. There was a green canvas screen bisecting her body. She could hear the doctors murmuring to each other, could see the tops of their heads, could feel their hands in her innards. Ted was nearby, at her left, perched on a stool. And there was a great heave and suck and she almost cried out, *what are you doing,* before she realised, before she heard the sharp, angry cry, surprisingly loud in the hushed room, before she heard the anaesthetist, behind her, saying, *a boy.* Elina repeated this word to herself as she stared ahead at the tiled ceiling. Boy. A boy. Then she spoke to Ted. *Go with him,* she said, *go with the baby.* Because her mother and her aunts had discussed in hushed voices stories about babies being given to the wrong mothers, babies disappearing into the labyrinths of hospital corridors, babies without name-tags. Ted was getting up and going across the room.

Then she was alone on the table. The anaesthetist somewhere behind her. The doctors below her. The screen cutting her in half. She lay, her hands folded on her chest and she had no control over them, couldn't move them if she wanted to and she didn't want to. There was a sound like a Hoover on the other side of the screen but she wasn't thinking about that because she was thinking, a boy, and listening for sounds from across the room, where two nurses were doing something to the baby and Ted was watching over their shoulders. But then something happened, something went wrong. What was it? It was hard for Elina to order her thoughts. The doctor, the student, the woman, said, *oh*. In the kind of voice you'd use if someone barged in front of you in a queue: a tone of disappointment, of dismay. Just after this, Elina had felt a cough rising in her throat, which exploded from her lips with quick force.

Was that right? Or was it the other way round? Did she cough and then afterwards the doctor said, *oh*?

Either way, what came next was the blood. So much of it. An unaccountable amount. Over the doctors, the screen, the nurses. Elina saw it falling to the floor, fanning out over the tiles, forming rivulets and gullies in the grouting; she saw people treading it as footprints around the table; she saw a plastic bag hanging from the wall filling with red-soaked cloths.

Her heart reacted almost instantly, setting up a rapid, panicked knocking in her chest, as if trying to attract someone's attention, as if trying to communicate that there was a problem and would someone please help? It needn't have worried. The room was suddenly swarming with people. The student doctor was calling for assistance, the anaesthetist was standing up, peering over the screen, a frown on his face, and then he was making an adjustment to the clear bag suspended above Elina's head, and a moment later she felt whatever it was hit her veins. She seemed to swoon, her vision wavering, the ceiling moving above her like a conveyor-belt, and the thought occurred to her that perhaps this wasn't the drug, that perhaps it was something else, that she mustn't whatever happened lose consciousness, she must stay, she mustn't go anywhere, and part of her wished someone would come and speak to her, to tell her what was happening, why she could feel people's hands far up inside her skin, up by her ribs, why someone was shouting, *quickly now, quickly,* and where the baby was and where Ted was, why the student doctor was saying, *no, I can't, I don't know how,* and the other doctor was saying something to her, something cross-sounding, and why Elina was being pushed by something or someone to the top of the table so that it felt as if her head might tip off the end.

With the rim of the table pressing into her skull, with the female doctor calling for assistance, she felt herself almost go again, as if she was in a train that had swerved on to a new track, as if clouds had been blown across her brain. To go would be such a relief. She longed to loosen her grip, to release herself to that down-pulling force. But she knew she must not. So she screwed her eyes shut and popped them open again, she drove the nail of one hand into the fingertip of the other. *Help me,* she said to the anaesthetist, because he was the nearest person, *please.* But her voice came out as a whisper and, anyway, he was talking to a new man who'd appeared above her and this man was carrying small clear sacks filled with fluid of an incredible red.

She turns from the mirror. Downstairs, the noise is starting up: *ha-nggg, ha-nggg.* Elina takes the stairs, clutching the banister for support, along the hall, where the noise has tipped into *uhHggg uhHggg,* and then she goes out through the front door.

Outside, on the step, she feels curiously like two people. One is standing on the threshold and is feeling very light, as if she might take off in her pyjamas and sweatshirt, float up and up into the sky, disappearing into the clouds and beyond. The other is calmly watching her, thinking, so this is what it is to be mad. She sets off down the path, opening the gate and stepping on to the pavement in her bare feet. She is going, she is leaving, she is off. You're leaving, the calm Elina observes. I see. The other Elina's lungs inflate and her heart seems to answer them, tripping into a fast, fluttering pound.

At the corner, she is pulled to a stop. The street, the pavement, the lampposts seethe and swing in front of her. She can go no further. It is as if she is tethered to the house, or to something in the house. Elina turns her head, first one way, then the other. She is interested in this. It is a curious feeling. She bobs there for a moment, like a tugboat at the end of its rope. Rain is soaking through the sweatshirt, gluing the pyjamas to her skin.

Elina turns. She is, she feels, no longer two people, but one. This Elina goes back along the pavement, holding on to the wall, up the path and into the house. She leaves wet footprints on the floorboards as she walks.

The baby is tussling with the blanket in his cot, fists clenched around wool, his face screwed up with effort, with need. Then he sees Elina and forgets all about his fight with the blanket, his hunger, his want for something he cannot express. His fingers uncurl like petals and he stares in amazement at his mother.

'It's all right,' Elina tells him. And she believes herself, this time. She reaches to lift him and his arms shudder with the surprise of being airborne. She settles him against her body. She says it again: 'It's all right.'

Elina and the baby walk together to the window. They don't take their eyes off each other. He blinks a little in the bright light but stares up at her, as if the sight of her to him is like water to a plant. Elina leans against the windows to the garden. She raises the baby so that his forehead touches her cheek, as if anointing him or greeting him, as if they are starting all the way back at the beginning.

Here is Lexie, standing on a pavement at Marble Arch. She is adjusting the back of her shoe, smoothing her hair. It is a warm, hazy evening, just after six o'clock. Men in suits and women in heels and hats, pulling children by the hand, flow around her as if they were a river and she were a rock in their path.

She has been at her new job two days. She is a lift attendant in a big department store. The labour exchange sent her there after a dismal result in the typing test, and she's been saying, 'Which floor, madam?'; 'Going up, sir'; 'Floor three, household goods, haberdashery and millinery, thank you.' She had never known anything could be so dull. Or that it was possible for her to hold the layout of an entire seven-floor shop in her head. Or that one person could buy so many things – hats, belts, shoes, stockings, face powder, hairnets, suits. Lexie has seen the lists, clutched in gloved hands, over people's shoulders. But she knows it's just a start. She is here, she is in London: any minute now the technicolour part of her life will commence, she is sure, she is certain – it has to.

Look at her, standing there on the pavement. She looks different from the Lexie in Innes's room, the one naked under a candy-striped shirt. She looks different from the Alexandra in a blue dress and yellow kerchief, sitting on a tree stump in her parents' garden.

She'll have many incarnations in her time. She is made up of myriad Lexies and Alexandras, all sheathed inside one another, like Russian dolls.

She has her hair pinned up. She is wearing the red and grey livery of the shop, the regulation red scarf tied around her throat, the corded hat stuffed in her pocket. Her coat is belted at the waist and is rather hot for this warm afternoon. Look at how high, how tense her shoulders are. You can't be unflinchingly polite to people all day without feeling the strain. She's loosening the scarf from her neck, pulling it free and stuffing its scarlet length into her other pocket. She is rubbing her shoulders, trying to ease the stiffness. She smiles at two other lift girls as they come out of the door. She watches as they head, arm in arm, up the crowded pavement, wobbling a little on their patent-leather heels. A bus chunters past, the sound of its bell creating a clear, widening circle in the air.

She breathes in. She breathes out. Her shoulders lower a fraction. She looks up at the bright strip of sky balanced on top of the buildings, then sets off across the street, leaving the department store, the lift, its buttons, its dinging bell, behind her until tomorrow. She has to dash because another tram is coming, a car hoots just as she reaches the pavement and she has to sidestep a man pushing a cart full of flowers, and she feels something like laughter crowd up into her throat. Or not laughter. What is it? She turns the corner and is suddenly drenched in low evening sun, the pavements and streets striated by long, spiked shadows. A newspaper seller is coming towards her, repeating two drawn-out syllables: *'Eeeeeee Nuuuuuuus, Eeeeeeee Nuuuuuuus.'* And Lexie decides: glee. What she feels is utter, unadulterated glee. She is on her way to meet a university friend who has been in London a year, and they are to go to the pictures together. She is working for herself, she has a place to live, she has made it to London and the feeling is glee.

'Eeeeeee Nuuuuuuus,' the newspaper seller calls again, the sound behind her now. She leaps off the pavement, with a glance over her shoulder, and crosses the road, and when she gets to the opposite pavement, she begins to run, swinging her bag, opening her coat. Ah, the delirium of first realising you can do exactly what you want and that no one is going to stop you. People turn to look at her as she runs, an old woman tuts and she can still hear the long, mournful cries of the newspaper seller: *'Eeeeeee Nuuuuuuus . . .'*

She gets back to Kentish Town late, but not so late, she is relieved to find, that Mrs Collins has bolted the door. She struggles for a minute with the key, then the lock gives, she steps inside and closes the door carefully behind her. But instead of the dim, hushed hallway she was expecting, the lights are blazing and there is a cacophony of chatter and laughter coming from somewhere. A number of people are sitting on the stairs. Lexie recognises several women who have bedsits in the house.

Puzzled, she heads towards them. Is someone having a party? Does Mrs Collins know about this? Maybe she's out for the evening.

'Oh, here she is!' someone cries, as Lexie comes towards them.

'We were getting worried,' Hannah says, leaning round someone else's back. She has a glass in her hand, Lexie notices, and her cheeks are a little flushed.

Lexie, unable to go any further even if she might have wanted to, starts to take off her coat. 'I'm fine,' she says, surveying them all. 'I went to the pictures with a fr—'

'She went to the pictures!' Mrs Collins who, Lexie now sees, is perched on a chair on the landing, is calling up to unseen people on the next flight of stairs.

'What's going on?' Lexie says, with a smile. 'Are we having a house party?'

'Well,' Mrs Collins says, with a hint of her usual severity, 'someone had to entertain your visitor.'

Lexie looks at her. 'My visitor?'

Mrs Collins takes her arm and propels her through the thicket of legs and people. 'Such an amusing young man,' she says. 'I don't usually ask gentlemen in, as you know, but he did say he'd made an appointment with you and, to be frank, I was embarrassed on your behalf that you hadn't seen fit to honour it and—'

Lexie and Mrs Collins and Hannah turn the corner to the next flight up and there, sitting on the fourth step, is Innes.

'And what did he say when you told him?' he is saying to a mousy girl with prominent gums. 'I hope he was excessively sorry.'

'Mr Kent has had us all playing a game,' Mrs Collins says, squeezing Lexie's arm. 'We had to tell him about our most embarrassing moment ever. And he is going to decide which is the worst and whoever it is wins.' She laughs wheezily, then seems to think better of it and covers her mouth with her hand.

'Is that so?' says Lexie.

Innes turns towards her. He looks her up and down. He gives a slight gesture with the hand that holds a cigarette which could be a wave or perhaps a shrug. 'There you are,' he says. 'We were wondering what had happened to you. Did you walk through the wrong door again? A portal to another world?'

Lexie puts her head on one side. 'Not today, no. Just the door to the pictures.'

'Ah. The lure of celluloid. There was some talk of you being abducted but I said you were the kind of girl who could see off any potential abductors.'

They regard each other for a moment. Innes narrows his eyes as he puts his cigarette to his mouth.

Hannah steps in. 'Mr Kent was telling us he knew you from university.'

Lexie raises an eyebrow. 'Was he indeed?'

'That's right,' Innes cuts in, 'and then these kind people took pity on me and invited me in. Someone had some brandy and your gracious landlady even provided me with some rissoles to eat. And there you have it. The whole story.'

Lexie can't think of what to say next. 'How were the rissoles?' she comes out with.

'Like none I have ever eaten.' He stands, stretches, grinds his cigarette into an ashtray balanced on the step below him. 'Well, I must be off. I'm sure you all need your sleep. Ladies, it has been a pleasure. I hope we can repeat it soon. Mrs Collins, you win the prize for the most embarrassing story. And perhaps you, Lexie, will see me out?' He proffers his arm.

Lexie looks at the arm. She looks at him. All around her are cries of 'Must you really leave?', 'What does Mrs Collins win?', 'What was Mrs Collins's story again?' She takes the arm and they walk together out into the hall. The crowd of women follow them to the bottom step, where they tactfully but reluctantly drop back.

Lexie thinks they will say goodbye at the front door but he pulls her through it. As soon as they are outside, Innes says, in a low voice, 'Truthfully, they were the worst things I have ever eaten. The texture of sawdust, the taste of shoe leather. Don't ever ask me to eat rissoles again.'

'I shan't,' she says, then catches herself. 'And I never asked you to in the first place.'

He ignores this. 'What are rissoles anyway? What are they for? You'll have to make it up to me.'

Lexie pulls her hand away from his arm. 'What do you mean? And what are you doing here? How did you ever find me?'

He turns to her. 'Do you know how many women-only rooming houses there are in Kentish Town?'

'No, how would I know such a—'

'Two,' he says, 'so it was really not that difficult. A simple process of elimination, balanced against chance. I knew you'd come soon, you see, knew you wouldn't last much longer there. But I couldn't be sure exactly when. All this is beside the point, anyway, because the point is, when are you coming to lunch with me?'

'I don't know,' Lexie says, lifting her chin. 'I'm rather busy.'

Innes smiles and moves a shade closer. 'How about Saturday?'

Lexie pretends to be straightening her cuff. 'I don't know,' she says again. 'I work on Saturdays, I think.'

'As do I. How about one o'clock? You're allowed lunches, aren't you? Where are you working? Did you reach your sixty words per minute?'

She stares at him. 'How did you remember about the sixty words per minute?' She starts to laugh. 'And how on earth did you remember I was planning to live in a rooming house in Kentish Town?'

He shrugs. 'I remember everything. It's either a disability or a form of genius. I can't decide which. Tell me something once and it's there,' he taps his head, 'never to leave.'

She glances involuntarily at his cranium and imagines it, beneath his thick hair, teeming with information. 'I don't know what time I'll finish. It's my first week, so—'

'All right, all right. I'll tell you what. You come and find me. I'll be at my office, in Soho. I'll be there all day and probably all night. So any time. Come whenever you're finished. I gave you my card. You still have it?'

Lexie nods.

'Good. The address is on there. So I'll see you Saturday?'

'Yes.'

He smiles and hesitates for a moment. Lexie wonders if he is going to kiss her. But he doesn't. He goes down the steps without a wave and crosses the street.

When Lexie reaches the fringes of Soho, she stops. She feels for Innes Kent's note and business card, which she has kept in her bag since the day she met him. She doesn't need to look but she does anyway. *Editor,* it reads, *Elsewhere Magazine, Bayton Street, Soho, London W1*.

Mrs Collins had been shocked that morning when Lexie came upon her on the stairs and let slip she was going to Soho later in the day. Lexie had asked her why. 'Soho?' Mrs Collins replied. 'It's full of bohemians and inebriates.' Then she narrowed her eyes. 'You,' she said, and pointed at Lexie, 'you're always asking why, aren't you? Curiosity killed the cat.'

Lexie laughed. 'But I'm not a cat, Mrs Collins,' she said, and ran the rest of the way down the stairs.

Lexie looks up the street that on her map is marked as Moor Street. It seems quiet for a place full of inebriates. There is one car parked at the side of the road; a man is standing in a doorway, reading a newspaper; there is an awning half closed above a shop; in a third-storey window a woman is leaning out to water some flowers in a window box.

Lexie takes one step into Soho, then another, and another. She has the odd sensation that she is motionless, that the pavement is moving under her and that the houses and buildings and street signs are reeling past. Her shoes make a clear *toc-toc* sound as she walks. The man with the newspaper looks up. The woman in the window pauses with her watering.

She walks past a shop with cheeses, big as wheels, stacked in the window. A man in a white apron is standing on the doorstep, shouting something in a foreign language to a woman with a baby across the street. He grins and nods at Lexie as she passes and she smiles back. Around the corner is a coffee-house, with men standing on the pavement outside, talking in a different language. They part, just enough to let her through, and one of them says something to her but she doesn't look back.

The buildings are crowded together, dark brick, the roads narrow. The gutters run and ripple with the earlier rain. Around another corner, and another, past a Chinese grocer's, where a woman is stacking pitted yellow fruits into a pyramid, past a doorway where two African men are sitting on chairs, laughing. A gaggle of sailors in blue and white uniforms are walking down the middle of the road, singing in staggered, off-key unison; a delivery boy on a bicycle has to swerve to avoid them and he turns to shout something over his shoulder. Two or three of the sailors seem to take exception and dart after him but the delivery boy pedals hard and disappears.

Lexie watches all this. She takes it all in. Everything she sees seems freighted with significance: the fluttering ribbon on one of the sailor's hats, a marmalade cat washing itself on a window, the billow of steam that gathers in the air outside that bakery, the chalked words – Italian? Portuguese? – on a board outside a shop, the strains of music, interspersed with laughter, that wreathe up from a grating in the pavement, the fur-collared coat and gold-clasped bag of a woman passing on the opposite pavement. Lexie drinks it in, every detail, with a feeling between panic and euphoria: this is perfect, this is all perfect, it couldn't be more perfect, but what if she can't remember it all, what if even the tiniest element were to slip from her?

She arrives rather suddenly outside the address in Bayton Street. It is a building squeezed between two taller buildings, with a symmetrical arrangement of sash windows and steps up to the door. Paint is peeling in curls off the sills and gutters. A pane on the second floor is missing.

Beyond the windows on the ground floor, Lexie can see a great number of people. Two men are peering at something they are holding up to the light; there is a woman on the phone, nodding, writing. Another woman is measuring a piece of paper with a ruler, talking over her shoulder to a man at the desk behind hers. In a corner of the room a group of people are bunched together, crowding round to look at some pages pinned to the wall. And there, next to the men holding something up to the light, jacketless, with his sleeves rolled up, is Innes.

Innes is, at this very moment, electrified by his magazine. The whole thing is being redesigned – the look, the content, the feel of it. The relaunched issue will feature an artist whom Innes believes will make an impression, will leave her footprint on history, will be remembered long after all these people have crumbled to dust.

And dust is something that is preoccupying him greatly today. Because this artist works with white clay, brushed and planed so smooth it assumes the texture of warmed infant flesh, making it imperative that—

Flesh? Innes's thoughts trip and stumble on the word. 'Flesh' is not a good word. Does it necessarily denote death? No, he decides, but the implication is enough to banish it from the paragraph he is privately composing in his head as he points out to the photographer that his lens must have been covered in dust when he shot this roll because the clarity, the slightly impure white that is the artist's signature, is by no means apparent.

Innes's mind is running on several planes. He is thinking, will the magazine masthead be all right at an angle like that, will it set off the plainness of the new font, I want the font to be plain, Helvetica perhaps, or Gill Sans, definitely not Times or Palatino, it must not fight for attention with the shot of the sculpture. He is thinking, warmed infant skin? No. Does he need the word 'infant' at all? Warmed skin? Warmed flesh? Does the juxtaposition of 'warmed' with 'flesh' expunge any overtones of death? He is thinking, will I trust Daphne to call the printers or shall I see to it myself?

As he crosses the room he looks out reflexively at the street, and so preoccupied is he with his magazine, with the impending font decision, with his article, that the image of the woman outside enters his mind and takes up a place there as a noise from the external world will incorporate itself into a sleeping man's dream. Innes immediately pictures this woman sitting with a typewriter at the desk next to his, her neat ankles crossed, her hand supporting her chin, that neck of hers turned so that she can look down at the street.

He stops in his tracks. The masthead must not be at an angle after all. It must be straight and at the bottom of the cover, justified right. It's never been done before! The font must be Gill Sans, bold, forty-eight point, lowercase, like so:

elsewhere

and the shot of the sculpture will float above as if the masthead, the name of the magazine itself, is the floor, the essential strut, the jumping-off point for the work. Which, in a way, Innes tells himself, it is!

'Stop!' Innes cries, at the layout man. 'Wait. Put it here. At the bottom. Like this. No, here. Gill Sans, bold, forty-eight point. Yes, Gill Sans. No. Perfect. Yes.'

The men with the contact sheet, Daphne on the phone, the visiting film critic and the layout man watch, unsurprised, as Innes stares at it for a moment, then bursts out through the door.

Suddenly Innes Kent is leaping down the steps. 'You,' he is saying.

'You took your time. Come here this instant.' He throws his arms wide.

Lexie blinks. She is still holding her map and his business card. But she moves towards him – how can she not? – and he envelops her in an embrace. Her face is pressed against the cloth of his suit and it registers somewhere that its nap is something familiar. She touches it with a fingertip, then pulls back to look. 'Felt,' she says.

'I beg your pardon?'

'Felt. Your suit is made of felt.'

'Yes. You like it?'

'I'm not sure.' She takes a step back to consider. 'I've never seen a suit made of felt before.'

'I know.' He grins. 'That's the point. My tailor wasn't at all sure either. But he came round to my way of thinking in the end.' He seizes her hand and sets off along the pavement. 'Right. Lunch. Are you hungry? I hope you're not one of those girls who doesn't eat.' He is talking almost as fast as he is walking. 'You don't look like you eat much. But I'm famished. I could eat a flock of sheep.'

'You don't look like you eat much either.'

'Ah, but I do. Appearances being deceptive, sometimes. You'll see.'

They pass at a fair pace along the street, down an alley, round a corner, past a man holding hands with two women, one on each side, both in shiny leather belts, all three of them laughing, past a shop with foreign papers in turning racks, past a group of girls carrying heavy sacks. Innes stops outside a restaurant. The sign above the door reads 'APOLLO', then nothing, 'APOLLO', then nothing, the word flashing on and off in blue neon. He opens the door. 'Here we are,' he says.

They go out of the sunshine, down a dark, twisting staircase to a low-ceilinged room. People are hunched at tables, with candles stuck into wine bottles flickering beneath their faces. In a corner, a man wearing a woman's feathered hat is playing the piano rather badly. Two other men sit squeezed on the stool with him and they are conducting a loud conversation above the player's head. It could, Lexie thinks, be any time of day at all outside – mid-afternoon, the dead of night – but down here you'd never know. There is a group of men, sitting around three small tables that have been pushed together. They greet Innes with shouts, raised wine glasses, expansive waves. Someone says, 'Is that a new one?' And 'What's happened to Daphne?'

Innes takes Lexie's arm and leads her to the back of the room. Catcalls and whistles follow them. They sit opposite each other in a booth.

'Who are they?' Lexie asks.

Innes turns to survey the group of men, who are now throwing candle stumps at the pianist and calling for more wine. 'They have many names,' he says, turning back. 'They call themselves artists but I'd say only one of them, no more than two, deserves that appellation. The rest are alcoholics and hangers-on. One is a photographer. One,' he says, leaning in close, 'is a woman who passes for a man. But only I know that.'

'Really?' Lexie is fascinated.

'Well,' he shrugs, 'me and her mother. And her lover, I'd imagine. Unless she's a very dim sort of girl. Now, what shall we eat?'

Lexie tries to look at the menu but she finds instead she's looking at Innes, at his blue felt suit, at his frown of concentration as he reads the menu, at the artists or alcoholics, one of whom now has the waitress – a florid, large woman in her fifties – on his lap, at the row of empty wine bottles that line the shelves, at the swirling patterns on the table-top.

'What's the matter?' Innes is touching her sleeve.

'Oh, I don't know,' she bursts out. 'I wish . . . I don't know. I wish I had a pair of red heels and some gold hoop earrings.'

Innes pulls a face. 'You wouldn't be sitting here with me if you did.'

'Wouldn't I?' She sees Innes is getting out his cigarettes. 'May I have one?'

He puts two into his mouth, watching her, strikes a match, holds it to the cigarettes until they ignite, then hands one over to her, all without taking his eyes off her face. 'You think you want hooped earrings but you don't.'

Lexie puts the cigarette to her own mouth. 'How do you know?'

'I know what you need,' he says, in a low tone, still looking her in the eye.

She stares at him, then bursts out laughing, without quite knowing why. What can he mean? Then she stops laughing because she has felt an unfamiliar sensation, low in her body, a kind of pull or drawing down. It is as if her blood and bones have heard him and are answering him. Then she laughs again and, as if he has understood, he laughs too.

He reaches out, cups a hand around her face, runs his thumb along her jawline.

Something unusual has happened to Innes. He does not fully understand it. But he can pinpoint when it began, this slight madness, this possession. When, a little over two weeks ago, he peered over a hedge and found a woman sitting on a tree stump. He looks at the restaurant table, at the floor, how it seems to feed and feed itself under all the furniture in the room. He feels for a moment the vastness of the city, the whole breathing breadth of it, and he feels as if he and this girl, this woman, are sitting together in its very centre, at the very eye of its storm, and he feels as if they might be the only people who are doing this, who have ever done this. He steals a half-glance at her, but only to be able to see her wrists, the way the sleeves drape over them, the way her hands are crossed over each other, the handbag placed on the bench next to her.

It seems at once peculiar and utterly right that she should be sitting there with him. He registers a vague desire to buy her something – anything. A painting. A coat. A pair of gloves. He would like, he realises, to watch her unwrapping a gift, to see her fingers negotiating the ribbon and paper of a present. But he pushes the thought from his mind. He cannot mess it up, not this one, not her. He doesn't know why but he recognises that this one is different, this one is necessary to him. It's an unaccountable thought.

To distract himself, he talks. He tells her about his magazine, about his recent trip to Paris, where he bought several paintings and two sculptures. He does a little dealing in art, as a sideline. Has to, he says, because the magazine makes no money at all. He tells her the sculptures were by unknown artists and that this is what he finds exciting. Anyone, he says, can buy work of an established artist. She interrupts at this point to say, anyone with money, and he nods and says, true. But it takes skill and a degree of recklessness to take a punt on an unknown. He says he can't describe the feeling of walking into an artist's studio and thinking, yes, this is it, this is something. And then he spends a long time trying to describe just that.

He explains how he has ordered the work to be packed, in sawdust and then in newspaper and then in crates. When it's unpacked he has to take a soft brush, made from the hair of small mammals, and dust off the bits of sawdust. He doesn't trust anyone else with this job, which is, he admits, a little ridiculous. It means, he says, I spend most of my evenings in the back room at the office with a tiny paintbrush in my hand. Painting a painting? she says, and he laughs. Yes, I suppose so.

She doesn't ask much but she listens. God, but does she listen. She listens to him like he has never been listened to before. She listens as if every single word he says contains oxygen. She listens with widened eyes and an incline to her body. She listens so intently that he would like to lean towards her until their heads meet, at which point he would whisper: what? What is it you're hoping I'll say?

His father, he tells her, was English, but his mother was a mestizo from colonial Chile. Half Chilean, half Scottish, he explains, hence his Hibernian Christian name and also his black hair. This causes Lexie's eyes to widen the most. She was from Valparaiso, he says, and he watches Lexie mouth the word to herself, as if committing all this to memory. His father was sent out there to make his fortune. He was, Innes tells Lexie, the second son of a wealthy family. And he returned with a fortune and also a somewhat exotic wife. He died in a motor accident when Innes was two. Do you remember him at all, Lexie asks, and Innes says, no, he does not. His mother talked about returning to Chile then, he says. She never did. She wouldn't have been able to. Why not? Lexie wants to know. She always wants to know, it seems. Because there was nothing there any more, he says, nothing she knew. It's a different country now.

Ted walks, pushing the pram in front of him. He doesn't think he's ever been out on the Heath this early in the morning. Some time after five a.m. he had been woken by a hand on his arm, and for a moment he couldn't work out what was happening, why a woman was swaying above him in the dark room, why she was crying, what she wanted from him. Then it had all come back to him. It was Elina, holding their son, and she was asking, please. Please can you take him.

Ted hadn't quite been able to make sense of what she was saying – a broken jumble of English and Finnish, with possibly some German mixed in, was coming out of her mouth, something about sleep, something about crying – but the sense of it was clear, what he had to do was clear. He took the baby she was holding out to him; she collapsed on to the bed and, within seconds, she was asleep, her head not quite on the pillow.

And now Ted is pushing his son up Parliament Hill, slowly, slowly, because there is no rush, they aren't going anywhere special, he and his son, they are just walking for the sake of walking. The sun has risen to make the dew on the grass glint like shattered glass and Ted finds himself wishing that the baby was old enough for him to point this out, finds himself looking forward to a time when he and this child can walk together and discuss the visual effect of early-morning sun on dew, the astonishing number of people out jogging and dog-walking at this ungodly hour, the way you can already see that the day is going to be a hot one. It gives Ted a sting of pleasure to know that this will happen, that this child will be here, with them, that he is theirs. It seems an impossible concept. Ted still half expects someone to come along and put their hand on the pram handle and say, I'm sorry, you didn't really think you could keep him, did you?

A man – older than Ted, perhaps in his forties, with skin tanned to the hue of oiled teak – jogs past and gives Ted a quick, rueful smile. And Ted sees that the man, off down the path now, is a father too, that in his time he has probably done exactly what Ted is doing, the early-morning shift while the woman sleeps after a long night, the circuit with the pram and the sleeping baby. Just for a moment, Ted would like to run after him, would like to say something to him, to ask, does it get easier, does it pass?

Instead, he looks down at the baby. He is dressed, parcelled up, in a striped all-in-one. Alternating red and orange bands with green poppers running the length of his stomach and down his legs. Elina has said she doesn't understand why people dress babies only in white and pastels. She loathes pastels, Ted knows: the diluted cousins of real colour, she calls them, claims they make her teeth ache. Ted can remember the day they bought this outfit. Elina was only just pregnant, they were still speechless with the shock of it, when they passed a shop with tiny outfits strung from mock tree branches. Somewhere in East London it was; they were on their way to an exhibition at the Whitechapel Gallery. They'd spent several minutes looking in at them, bemused, side by side but not speaking to each other. A green one with orange spots, a pink one with blue zigzags, a purple one, a turquoise one. Ted couldn't decide whether they seemed astonishingly small or unaccountably large. Then Elina had said, 'Right.' Bitten her lip. Folded her arms. Ted saw that she was steeling herself, she was making up her mind; he knew then that they were going to have this baby, that this child would be born, and he realised that up until this moment he hadn't been sure what Elina would decide, whether she did want it, whether she would go through with it. 'Right,' she said again, took two steps towards the shop door and pushed it open. Alone on the pavement, he felt his face break into a smile. They would be parents and their baby would always be dressed in colour. He watched through the window as Elina selected two outfits, still biting her lip, still with her arms folded, like a woman psyching herself up for a high dive, and he saw that she would stay with him, that she wasn't going to disappear off to New York or Hong Kong or wherever, as he sometimes feared. He remembers feeling as though he had X-ray vision, watching her there in the shop, that he could look at her and see through her body to the curled being suspended inside.

He is smiling now, thinking about it, as he looks down at his son. The baby's eyes waver towards his, seem to lock with his, and then they waver away to focus on something just past Ted's head. Ted cannot imagine, cannot comprehend what it is like to see the world for the first time. To have never seen a wall, a washing-line, a tree. He is momentarily filled with a kind of pity for his son. What a task lies ahead of him: to learn literally everything.

Ted reaches the apex of Parliament Hill. Ten past six in the morning. He inhales a lungful of air. He glances down at the tiny, bundled form in the pram and sees that the baby has fallen asleep, arms flung wide. He sees that inside the pram are pinned abstract black and white sketches, geometric shapes, probably done by Elina. She said something the other day about how babies of this age only see in black and white and, as Ted is stepping backwards to sit down on a bench, he is wondering how scientists can possibly know this.

He is stepping back. Three or four steps. Towards a bench he knows is there. He recalls this later. Because although he is sure of what he is and what he is doing – a father of a young baby, out for a walk – he cannot be entirely sure that he isn't a child, standing at the window of his yellow-curtained bedroom, listening to the surprising sound of his mother arguing with someone who has come to the door. Ted stands at his window, gripping the fabric of the curtain, looking down into the street, where a man is stepping backwards, three or four steps, off the pavement and into the street, and the man is looking up at the house, scanning the windows, his hand shading his eyes, and when he sees Ted, he waves. There is something frantic, urgent, in the way he waves. As if the man has an important message for him, as if he is beckoning him down to the street.

Ted lands on the bench with a thud. The recollection is gone. The image of the man walking backwards outside his house is gone. Ted looks at the silver pram handle, where the sun is glancing off it in sharp rays; he looks at the grass, the long swaths of it still glistening; he looks at the ponds at the bottom of the hill, and as he looks he is aware that there is a space at the centre of his vision. The periphery is clear but he cannot see the very thing he looks at, as if a hole has been burnt in the centre of a lens, as if he is looking through a shattered windscreen, and he realises that he is having one of the visual disturbances he used to suffer from as a child. A 'bizzy', his mother used to call them. This hasn't happened for years, and the old familiarity of it almost makes him laugh. The crackling, fiery bonfire that flares in front of his eyes, illuminating whatever he looks at, the prickling sensation down his left arm. He can't remember the last time this happened – when he was twelve, perhaps, thirteen? Ted knows it will pass, that it means nothing, that it's just a neurological blip, a momentary confusion of pathways. But he keeps a firm hold of the pram handle, as if to ground himself. He is tempted to ring his mother and say, guess what? I'm having a bizzy. Bizzies once united him and his mother. She watched him, eagle-like, and if he so much as closed his eyes, she would be there beside him, saying, 'What is it? What's wrong? Is it happening again?' She took Ted to doctors, optometrists, consultants. She tracked down specialist after specialist with detective zeal. He had examinations, scans, referrals, X-rays, and after each of these appointments – which meant a day off school for Ted – he and his mother would go for tea. So instead of maths or chemistry or history, he would be sitting in Claridge's or the Savoy, eating sandwiches and cream cakes as his mother poured the milk. The doctors could find nothing wrong with him, they told his mother. It's just one of those things. He'll probably grow out of it. And meanwhile his mother wrote notes to the school, excusing Ted from games, from rugby, from swimming lessons. Ted told his father once that it was like seeing angels, like watching sunlight on moving water. His father had fidgeted in his chair, asked him if he wanted to bowl a few cricket balls. He didn't go in for fanciful talk.

Just as Ted knew it would, the refracting blaze at the centre of his vision breaks slowly into pieces and these pieces float to the edges of what he sees and then, finally, vanish. And Ted is back to the way he was, a man sitting on a bench, holding on to a pram. The baby is stirring in his wrappings, a hand flailing out, curled fingers brushing against the sketches done by his mother. Ted, taking this as a sign from the baby, stands and starts to push him back down the hill.

Elina is in the garden. Daytime. The sun horizontal above her, the plant pots, the coiled hose, that old tin bucket all standing in inky pools of their own shadows. She is sitting cross-legged on a rug and, on the grass next to her, her shadow is struggling to hold its shape.

She watches it for a moment, fighting a losing battle with its surface, the millions of blades of grass all growing in different directions, at different rates. The shadow's edges are splintered, ragged, like something lost at sea.

Elina looks away from it and, as she does so, sees that she is holding a rattle in her right hand: a complex thing of coloured rods, bells, strips of elastic, beads inside balls. Beneath where it is suspended, the baby is lying. On his back, his eyes fixed on her. The frank interrogation of his gaze gives her a start.

She moves the rattle from side to side and the coloured beads ricochet around inside their clear globes. The effect on the baby is instantaneous and remarkable. His limbs stiffen, his eyes spring wide, his lips part in a perfect round O. It is as if he's been studying a manual on how to be a human being, with particular attention to the chapter, 'Demonstrating Surprise'. She shakes it again and again and the baby's limbs move like pistons, up, down, in, out. She thinks: This is what mothers do.

A clashing noise from the house makes her look up. And there is Ted, in the kitchen window, framed in the act of lifting a pan from the stove. He is here this week, she remembers now, he's taken time off work.

She turns back to the baby. She touches the hair on his temples, which is inexplicably turning from dark to light, she strokes the curve of his cheek, she rests a hand on his chest and feels his lungs fill, flatten, fill, flatten.

A squirrel with a grey-flecked tail darts from a flowerpot to the wall of her studio, its clawed feet gripping the wood as it shunts itself up to the roof and then away. The scrolled white petals of the calla lilies in the pot shiver with the vibrations.

She must have turned her head too quickly because the colours of the garden, of the baby's suit seem to blaze brighter for a few seconds. And now Ted is coming out of the house and, in the bright sunlight, the shape of him seems to shimmer and bifurcate and, for a moment, it is as if there is another person there, hovering just behind him. He walks across the grass and the shape seems to follow him.

'OK,' he is saying, 'get this down you. *Pasta al limone,* made with fresh—' He catches sight of her face. 'What's up?'

'Nothing.' Elina pulls her mouth into a smile. It is important to reassure him. 'I think I need my sunglasses.'

The house is dark and shadowed after the glare of the garden. Unfamiliar, almost. She stares about her as if seeing it for the first time. That vase, the orange bowl, the jute rug with a million tiny loops. She tiptoes past all these things that are hers but don't look like hers, through the kitchen and up the stairs. On the landing, she thinks: I am alone in the house. She stops for a moment, one hand resting on the banisters. She feels light, insubstantial, the air circulating around her empty arms.

She has tried to talk to Ted. She had thought it might help. He is at home this week, and the next. They are together, all day and all night, the two of them and the baby. She sits on the sofa, mostly, and breastfeeds. Ted cooks. Ted loads the washing-machine. Ted takes the baby out for walks in his pram and then she can sleep. She sleeps in short, snatched bursts – on the sofa, in a chair, in bed if she's lucky – and these naps are animated by hectic, speedy dreams, most often on the subject of losing the baby or being unable to reach the baby, or sometimes there are abstract images of fountains. Fountains of red liquid. These she wakes from with a jolt, with a galloping heart.

So Ted is at home, with her, the shoot is over, and she has tried to talk to him. She tried last night as they sat at the table, eating a takeaway. Ted had been cradling his son, hand bent back on itself so that the baby was able to keep his grip on Ted's thumb and she had liked to see that, that Ted had thought that the baby needed to hold his thumb and should continue to do so. And she had been close to him and she had put down her fork and touched his arm and said, 'Ted, do you know how much it was that I lost?'

'How much of what?' he'd said, without looking up from his plate.

'You know.' She waited before saying: 'Blood.'

His head swung up to look at her and she had waited some more. But he hadn't said anything.

'I mean,' she prompted, 'at the birth. The caesarian. Did the doctors tell you because—'

'Four pints,' he said flatly.

There had been a pause. Elina pictured those four pints lined up, as if in milk bottles: clear, greenish glass holding that startling, jewel-scarlet liquid. In the fridge, placed on a shelf, on a doorstep, in a supermarket display cabinet. Four pints. She toyed with her food, took a mouthful, stole a glance at Ted. He was sitting with his head bent, looking either at the baby or at his plate, she couldn't tell which, his hair obscuring his face.

'I couldn't see you at the time,' she'd tried again. 'You must have been over near the baby.'

He gave a noise of assent.

She picked up a silver-foil carton and, seeing it was full of chopped onion, put it down again. 'Could you see much?' she had asked, because she wanted to know, she wanted to hear him say it, she wanted to get whatever was in his head out so they could look at it together, so they could try to thaw this thing that had seemed to solidify between them. He hadn't answered so she had said, 'Ted? How much did you see?' He had put down his fork and said: 'I don't really want to talk about this.'

'But I do,' she'd said.

'Well, I don't.'

'But it's important, Ted. We shouldn't just brush it away as if it never happened. I want to understand – is that so bad? I want to know why it happened and—'

He pushed back his chair and left the table. In the kitchen he turned, the tiny form of the baby clutched in his arms. His face had been stricken, unrecognisable, and Elina had felt a hot pulse of fear – for him, for the baby. She wanted to say, OK, forget it, let's not talk about it, just sit down. Most of all, she wanted to say, Ted, give me the baby.

'They don't know why it happened.' He was almost shouting. 'I – I – I asked them the next day and they said they didn't know, that it was just one of those things.'

'All right,' she tried to say soothingly. 'It doesn't—'

'And I said, you can't say that, don't you dare say that. She nearly died, for Chrissake, and all you can say is *just one of those things*? You let her go for three days before realising the baby's jammed in some impossible position and then you let some fucking student carve her up and—'

He had stopped short. He stood in the kitchen and she had thought for a moment that he might cry. But he didn't. He came towards her, where she sat at the table. He handed her the baby and, without looking at her, he left the room. She heard him go upstairs. There was silence for a while. Elina sat tight on her chair. Then she had heard him opening cupboards, shutting doors and from these sounds she had known he was getting ready to go out for a run. She had heard him descend the stairs, then the front door slam and she had heard his feet, pounding the pavement, as he sprinted away up the street.

She finds the sunglasses on the bathroom shelf and is just about to pick them up when she realises that her body is moving quickly: it is turning and walking her towards the door, it is starting to carry her down the stairs. It takes her a second or two to work out why. The baby is crying, a thin, winding cry snaking in through the bathroom window. It surprises her that her body had heard and recognised this before she was aware of it.

Out in the garden, Ted is sitting on the rug. He has picked up the baby and is holding him gingerly in both hands. The baby is a tiny, angry automaton, legs and hands working like levers in the air, the cries regular, each one crescendoing at shriek-pitch.

Elina moves over the grass, bends and lifts him with one movement. His body feels rigid and his cries broaden into outrage. *How could you?* he seems to be saying. *How could you leave me like that?* She places him over her shoulder and walks to the garden wall and back, saying, 'Sssh, sssh, it's all right, sssh, sssh.'

'Sorry.' Ted is standing up now. 'I didn't know what to . . . I wasn't sure if he was hungry or not or whether . . .'

'It's all right.' She passes him on her way back to the wall and sees that he is watching her, anxiety gathered in his face.

'Do you want me to take him?' Ted says.

The baby's cries are subsiding into shuddering breaths. Elina shifts his position so that he is looking up at the sky. 'No,' she says. 'Don't worry.'

'Is he hungry?'

'I don't think so. He only fed . . . I don't know . . . half an hour ago.'

They sit down again on the rug and Elina sees the bowl of pasta. She'd forgotten about it. She puts on the sunglasses and, placing the baby so that he is looking over her shoulder, starts to eat with her spare hand. He clutches at the collar of her shirt, snuffs his wet mouth into the skin of her neck, his breath sounding hot in her ear.

'It's amazing how you can do that,' Ted says.

'What?'

'That.' He indicates the baby with his fork.

'What do you mean?'

'He's crying – really crying – and you come along and pick him up and he stops. Like magic. Like a spell. It's only with you. He doesn't do it with me.'

'Doesn't he?'

'No. I can't get him to stop like you can, it's—'

'That's not true. I'm sure you can—'

'No, no.' Ted shakes his head. 'It's a special thing you have with him. It's like he has this internal timer that measures how long he hasn't seen you and without warning it can just go off and nothing else will mollify him.' He shrugs. 'I've been noticing it this week.'

Elina thinks about this. The baby, sucking her shirt, seems to be thinking about it too. 'It's probably just these,' she says, gesturing at her breasts.

Ted shakes his head again, grinning. 'No, although I wouldn't blame him. But it's not that, I promise you. It's like . . . it's like he needs a dose of you at regular intervals. To check you're still there. To check you haven't gone anywh—' He breaks off in mid-sentence. Elina glances up at him. Ted is kneeling on the rug, a forkful of pasta halfway to his mouth. He is motionless, his face screwed up.

'Hey,' she says, 'are you OK?'

He puts down his fork with a clatter. 'Fine . . . Just feel a bit . . .'

'A bit what?'

'Just . . .' He presses both hands to his eyes. 'I just get this . . . thing sometimes where . . .'

Elina puts down her own fork. 'Where what?'

'Where my eyes go a bit funny.'

'Your eyes?'

'It's really nothing,' he murmurs. 'It's fine. I've . . . I've had it . . . all my life.'

'All your life?' she repeats. What can he mean, all his life? She puts down the baby on the rug and crouches next to Ted. She touches his back, moves her hand up and down his spine. 'How long does it last?' she asks, after a while.

Ted is still hunched into himself, shielding his eyes. 'Not long,' he gets out. 'Any minute now. Sorry.'

'Don't be silly.'

'It's weird, it hasn't happened for—'

'Ssh,' she says. 'Don't talk. Shall I get you some water?'

When she comes back with a glass he has straightened up. He is sitting staring at the baby, his head tilted, frowning. She hands him the water. 'How are you? Are your eyes OK again?'

He nods.

'What was that?' She touches her hand to his forehead. 'Ted, you're freezing and – what's the word – damp?'

'Clammy,' he mutters.

'Clammy,' she says. 'I think you should go to the doctor.'

He takes a sip of the water and grunts.

'You must.'

'No, it's fine. I'm fine.'

'You're not fine.'

'I am.' He shakes his hair out of his eyes, looks up at her. 'I'm fine,' he says again. 'Really.' He puts his arm around her, kisses her neck. 'Don't look so worried. It's nothing at all, just—'

'It doesn't sound like nothing.'

'It is. I used to have them all the time when I was a child. Haven't had one for years and years until the other day and—'

'This happened the other day? And you didn't tell me?'

'Elina,' he takes both her hands in his, 'it's nothing. I promise.'

'You need to see a doctor.'

'I've seen every doctor there is to see about this. When I was young. I've had eye-scans and brain-scans and everything-scans. Ask my mother.'

'But, Ted—'

At that moment, the baby starts to sob from his position on the rug.

'Look,' Ted says, 'the internal timer's gone off.'

And later that day, or perhaps the next – it's hard to tell because she hasn't been to sleep – Elina sits on the sofa, the length of her spine resting against cushions, her feet planted together on the carpet. In one hand, she is feeling the heaviness of a glass paperweight.

It is a near-perfect sphere, flattened out at the base so that it sits without rolling on a table-top. It has hundreds of tiny bubbles in it. Elina holds it up to her eye and peers through it at a murky, distant, greenish place with holes in its atmosphere the shape of tears.

She likes this paperweight, the cold, clear heft of it. She likes the way that the air from the room in which it was made, on the day it was made, is trapped inside it for ever. Perhaps even air breathed out by the person who made it. It fits so exactly to her palm and it must be the size of the head of an unborn baby at – what? – six months? Five? She would like to photograph it, from very close range. She must do that soon. One day. Where is her camera anyway? Out in the studio? She should look for it, put it somewhere safe. She would like to capture the secret, still space inside the paperweight. She would like to squeeze inside it.

She laces both hands underneath it and lets her gaze drift up into the room.

'And I tried to tell her,' Ted's mother is saying from the other sofa, twisted round to address Ted, who is in the kitchen, 'that the reason why she hasn't received a card from me is that you just will not decide on a name. But she wasn't having any of it. Very mardy, she was.' Ted's mother twitches then smooths the cuff of her blouse and Elina sees that she is trying to mask her irritation. 'Have you had any more thoughts on what you'll call him?'

Ted makes some unintelligible reply from inside the fridge.

Elina blinks. She is experiencing, just for a second, the sensation of having someone's hands up inside your skin, near your ribs, pushing, pushing at something. She blinks again to make it go away.

Ted's mother turns back to the room, shifting herself against the sofa. She'd said when they'd first bought it that it would never be comfortable as there was no head support. Elina wonders now if she is feeling the lack of cushioning in her cranial area.

'Well,' she says, 'I never thought that by the time my grandson was almost a month old I still wouldn't be able to send out cards. All my relatives are dying to get one.'

'Why don't you just send them?' Ted's father says, with only a hint of gritted teeth, from behind a newspaper. And Elina is surprised to see him because it's rare for Ted's parents to come together: they usually operate on separate schedules.

'Yeah,' Ted says, as he comes in, carrying a tray. 'They don't have to have his name on, do they?'

His mother gasps, as if they are suggesting something lewd. 'Not have his name on? Of course they must have his name on!'

Ted shrugs and starts to pour the tea.

'What about Rupert?' his mother says brightly. 'I've always loved the name Rupert and it's an old family name on my side.'

'Sounds like . . . a whatdyoucallit?' Ted's father says, folding up the newspaper and tossing it to the floor.

'What?'

'A . . .' Ted's father puts his hand to his brow '. . . you know . . . a thing that children take to bed. Um . . . *Brideshead* . . . um . . . teddy-bear! That's it. A teddy-bear.' He reaches down and picks up the newspaper again. 'It sounds like a teddy-bear,' he says, as he scans the front page for the second time.

'What does?' his mother says.

'The name Rupert.'

Elina hears the word: clamp. She hears: rupture. She hears: stargazer presentation.

Ted makes another uninterpretable noise, then says, 'Here's your tea. How have things been with you? Been busy this week?'

'Or Ralph. How about Ralph? He looks like a Ralph. And it was my grandfather's middle name. It has a lovely ring to it. It would go well with the surname, too.'

'Um.' Ted glances at Elina. She keeps her face very still; she shifts the paperweight in her hands. The glass surface has become warm to the touch. She can see Ted debating whether to broach this or not, then she sees him decide to take the plunge. 'Actually,' he says, handing his parents cups of tea, 'we've decided to give him Elina's surname. He'll be a Vilkuna.'

When Ted's mother came to visit at the hospital, the baby was three hours old. Elina can remember it all now. With her one free arm, Elina was holding him against her chest, where he was asleep, his limbs folded under him, his face pressed up against her skin. Her other arm was bandaged and wrapped into a mysterious chrysalis. Tubes came in and came out again. Various bags were suspended above her head. From under the blanket, there were more tubes entering and leaving her. She wasn't yet allowing herself to think about where those ones were going in.

She appeared to be banked up on numerous pillows. Something – she wasn't sure what, the morphine, perhaps – was making her eyes roll backwards in their sockets every few minutes. It made the room lurch and pitch and Elina had to struggle to stay in the here and now, not to give in to the medicine's dragging force. It was like a strong current in the sea, pulling her down.

Ted was across the room, a long way off, it seemed, in a chair. He had a pen in his hand and he was filling in some forms. As she looked, he raised his head, and Elina almost gasped because his face was such a shock: drawn, grey, tense, it was a skin-covered mask. She felt that he might be a stranger, might be anyone. What's happened? she wanted to say. Why do you look like that?

The door swung open and Elina turned her head and suddenly Ted's mother was in the room.

'Ohhhh!' she squealed. 'Ohhhh! My darling!' She swooped across the room and for a disconcerting moment, Elina thought she meant her. But Ted's mother wasn't looking at her. She was lifting up the baby and settling him in her arms. 'You,' she said, and Elina wondered why she was talking so loudly, 'just look at you.'

She had her back to the bed now and was walking away towards the window. Where the baby had been on Elina's chest felt damp. She could feel the outline of the baby on herself, where warmth had generated between them. She saw her hand, her chrysalis hand, raising itself from the bed, as if she would speak. But she wasn't sure what she would say and Ted was getting up from the chair and her eyes were doing that rolling thing so that all she saw before she forced them down again was the ceiling, the bags of fluid hanging above her.

'. . . just terrible,' Ted was saying, with his new, grey face, and Elina had to strain to hear him, '. . . lost his heartbeat and . . . whisked into theatre . . . but then everything just . . . everywhere, an unbelievable . . . Elina nearly—' Ted came to a halt, swallowing his final word.

For a moment, no one spoke. There was the slight, impossible sound of the baby's breathing: a rapid, fluttering in–out. The silence in the room seemed as fragile, as intricate, as frost.

'Mmm, oh dear,' Ted's mother said. 'Get my camera, would you? It's in my bag there.' She was gazing down at the baby. Her expression was hard to read. It was rapt, fierce, complicated. It was one of covetousness or avid desire, and it sent a pulse of fear through Elina. And the baby, as if sensing this, let out an abrupt high-pitched cry.

From the bed, Elina saw her arm rise up again. This time Ted saw. He came over and leant his head towards her, his hand taking hold of hers. 'What is it?' he said. 'Are you OK?'

'The baby.' Elina was surprised at how hoarse her voice was. 'I want the baby back.'

And here she is again, Ted's mother, sitting on the sofa she'd complained about, waiting for the baby to wake up so she can 'have a hold'.

'Vilkuna?' she is saying, as if it's a swearword. 'He'll be a Vilkuna? You're not going to give your son his proper name?'

Ted adjusts the angle of his mug, keeping his eyes on the rug under his feet. 'There's no reason why a child should have his father's name instead of—'

'No reason? No reason? There's every reason in the world. People are going to think he's a . . . that he's illegitimate, that he's—'

'Well, he is,' Elina says.

Ted's mother turns her head with a jerk, as if she'd forgotten Elina was there and the sound of her voice had given her a fright.

'In my day,' she begins in a shaking voice, 'that was not something people broadcast. In my day—'

'The world's changed, Mum.' Ted stands, picking up his mug. 'Let's face it. More tea?'

After his parents leave, tucking themselves into their neat little silver car and driving back to Islington, Ted returns to the sitting room. There isn't a surface that isn't covered with the flotsam and jetsam of the day: nappies have washed up all over the floor, coffee cups on the tables, a breast pump on the television, cards brought by his mother, a half-eaten plate of biscuits on the bookshelves, a baby-care manual face down on a chair.

Ted sighs and slumps on to the sofa. He had had no idea that having a baby would entail so much entertaining, so many visitors, so many phone calls and emails, so many pots of tea to be made, served, cleared away, washed up, that the mere act of procreation meant that people suddenly wanted to come around several times a week and sit in your house for hours on end.

Ted clears away the tea tray. He walks about the sitting room, past Elina, who is wiping something off one part of the baby's body while simultaneously smearing something on another, picking his way through toys, rattles, nappies, wipes, muslin squares. He gathers up stray coffee cups, cake plates, moves them from the sitting room to the kitchen. Elina hands him the baby before getting down on her hands and knees and scrubbing at a stain – milk? sick? shit? – on the rug.

Ted holds his son to his chest and does circuits of the room, round and round the table. The baby's eyes roll in their sockets, he sucks absently on his thumb – surely he'll sleep. Ted walks on, listing from side to side, a ship in calm seas. The baby's eyelids droop, his sucking slows, but as soon as he falls asleep his thumb drops out and he jerks awake again, his eyes rolling open in dismay. Suck, suck, eyes close, thumb falls out, eyes open and round they go again, past Elina, who is now folding muslin squares, through the toys, over the changing mat, through the nappies. Ted adjusts his position so that the thumb arm is wedged against him, immovable, but the change seems to remind the baby of something because he starts, back stiff, neck twisting, alert to the possibility of food.

Ted tries a bit longer to get him to sleep but all he wants now is to eat – he cries, he frets, he strains and struggles – and eventually

Ted taps Elina on the shoulder. Without a word, she sweeps a mess of wipes, instructions for sterilisers, baby socks, unopened cards off the chair on to the floor and sits, lifting her blouse.

Ted is surprised at how smoothly and quickly she does the latching on: unsnaps her bra with one hand, while the other does a swift tilting motion with the baby. He gives a final, high cry of relief and is then silent. Elina settles herself deeper into the chair and lets her head fall back to the wall. Ted registers again how pale she is, how dark and deep are the circles around her eyes, how thin her limbs look. He is possessed with an urge to apologise – for what he isn't sure. He scans his mind for something to say, something light and perhaps witty, something to take them out of themselves, to remind them that life is not all like this. But he can't think of anything and now the baby is rearing back, crying, fidgeting, fists flailing, and Elina is having to open her eyes, sit up again, lift him to her shoulder, rub his back, untangle his hands from her hair and Ted cannot bear it. He cannot bear to watch her having to rouse herself, to lift that tired head from the wall, to rev herself into action. He lunges for a forgotten cake plate and makes for the kitchen.

The baby cannot settle to his feed. Elina pushes herself into a standing position. Sometimes the only thing that works is feeding him while she walks around. The movement seems to soothe him, seems to allow him to digest. Or something. She walks slowly, slowly to the window, then back. The baby fusses, turns his head this way, then back, and finally latches on. Elina keeps walking, letting out her breath a bit at a time. Ted is in the kitchen now, his hands in the washing-up bowl.

'Ted,' she says, as she passes on the way to the television, where she turns round and walks back, because she wants to say something to him, wants them both to recall that they are more to each other than just parents of the same child.

'Mmm?' He lifts a dripping cup from the water.

The problem is she can't think of what to say. 'How are you doing?' she tries.

He looks at her, surprised. 'I'm fine. How are you doing?'

'I'm fine too.'

'Good. Tired?'

'Of course. You?'

'Of course.' He extracts a plate from the sudsy water and lays it on top of the cup. 'Maybe you should have a nap when he's finished.'

'Maybe,' she says. 'He might sleep. Then we could all have a nap.'

Ted nods. 'Sounds good.'

Elina cannot bear it. Why are they talking to each other like this? What has happened to them? She tries to think of one thing, one interesting thing to say, to snap them out of it, but her brain fails her. She turns and marches through the room with the baby – how can it be that she has produced a child who can only eat on the move? – from the sofa, past the table, through the kitchen and to the window.

It was not always like this. She would like to set this down: they were not always like this.

She puts the baby to her shoulder, his forehead falling into the curve of her neck, the damp warmth of his breath spreading into her collar. She'd met Ted because she was looking for somewhere to live; she was looking for somewhere to live because she'd decided to leave Oscar; she decided to leave Oscar because he never bought his own materials and constantly stole hers, because he couldn't cook anything other than a bacon fry-up, because he'd slept with a waitress; he'd slept with the waitress, so Oscar said, because he felt threatened by the success of Elina's last show. And so because of all this – a chain reaction of bacon, pilfered paintbrushes, sex with waitresses, and a place to live – she had rung the number advertising a room in Gospel Oak. Near the Heath, it had said, which was why she chose it. And there, in the house near the Heath, was an attic room up a ladder, with the best kind of washed, level, London light. The man, Ted, had helped her carry in her toolboxes, her paint, her unstretched canvases. There was a garden, out the back, a kitchen painted blue and, sometimes, a girlfriend called Yvette, a thin woman with the watchful gaze of a cat. Elina worked and slept in her attic room, she gave up smoking, she avoided calls from Oscar, she had another show, bigger this time and just for her, she took up smoking again, Ted came and went downstairs, as did Yvette. If Elina heard them in the bedroom below, she put on her headphones and turned up the volume. And then suddenly Yvette was gone. Had left Ted for an actor. Ted came up the ladder to tell Elina. Elina said, never trust an actor. She took Ted out to a private view of photographs of drag queens and afterwards they went to a bar. Ted got drunk. Ted fell down. Elina called a cab and helped him into the house. The next day they looked up the actor on the Internet, using Elina's laptop – Elina said he had the kind of looks that don't last and, also, weren't his trousers pulled up slightly too high? Ted began to visit her in her room. He liked to lie on her bed and tell her about the film he was working on, the rushes he'd edited that day. Elina had to stop work – she couldn't work with anyone watching – but she could always clean her brushes, stretch a canvas, tidy her bench.

Sometimes they went for walks on the Heath in the dusk. Sometimes they went to the cinema. They talked about the films. He lent her books. They talked about the books. He cooked for her, if she was in; if she was out, he left a note for her, saying that supper was in the fridge. She picked up the shoes he left in the sitting room, lined them up in pairs on the shoe rack. She replaced his keys on the hook. She liked to draw on the mirror in the steam of his morning shower, after he'd left for work – abstract lines that flowed to a single centre. She liked coming down in the morning and finding the water in the kettle still warm from his cup of tea. Once, finding herself cold in the late afternoon, she put on the first thing she found – a jumper of his left on the stairs – and returned to work. But she couldn't concentrate, couldn't make the paint work the way she wanted it to, couldn't be anything other than what she was: a woman in a room with a brush in her hand. She flung down the brush and stalked to the slanted window and there she discovered she was holding up the jumper sleeve to her nose, breathing in, breathing in. The smell of him filled her face, surrounded her. She yanked the jumper over her head, shocked, and dropped it down the hatch to the floor below. For a week she avoided him, made sure she was out, lived her evenings in cafés, in bars, in galleries. She ate his dinners in the middle of the night, slept until lunchtime, worked in the afternoons. She collected the notes he wrote her, cooking instructions, a request for the gas money, a phone call she'd missed, and shut them inside the pages of her books. She began a series of smaller paintings, all in blacks and reds. Then one day, another note, longer this time, saying he was going to Berlin, to the film festival, had an extra ticket and did she want to come? She went. Berlin was cold, the air filled with sleet, the trams powering through mounds of dirty snow. They ate apple cake in cafés, saw films in the afternoons, went to look at the remains of the Wall. They stayed in a hotel with twin beds and tinted-glass windows that made the sky appear tea-coloured. The bedcovers were nylon and slid off in the night. Elina listened to his breathing as he slept. She peeped at his passport photo while he was in the bathroom. She looked at his empty clothes, crumpled on a chair. They went to the art gallery, more films, some parties where people were drinking frozen vodka that Ted said made his teeth ache; she watched as he chatted to a producer from Canada called Cindy and as they exchanged email addresses. Elina got drunk. Elina fell down. Ted helped her back to the hotel and put her under the bedcovers. He brought her water to drink in the morning. They went to find Potsdam Square and found only a shopping arcade. They ate tortillas that were too greasy, they wrote postcards. She asked Ted who his were to and he told her; he didn't ask about hers. They saw another film, they ate more apple cake, they went to another party. She listened to his breathing as he slept. Both their bedcovers slid off during the night, into the space between their beds. Elina woke early, the sky a dark tannin brown, to find them there, jumbled together. They went home. Back in her attic room, she propped the black and red paintings against the wall, facing in. She mixed some paint but let it dry on the palette. She shook the notes out of the books into the bin. She lay on her bed, head tipped over the end, smoking, looking out of the skylight. She was smoking in the garden when Ted got back. She heard him come in, heard him move through the house, turning on lights, opening the fridge. After a while, he came out into the garden. He called her very softly, Elina, with a lilt at the end, which made a question of her name. But she didn't turn round. He said: I didn't think there was anybody here. He came across the lawn, his bare feet soft in the grass and he picked up the end of her belt – a long, fabric belt it was, connected to her top, that wound round and round her, many times – and he pulled her towards him, hand over hand, like a man hauling himself from deep water.

So they were not always like this. Elina tells herself this as she watches Ted tip out the washing-up water, as she coaxes the baby towards sleep, as she surveys the wreckage of the room.

Lexie doesn't hear from Innes as soon as she thought she might. At the end of their dinner, he had walked her to Leicester Square Tube station, talking the whole way. He was still talking – about a painting he'd bought once in Rome, about a flat he'd lived in near here, about a book he was reviewing that he thought she ought to read – as he kissed her cheek, the lightest possible kiss, a graze of his mouth on her skin, as he adjusted the scarf about her neck, as she waved goodbye and walked down the steps to the Underground.

She works on Monday and Tuesday: going up, going down, going up again, and again, and again. On Wednesday, she accepts a lunch invitation from a man in Accounts. He tells her he is about to leave to work for a company that is buying up the City's remaining bombsites. They go to a café – an Italian café, and Lexie thinks of Mrs Collins as she orders – to eat cutlets smothered in gravy. The colleague drops gravy from his fork on to his suit and enumerates the different types of bombs used during the war and the particular sorts of damage caused by each. Lexie nods as if interested but she is thinking about the bombsites she has seen around London – blackened craters choked with nettles, terraces with a sudden raw gap, windowless buildings with that sightless, vacant appearance – and she is thinking she wouldn't go anywhere near them, wouldn't have anything to do with them.

She works some more. She ferries people from footwear to electrical goods, from millinery to corsetry, from gloves and scarves to the café on the top floor. On Thursday, she gets out Innes's business card from her bag and looks at it. She puts it into the pocket of her uniform. She touches it, every now and again, between operating the lift's machinery. At the end of the day, she puts it back. Friday, she refuses another invitation – for a walk in Hyde Park – from the man in Accounts.

At the weekend, she goes to the Tate Gallery; she walks along the river. She goes to the pictures in Hampstead with Hannah. She rearranges the furniture in her room again, polishes her shoes, writes a shopping list. The weather turns humid and heavy, and Lexie sits at her open window, her stockings drying on the ledge, staring up at the sky, struck by how oddly like the sky at home it looks.

At five past six on Monday evening Lexie walks out of the doors of the department store with the accountant and there, parked half on, half off the kerb, is a silver and ice-blue MG. Its owner is leaning against the bonnet, reading a newspaper, cigarette smoke drifting from him like a scarf. He is wearing curious pointed boots with elasticated sides and a turquoise shirt.

Lexie stops. The young accountant is holding her elbow, imploring her to accompany him to a pub in Marble Arch. Innes looks up. His gaze passes over her and across to the accountant. There is a minuscule alteration in his expression. Then he tosses aside the cigarette and, as he comes over the pavement, he is folding the newspaper.

'Darling,' Innes says, putting his arm around Lexie's waist and kissing her full on the mouth. 'I brought the car. Shall we go?' He opens the passenger door of the MG and Lexie, stupefied by the kiss, by how fast events seem to be moving, by his extraordinary shirt, gets in. 'Goodbye.' Innes waves to the accountant as he slides himself in behind the wheel. 'So nice to have met you.'

Lexie is determined not to speak first. How dare this man shoehorn her into his car? How dare he disappear for more than a week and then kiss her on the mouth?

'Who's the troll?' Innes murmurs, as they screech away from the kerb.

'The troll?'

Innes jerks his head towards the pavement. 'Your friend in flannel.'

'He . . . I . . .' She tries to think what it is she wants to say. 'He's not a troll,' is what comes out, rather haughtily. 'He's actually a very interesting man. He's going to buy up as many bombed-out sites as he can—'

'Oh, a businessman.' Innes lets out a long, loud laugh. 'I might have guessed. The classic mistake for someone in your position.'

'What do you mean?' Lexie shouts, furious in an instant. 'What mistake? And what do you mean, my position?'

'A young girl just arrived in the big city. Dazzled by the cut and thrust of the business world.' He shakes his head as they turn on to Charing Cross Road. 'It happens every time. You know,' he says, and reaches over to take her hand, 'I have every right to be offended.'

'Why?'

'I turn my back for five minutes and you start running about with property speculators. I mean, what about our—'

'Five minutes?' She snatches her hand away. She is shouting again. She would like to stop but she seems to be unable to speak in a normal way. 'It's been more than a week. And, anyway, you have no right at—'

But Innes is smiling to himself, rubbing his hand over his chin. 'Ah, you missed me, did you?'

'I certainly did not. Not at all. And if you think—' She stops. The car has swung into a narrow street with darkened windows and dim signs above the doors. 'Where are we going?'

'A jazz club, I thought. But not until later. I need to go back to the office for a bit first.' For the first time, he looks faintly anxious. 'Do you mind? I can't walk out on my staff on distribution day, you see. You can sit and read a book, if you like, until I've finished. It shouldn't take long. There are plenty of books about, unless of course you have one of your own on you. It's not much of an offer, I know, but I did want to be sure of catching you.'

Lexie twists a finger of her glove. She looks out at the wet streets of Soho, at the lights from the rooms above as they glide by, at a man on a bicycle with a basket piled high with newspapers. She doesn't want to admit to him how keen she is to see inside the magazine offices, to be in that frenetic room she caught a glimpse of the other day. 'As you like,' she says carelessly.

The *Elsewhere* office is quiet when they arrive. For a moment, Lexie thinks no one else is there. But Innes strides through the spaces between the cramped desks and says, 'How are you getting along?' to someone, and Lexie moves forward to see three people – a man and two women – crouched on the floor, surrounded by piles of magazines and envelopes. She watches as Innes kneels down among them, reaches for a magazine, stuffs it into an envelope and tosses it on to a pile.

'Innes, for God's sake!' one of the women cries, raising her hands to her hair, rather too dramatically Lexie feels.

'Over here,' the man says, tapping a different pile. 'The finished ones go here. Daphne's got the list. She's got the best handwriting. We did a test and hers was by far the most legible.'

Innes puts another copy of the magazine into an envelope and tosses it towards the woman with her back to Lexie.

'Can I help?' Lexie says.

All heads turn to look at her. Daphne, the woman with the list, takes the pen from her mouth.

'Everyone, this is Lexie,' Innes says, gesturing towards her. 'Lexie, this is everyone.'

Lexie raises her hand in a wave. 'Hello, everyone.'

There is a short pause. The man clears his throat; the woman glances at Daphne, then away. Lexie straightens her lift-attendant jacket, pushes the hair off her brow.

'Come and sit here.' Innes pats the space on the floor next to him. 'You can help me stuff envelopes, but only if you want to. Lexie is a slave within the machine of a department store,' he says to the others. 'We don't want to wear her out but we never knowingly refuse assistance, do we?'

Lexie and Innes put the magazines into the envelopes, Daphne addresses them, working her way down her list. The man who introduces himself as Laurence sticks on the stamps. The other woman, Amelia, fetches more copies, more envelopes, makes everyone cups of tea, gets the bottle of ink when Daphne's pen runs out. Innes tells them a story about a gallery owner he had lunch with the day before and how the man had dyed his hair since Innes last saw him. Laurence asks Lexie about her job and where her digs are. Innes gives them all a description of Lexie's rooming house, saying it's like something out of Colette. Laurence and Amelia get into an argument about an exhibition in Paris. Daphne tells them they're both talking rubbish. It's one of the few things she says, and Lexie takes the opportunity to give her a covert examination: a petite woman with a head of neat, dark hair, she's wearing a long, loose, dirndl dress. She turns her head and catches Lexie looking.

When all the envelopes are addressed and all the stamps stuck, Laurence slides them into a big mail sack. He then puts on bicycle clips over his trousers and waves goodbye. Amelia's boyfriend meets her at the door. Daphne takes a long time to collect her things, pull on her coat, slide a comb through her hair. Lexie and Innes are silent as she does this, Lexie staring at the grimy blue flowers on the carpet. Just as Daphne is about to go out of the door, she turns. 'By the way, Innes,' she says, a slight smile on her face, 'your wife telephoned today.'

If Innes is disconcerted by this, he does not show it. He is shuffling through a file. 'Thank you, Daphne,' he says, without looking up.

Daphne steps a little further into the light. 'I meant to tell you earlier,' she says, chin raised, 'but I forgot. She said could you please phone her.'

'I see.' He turns a page in the file. 'Well, goodnight. Thanks, as ever, for your hard work.'

She leaves, her coat flapping out behind her. Innes replaces the file on a shelf. He runs a finger along the mantelpiece. He sits down in a chair, then gets up again. Lexie continues to sit in her chair, legs crossed, hands in her lap. She stares at the blue flowers, which seem to be moving of their own accord, petals trembling against the grey background, the blue stamen quivering.

She is aware of Innes coming to sit opposite her, a desk between them.

'So,' he says, in a low voice, 'cards-on-the-table time, I think.' He takes a stack of business cards from the desk and starts to shuffle them as if they are about to play a game. He does it well, the cards whirring and clacking as he stretches and pulls them between his palms.

He places a single card on the desk, face down. 'Number one,' he says, 'I have a wife. I was going to tell you but Daphne, minx that she is, got in first.' He pauses for a moment, then continues, in a careful voice, 'I married Gloria when I was very young, as young as you, in fact. It was during the war and it seemed a good idea at the time. She is . . . How can I put this without sounding ungallant? She is the most monstrous person you could ever have the misfortune to meet. Any questions so far?'

Lexie shakes her head. Innes deals another card.

'Two,' he says, 'you should know that there is a daughter. Mine in name only.' He places a third card on the desk. 'I have very little money and I rarely sleep.' A fourth card is laid alongside the others. 'I'm told I work too hard, too much of the time.' He puts a fifth card close to Lexie's hand. 'I am completely infatuated with you and have been since I first saw you. You may have noticed this. I think the word is "struck". I am Lexie-struck.'

She looks at him, his hand gripped in his hair, his shirt collar all skew-whiff. 'Are you?' she says.

He sighs. 'Yes.' He puts his hand over his heart. 'Absolutely yes.'

'Tell me something.'

'Anything.'

'Have you been to bed with Daphne?'

'Yes,' he replies instantly. 'Any other questions?'

'Were you in love with her?'

'No. And she wasn't with me.'

Lexie frowns. 'I think you could be mistaken about that.'

'No.' He shakes his head. 'Daphne's been in love with Laurence for years. But Laurence isn't inclined that way. He doesn't go in for girls.'

Lexie says: 'What about Amelia?'

He gives a minute, telling hesitation. 'What about her?'

'Have you been to bed with her?'

He looks gloomy for a moment, then nods. 'A long time ago.' He seems to brighten with a sudden thought. 'And it was only once.'

Lexie gathers up the cards he has laid on the desk. She turns them over in her hand, looks at his name printed there, thinks about a dense green hedge hundreds of miles away. She lines them up longways and then again sideways. She looks at Innes, who is lighting a cigarette. She notices that his hands are shaking slightly. She looks again at the cards.

She places one on the desk and lays another over it, at an angle. She is relieved, at that precise moment, that last year she went to bed with a boy she knew at university. Virginity had always seemed to her an inconvenient, unenviable state, something to be got out of the way. She had chosen the boy on the criteria that he washed frequently, that he was funny and that he was keen. She lays a further card on top of that one, and another and another, forming a fan shape. In a way, they had both been satisfying their curiosity. Her memory of it is of something earnest and brief, achieved and negotiated through complex layers of clothes, in the long grass of a damp meadow. She remembers a prolonged struggle with the unfamiliar straps and fastenings of each other's underwear, the way her hair got caught on his shirt button, the not unpleasant rocking, sliding sensation of it, eventually. But something tells her the experience with Innes will not be the same at all. She pushes the cards together, closing the fan, so that they all align underneath the top one.

'Look here,' he says, dropping ash over the desk, 'this has been a very poor sort of evening for you. What must you think of me? I take you out and make you work like a dog in my office, then I reveal my sordid past to you. It won't do at all. You haven't even had supper. Shall we go to this club? I'm sure we can get something to eat there. Or, if not, on the way. What do you say?'

'I say . . .' She considers him, for a moment. He looks wretched, his hair disarrayed, his cigarette burnt down to a stub, his eyes anxious, on hers.

'Oh, God,' he bursts out, 'you're not going to run out on me, are you? I've completely messed it up, haven't I? I mean, I bring you here and then you have to listen to all that.' He gestures wildly around him. 'You probably think I'm a depraved, immoral idiot, don't you? And you're still a child, really, an *ingénue,* an—'

She is riled now. 'I am no such thing,' she snaps. 'I am twenty-one and I am not an *ingénue*, I have—'

'She's twenty-one,' he appeals to the ceiling. 'Is that old enough? Is that even legal?' He leans over the desk towards her, close enough so that she can catch the scent of him – hair-oil, a whiff of soap, fresh cigarette smoke. She sees the way his hair grows straight up at the front, the emerging stubble on his chin, the widening and narrowing of his pupils. 'I am thirty-four,' he murmurs. 'Is that too old for you? Do I still have a chance?'

Her heart is hammering so hard it feels painful in her chest. The proximity of him is making her think about that sensation of his lips pressed against hers, and she finds she wants to feel it again, but harder this time and for longer. 'Yes,' she gets out.

He smiles, abruptly and broadly. 'Good.' He seizes her hand in both of his. 'Good,' he says again.

'I think,' she takes a deep breath because her throat feels so tight that the words will hardly come out, 'we should skip the jazz club. Let's go to bed instead.'

Innes became very brisk, very efficient. He led her into the back room, he cleared all the papers and coffee cups and pens off a sofa in there. He sat her down. He kissed her, lightly but firmly. Lexie imagined that it, the act, would commence quickly and soon. It had been like that with the boy in the meadow – as soon as she'd proposed it, the boy had started yanking off his shoes. But Innes seemed in no hurry at all. He touched her hair, he stroked her neck, her arms, her shoulders, and he talked, keeping up his usual stream about nothing and everything. And while he talked he removed her clothes, the lift-attendant uniform it was, piece by piece: the jacket with brass buttons and the name of the store embroidered in gold, the red scarf, the blouse with the itchy neckline. It was all done so gradually and so nicely. They chatted some more, about the magazine, about where she'd bought her shoes, about how she'd got to work that day – there had been some problem or other on the Tube – about a leaking pipe in his flat, about a bookshop he was planning to approach about stocking *Elsewhere.* At the time it seemed so natural. There they were, talking as people usually did, and it seemed oddly not at all odd that she had no clothes on, that he was nearly naked, that he was – my God – completely naked, that he was there, beside her, around her and inside her. He cradled her head in his hands. He said, 'my darling'; he said, 'my love'.

Even afterwards, he kept on talking. Innes could always talk. Lexie listened to him describing one of his mother's Pekes, the way it used to be allowed to wander over the table-top during dinner; she crossed the room to find a blanket because that back room was draughty. She returned, and pulled it over them both. He settled his arms around her again, asked if she was comfortable, then returned to a story about a visiting Russian who offered to shoot the Peke with a cap-gun. He lit two cigarettes, passing one to her, and as she took it from his mouth and put it to her own it was as if, in that moment, the magnitude of what had happened caught up with her. She felt tears stand to attention in her eyes. What was she doing, lying naked on a couch with a man? A man with a wife and daughter? She had to swallow and pull at the cigarette.

He must have noticed because the arm around her waist tightened, pulling her closer. 'You know something?' he said, and he kissed her hair. 'I think—' He broke off, adjusting his position on the sofa. 'This thing is damned uncomfortable. We'll make love in a bed next time. It'll have to be my place. I doubt your landlady would allow such things.' He paused to kiss her temple. 'I think you should come and work for me.'

She sat up, spilling ash all over them and the blanket. 'What?'

Innes smiled and took a long draw of his cigarette. 'You heard me.'

He extended an arm and, twitching the blanket off her shoulders, exhaled a happy sigh. 'You know, I've been dying to know what your breasts look like naked and I have to say they by no means disappoint.'

'Innes—'

'Not too small, not too large, they have the most perfect under-curve – did you know that? I had a feeling they might. I've always been an admirer of breasts that tilt up to look at the ceiling, like yours. Never been fond of floor-gazers.'

She touched his arm. 'Listen—'

He instantly put his hand over hers, trapping it there. 'You should come and work here,' he said. 'Why not? You're wasted on those purveyors of luxury tat. Anyone can see that. And I don't like the way that colleague of yours looks at you.' He pulled a grotesque face, like a bulldog's. 'It wouldn't be terribly stretching work, at least not at first. Girl Friday things, you know. Typing and running about the place. How is your typing, by the way?'

'It's better,' she said. 'I've been practising. I'm on chapter four of my manual. I've been learning to set margins for laundry lists.'

'Perfect. That'll come in handy at *Elsewhere*.'

She leant forward so that her face was close to his and he held her gaze steadily. 'Don't say no,' he murmured. 'I hate being turned down, you must know that by now, and I never take no for an answer. I'll pester you and pester you until you agree. Let's ring the tat purveyors in the morning and hand in your notice.'

'Hmm,' she said, sitting upright again. 'Maybe.' She cleared the hair from her face, swung it over her shoulder. 'It depends, though.'

'On what?'

'On what you're going to pay me.'

Innes's face clouded for the first time. 'You mercenary little so-and-so. I offer you the opportunity of a lifetime, a chance to lift yourself – so to speak – from the deadliest of deadly jobs and—'

'It's not mercenary at all. Merely practical. I can't live on thin air. I've got to pay my rent, I've got to eat, I've got to buy my Tube tickets, I've got to pay for—'

'All right, all right,' he said testily, 'spare me the inventory of your spending habits.' He lifted the cigarette to his mouth and inhaled. 'Hmm,' he said, addressing the ceiling. 'She wants paying.' He thought a bit more. 'There's no money, of course, none at all. I suppose I could sell one of my paintings. That ought to keep you in nylons for a while and—'

'I don't wear nylons,' she put in.

He looked at her. 'Don't you? Good. Can't abide them.' He looked back at the ceiling. 'So. I sell a painting. We can pay you out of that until I come up with a better solution. And, of course, you'll have to move in with me.'

'What?'

'To save on your rent. I shan't charge you for bed and board.'

'Innes, I can't possibly—'

'We all have to make sacrifices.' He was grinning, one hand behind his head. 'I'm going to sell my Hepworth lithograph of the bisected sphere. The least you can do is bunk up with me for a while.'

'But . . . but . . .' She floundered. Innes used the opportunity to put his hand up and caress her right breast. 'Stop it,' she said, 'I'm trying to have a serious conversation.' She pushed his hand away. 'But what about your wife?' she came up with.

The hand was back. 'What about her? I don't need to ask her permission about who I employ,' he murmured, starting to nuzzle the underside of her breast.

'I meant about living with you.'

'Oh.' He flopped back to the sofa. He exhaled a stream of smoke and stared for a moment at the drifting coils, then reached out and started to grind his cigarette into a saucer. 'You don't need to worry about that. We don't live together – haven't for a while. It's none of her business.'

She said nothing but began to plait the tassels of the blanket together.

'It's none of her business,' he said again.

Lexie continued with her plaiting. 'Do you often ask girls to live with you?' she asked, without looking at him. She didn't care about the other women but she did rather want to know where she came in the order of things.

'Never,' he declared. 'I've never asked anyone else. I've never had anyone else back to my flat before, even to spend the night. I don't like to clutter the place up with . . . with . . .' he waved a hand in the air, '. . . people.' They both reflected on this for a moment and then, without warning, Innes leapt from the sofa. 'Let's go,' he said, starting to pull on his clothes.

'Go where?' she asked, bewildered. She had not, as yet, got used to Innes's abrupt changes of course.

'To pick up your things.' He took hold of her hand and pulled her from the sofa.

'What things?'

'From your bedsit.' He handed her her coat, seemingly unmindful of the fact that she was still naked. 'You've lived in that shrine to virginity long enough. You're coming to live with me.'

Innes's flat today is no longer a flat. At first glance, it is unrecognisable, fifty years on. But the door jambs are the same, the window fastenings, the light switches, the ceiling covings. The raised grain of his wallpaper is just discernible under the awful lilac paint that has been daubed on the walls. There is still the loose board on the landing, which always tripped people up, now covered with beige carpet, and no one who lives here now knows that under there, still, is a spare key for the *Elsewhere* offices. The fireplace has survived the rooms' various renovations and incarnations. It is still the same narrow, early-Victorian affair with the outlines of leaves and stems pressed into the iron. There is a scorch mark on the left-hand side from an accident with a candle that Lexie lit in the winter of 1959, when they'd run out of sixpences for the meter. Under the carpet by the door there is a stain on the floorboards, which appeared during a party they held the same year. There is a strong sense of them both in these rooms – that and the hope that time might blur and collapse and, if one were to turn round fast enough at the right moment, one might catch a glimpse of Innes. Sitting in a chair, a book in his lap, his legs crossed, cigarette smoke spiralling to the ceiling. Standing at the windows, looking down into the street. Sitting at the desk, swearing as he struggles to fit a new ribbon into the typewriter.

But he is gone. And so is Lexie. A young woman from the Czech Republic lives in these rooms. She plays tinny electronica music on the stereo and writes letters in blue biro on squared notepaper. She's the au pair for the family who lives in the house – the flat has reverted to being the attic of a large house, which would interest Innes. He was always saying that they lived in what would have been the servants' quarters.

It is a different place, these days. Different and yet the same. It has radiators, painted walls, carpets, blinds on the windows. The tiny kitchen, which had a gas stove, a temperamental water-heater, a tin bath, is gone, knocked through to make the landing bigger. The small room at the back, where they used to eat and Innes used to work, is now a bathroom with an enormous corner bath. The panelling that separated their door, with its rusted latch and lock, from the other flats in the building is gone and, these days, the children of the house run up and down the stairs. The au pair sometimes sits in the place where Innes kept his doormat, to talk on her mobile phone in lachrymose Czech to her faraway boyfriend.

Lexie didn't move in with Innes that night. Innes was far too used to having his own way, to people jumping when he called, jump. Lexie dug in her heels. They were a good match, in terms of stubbornness. He drove Lexie back to her digs. They had a furious argument in the car when she refused to pack her case. The argument continued on the steps to the house and she flounced through the front door. He and his MG were back outside the department store the following evening. They had another session on the *Elsewhere* sofa and this time they managed to have supper as well. Lexie handed in her notice and went to work at *Elsewhere.* She did not give up her bedsit.

At *Elsewhere,* she began by answering the phone and running errands, to the printers and back, to various bookshops and galleries and theatres. All the way there and all the way back she would turn over in her head the things she had overheard, the things they had said to each other, the things she had yet to learn.

'Your shittiest standfirst ever,' Daphne had hurled at Laurence.

'Where's the galley?' Innes sometimes stood up and demanded.

'There's no kicker,' Laurence said, as he pointed at what she'd learnt was called a 'page proof'.

Set, widow, justified, puff, credit: all these words had their own elusive meaning inside the *Elsewhere* office and ones she had yet to pin down. So she walked about the blue-flowered carpet, holding this new vocabulary in her head, and she made cups of tea (this, with bad grace and often sour milk) and, after a few weeks, she was allowed to type up the handwritten copy for the magazine. Typing never was her strong point. It used to make Innes shout. 'What's Dructuralism, Lex?' he'd bawl across the tiny office. 'Anyone heard of Dructuralism? And "piminal"? What the hell is a "piminal space"?'

Laurence became very good at decoding her mistakes. 'Liminal, Innes,' he'd reply, without looking up from his own work. 'She means "liminal space".' And she'd make him a cup of tea, unasked, unsour, to say thank you.

Innes was constantly furious that Lexie refused to move in with him. But she didn't like to give him the upper hand. He was her boss, she would tell him, what more did he want? Why did he want to be her landlord as well? Lover, yes, he'd reply, but landlord never. So Innes and Lexie ricocheted like metal balls in a pin-machine, arguing over the matter of where she lived and why, from the settee in Bayton Street, to jazz clubs, to eating houses, to Innes's flat, to gallery openings, to Jimmy's on Frith Street, to poetry nights in a smoke-hung basement where thin girls with black polo-necks and parted hair circled like moths around the poets with beards and pints. On the pavement outside the Coach and Horses they once saw her erstwhile colleague pass arm in arm with a girl Lexie recognised from the perfume counters. Could have been you, Innes remarked, placing his hand on her thigh under the beer-ringed table. Lexie leant over and stole the cigarette from his mouth.

Like a traveller across continents, she had to shift her hours. She would get up late, aim to be in the office by mid-morning or occasionally lunchtime. Mrs Collins was regularly horrified by the sight of Lexie making her way to the bathroom at ten or eleven a.m. 'I knew it,' she shrieked at her one morning, 'I knew you'd turn!' Lexie had shut the door, turned the tap on full, smiling to herself.

At Elsewhere, they would work until the evening and then they would head out into the streets to Soho – sometimes all together, sometimes in splintered groups of three or four – to see where they might end up. Laurence preferred the Mandrake Club, where they could find a table and listen to whoever was on stage, but Daphne complained that Laurence became 'a crashing bore' as soon as he stepped over the Mandrake threshold because he was so mesmerised by the music he wouldn't converse. She always campaigned for them to come with her to the French Pub: she liked the close, fetid interior, the hordes of whores and sailors, the way the proprietor greeted her with a kiss on the hand, and the contraption on the bar that dripped water through a sugar lump into a glass of absinthe. Innes always voted for the Colony Room. He was not a big drinker, as a rule, but he argued that a great deal of work could be achieved within its green and gold walls. Laurence, however, had fallen foul too many times of the proprietress's acid tongue, and Daphne referred to her as 'that twisted Belcher bitch'. The Elsewhere staff would regularly be seen arguing on street corners as to who was going where and whether they would meet up again later.

These nights tended to end at two or three in the morning, so Lexie regularly missed Mrs Collins's curfew. After a week when she was absent from her room every night, Lexie collected her things while Innes waited in the MG at the kerb, smoking behind his sunglasses, the engine running. Mrs Collins was so outraged she wouldn't speak to Lexie or even look at her. She shrieked, 'Jezebel!' as Lexie closed the front door, which made Innes roar with laughter. For years afterwards he often called her that.

Innes's flat was a revelation to her. It was like nowhere she'd ever been. It had no curtains at the windows, the floors were bare boards, the walls were whitewashed, and what little furniture there was was of smooth, light-coloured wood, curved to form a seat, a shelf, a sideboard. Scandinavian, Innes threw over his shoulder, when she ran her fingers over its planed surface, like someone stroking a dog. He had a bookshelf that ran around the entire place, at the level of the ceiling. 'So no one bloody well steals them,' he said, when she asked why. The walls were hung with art: a John Minton, he pointed out, a Nicholson, a de Kooning, a Klein, a Bacon, a Lucian Freud, a Pollock. Then he took her hand. But enough about them, he said, come and see the bedroom, it's through here.

Innes took her to a shop in Chelsea and bought her a scarlet coat with outsized fabric buttons, a dress in green wool crêpe with ruffles at the wrists, a pair of peacock blue stockings – 'You are a blue stocking,' Innes said, 'so you might as well wear them' – a sweater with a draped cowl neck. He took her to a hairdresser and stood beside the chair. 'Like this,' he instructed, sweeping a finger along her jaw, 'and this.'

When her parents heard that Lexie was living with a man, they told her she was dead to them, that she should never contact them again. And so she didn't.

It is hotter than Elina had thought. Inside, before they left, the house had been its usual temperature – cool, slightly damp, the air still and unmoving. Now she is outside, in her jeans and red sandals and blouse with a pattern of apples, she is too hot. Sweat rises to the surface of her skin; she can feel it coursing down the groove of her spine. The jeans she has on are from before – they have no elastic waist, they are ordinary jeans, worn by ordinary people. The waist-band is a little tight but she has them on. She is wearing proper clothes. In them, she gets a hint, a whiff, of the possibility of feeling normal again.

Beside her, Ted carries the *A–Z*, into which is tucked a letter from the doctor. They are going for the baby's check-up to a health centre on the other side of the Heath. Ted had suggested they walk, but Elina hadn't told him that, two days ago, she'd tried to take the baby out in his pram and only got as far as the corner before she saw the sides of the pram waver, the stars on the blanket shimmer and break free. She'd had to sit down on the kerb, her feet in the gutter, her head between her knees, before she could make it back to the house. Instead she said: 'Let's call a cab.'

Neither of them is familiar with this area, a grid of streets, hidden behind a busy road going north. Dartmouth Park, Ted says it is called.

The taxi driver dropped them on the main road, pleading one-way systems, and now they are walking down a street, looking for the health centre. Ted is sure it's this way. Then he changes his mind and says it's the other way. They have to double back. He hands the baby to Elina as he consults his map.

'Over here,' he says, and strikes out over a road. Elina trails after him, worrying that the baby is in the sun, that the blanket is too hot, that she might faint in this heat if Ted makes her walk much further.

At the next corner Ted comes to a stop. He looks up the street, he looks down. The map dangles in his hand. Elina waits. She takes a deep breath and the air seems to burn her throat. She is not going to faint. Everything is fine. Nothing that shouldn't be moving is moving; the stars on the baby's blanket are just pieces of embroidery, nothing more. The baby is sleeping, mouth in a pout, one hand curled by his cheek, as if holding an invisible telephone receiver to his ear. Elina is smiling at this thought when she hears Ted mumbling: '. . . somewhere else . . .'

'Sorry?'

He doesn't answer. She watches as the letter slips out of the *A–Z* and on to the pavement. He doesn't bend to pick it up but just stands there, his back to her, hands at his sides.

Elina frowns. She crouches and scrabbles for the letter, carefully balancing the sleeping baby on one arm. 'Ted?' she says. She touches his sleeve. 'Ted, we should get a move on, the appointment's in two minutes.' She takes the *A–Z* from him. She looks at the letter, she looks at the map. 'It's along here and then left.'

He turns the wrong way and seems to be gazing over the road at a fence.

'Ted!' she says, more sharply. 'We've got exactly two minutes before our appointment.'

'You go,' he says, without turning round.

'What?'

'I said you go. I'll wait here.'

'You're telling me . . . you're . . . you don't want to come to—' Elina is so cross she cannot finish the sentence. She cannot be in his presence a minute longer. She hefts the bag strap further up her shoulder, spins round and marches off up the street, clutching the baby to her. Her red sandals seem to burn her feet and she feels more sweat soaking into the waistband of her jeans.

'"I'll wait here,"' she is muttering to herself, as she pushes her way through the swing doors. '"I'll wait here" indeed, selfish pig of a—' She breaks off because she has to give her name to the receptionist. The interior of the centre is cool and smells of lino. Elina sits on a plastic chair, still seething, still half expecting Ted to appear. She surveys the notices about breastfeeding, smoking, meningitis, vaccinations, all the while composing speeches on the subject of paternal involvement, to be delivered when Ted decides he can spare the time to show up. She has just hit on the phrase *abdication of responsibility* when she is called for her appointment.

'Name?' the nurse says, bending towards her computer screen.

'Um,' Elina fidgets with the bangle on her wrist, 'we haven't decided yet. It's ridiculous, I know,' she hears herself give a strained laugh, 'I mean he's almost six weeks old but—'

'I meant your name,' the nurse says.

'Oh.' That strange high laugh again. What is wrong with her? 'It's—' Elina finds, to her surprise, that her adolescent stammer seems to have momentarily resurfaced. She always had trouble with words beginning with E, could never get them out, never force them beyond the area of her tonsils. She swallows, then coughs to cover it and manages to get out, 'Elina Vilkuna.'

'Swedish, are you?'

'Finnish.' Her voice seems normal, she is relieved to hear. Perhaps the stammer has gone back to wherever it's been hiding. 'My mother's Swedish, though,' she adds, without knowing why.

'Oh. You'll have to spell it for me.'

Elina does, and has to point out twice that Vilkuna has a k, not a c.

'You speak very good English,' the nurse says, as she takes the baby from her.

Elina watches as the woman flexes the baby's arms, his legs, touches the top of his head. 'Well, I've lived here for a while, you know, and—'

'In London?'

'Mostly.' Elina is weary of telling this story, weary of people trying to sniff out her origins. 'But all over, really,' she says vaguely. 'Different places.'

'I couldn't work out what your accent was. I thought you might be Australian at first.' The nurse hands the baby to her. 'It's fine,' she says. 'He's fine. You have a beautiful healthy boy.'

Elina floats out of the health centre; she has the baby in her arms, the blanket draped over him to shield him from the glare. She loves that nurse, she loves her. The words *beautiful* and *healthy* and *boy* circle her head like butterflies. She would like to say them aloud; she would like to go back in and ask the nurse to tell her that again.

She walks back towards the main road and she is saying the words, under her breath, through her mouth, which is the shape of a smile, and she is thinking about how you can always tell if someone on the phone is smiling by the sound of their voice, and how the shape of your lips must determine this.

At the corner, where she'd left Ted, she stops and looks around. *Beautiful*, she hears again, *healthy*. She turns left, she turns right. No sign of Ted. The sun is beating down on her shoulders, on the part of her neck not covered by her apple blouse. She frowns. Where is he? She crosses the road, puzzlement giving way to her earlier irritation. Where the hell has he gone? And what is wrong with him today?

She turns a corner and there he is, standing on the pavement gazing up at something, shielding his eyes. 'What are you doing?' she says, as she reaches him. 'I've been searching everywhere for you.'

He turns and looks at her as if he's never seen her or the baby before.

'What are you doing?' she asks again. 'What's going on?'

He squints up at the tree behind her, into the sun. 'Do you know that song,' he says, 'about three crows?'

'What?'

'You know,' he says and then he sings, in a cracked voice, '"Three crows sat upon a wall, sat upon a wall, three crows sat upon a wall on a cold and frosty morning."'

'Ted—'

He lowers himself to a garden wall behind him. 'The next bit goes, "The first crow was greeting for his ma, greeting for his ma" – and so on. But I can't remember what comes after that.'

She shifts the baby to the other arm, rearranging the blanket. Despite herself, she is picturing three crows perched on the wall next to Ted, lined up, their feathers glossy, greenish black, their beaks hooked, their scaled feet gripping the brick.

'It must start, "The second crow".' Ted closes his eyes. Then he opens them and places first one hand then the other over them, as if checking his eyesight. He shakes his head. 'I can't remember.'

Elina comes to sit next to him. She puts her hand on his leg, feels the muscles quivering under the fabric. 'Are you OK?'

'Am I OK?' he repeats.

'Are you having one of your things? With your eyes?'

He is frowning, as if giving this question great consideration. 'I thought I was,' he says slowly, 'or that I was about to. But it seems to have gone away.'

'That's good.'

'Is it?'

Elina swallows. She is seized by an urge to cry. She has to turn her head away so that he doesn't see. What is wrong with him? Maybe some men lose the plot when women have babies – Elina doesn't know and she can't think who to ask. Perhaps it's normal for them to become a little distracted, a little withdrawn. It seems that just as she is beginning to rise, to struggle, blinking and gasping, to the surface, he is starting to sink. She grips his leg tighter, as if to transmit something of herself to him. Please, she wants to say, please don't be like this, I can't do this alone. Another part of her wants to shriek, get up off that wall, for God's sake, and help me find a taxi. But she forces herself to speak in an even voice. 'Why "greeting for"?' she says. 'Why the "for"?'

'It means crying,' he says, still covering one eye, then the other. 'I think. It's slang or dialect or something. It means he's crying for his mother.'

'Oh.' Elina looks down and almost jumps because the baby has woken up. His eyes are wide open and he is staring straight at her.

'My mum used to sing it,' Ted is saying, 'when I was little. She'd know about the other verses. I'll ask her, next time I see her.'

Elina nods, touches the baby's cheek with her finger and Ted leans in to see.

Ted is thinking about paternity leave. It is an idle, meandering train of thought he's been having ever since he left the house with a list of things Elina needs for the baby. Or a list of things they need. Wipes, cotton wool, barrier cream – on and on it goes. Who would have thought that a person so small could generate such heaps, such mountains, of stuff, of needs?

He has been reflecting that his role, as a new father on his two weeks of paternity leave, is akin to that of a runner on a film set. The baby is the star, undoubtedly, with its every whim instantly met, its demands and timetable slavishly adhered to at all times. Elina is the director, the one responsible for proceedings, the one trying to keep everything on track. And he, Ted, is the runner. There to fetch and carry, to assist the director in her work, to mop up spillages, to make the tea.

Ted is rather pleased with this analogy. He is smiling to himself as he walks along the pavement, weaving in and out of the plane trees, sidestepping the odd mound of dog shit, swinging the shopping bags at the ends of his arms.

He turns into his front garden, fumbles for his keys. He unlocks the door and scrapes his feet on the mat, shouting, 'Hi. It's me. I got the stuff. All of it except the biodegradable wipes. They didn't have them. So I got the ordinary ones. I know you won't like them but I reckoned it was better than getting none at all.' He pauses to let her answer. But the house is silent. 'Elina?' he calls. Then he stops. She might be asleep. He takes the shopping bags into the kitchen and dumps them on the counter. He puts his head around the sitting-room door, but there's no one in there, no one stretched out on the sofa. The pram stands in the hallway, empty, the sheets rumpled, as if the baby has only just been taken out of it. Ted puts his hand to where the baby's head lies, and is it his imagination or does it still feel a little warm?

A sound – something being dropped, a footfall, a click – from the floor above makes him look up. 'Elina?' he says again. But, again, there's no answer.

He takes the stairs, slowly at first, then two at a time. 'El,' he says, on the landing, 'where are you?' She has to be here somewhere, she can't possibly have gone out.

And yet the bedroom is empty, the duvet pulled taut over the pillows, the wardrobes shut, the mirror above the mantelpiece blank and silvery. In the bathroom the window has been left open and the curtain is drifting into the room like smoke.

He stands again on the landing, perplexed. Where can she be? He checks the bedroom again, the living room, the kitchen, just to be sure she hasn't fallen asleep somewhere. After a moment's thought, he checks the space behind the bed, too, just in case. He doesn't allow himself to register what the 'just in case' might be. But she's not there either. She's gone – and the baby too.

In the hallway, he fumbles in his back pocket for his mobile phone. As he fiddles with the buttons, scrolling down for her number, he catches sight of the pram again. Where would she go, he thinks, with the baby but without the pram? He clears his throat as he lifts the phone to his ear. He must, he decides, be careful to come across as relaxed, casual; his voice mustn't sound panicked; he mustn't communicate how terrified he is.

He hears the line click and then the tinny sound of ringing. And, then, somewhere nearby, an echoing ring. Ted takes his phone away from his ear and listens. In the next room another phone is ringing and ringing. Ted shuts off his phone and he hears Elina's fall silent. He lowers himself to the stairs and sits with his elbows resting on his knees, head gripped in his hands. Where can she be? What should he do? Should he call the police? But what would he say? He tells himself to stay calm, he has to stay calm, he mustn't panic, he has to think this through, but all the time his mind is shouting, she's gone, she's taken the baby, she's disappeared, and she's so weak she can't even walk as far as—

A deafening, shrill noise makes him leap off the stairs. For a moment, he can't think what it is or why it is so loud. Then he realises it's the doorbell, ringing right above his head. It's her. She's back. Relief surges through him and he seizes the door handle and wrenches it open, saying, 'God, you scared me. I was—'

He stops. On the doorstep is his mother.

'Darling,' she says, 'I was just passing. I met Joan – you remember Joan from across the way, with the cocker spaniel – for coffee in South End Green. There's that lovely new café, have you been?' She clips over the threshold, presses her cheek to his, clutching at both his shoulders. 'Anyway, I just couldn't pass the end of your road without coming to see you all and without a cuddle with my grandson. So,' she holds her arms aloft, as if presenting herself on stage, 'here I am!'

'Um,' Ted says. He runs a hand through his hair. He grips the edge of the door. 'I've just got back,' he mumbles. 'I . . . er . . .' He goes to shut the door, then looks out of it, at the path, at the pavement, just to see if she's there, if she's coming. 'I'm not sure,' he begins carefully, as he shuts the door, 'where Elina is.'

'Oh.' His mother unthreads the silk scarf from around her neck, unbuttons her jacket. 'Popped out, has she?'

'Maybe.' He leans his back against the door and stares at his mother. Something is different about her and he's not sure what it is. He looks at her hair, her cheeks, her nose, the skin on her neck, her hands as they hang her coat on a hook, her feet, shod in patent-leather heels. He has the odd sensation that he doesn't recognise her, that he doesn't know who she is, that she is a stranger to him, rather than the person he's spent more time with than anybody else in the world. 'I don't . . . um . . . I don't— You look different,' he blurts out. 'Have you done something to yourself?'

She turns towards him, brushing down her skirt. 'What kind of thing?'

'I don't know. Your hair. Have you changed your hair?'

She raises a self-conscious hand to her helmet of platinum blonde. 'No.'

'Is that new?' He points at her blouse.

'No.' She makes a small movement of impatience – a touch to her eyebrow with the side of her finger – and Ted recognises that. 'When are you expecting Elina back?'

He still stares at her. He can't put his finger on what it is. The mole on her neck, the line of her jaw, the rings on her fingers: it's as if he's never seen them before.

'She's taken the baby with her, I suppose?' his mother is saying.

'Uh-huh.'

'Darling, could you possibly phone her and tell her I'm here? Because I have to be back by six tonight. Your father needs his—'

'She hasn't taken her phone.' Ted gestures towards the living room. 'It's in there.'

His mother lets out a small, irritated sigh. 'Well, that is a shame. I did so want to have—'

'I don't know where she is, Mum.'

She looks at him sharply. She hasn't missed the tremor in his voice. 'What do you mean?'

'I mean she's gone. I don't know where.'

'With the baby?'

'Yeah.'

'Well, she's probably taken him for a walk. She'll be back soon. We'll have a cup of tea in the garden and—'

'Mum, she can barely even make it up the stairs.'

She frowns. 'What are you talking about?'

'Since what happened. The birth. You know. She's very . . . weak. She's very ill. She nearly died, Mum. Remember? And I come back from the shops and she's not here and I've no idea where she's gone or how she'd get there because—' Ted stops. 'I don't know what to do.'

His mother walks into the living room, walks out again, walks into the kitchen. 'Are you sure she's not here?'

Ted rolls his eyes. 'Yes.'

His mother goes to the sink, turns on the tap and starts filling the kettle.

'Mum, what are you doing?' he says, aghast. 'How can you make tea when—' He stops again. He has suddenly seen that the key is in the back door. It's not hanging on its hook. It's in the door. Ted darts towards it. He pushes the door open and the smell of the garden rushes to meet him. He steps out on to the decking and he sees that the studio door also has a key in it and his heart seems to pound with joy as he runs over the grass to the studio window.

Through it, he sees something incredible. Elina, in profile, standing at the sink. She is wearing her overalls and she is doing something, mixing a colour, perhaps, or washing a brush, Ted can't see exactly what. But her movements are deft, practised, and the look on her face is one of absorbed serenity. She looks, Ted sees, like she used to. Like she did when he first met her, when she arrived at his house in some battered van she'd borrowed, all alone, perfectly prepared to lug astonishingly heavy boxes and equipment up two flights of stairs to the attic. He'd watched this slight, pixie-like woman with cropped, bleached hair calmly labouring under the weight of an enormous lightbox and he'd gone out and offered to help. She'd seemed surprised. 'I can manage,' she'd said, and he'd wanted to laugh because she clearly could not. He'd watched her come and go during the weeks that followed – out in the evenings, he didn't know where, up and down to the attic, coming into the kitchen to eat at odd hours. He'd hear her walking about above his head in the middle of the night and would wonder what she was doing, had felt oddly privileged to be able to witness the private workings of this unusual life. Often, after one of those walking-about nights, she'd had that look the next day: a woman preoccupied, a woman with a satisfying secret, and he'd wanted to ask her, what is it, what is it you're doing up there?'

He loves that look. He's missed it. It was what made him realise what had to happen, what he must do. After a while, he began to see that Elina reminded him of nothing so much as one of those balloons children have – the bright ones, filled with helium, that bob and tug at the end of their string. One moment of inattention and off they go, skywards, away, never to be seen again. He saw that Elina had lived everywhere, all over the world, that she arrived and left and moved on. That secret thing she had, what she did up there in the attic when no one was looking, with her paints and her turpentine and her canvases – she only needed that, she didn't lack anything else, any anchor, any gravity. And he saw that if he didn't take hold of her, if he didn't tether her down, if he didn't bind her to him, she would be off again. And so he did it. He laid hold of her and he held on tight; he sometimes pictures this as him tying the string of a balloon to his wrist and getting on with his life while it floats there, just above his head. He has been holding on tight ever since. In their early days, it took him a while to get used to waking sometimes in the night and finding that she'd gone, that the bed was empty. At first, it had made him start awake and run about the house in a panic. But then he had learnt that she sometimes slipped away in the night, to work, to lead her other life. He always checked, always looked out of the back windows of the house, to see the light on in the studio and then he would return to bed, alone.

The look is back! He has to suppress the urge to clap his hands as he watches her through her studio window. She will be all right again, he sees, she has survived. None of this – the carnage at the hospital, his whisper of *let's not bother* – has vanquished her. She will be all right. He can see the special look on her face, in the workings of the muscles of her shoulders, in the set of her mouth. She's working. He feels the excitement radiating from her. She's working.

Then he hears a voice to his left: 'In here, is she?' and Ted is so caught up in what he has been seeing through the window that he fails to catch on quickly enough to prevent his mother pushing open the studio door and stepping inside.

Several things happen at once. The studio door, always a bit loose on its hinges, slams back against the wooden wall with a crash. Ted sees Elina whirl round from the sink, knocking a china saucer to the floor, which smashes. The baby, somewhere in the room with her, wakes with a start and lets out a piercing screech.

'Oh,' Elina cries, a blue-stained hand clutched to her chest, 'what are you doing here?'

Ted is through the door in seconds, talking over his mother, trying to explain, but Elina is rushing to pick up the baby and she steps on the pieces of broken china in her bare feet so Ted picks up the baby, but the baby is furious, woken from his nap, and Elina is sitting on a chair, trying to pull the bits of china out of her foot with her blue hands and she is saying, I can't believe you woke him up, I'd just got him off, and her foot is bleeding and she sounds as if she might cry. She lets out a Finnish word that sounds to Ted like a curse, as she pulls a shard of saucer from her heel.

'You go back to work,' Ted says unconvincingly, above the noise, trying not to look at the blood dripping out of her wounds, 'if you like. We'll take the baby and—'

Elina mutters a different Finnish curse and hurls a piece of china into the bin. 'How can I go back to work?' she cries, gesturing at the screaming baby. 'Are you going to feed him? Is your mother?'

Ted bounces his son up and down. 'It's not our fault,' he says, over the noise. 'We didn't know where you were. I got back and you were gone. I was really worried about you. I looked everywhere and—'

'Everywhere?' Elina repeats.

'I thought . . . I thought . . .'

'You thought what?' They stare at each other for a moment, then both drop their eyes. 'Give me the baby,' she says quietly, and begins to unbutton her overalls.

'Elina, come into the house. You need to put a plaster on that and—'

'Give me the baby.'

'Feed him in the house. My mother's come to see us. Come into the house and—'

'I will not!' she shouts again. 'I'm staying here. Now give me the baby!'

Out of the corner of his eye Ted sees his mother, standing near the door. She is shaking her head. 'Goodness,' she says, 'what a noise.' Ted sees Elina flinch at the sound of her voice and he feels guilty because he knows that she doesn't like anyone in her studio, anyone at all, not even him, not even her dealer. But Ted's mother isn't looking at the work, she isn't looking at the rough sketches and stretched canvases and the photographs and the transparencies on the lightbox and the tools on the walls, she's only looking at the baby, in that hungry, needful way she has.

'What's wrong?' his mother croons to the baby. 'What's wrong, little man?' She lifts him out of Ted's hands; he feels the rasp of her frosted fingernails against his palms as she takes hold. 'Are you upset because Mummy and Daddy are shouting? Are you? Don't you worry. You come along with Grandma and everything will be all right.'

She disappears out of the door with him. Ted and Elina look at each other across the empty studio. Elina's face is chalk white, her mouth slightly open, as if she's about to say something.

'I was worried about you,' Ted says again, scuffing his shoe against the lip of the rug.

Elina springs from the chair and comes right up to him. 'Do you know what, Ted?' She takes hold of his face in her hands. 'I'm fine. I really am. I wasn't for a while but now I'm doing OK. You're the one we need to worry about.'

He gazes into her eyes, mute. He sees the familiar slate blue of them, the left one slightly darker than the right, he sees a miniature version of himself looking back out at him. They stand like that for a long moment. From the open door, they can hear the baby's screams redoubling, sharpening.

Ted pulls away from Elina's grasp. He drops his gaze. He half turns. Elina, he knows, is still looking at him. He steps out of the studio. 'Baby's hungry,' he mutters, as he goes. 'I'll get him back for you.'

Lexie had been working at *Elsewhere* for a few months, and living with Innes for a few weeks. They arrived together each morning, roaring down Wardour Street, turning into Bayton Street, in the MG; Lexie would always associate these morning rides with a pleasantly sore ache in her groin, her upper thighs – Innes liked to make love at night and again in the morning. He said it cleared his head. 'Otherwise,' he said, 'I'd be thinking about sex all day, instead of work.' It was, he said, particularly difficult since Lexie, the object of his lust, worked with him. 'There you are, you see, walking about, taunting me, all day long, naked under your clothes,' he'd complain.

'Just park the car, Innes,' she would say, 'and stop whining.'

One afternoon, the usually busy office was quiet – Laurence had gone out to the printer's, Daphne was off on an assignment, Amelia had gone to supervise a photographer. Lexie and Innes were working alone. They were not speaking. Or, rather, Lexie was not speaking to Innes. She was bashing crossly at a typewriter, not looking in his direction. He, she knew, was sitting at his desk, reading through a newspaper, an infuriating half-smile on his face.

Lexie slammed back the carriage on the typewriter, then leant her head in her hands, staring down at the pleats of her green wool dress.

'A journalist was not made in a day, Lex,' Innes observed, from across the room.

She let out a sound halfway between a growl and a scream, yanked the page out of the machine, scrumpled it in her hands and hurled it at him. 'Shut up!' she shouted. 'I hate you!'

The ball of paper fell in a pathetic arc to the carpet, nowhere near its destination. Innes turned a page with a flamboyant rustle. 'No, you don't. You love me.'

'I don't, I don't. I loathe the very sight of you.'

He smiled, folded the newspaper and laid it on his desk. 'You know, if you can't take the criticism – the constructive criticism – of your editor, you'll never make it. You'll be an overqualified typist for the rest of your life.'

Lexie glared at him. 'Constructive? You call that constructive? It was mean and hateful and—'

'All I said was that you were still in undergraduate gear, that—'

'Stop it!' She held her hands over her ears. 'Don't say it! Don't speak to me!'

He laughed again, got up from his desk and walked across the office to the little back room. 'Well, I'll stay out of your way. I'll be in here, if you need me, but I want two hundred words by lunchtime.'

She let out another growl at his back. Then she looked again at the typescript she'd shown Innes last night. He'd said it was time for her to 'try her hand' at writing something. He'd sent her along to a small show at a gallery and told her to produce a two-hundred-word review. She'd arrived early, circled the space, looked at each painting carefully and noted down what she saw on her pad. She overheard someone asking who that was and when she heard the reply from the gallery owner – 'Kent's new girlie' – turned and flashed a furious look on him. Girlie, indeed. She had returned to scribbling on her pad, as if she didn't care, and had ended up with pages and pages of indecipherable scribbles. She'd spent a week writing and rewriting it. Then Innes had spent perhaps five minutes reading it before returning it to her, covered with blue pen.

What did he mean, anyway, 'undergraduate gear'? And what was wrong with the phrase 'vibrant hue'? What did he mean by 'a more arresting opening'?

She sighed, rolling another sheet of paper into the typewriter. As she did so, the door to the office opened and in stepped a woman. Or perhaps 'lady' was more the word. She had on a red pillbox hat with a net veil covering half of her face, a navy coat with a nipped-in waist, navy shoes. She clasped a shiny bag in her gloved hands. Her face was pale, flawlessly powdered, her lipsticked mouth parted, as if she would speak if only she might find the words.

'Good morning,' Lexie said. The woman, surely, any second now, would realise she was in the wrong place. 'May I help you?'

The woman gave her a quick, narrow look. 'Are you Lexie?'

'I am.'

With one hand on her hip, the woman proceeded to examine her as if Lexie were a store mannequin and she the discerning buyer. 'Well,' she exclaimed, when she'd finished, letting out a peal of brittle laughter, 'all I can say is that they get younger every time. Wouldn't you agree, darling?' At this the woman turned, and Lexie was astonished to see that behind her was a girl of twelve or thirteen. She was pale, with hair that had been coaxed into ringlets – Lexie imagined she would have had to sleep in rags all night to achieve the effect – and had her mouth open, as if nasally afflicted.

'Yes, Mother,' she muttered.

Lexie drew herself up to her full height, which was, she was pleased to notice, a great deal more than the woman's. 'I beg your pardon, but may I enquire what is your business here?'

'I say,' the woman said, with another burst of laughter, 'you *are* a cut above the rest, aren't you? He's done rather well for himself, this time, to bag a chit so youthful and well-spoken. "What is your business here?"' she mimicked, glancing back at her daughter, who continued to glare, open-mouthed, at Lexie. 'Wherever did he find you? Not in some seedy drinking-hole, like all the others, I'll warrant. Have a good look, my darling,' she said, turning again to the daughter. 'This is whom your father has left us for.' With the final words, her perfectly made-up face began to crumple. Lexie watched, appalled, as Gloria – for it had to be her – bowed her head and searched for something in her handbag, bringing out a handkerchief and crushing it to her face.

There was the sound of a door slamming behind them and feet pounding across the floor. Innes had appeared from the back room and was bearing down on them, his face rigid with fury.

He came to a stop beside Lexie. He surveyed his wife for a moment, taking in the hat, the handkerchief, the tears. He took the cigarette from his mouth. 'What are you doing here, Gloria?' he said, through gritted teeth.

'I had to come,' Gloria whispered, reaching under her veil to dab at her eyes. 'Call me foolish but a woman has to know. I had to see her. Margot had to see her.' She cast her gaze imploringly up to Innes's face but he looked over her shoulder.

He nodded at the girl. 'Hello, Margot,' he said quietly. 'How are you?'

'I am well, thank you, Father.'

He seemed to wince slightly at this but he stepped sideways to see the girl better. 'I hear you're at a new school. How is everything there?'

Gloria swirled round, her navy skirts swishing against Innes's trouser-legs. 'As if you care,' she spat and, without looking at her daughter, said, 'Don't answer him, Margot.' She and Innes glared at each other from their new proximity. 'Don't tell him anything. Why should you, when he treats us like this?'

'Gloria—' Innes began.

'Ask him, my darling,' Gloria said, and Lexie watched, horrified, as Gloria reached behind her, seized her daughter by the arm and propelled her forward. 'Ask him what we came here to find out.'

Margot could not meet her father's eyes, her lids cast down, her face like stone.

'Ask him!' Gloria urged. 'Because I cannot.' More fluttering and dabbing with the handkerchief.

Margot cleared her throat. 'Father,' she began, in a monotone, 'will you please come home?'

Innes made a small movement with his hand, as if he were about to take a draw on his cigarette but had then changed his mind. He looked for a long moment at the girl. He then rested his cigarette in an ashtray on Lexie's desk. He folded his arms about himself. 'Gloria,' he spoke in a low, tight voice, 'this display is most ill-judged. And involving Margot like this. It is really too—'

'Display?' Gloria shrieked, thrusting the girl behind her again. 'Do you think I'm made of clay? Do you think I have no feelings? The others I could overlook – and God knows there have been enough of them – but this! This is too much. It's all over town, you know.'

Innes sighed, pressed his fingers to his brow. 'What is?'

'That she's living with you! That you've left us to set yourself up with a mistress. A girl half your age. In the flat that by rights should belong to us, to me and Margot. And when you should be with us, with your wife and child—'

'First,' Innes began, in an even tone, 'half of thirty-four, as I'm sure you're aware, is seventeen.' He gestured towards Lexie. 'Does she look seventeen to you? Second, I have not left you to set myself up with her, as you well know. You and I have been living separately for some time now. Let's not pretend otherwise. Third, the flat is in no sense your property. You got the house – my mother's house, need I add? – while I took a flat. That was our agreement. Fourth, Gloria, I fail to see what business all this is of yours. I let you live your life. You must return me that favour.'

During this speech, Lexie had stolen a covert glance at Margot. She felt an odd sense of alignment between them – both observers to what seemed to be a well-trodden argument. When her eyes met Margot's, the girl didn't look away. She didn't flinch, she didn't move a muscle. She just kept Lexie fixed with a chillingly still, open-mouthed gaze. After a second or two, Lexie was forced to look away, back to Gloria, whose hat was now slightly askew; she was screeching about decency and propriety.

'Gloria,' Innes spoke across her, with a deathly, low tone, 'if Margot weren't present, there are many rejoinders I could make to your accusations of moral turpitude. It is for her sake and her sake alone that I restrain myself.'

There was a short silence. Gloria looked up at her husband, panting lightly. It was a peculiar tableau, Lexie reflected. Minus sound, minus speech, minus the child standing behind them, it might have looked like the height of passion instead of its inverse. It looked as if Innes and Gloria were about to lock each other in a frenzied embrace.

Innes broke away first. He took two strides to the door and yanked it open. 'I think perhaps you should leave,' he said, addressing the floor.

Gloria swirled again, her skirts rustling, towards Lexie, as if for a last look. She surveyed her, up and down, patting her hair, righting her hat, clearing her throat. Then she swirled back and, taking her daughter's arm, swept out of the door Innes was holding open.

He nodded, almost bowed, to the girl. 'Goodbye, Margot. It's been nice to see you.' There was no reply. Margot Kent walked after her mother with her head bent.

Innes pushed the door to. He inhaled deeply, then sighed out the breath. He took several quick steps into the room, then drew back a foot and kicked a wastepaper bin. The bin and its contents went skittering over the floor.

'That,' he said, apparently to no one, 'was my wife. My dearly beloved. What a sight, eh?' Arriving at a wall, he proceeded to slam his hand against it, once, twice. Lexie watched, unsure what to do.

Innes shook his hand, flexing the fingers. 'Ow,' he said, and his voice was surprised. 'Damn.'

Lexie walked over to him. She took the hand in hers and began to rub it. 'You idiot,' she said.

He pulled her towards him and wrapped his good arm around her. 'For hitting the wall?' he mumbled into her hair. 'Or for marrying that maenad?'

'Either,' she said. 'Both.'

He embraced her tightly, then pulled away. 'Christ,' he said, 'I need a drink after that. How about you?'

'Um,' Lexie frowned, 'isn't it a bit early for—'

'You're right! Damn it. Will anywhere be open?'

'No, I meant—'

'What time is it?' He was glancing at his watch, feeling his pockets for change. 'The Coach and Horses? No. Not at this time. We could try the French Pub. What do you think?' He seized her by the hand and wrenched open the door. 'Let's go.'

They marched along Bayton Street and at the end, where it met Dean Street, Innes stopped. He looked up Dean Street, he looked down. He fumbled in his pocket for a cigarette. 'We'll try Muriel,' he muttered. 'She owes me a favour.'

'What for?' Lexie asked, but Innes was off again, striding down the pavement.

Minutes later, they were sitting in a corner of the Colony Room, Innes knocking back a whisky. The curtains were drawn against the afternoon light and Muriel Belcher sat surveying her empire from a stool by the door. 'What's up with Miss Kent today?' she'd remarked, as Innes marched in.

Lexie watched coloured fish circling each other in a tank above the cash register and wrote her name over and over again with a swizzle stick in gin and tonic on the sticky table-top. A man with a wide, asymmetric face was sitting at the bar, engaged in a loud, somewhat sneering conversation with someone Innes had greeted as MacBryde. In the corner a rather beautiful tall man was dancing alone to a wind-up gramophone. An elderly woman in a bedraggled coat sat at the next table, surrounded by her bags, muttering to herself and sucking up the drink that Innes had bought her.

'You weren't fooled, were you?' Innes said suddenly.

Lexie looked up from her swizzle stick. 'By what?'

'The histrionics.'

Lexie did not reply but dipped the stick into her drink again.

Innes ground out his cigarette. 'She's a consummate actress. You can see that, can't you? The tears and the tantrums are just an act. It's all about the game with her. She doesn't care either way about me. She just doesn't like being seen to lose. She can't bear the idea that I'm living with you.'

Lexie still did not speak.

'She doesn't care about me,' Innes insisted.

Lexie took a sip of her gin and felt its heated path sink down through her body. The dancing man had changed his record and was now gyrating to a hectic, fast tune, his head snapping back and forth on his neck. 'I'm not so sure about that.'

'Well, I am.'

'What about Margot?'

Uncharacteristically, Innes was silent. He picked up his glass and drained it. 'She's not mine,' he said eventually.

'Are you sure?'

'One hundred per cent.'

'How can you be so certain?'

He looked up. He smiled quickly, then looked down at the table again. He reached out and took his empty glass in his hands, rolled it between them. The elderly woman chose this moment to lean across the gap between their tables and rattle a tobacco tin in Innes's face. 'Could I trouble you,' she said, in arch, upper-class tones, 'for the price of a drink?'

Innes sighed but dropped a shilling into the tin. 'There you are, Nina,' he said. Then he turned back to Lexie. 'I'd been away for two years,' he said, 'by the time Margot was born.'

'But she doesn't know that you're not her father?'

Innes played with a strand of Lexie's hair, putting it behind her ear, then pulling it free.

'Innes,' Lexie persisted, pulling away, 'why doesn't she know?'

'She . . .' Innes began, then stopped. 'Because I've always thought the alternative would be worse for her. It's not her fault, after all. If I were to disown her, there would be no father at all. And having someone, no matter how feckless, is better than no one. Don't you think?'

'I don't know. I really don't know. I feel she ought to know the truth.'

'Ach.' Innes waved his hand and got up to go back to the bar. 'You young people are always so obsessed with truth. The truth is often overrated.'

*

Innes's marriage was, largely, a mystery to Lexie. He didn't talk about Gloria much; when he did, it was generally to swear and curse and think up more and more elaborate insults for her.

Lexie was able to glean only the barest facts. That Innes had been seventeen when the war started, that his mother Ferdinanda had refused to leave the house in Myddleton Square, even though air-raid sirens were sounding all round them. He went to school; Ferdinanda stayed at home with her maid Consuela. What did they do? Lexie asked Innes one night, when the window to his past was briefly opened. Embroidery, he replied, of samplers and the truth. At eighteen he went up to Oxford, to study art history. At twenty he came down again, conscripted into the RAF.

Imagine a twenty-year-old Innes in his blue serge uniform, in formation at some training camp, forced away from the study of art to perform drills on an airstrip in the Home Counties. His misery would have emanated from him like an odour. He did not have the temperament for the RAF, for war.

So, these are the bare facts. But in between are layer upon layer of subtleties, strata of unknowns. Lexie never knew for certain how Innes looked, what he was wearing, whether he was sitting or standing or walking when he had first met Gloria.

It was at the Tate Gallery, he once gave away, and he was home on leave. They were in front of the Pre-Raphaelites, looking at Beatrice with her flaming hair. Let us imagine Gloria before the painting of Beatrice with her hair spread about her shoulders. Drabber than usual – this is wartime Gloria, don't forget – in low, laced shoes, a Utility coat. Her hair would have been curled at the ends, set in a side parting. She'd have been wearing bright scarlet lipstick. A scarf, perhaps. A crocodile handbag over her arm.

Would she have felt his presence? Been aware of him sidling towards her? Might she have turned her head once, quickly, then turned it back to the painting? Innes would have approached her first. What would have been his opening gambit? Something about the painting? They fell into conversation, they walked into the next room, they might have consulted the gallery map together. They might have had tea and a bun in the café next. And then, perhaps, a walk along the river.

A month later they were married. Innes got shifty and irritable if questioned about why, whether he loved her, what he had been thinking at the time. It's possible that his imminent posting was uppermost in his mind but he would never say. He didn't like to admit to fear of any kind, liked to think he was invincible, unshakeable.

Ferdinanda, excited by the prospect of grandchildren, gave them the basement of the house to live in. Her new daughter-in-law would be company for her. Lexie never met Ferdinanda – she had died before her time – but let's have her as a tall woman with steel-grey hair pulled away from her face, sitting in a silk wrap in the upstairs room in Myddleton Square (a fine room with floor-length double windows opening out over the square, the trees, the benches there), with Gloria in a chair opposite and Ferdinanda directing her faithful servant to pour the tea.

Innes was posted shortly afterwards to an airfield in Norfolk. In his second week he was taking part in a raid over Germany when the plane was shot down. Everyone was killed, apart from Rear Gunner Kent, aged twenty-one, who opened his parachute and floated like thistledown into enemy territory.

Actually, it wouldn't have been like thistledown at all. It must have been fast, furious, terrifying, the cold night air rushing, rushing into his face, his injured leg, which had swallowed up broken bits of the fuselage and bits of the splintered cranium of his fellow gunner, smarting and throbbing, and all the time he was hanging from his straps, like a puppet, watching as the treetops rose up to meet him.

For the next two years, until the end of the war, Innes was in a prisoner-of-war camp. He would never talk about this, ever, no matter what wiles Lexie employed. 'You don't want to hear about that,' he would say.

'I really do,' she'd reply, but he was immovable.

What is known is that when he returned to Myddleton Square he found Gloria occupying the whole house. Ferdinanda was gone, put into a home for the elderly run by the Church. Consuela had disappeared into the confusion of wartime London. Gloria had cleared out the entire house: all Ferdinanda's clothes, photographs, ostrich-feather fans, hats, shoes had been burnt in the back garden. The blackened circle was still there to see on the grass. Also in residence was a four-month-old baby and a lawyer called Charles. When Innes arrived and opened the front door with his key, Charles appeared at the top of the stairs, wearing Innes's father's dressing-gown, demanding to know who Innes was.

The details of the scene that ensued are not known but Innes became remarkably articulate and verbose when riled. There would have been long, vicious speeches from Innes, tears and shrieking from Gloria, confused interventions from Charles. Anyway, Gloria agreed to a separation but not a divorce. She kept Myddleton Square and lived there with the baby, Margot. There must have been some money from somewhere – Gloria's, perhaps? – because Innes took a flat on Haverstock Hill to live in and, for a while, Ferdinanda lived there with him.

She was the real casualty of this story. When Innes went to find her, she no longer recognised him. Gloria had told her that Innes was dead, killed in action, slaughtered in the night-time German sky. Here is the nub, the rub, the font of all Innes's hatred and bitterness towards his wife. Why had she done it? Only Gloria knew, and she wasn't telling. She might have thought her young husband wasn't coming back, she might have taken a fancy to that beautiful big house. Perhaps Ferdinanda irritated her, plagued her. Perhaps when she got pregnant she knew it would be impossible to pass off the baby as Innes's with Ferdinanda around. Ferdinanda kept a calendar, ticking off the days, measuring how long it had been since she'd seen her beloved son. She would never have been fooled by a twenty-month pregnancy. So, she had to be got out of the way.

The news of her son's death caused Ferdinanda's mind to wander off and not come back. Innes took her from the Catholic home and looked after her until she died. She was always, he said, distant but unfailingly polite. She addressed him as 'young man' and would tell him stories about her son who'd been killed in the war.

The presence of Lexie in Innes's life seemed to torment Gloria, in a way that none of his other women had. She began appearing at their office at regular intervals, sometimes crying, sometimes demanding money; she called at the flat early in the mornings. She made scenes in stairways, in restaurants, in the foyers of theatres, in the doorways of bars, weeping and accusing, her daughter standing mute behind her. They seemed to come in waves, these visitations: there might be two in a week and then they wouldn't see Gloria for months. Then she would appear again, the sound of her heels clipping up Bayton Street. She wrote letters to Innes, entreating him to remember his legal vows. These, Innes shredded into pieces, which he then fed into the fire. For a while one summer, when Lexie left the house in the morning, she would often see the daughter sitting on a wall on the other side of the road. Margot never spoke to her or approached her and Lexie never mentioned these incidents to Innes. Once Lexie looked up from a newspaper on the Tube to find the girl sitting in the seat opposite her, a school satchel clutched on her lap, those pale eyes fixed on Lexie's face.

Lexie stood and gripped the handrail above them. 'Why are you doing this?' she said to her, quietly. 'What do you want from me?'

The girl moved her stare from Lexie's face to the area of her shoulder. Her waxen cheeks began to stain red.

'Nothing can be gained from this, Margot,' Lexie said. The train lurched around a corner and Lexie had to cling tight to the rail so as not to be thrown forward on to the girl. 'I am not to blame for this situation. You have to believe me.'

This seemed to sting the girl. She looked up, clutching her satchel tighter. 'But I don't,' she said. 'I don't believe you.'

'I promise you that it's not my fault.'

Margot started up from her seat. The train was pulling into Euston. 'It is your fault,' she hissed. 'It is. You took him away from us and I'm going to make you sorry. I am. You see if I don't.' Then she was gone and Lexie did not see her again for a long time.

For the final two hundred yards or so, after he turns off the main road, Ted pushes himself into a sprint. His feet work against the pavement, his arms slice back and forth, back and forth, the blood screeches around his body and his lungs snatch at air. He arrives at his parents' door with a scattering of gravel and sweat and he has to hold on to the railings, allowing his lungs to fill and flatten, fill and flatten, before he can straighten up and ring the bell.

His mother takes a long time to answer.

'Darling,' she says, automatically proffering her cheek for him to kiss before she takes in her son's jogging clothes. She retreats, nose wrinkled. 'Would you like to use the shower?'

'No, it's OK.' Ted shakes himself, like a dog exiting a river, pushing his hair off his brow. 'I can't stay. I just came because Dad said—'

'Did you run all the way?' she asks, as she leads him down to the kitchen.

'Yeah.'

'From work?'

'Uh-huh.'

'Is that wise?'

'Wise?'

'With all the . . .' she shrugs a cashmere-clad shoulder '. . . I don't know, pollution. And your joints.'

'My joints?'

'Yes, I'm told that jogging can be very bad for you.'

Ted slumps into a chair at the table. 'Mum, I think you'll find the general consensus is that exercise is, in fact, very good for you.'

'Well,' his mother looks doubtful, 'I don't know about that. Are you sure you wouldn't like to have a shower?'

'I'm sure. I can't stay. Got to get home.'

'We have towels. They're in the—'

'I know you have towels, Mum, and I'm sure they're very nice but I can't stay. Dad said he had some papers he wanted me to sign so I've come for that and then I have to go.'

'You don't want dinner?'

'I don't want dinner.'

'You'll have coffee, though. How about a sandwich? I can make you a nice ham and—'

'Mum, I'd love to but I can't.'

'You'll pop upstairs and see your grandmother, won't you? It would make her day, darling, you know it would.'

'Mum,' Ted holds his brow in his fingertips and massages his temples, 'another time, I promise. Right now, I have to go. Elina's been on her own all day—'

'Well, so has your grandmother.'

Ted takes in a breath and lets it out again. 'Elina's been on her own with a small baby. The feeding's not going so well and—'

'Really?' His mother turns from the coffee-maker, her face ablaze with alarm. 'What's happened? What's wrong?'

'Nothing's wrong. He's—'

'He's not eating? He's losing weight?'

'He's fine. He's just crying a lot, that's all. It's just wind or colic, Elina thinks.'

'Colic? Is that serious?'

'No,' he says, 'lots of babies get it. I probably had it. Don't you remember?'

His mother turns back to the coffee-maker and flicks a switch, her reply drowned by the grinding of beans.

'What did you say?' Ted sits forward in his seat. 'Actually, you know what? I'll have just water. That would be great.'

'Not coffee?'

'No. Water.'

His mother opens the fridge. 'Still or sparkling?'

'Was I breastfed or did you—'

'Still or sparkling?'

'Either. Anything. Just tap water's fine. I don't know why you buy that crap anyway.'

'Language, Ted.'

'So, was I?'

His mother is searching in a high cupboard for a glass, her back to him. 'Were you what?'

'Breastfed.'

'Do you want lemon?'

'Yes, OK.'

'Ice?'

'Anything. Doesn't matter.'

She puts down the glass and starts rummaging in the freezer. 'I told your father to fill the ice-trays the other day but I bet he didn't.' She extracts a whole fish, frozen solid inside its wrapping, a plastic box of some clear, brackish fluid. 'Here's one,' she mutters, 'empty, of course, but where's the other?'

'Mum, forget the ice. I'll have it just as it is.'

'I ask him to do these things and it's as if he doesn't even— Aha!' She holds aloft an ice-tray triumphantly. 'Here am I, maligning your poor father, and look – ice.' She drops three cubes into Ted's water and they split on impact. She replaces the frozen fish before handing Ted his glass.

'Thank you,' he says, and takes a long drink. 'So, was I breastfed?'

His mother sits opposite him at the table. She shakes her head, her mouth pursed with distaste. 'I'm afraid not. It was bottles all the way with you.'

'Really?'

His mother jumps up again. 'Now, where did I put those papers?'

'It's funny,' Ted says, as she moves a pile of newspapers from a chair, then puts them back, 'they tell you nowadays that you have to breastfeed for their immune systems. Elina's always saying I'm more resistant to illness than anyone she's ever met. And if I wasn't breastfed that just disproves the whole theory, doesn't it?'

His mother opens a cupboard door, peers inside, then shuts it. 'I know they're here somewhere, I had them only this afternoon, but where . . .' She darts forward and pounces on a sheaf of white documents. 'Here they are! I knew they were here somewhere.' She puts them down in front of Ted.

'What are these, anyway?'

'Some financial dealing of your father's.'

'Yes, but what?' Ted drains his glass then picks up the paper on top of the pile.

'Don't ask me, darling. He doesn't discuss these things with me. Something about a trust. For the baby. You get some money back from the government or something.'

'He's setting up a trust for the baby?'

'I think that was it. We both worry sometimes, you know. Especially now you have the baby.'

'Worry about what?'

'Well, you know. Yours and Elina's income is so . . .'

'So what?'

'Unreliable.'

'Unreliable?'

'Not unreliable. Irregular. Erratic. So we thought we would sort out some money for the baby, just in case.'

'I see,' Ted murmurs, trying to hide his smile. He restrains himself from asking, in case of what? 'That's very kind of you. Have you got a pen?' His mother hands him a fountain pen and Ted scribbles his name in the box marked 'consent'.

At the door, his mother is still talking about the shower and towels and popping up to see his grandmother.

'Sorry,' Ted says, kissing her cheek, 'got to go.'

'You're not going to jog all the way to Gospel Oak, are you?'

Ted walks backwards, waving at her. 'No. I'll get the bus.'

'The bus? I'll give you a lift. You don't have to get the bus. I'll drive you, then I can see—'

'I'll get the bus,' Ted says, still waving, still walking. Then he stops.

His mother regards him, the door held in one hand. 'What's the matter?'

'Do you remember . . . ?' he asks, then has to break off to think. 'A man came to the house once. And you . . . you sent him away. I think. I'm sure you did.'

'When?'

'Years ago. When I was small. A man in a brown jacket. Sort of untidy hair. I was upstairs. You were arguing with him. You said – I remember this – you said, "No, you can't come in, you have to leave." Do you remember that?'

His mother gives an emphatic shake of her head. 'No.'

'Who would he have been? He was looking up at the house as he walked away. And he waved at me. You don't remember?'

She isn't looking at him. She is running her hand over the paintwork of the door, as if checking for cracks. 'Not at all,' she says, with her face turned away.

'He waved at me as if he—'

'Sounds like a travelling salesman or something. We used to get a lot of them coming to the door in those days. A pushy lot, they were.' His mother turns to him, teeth bared in a smile. 'That's the most likely explanation.'

'Right.'

'Goodbye, darling. See you soon.' She shuts the door quickly and, after a moment, Ted turns and sets off across the street.

Elina doesn't hear Ted's key in the lock because the baby is screaming again, his fist rammed into his mouth, his head buried in her neck. She is doing circuits of the living room in that special slow-bouncing walk, like someone on the moon, Elina thinks, or someone in deep snow. The baby has fed for two thirty-second bursts in the last hour: he latches on with gusto but then pulls away, shrieking. Is he in pain? Is there something wrong with her milk? Doesn't he like it? Is there something wrong with him? Or is there something wrong with her?

Elina eyes the baby book on the sofa. She'd bought it because the woman in the bookshop had told her it was the 'absolute baby Bible'. She's looked up 'wind', she's looked up 'crying', she's looked up 'feeding problems' and 'colic', she's looked up 'despair' and 'agony' and then 'fathomless grief', but she can't find anything helpful.

She changes the baby's position so that he is lying along her forearm, his head cradled in her palm. She rubs her other hand up and down his back. He seems to accept this change with a seriousness, a concentrated frown, as if to say, yes, let's try this, maybe it will work. Lasse, she makes herself think, as she looks down at his silken head, Arto, Paarvo, Nils, Stefan. How are you supposed to choose one name for your child? How does anyone decide? Does he look like a Peter, a Sebastian, a Mikael? Or is he a Sam, a Jeremy, a David? She is feeling, along the tendons and veins of her arms, minute adjustments, peristaltic gurgles, catches, releases of his tiny alimentary canal and she is focusing so entirely on these that when she raises her head, and sees the outline of two faces in the darkened window before her, she lets out a shriek, whirling round, clutching at the baby so as not to drop him.

It's Ted, who has come into the room behind her, a wry smile on his face, dressed in his jogging clothes, flinging his keys to the sofa. 'Well,' he is saying, 'that's quite a greeting.'

The baby, frightened by her shriek, begins to wail again. Not with the rasped, raw shouts of the last hour but a new, tense, spiralling cry.

'You scared me,' she mouths over the noise.

'Sorry,' he mouths back. 'How are you two?'

She shrugs.

'Do you want me to take him?'

Elina nods, hands over the baby. Her arms feel light, oddly numb, as in that game where you stand pressing your hands to the doorframe, then step back and your arms float, of their own accord, up into the air.

She slumps down to the sofa, closes her eyes and rests her head on the low cushions. After two, perhaps three seconds of this oblivion, she feels a hand on her arm. 'I think he's hungry.' Ted is handing the baby back to her. 'Maybe you should feed him.'

'For God's sake,' she screams, as she yanks at her shirt, trying to pull it up and hook it under her chin while she fumbles with the catch of her bra, the pad, the angle of her nipple, the baby's fist, which is flailing dangerously close to the swell of her rigid, hot-skinned breast. 'What do you think I've been trying to do for the last hour?'

Ted gazes down at her, perplexed by her sudden anger. She sees him take a deep breath before he speaks. 'I wouldn't know,' he says, in a slow, placatory voice. 'I've only just got in.'

The baby is slippery in her grasp, he is puffing and writhing with anxiety, with hunger, she wants nothing more than to lie down, to apologise to Ted, to have this breast drained of its sore, scalding milk, for someone to bring her a drink of water, for someone to tell her it's all going to be all right. The baby is staring at the breast, hesitating, then his gums clamp down firmly and Elina's whole body curls with the pain of it. He seems to think for another few seconds and then, at last, he begins to suck, with the absorbed air of someone getting down to business, his eyes moving back and forth, as if reading invisible text in the air.

She lowers her shoulders, very slowly, a bit at a time. She looks up into the room. Ted is sitting in the chair opposite, watching them, frowning, one leg crossed over the other. She attempts a smile at him and she sees that, in fact, he is not watching them but looking at something near them. He has that odd, unfocused look in his eyes.

'Are you all right?'

He blinks and focuses on her, bemused. 'Huh?'

'Are – you – all right?'

He seems to shake himself. 'Of course. Why do you ask?'

'No reason. Just, you know, checking.'

'Well, I wish you wouldn't.'

'Wouldn't what?'

'Keep checking. Keep asking me if I'm all right.'

'Why?'

'It's annoying. I keep telling you I'm fine.'

'Annoying?' she repeats. 'It's annoying that I care about you, is it?'

Ted pushes himself to his feet. 'I'm going to have a shower,' he mutters, and walks off.

They lie on the bed, all three of them, on their backs, Elina staring at the ceiling, the baby asleep between them, arms spread wide.

'I wonder,' Ted begins, 'when he'll start remembering things.'

She turns to look at him. Ted has his head propped up on his elbow and is gazing at the baby. 'It varies, doesn't it?' she says. 'Around three or four, I think.'

'Three or four?' he murmurs, regarding her with raised brows.

She smiles at him. 'I'm not talking about you, Mr Amnesiac, I'm talking about normal people with normal brains.'

'What is a normal brain, Ms Insomniac?'

She ignores him. 'I remember my brother being born—'

'How old were you then?'

'Um . . .' she has to think '. . . two. Two and five months.'

'Really?' Ted is geniunely surprised. 'You remember something from the age of two?'

'Uh-huh. But it was a big thing. Thc arrival of a brother. Anyone would remember that.'

He curls a hand around the baby's foot. 'Not me.'

'I've read that people with younger siblings have better memories because they've been, I don't know, exercised more. They can pin down their memories more easily.'

'That's me stuffed, then.' He grins, lets go of the baby's foot and lies back on the bed, his hands behind his head. 'It's a perfect excuse for my rubbish memory, though. No siblings.' Elina looks over at him.

She sees the tan lines on his arms, around the wrist where his watch goes, the muscles pushing up from under the skin of his legs, the way the dark hair gathers at the navel, the chest. It's a hot night and he's wearing only a pair of shorts. How strange, she thinks, that he is so physically unchanged. When I am unrecognisable.

Ted is speaking again. '. . . something about having him, about watching you and him together that means I can suddenly almost see these things. Almost but not quite. I remembered this thing the other day – it's not much, don't get excited – but I remembered walking down a path and my hand was being held by someone much taller than me, someone in green shoes, you know those high ones, not stilettos, with a kind of thick sole.'

'Platform shoes?'

'Yes. Green ones, with a wooden sole.'

'Really? What else?'

'That was it. I just remembered the sensation of having my arm straight up above my head.'

'Don't tell me,' she turns over, reaches out a hand and lays it on his chest; he covers it immediately with both of his own, 'that your memory is improving. Can it be possible?'

'Apparently,' he says. He lifts her hand to his mouth and kisses it absently. 'Miracles do happen.'

One night Lexie was left alone at *Elsewhere.* Innes had disappeared, muttering something about viewing a new triptych in someone's studio, and Laurence had gone to the Mandrake. Lexie was determined not to leave until she had cut a further two hundred words from a rather verbose piece about George Barker. She gripped a blue pencil between her teeth and bent over the closely typed copy.

'The quintessential quality, tone and distinctiveness of Barker's cadences . . .' she read. Did it need 'quality' and 'tone'? And 'distinctiveness'? Didn't 'quintessential quality' mean the same as 'distinctiveness'? Lexie sighed and bit down on the end of the pencil, tasting lead and wood. She had read this so many times that the piece was losing sense, the words so familiar that none of them meant anything any more. Her pencil end hovered over 'distinctiveness' and then 'quintessential quality', then back, until she sighed again and finally made her decision. She scored out 'distinctiveness', on the grounds that it was an ugly word, made up of—

The door screeched open and Daphne stepped in, shaking rain from her coat and hair. 'God,' she was exclaiming, 'it's a filthy night out there.' She looked around. 'Where is everyone? What happened? Are you here all alone?'

'Yes,' Lexie said. She and Daphne regarded each other, the desk between them. Lexie put down her blue pencil, then picked it up again. 'I'm just finishing this and then I'm going to—'

Daphne came to look over her shoulder. 'Is that Venables's book review? His copy's always a dog's dinner. I don't know why Innes keeps using him. He's cheap, I suppose, but that's all that can be said for him. Hanging clause.' Daphne pointed with a bitten-down fingernail at the second paragraph. 'The word "stanza" twice in one sentence.' She pointed elsewhere on the page. 'The lazy bugger. Sometimes I wonder if he even reads them over when he's finished.'

Daphne drew herself up to sit on Lexie's desk and Lexie, hotly aware of Daphne's gaze, began to rearrange the hanging clause.

'Quite something, though, that you've been given that,' Daphne remarked.

Lexie looked up at her, at her lipsticked mouth, pursed in contemplation, at the green ring encircling a thumb. 'Do you think?'

Daphne examined a nail, bit it, then examined it again. 'Mmm,' she said. 'If he gives you Venables's rubbish to resuscitate, he must rate your abilities.'

Lexie yawned, suddenly overcome with fatigue. 'I don't know why,' she said. 'I don't feel as though I have any abilities at all.'

Daphne reached out and plucked the pencil from her fingers. 'Come on,' she said. 'Enough. I think we both need a drink.'

'I need to finish this,' Lexie protested, because it was the truth and also because she'd never been out with just Daphne before and she wasn't sure she wanted to. 'I've still got a hundred and thirty words to cut. I promised Innes I'd—'

'Never mind Innes. What do you think he'll be doing with Colquhoun if not downing the best part of a bottle of whisky? Let's get out of here.'

They tried the French Pub – Daphne's first choice – but it was so full that people had spilled out on to the pavement. 'It'll take years to get served,' Daphne muttered, as they surveyed the scene from the opposite pavement. They considered the Mandrake, but rejected the idea. At the door of the Colony Room, Muriel Belcher stopped them with a glare. 'Members only, I'm afraid,' she rasped.

Daphne removed the cigarette from her mouth. 'Ah, go on, Muriel, just this once.'

'You two donnas don't, as I recall, have the honour of membership here.'

'Please,' Lexie begged, 'it's late. Everywhere's packed. We won't stay long. We'll be on our best behaviour, we promise. We'll buy you a drink.'

'Where's Miss Kent tonight?'

'Off with Colquhoun,' Daphne said.

Muriel raised an eyebrow and looked at Lexie. 'I see. Going over to the other side, is she?'

'Um,' Lexie floundered, not entirely following Muriel's meaning, 'well . . .'

Daphne came to her aid. 'That's about as likely as the earth becoming flat,' she interjected.

'Well, you two should know.' Muriel cackled. 'You should know.'

'So can we come in?' Daphne said. 'Please?' She was pushing Lexie forward so that she was almost on top of Muriel. Lexie had to push back so as not to land in the landlady's lap. 'She's trading with a member,' Daphne said, still shoving Lexie in the ribs; Lexie trod down hard on Daphne's toe. 'Couldn't that count?'

Muriel looked them both up and down. 'All right, but only this once. Make sure your dilly boy is with you next time.'

'Dilly boy?' Lexie whispered, as they stepped through the tables to the bar.

'She means Innes,' Daphne whispered back.

The phrase in connection with Innes struck Lexie as particularly funny and she began to giggle. 'Why does she call him that? And why does she refer to him as "she"?'

'Hush,' Daphne gripped her arm, 'she'll think you're laughing at her. And she'll throw us out.'

Lexie couldn't stop laughing. 'Will she?'

'Dear God,' Daphne moaned. 'And you haven't had anything to drink yet. She calls all men "she". Have you never noticed?'

'But why?'

'She just does,' Daphne let out impatiently. 'Now,' she said, as they reached the bar, 'what'll we have? Gin, I think. I've got no money at all – how about you?'

They sat at a table near the bar, squashed between a man in a filthy sheepskin coat, two young men, one carrying a beautiful patent-leather handbag over his arm, and the old woman Lexie had seen in here before.

Lexie pushed a gin towards Daphne, stirred her own and said, 'Bottoms up,' before downing the lot. The alcohol flooded the back of her throat, making her cough and her eyes water. 'Ouf,' she said, spluttering, 'ah. Shall we have another?'

Daphne eyed her and took a sip of her own drink. 'You don't do things by halves, do you, Lexie Sinclair?'

Lexie hooked an ice cube out of her glass and dropped it into her mouth. 'What do you mean?'

Daphne shrugged. 'You throw yourself into everything.'

'Do I?'

'Yes.' She sucked meditatively on her swizzle stick. 'It's obvious why you and Innes are . . . you know . . . a success. He's just the same.'

Lexie crunched down on the ice cube, feeling it splinter between her teeth. She ground it into smaller and smaller pieces. She looked at Daphne, at the green thumb ring, the smooth skin of her brow, her wide mouth as she sipped from her glass. She was presented, for a fleeting moment, with an image of Innes above Daphne in bed; she pictured his hands, his lips touching that skin, that hair, their mouths meeting. Lexie gulped down the particles of ice and took a deep breath. She felt that the time had come to speak, that if she and Daphne were to continue, the thing needed to be said.

'I'm sorry,' she began, 'if, well, I got in the way or . . . or . . . or stepped on your toes. With you and Innes, I mean . . . I never meant for it to—'

'Oh, please,' Daphne flicked her wrist, as if waving away a fly, 'there's nothing to apologise for. Me and him were . . . Well, it was just a convenient arrangement. Not like you and him. You and him are different, aren't you? Anyone can see that.' Daphne grinned at her, as if pleased by the turn in the conversation. 'He's a different man since meeting you.'

'Me too,' Lexie said. 'Although, I'm not a man, obviously.' She was once more struck by uncontrollable giggles. The sight of the Colony Room – the man with the patent handbag in the chair next to her, the old woman rattling her tobacco tin under the nose of the man in the sheepskin coat, the fish doing laps of their murky tank, Muriel shrieking at some hapless member to 'open up his beadbag', an artist she vaguely recognised with his arm around the neck of a woman in a tight purple dress – seemed so far from anything her upbringing had led her to expect that all she could do was laugh.

Daphne rolled her eyes. 'What's so funny now?'

'I don't know,' Lexie managed to get out, 'I don't know. Sometimes I find it hard to believe that I used to live in Devon.'

'What?' Daphne stared at her, baffled. 'What's Devon got to do with anything?'

'Nothing!' Lexie leant over the table. 'That's just it!'

Daphne put a cigarette to her mouth and lit it, shaking out the match. 'You're a strange girl, Lexie.' Then she slapped the table. 'Well, more drink, I think. Deakin,' she called across the table, to the man in the sheepskin coat, 'lend us a bob or two, there's a love. I know you can spare it.'

Deakin turned towards them slowly, his lip curled. 'Fuck off,' he drawled. 'Buy your own.'

The *Elsewhere* offices are currently a café. Or a bar. It's uncertain which. It says 'The Lagoon Café Bar' above the door so you can take your pick. The lack of punctuation in that sign would have bothered Innes. It should be 'Café/Bar', he would have insisted, or 'Café, Bar', or at least 'Café-Bar', if you're using the term in its compound sense.

Anyway, it's the sort of place with a planed wooden floor, low lighting, dark blue walls, a candle on every table, sofas at the back. It has books and magazines scattered about, one of which is *London Lights*, ironically. *London Lights* is what *Elsewhere* is now called. A terrible name change. But the people who bought *Elsewhere* in the early sixties thought the original name 'too heavy'. It's unrecognisable as the magazine of Innes's day, of course. Four times the length, stuffed with adverts, filled with serried lines of listings, interviews with television stars disclosing run-of-the-mill secrets. The arts reviews, such as they are, are given very little space. Only the other week, a National Theatre production of *Medea* was dispensed with in a hundred words.

There is a table in the Lagoon Café Bar (or Café/Bar, or Café-Bar), roughly where Lexie's desk – an old kitchen table, covered with knife scars and ink spots – used to be, by the door, facing down the street. The door is different but this one also sticks in wet weather. The fireplace Innes boarded up – because in winter-time he couldn't bear the draught that reached down its icy arm – the café people have opened, polished, renovated. How things change. They don't use it as a fireplace but more as a kind of shrine, filled with candles. A shrine to what isn't certain. Some of the *Elsewhere* shelving has survived – remarkably, as it was inexpertly put up by Laurence and Lexie one weekend in 1960. It holds some of the café/bar's books and, at the back, rows and rows of glasses, inverted and dripping from the dishwasher. What was Innes's back room, where he kept paintings and his sofa and assorted junk, is now a kitchen. They grill panini, mix hummus and lay out olives in little bowls there – the Lagoon's cuisine is unspecified Mediterranean, and served by a mix of Bosnians, Poles and Australians. Innes would have loved it.

From the table where Lexie's desk used to be, there is a view of Bayton Street. It is unseasonably cold for July, grey curtains of rain falling aslant the tarmac, spattering the windows. The tables outside on the pavement are empty, a single abandoned coffee cup slowly filling with rain. The Australian waitress or 'barista', as her badge says, has put on an old Edith Piaf recording. It is early in the afternoon, just past the lunchtime rush. And sitting at the table where Lexie's desk used to be is Ted.

He comes here quite a bit. The editing house is just around the corner, on Wardour Street. He is eating his lunch, a panini of goat's cheese and red pepper. His fingers tap along to Edith ever so slightly and the vibrations can be felt through the wood. He seems to be staring at the place where Lexie's pinboard used to hang. An untidy array of notes, proofs, lists, postcards, transparencies that only she understood. But, of course, he's just looking at the rain.

The baby was awake a lot last night, he's just been saying, which would go some way to explaining his dazed appearance. He is wearing a shirt, the collar of which is skewed, a jumper with a frayed cuff.

'It's time you gave that child a goddamn name,' his companion, Simmy, says stridently. 'You can't still be calling him "the baby" when he goes off to university.'

Ted smiles, then shrugs and the skewed collar lifts up and down as he does so. 'He might not go to university.' He takes an enormous bite of his panini.

Simmy rolls his eyes. 'You know what I mean. What the hell are you—'

'For your information,' Ted interrupts, once he's swallowed his mouthful, 'we decided on a name last night.'

'Really?' Simmy is so surprised he has to put down his glass. 'What is it?'

Ted indicates with a circling gesture that he is chewing.

'Is it some unpronounceable Finnish thing?' Simmy persists. 'With seven vowels? Or is it really long, like James James Morrison Morrison Weatherby George Duwhatsit. Or is it Ted? Ted the Second?'

'It's Jonah,' Ted says.

Simmy considers this. 'As in the whale?'

'Yep.'

'You know,' Simmy says, 'that people are going to say that to him for ever more?'

'What? The whale thing?'

'Yes.'

Ted shrugs again. 'Well. He'll get used to it. All names have got some associations. Anyway, he looks like a Jonah. And I like the name Jonah—'

'Obviously,' Simmy cuts in, 'since you chose it.'

'And,' Ted continues, as if he hasn't been interrupted, 'it works well in Finnish and English. In English it's, well, Jonah; in Finnish it's pronounced "Jurnah." Or "Juor-nah". Something like that.'

'"Juor-nah?"'

'Apparently.'

'I wouldn't call that working well.'

'Sim,' Ted says amiably, 'no one's asking you.'

They eat in silence. Ted starts to drum his fingers again on the table and the glasses, the knives, the cups in the saucers set up an answering vibration.

'I like it,' Simmy mumbles, through a mouthful of breadstick. 'It's a good name.'

'Thanks.'

'How's Elina?'

Ted stops drumming his fingers. He fiddles with his napkin, unfolding and refolding it. 'All right.' He frowns in the middle of this phrase. 'She's . . . you know . . . tired.'

Simmy puts his head on one side. 'I expect she is.'

'I wish I could just bag this bloody film and then maybe take some more time off but—'

'There's really no one else you can get to do some of the editing?'

Ted scratches his head, yawns. 'I'm contracted. And, you know, he's a big client. He wouldn't like to be passed on to someone else. I have to finish it. And the baby came early and everything . . . I've been telling her that she should get in touch with her group.'

'Her group?'

'Yeah. You know. Birthing group, or whatever they call it. Birthing class. From the hospital. They're meeting once a week, I think. But she won't go.'

'Why not?'

'I don't know.' Ted tosses his napkin down to his plate. 'She's says she no good at groups, or something like that.'

'Maybe she isn't. I don't see Elina as a group person, somehow.'

'And she says Jonah will scream the whole time.' Ted frowns again. 'He's got colic, she thinks, and she says she can't feed him anywhere other than at home because he just screams and struggles and she's left with her . . . you know . . . hanging out until he calms down, which can take about an hour.' Ted stops to draw breath. The two men stare at each other.

'Right.' Simmy nods. 'Maybe I'll come over. At the weekend.'

'Most people would say, "Is it OK if I come over?" Not "I'll come over."'

'I'm not asking your permission. I'm not coming to see you. I'm coming to see Elina. And the newly named Jonah. You can go to hell in a handcart.'

Ted grins. 'Fine,' he says. Then he takes a glance at his watch. 'I've got to go.' He stands, throws some notes on to the table. 'Sorry, Sim. See you later.' Then Ted is gone.

He moves fast, always has done, his walk slightly bouncy, the balls of his feet lifting, propelling him along the pavement. On the way, he pulls out his phone and calls Elina. 'Hello . . . Yeah . . . How are you? How's Jonah? Has he fed OK? . . . Oh. Really? Oh, no. I'm sorry. Well, maybe— . . . I see. OK . . . I just saw Simmy. Yes. I told him about the name. He said— . . . Oh. All right. Speak to you later.' He snaps his phone shut, then turns into his building. In the lift, he stands watching the numbers change, and when he reaches his room, he flops into his chair. He rearranges some papers on his desk, puts a pen behind his ear, puts it down again; he drinks some water from a plastic bottle, adjusts the angle of his chair; he shakes out his right wrist. Then he gets to work.

In front of him are two screens: on both is the still image of a man, teetering on the edge of a building, about to fall.

Ted's fingers move the mouse against the desk and click the buttons with a quaver-crotchet rhythm and the film begins to edge forward, frame by frame, in slow motion. The man's feet lose contact with the building's edge, he tips lengthways, the fragile shell of his skull pointing down now, his arms beginning to flail in a circling motion, his clothes flap-flapping in the breeze – we don't see his face but we can imagine it, that frozen, wide-mouthed horror – as he passes the camera and we follow him, down, down, a dreadful plunge and this man doesn't have a parachute, there is no cord to pull, no opening silk billowing out to save him; he is heading, head first, limbs windmilling, for the unmerciful ground below.

Then Ted nudges his mouse again and clicks – three clear quavers – and the man is halted in his fall, just inches from the road. You can see his face now, from this camera angle; his teeth are bared, his eyes are shut, and who can blame him for that, and it's an expression of extraordinary ferocity and Ted has saved him. He is clicking again, the film is rewinding, the man is being hauled back up through the air, up and up and up, away from the ground and, there, he is back up on top of the building; now he is talking to the other man, a large man, the one who pushed him, and he really shouldn't get into conversations with large men on the roofs of skyscrapers again.

Ted rolls the film forwards, then backwards. We see from different angles the man teetering on the edge of the building, then stepping back. Forwards: about to fall. Back: towards the large man. Forward, back. Will he fall or will he stay on the building? Will he die or not? Will he die today or tomorrow? Ted can decide.

But he doesn't seem to want to decide at the moment. He is yawning, rubbing his eyes with the heels of his hands, sitting back in his chair. He clicks again on his mouse and the scene spools backwards. Ted massages the tendons of his right arm as he watches, yawns again, glances at the clock on the wall – the director will be here soon and wants to see this scene. Then he frowns and sits forward. Something has flickered for no more than a micro-second, at the top of the screen. Ted moves the mouse again and the images scroll forward, then back, at inching speed. Forward, back.

There! He has it! He knew it! A black flicker across the camera.

A piece of equipment, a dangling wire, a finger-end, who knows? But he's found it and, with a swift few clicks of the mouse, eliminated it.

Ted sits back, pleased with himself. He hates dirty shots, hates to miss them. Then he yawns again. He slaps his cheek gently, three times. He needs to wake up before the director gets here, he needs to get some coffee, he needs to call his father back, later maybe, he needs to—

For no reason at all, he suddenly thinks of his father. Pulling him down a street as a child. He, Ted, is dragging his feet, letting his legs buckle under him, in that way children do, and he is wailing, *no, no, no*. In that way children do. And his father? His father is saying, *come on* and *you have to* and *don't be silly* and all those other things fathers say. He must have been taking Ted somewhere without his mother because Ted can feel the sensation – so distant now – that consuming urge, that overwhelming need to see her, to go back to her, to grip and hang on to that metal railing until she hears him crying, until she comes for him.

Ted looks at the screen, the man suspended in the air like a dark angel. He looks at the postcard of Elina's painting. He shakes his arm, which feels stiff and is prickling with pins and needles – maybe it's time to go and see that osteopath again – and he stands. He looks at his hands, the scar on the back of his thumb, the numbers on the phonepad. He picks up the phone and holds it. He should call his father back. Or maybe he should call Elina again to see if she's OK. But Ted doesn't punch in any of their numbers. He sits at his desk, holding the receiver to his ear and listens to the sonic pulse of the dial tone, soothing in its monotony, like the wind through trees, like the sea over pebbles.

The doorbell is ringing, on and on. Elina is folding things in the spare room, small things – tiny vests, bodysuits, miniature socks. 'Ted?' she calls. 'Ted!'

There's no reply. The bell goes on ringing. She puts down the vest she's holding and leaves the room.

When she opens the door, Simmy is standing on the path. 'Little My,' he says, 'I've come to take you away.'

Elina laughs. She can't help herself. Simmy is wearing a straw hat and an enormous shirt printed with coloured deck chairs. 'You look . . . I don't know . . . like you should be appearing in a musical,' she says.

He opens his arms expansively. 'My whole life is a musical. Come on, let's go.'

'Go?'

'Out. Hurry, hurry.' He jangles his car keys. 'Haven't got all day.'

'But . . .' Elina tries to think '. . . where are we going?'

'Out, I told you. Where's that man of yours? Is he in?'

'He's in the garden with the baby.'

'You mean Jonah,' Simmy says severely, stepping into the hall, starting to rummage through the things on the coat rack. 'You've got to drop this habit of calling him "the baby". I don't call you "the woman", do I?' He hands her a jacket and a sunhat.

Elina takes them, helplessly, then lowers herself to the bottom step. 'What are you doing, Sim?'

'Don't you have a bag?' he demands, holding up a small green leather pouch with multiple zips, then casting it aside. 'One of those proper suitcase-like things. With stuff in.'

'What stuff?' she asks, as Simmy continues to ransack the coat rack.

'Baby stuff. Nappies, et cetera. You know. Those quilted monstrosities you people cart about.'

Elina points at the canvas bag beside the door.

'That?' Simmy says, poking it with his toe. 'You can't be serious. It looks like the thing my mother keeps horse-feed in.' He pulls it open. 'Hmm. Let's see. Nappies,' he says, 'check. Cotton wool, check.

Bottom-wipes, check. Unidentifiable small white things, check. What else do we need?'

'Sim, I can't just—'

'Bottles. How about bottles? Don't we need those?'

'No.' She gestures towards her chest. 'I'm—'

'Oh,' he wrinkles his nose, 'of course. You're doing all that business. Well, you can carry those yourself. Where's Ted? Ted!' Simmy shouts. 'Come on. Let's go.'

Let's go, Elina thinks, as they whiz in Simmy's car through streets full of people, of children on bicycles, of teenagers in groups, of trees in full bloom. It is one of her favourite expressions. Let's go. It seems to call to her from her other, old, life, when she was always arriving or departing or somewhere between the two. She feels sessile now, like a mussel shell, welded to the house, to the few streets around it. Let's go.

She holds Jonah's curled hand in the palm of her own. He sits in his car seat, awake, alert, his eyes wide. He seems to be as astonished as she is by this sudden outing. In the front, Ted and Simmy are arguing over which CD to play. Ted is wearing the straw hat now, set back on his head, and Simmy is driving with one hand on the wheel and the other over the slot in the CD player, preventing Ted from inserting whichever CD he's holding. Both men are laughing and the windows are all rolled down and warm air is streaming through the car.

They go to the National Portrait Gallery. Simmy insists on carrying Jonah in the sling and Ted has the canvas nappy bag so Elina can swing her arms lightly by her sides. Ted wants to head up to the café on the top floor but Simmy tells him not to be a Philistine. They are there to see a John Deakin exhibition, he tells them, not to drink overpriced cappuccino.

'Who is John Deakin anyway?' Ted grumbles.

'Little My?' Simmy turns to her.

'Um,' Elina has to think, 'a photographer. I think. A contemporary of Francis Bacon?'

'Full marks to you,' Simmy says. He takes them both by the hand. 'Children,' he announces, in such a loud voice that several people look over, 'we are about to enter the world of seedy, Bohemian post-war London. Are you ready?' He turns to Ted.

'No, I want to go for a c—'

'Are you ready?' Simmy turns to Elina.

'Yes,' she murmurs, holding in her laughter.

'Are you ready?' he asks, looking down at Jonah. 'No, you appear to be asleep. Never mind. Let's go.' And he pulls them along, through the doors, by their hands.

Elina first met Simmy in the living room, early one morning. She'd been renting a room off Ted for a month or so, she'd come down early before heading out to her teaching job in East London and there was a large, overweight, sandy-haired man asleep on the sofa, fully dressed, in an extraordinary ensemble of scruffy clothes. She tiptoed across the room, towards the kitchen, and filled the kettle as noiselessly as she could.

'Don't tell me,' a booming voice came from the sofa, 'you're making a pot of tea.'

She looked over and saw that the man was regarding her from above the sofa's back. 'Coffee, actually.'

'Even better. You complete angel. You couldn't spare me a cup, could you?'

Elina could. She brought it to him on the sofa and sat on the carpet to drink hers.

'Jesus,' the man gasped, after his first swallow, 'that's enough to take the skin off my throat.'

'Too strong?' Elina asked.

'Strong's not the word.' He massaged his neck. 'I may never speak again. So let's make the most of it.' He smiled at her and sat up, settling the rug about him. 'Tell me everything you know, Ted's Lodger.'

When she saw Ted that evening – he and his girlfriend Yvette were cooking dinner together – she asked him about the man on the sofa.

'Simmy?' Ted had said, without turning away from the wok. 'James Simpkin, to give him his full name. He stays here sometimes – he has his own key. I told him the attic was occupied so he probably crashed out on the sofa instead. I'm glad he remembered,' Ted added, 'and didn't burst in on you in the middle of the night.'

'Did he talk to you loudly about random things?' Yvette, dropping an olive into her mouth, had asked her. 'And was he wearing mismatched shoes?'

'No, but his trousers were held up with green garden string.'

'Don't be deceived by appearances,' Yvette said, rolling her eyes. 'His family owns half of Dorset.'

'Really?'

Ted had turned, selected a knife from the drawer. 'It's a prerogative of the very wealthy in this country, dressing like a tramp. Don't ask me why.'

At the exhibition, Elina stares into the hooded dark eyes of a famous Italian sculptor, the wide, kohled ones of a 1950s actress who later became famous for her drug problem. There is the gaunt, handsome face of Oliver Bernard. And Francis Bacon, close to the camera, as if about to kiss it. There are three men standing with their backs against a wall, unsmiling, their skin a silvery bromide sheen. She finds Ted in front of a portrait of a man and a woman. The man has his arm lightly about the woman's shoulders and with his other hand he holds a cigarette. She is in black, a scarf around her hair, the ends of which trail over her shoulder. The man is looking sideways at her but she looks out, with a candid, assessing gaze, at the viewer. The sign on the wall behind them reads 'elsewher', the end of the word obliterated by the man's head.

Elina lays her cheek, briefly, on Ted's sleeve, then moves along to see an unidentified man in a white shirt crossing a road in Soho, a side of meat over his shoulder, more pictures of Bacon, in his studio, on a pavement, standing with the same man from the picture with the sign and the woman.

Simmy appears at her side. 'You wouldn't have thought he was an incurable drunk, would you?' he says, in his version of a whisper.

'I don't know,' Elina muses, looking again at the man carrying the meat across a road, 'they all have a kind of starkness to them, don't you think? A kind of melancholy.'

Simmy snorts. 'That's because they're of the past. All photos of the past look melancholy and wistful precisely because they capture something that's gone.'

Elina reaches down to touch Jonah's head, to readjust his hat.

'Stop fiddling, will you? Leave the child alone,' Simmy says. 'And where's Ted? Let's get him that coffee.'

Ted is sitting in the café, with Simmy and Elina. Not the café he wanted to go to, the one up in the roof, with the views over Trafalgar Square, but the one in the basement. He is sitting at the table, drinking coffee, talking with his friend and his girlfriend and, without warning, something rears its head. The recollection of himself as a child on a woman's knee. The woman is wearing a red dress of slightly slippery material and it is tricky for him to stay in position: he has had to wind his arm into hers and this makes the woman laugh. He feels the reverberation of it through her chest, through the fabric of the dress.

This keeps happening, Ted finds, and more since Jonah was born. Flashes of something else, somewhere else, like radio static or interference, voices cutting in from a distant foreign station. He can barely hear them but they are there. A hint, a glimpse, a blurred image, like a poster seen from the window of a speeding train.

It must be, he decides, that having a baby leads you to relive your own infancy. Things you might never have thought about before suddenly emerge. Like the sensation of sitting, or trying to sit, on this woman's knee. He has no idea who she was – a friend of his mother's, perhaps, a visiting relative, a glamorous colleague of his father's – but he can recall the sensation of losing his hold on her with sudden, vivid clarity.

Someone behind him bumps into his chair. Ted is thrown forward into the edge of the table. He turns to see a man with a rucksack amble past, oblivious. Ted adjusts his chair so that it's away from the thoroughfare, closer to Elina. He picks up his cappuccino and takes a sip. The image of the woman in the red dress is gone. Transmission terminated. Simmy is shovelling walnut cake into his mouth, talking animatedly. Elina is leaning towards him, listening, holding Jonah on her lap. Jonah, his head wobbling, is looking at something on the table; he clings to Elina's thumb with both of his hands, fingers clenched tight, as if he will never let go. Ted feels a sudden empathy with his son, with his need of Elina. He feels a corresponding tug in his own chest, puts out a hand and lays it lightly on her leg. Actually, he really wants to pull her to him, so that her shoulder fits underneath his arm, so that her head is against his chest, so that she's as close as she can be, and then he would like to say, don't go, don't ever go.

Elina is getting up, Ted sees. She is still listening to Simmy but she is handing Jonah to Ted. As he puts out his arms to take him, he sees that she has to wrest her thumb free. 'Where are you going?' Ted says.

'To the toilet.' She turns back to Simmy. 'Yes, I see what you mean,' she says to him, as she slides behind Ted's chair.

Ted takes hold of her wrist. He feels that queasiness again, senses that flat, unending sea. For a moment, he sees a woman with long hair bending over him, her hair swinging into his face, putting a plastic cup into his waiting hands. He sees himself sitting on a landing with a green rug, its woollen strands between his fingers, listening to his father's voice downstairs, which sounds pleading and apologetic. Ted has to shake his head to rid himself of these impressions. Jonah seems to sense something, too, because he starts to sob, his face crumpling. Ted wonders what to say. 'Where is the toilet?' is what comes out.

Elina looks down at where he is holding her arm. 'Over there,' she murmurs. She looks at his face, perplexed. 'I won't be a minute.' And then she turns, her arm parting company with his fingers, and he watches her as she walks away from him and he tries not to see the operating theatre, her lying in that sanctifying white light, that featureless, heaving sea.

'Are you OK?' Simmy is asking him from across the table.

'Yeah,' Ted says, without meeting his eye.

'You look a bit . . . peaky.'

'I'm fine.' Ted stands, hoisting Jonah to his shoulder. 'I'm going to the shop.' He's suddenly remembered that there is a postcard he wants from the exhibition.

It was a busy time at *Elsewhere* – Lexie had persuaded Innes to expand the magazine, to get in more advertising. They had upped the number of their features and had stopped using low-grade matt paper. The pages were now glossy, slightly grainy to the touch, the photographs bigger. They had just launched a section for rock and roll, the first arts magazine to do so. Innes had been dubious but Lexie had insisted and even found a critic, a young man studying the guitar at the Royal College of Music. The magazine was, at the time, revolutionary. Unfortunately they had no more staff than before so they were rushed in what they did, working until after ten most nights. They were, that winter, all ill, to varying degrees. Someone had caught a cold and passed it round the rest of them. The office rang to the sound of sneezing and wheezing and coughing.

Lexie had to go to Oxford that day, by train, to interview an academic who had written a surprisingly racy *roman à clef* about life in the cloisters – all grizzled tutors and palpitating young undergraduates. She dashed around the office, collecting her pen, a pad of paper, a copy of the novel to look over on the train. She paused briefly behind Innes's desk. He was hunched over a page proof, his hands cupped over his ears (he always said their noise distracted him).

'Goodbye,' she said, and kissed one of his hands.

He straightened up and caught her by the wrist. 'Where are you off to?'

'Oxford. Remember?'

He tapped his fountain pen against his teeth. 'Ah, yes,' he said, 'the priapic lecturer. Good luck. Stay on the other side of the desk from him.'

She smiled, kissed him again, on the mouth this time. 'I will.' Then she frowned, touched his cheek, his brow. 'You're very hot,' she said. 'Do you feel feverish?' She felt his forehead again.

He waved her away, beginning to cough. 'I'm fine, woman, be off with you.'

'Innes, are you sure—'

He turned back to his proof. 'Away to your seat of learning. Come back unscathed.'

Lexie turned to Laurence and Daphne, who were on the other side of the room, leaning over some copy together. 'Will you keep an eye on him?' she said. 'Send him home if he gets any worse.'

Laurence looked up and smiled. 'We will,' he said, and she left, satisfied. Innes was lighting a cigarette when she looked back from the door, arranging his jacket about his shoulders, scoring a line through the proof.

There is no need to dwell on the details of Lexie's trip to Oxford, of the academic's inflated sense of self, the clumsy passes he made at her, how delayed her train was on the way back, that she was rehearsing in her mind how she would tell Innes all about the passes, that he would relish the details and make her tell him all over again. She was imagining them in bed, the only warm place in the flat that January; she would make him drink hot whisky with honey, tuck the covers about him, make him rest.

Lexie knew he'd still be at the office so, even though it was late when she made it back to London, she went there. The fog was thick that night. Walking from the tube to Bayton Street she almost lost her way several times and her hair was damp about her face. She was wrong, she remembers thinking, when she reached the office. Innes's desk was empty. She could see only Laurence through the window. She was pleased, thinking Innes must have gone home.

But Laurence stood up as she came in, reaching for his jacket.

'Oh, what a day I've had,' she was saying. 'I—'

But Laurence interrupted her: 'Lexie, Innes has been taken to hospital.'

They had a rapid review of their money situation. She had exactly ninepence in her purse, Laurence even less. Was it enough for a cab to the hospital? No. They rummaged through Innes's desk for the petty-cash tin, rattled it, were heartened by the sound of coins but couldn't find the key.

'Where would he keep it?' Laurence said to Lexie. 'Come on, you know him best.'

She thought about it. 'It'll be in the desk somewhere,' she said. 'Unless he has it with him.' She opened another drawer and swept aside paperclips, split and broken cigarettes, torn scraps of paper with bits of Innes's scrawl on them. She found a ha'penny and added it to the pile. All the time, her heart was squeezing painfully, painfully in her chest, and her hands, searching through the mess in Innes's drawers – was he really this untidy, why did the love of her life need so many paperclips, what did these scraps of paper say – were trembling. Innes in hospital, Laurence had said, and her mind turned over the other words: breathing difficulties, collapsed, called an ambulance.

'This is ridiculous,' she said finally. She marched to the back room and returned with a screwdriver. Steadying the petty-cash tin with her foot, she rammed the screwdriver end between the lid and the base. The lock made a grinding noise, then broke. Coins burst out, all over the desk, the chair, the floor. In an instant, she and Laurence were on their knees, gathering them up, filling Laurence's jacket pockets. Then they were running, through the door, out into the street, up the road, to where the taxis congregated.

At the hospital, they ran again, along the corridors, around the corners, up the stairs. At the ward door, there was a nurse with a clipboard.

'We're here for Innes Kent,' Lexie said breathlessly. 'Where is he?'

The nurse glanced down at the watch on her chest. 'Visiting hours ended half an hour ago. I've asked his *sister,*' she pronounced the word with a leaning sarcasm, 'three times now to leave but she says she won't until his *wife* gets here. Am I to take it that you are his wife?'

Lexie hesitated. Laurence jumped in: 'Yes, she is.'

The nurse looked at him. 'And who are you? His grandfather?'

Laurence, a slight, fair-skinned Anglo-Saxon, treated her to a dazzling smile. 'His brother.'

She regarded them both a moment longer through narrowed eyes. 'Ten minutes,' she said, 'and no more. My patients need their rest. I can't have this place filling up with the likes of you.' She pointed with her pen. 'Fourth bed on the left and no noise.' She turned away, muttering, 'Wife, my foot.'

Lexie slipped between the curtains, which had been drawn to make a cubicle, and inside was Daphne, sitting on a chair, and there on the bed was Innes. He had a mask strapped over his face, his hair was plastered back from his forehead and his skin was greyish white.

'Lexie,' he mouthed, from behind the mask, and she could see him smile. She immediately climbed on to the bed, put her arms around him, laid her head next to his on the pillow. She was aware of Daphne and Laurence disappearing at this point, of hearing their footsteps recede down the ward.

'I don't know,' she murmured into Innes's ear. 'I turn my back for five minutes and you go and get yourself admitted to hospital. That's the last time I'm going to Oxford.'

His arm came up to grasp her waist. He put his other hand up to her cheek, her hair. 'How was the academic?' he said, behind the mask.

'It couldn't matter less,' she replied, 'and you're not allowed to speak.'

Innes removed the mask. 'I'm absolutely fine,' he rasped. 'All this is a lot of fuss about nothing.'

'It didn't sound like nothing. Laurence said you collapsed.'

He made a dismissive gesture with his hand. 'I had a moment of . . . of pain but it was nothing at all, really. It's a touch of pleurisy, they say. I'll be back on my feet tomorrow.'

Lexie curled herself around him, pressed her ear to the side of his chest, heard the boom-swish-boom of his heart.

'Checking it's still going, are you?' he said.

This she couldn't bear. She clutched at him and felt tears prick her eyelids. 'Innes, Innes, Innes,' she muttered, like an incantation.

'Hush,' he whispered and his hand stroked her hair.

'Mrs Kent,' the nurse was suddenly there, 'the only people allowed in these beds are my patients. This is most irregular. I must ask you to get down immediately.'

Innes gripped her tighter. 'Does she have to, Sister? She's very slim, as you can see. She doesn't take up much room.'

'Her physique is irrelevant, Mr Kent. You are a very sick man and I must ask your wife to leave. And you!' She regarded Innes with a look of horror. 'You have taken off your oxygen tube! Mr Kent, you are a very bad man.'

'It's been said before.' Innes sighed.

Lexie slid reluctantly from the bed but Innes kept hold of her hand. 'Do I really have to go?'

'Yes.' The nurse was firm, smoothing the covers, snapping Innes's mask back into place. 'You can come back tomorrow, two p.m.'

'Can't I come in the morning?'

'No. Your husband is ill, Mrs Kent. He needs to rest.'

She bent to kiss Innes's cheek. 'Goodbye, husband,' she murmured.

Innes seized her, pulled her back down towards him and, removing the mask, kissed her full on the mouth. They drew apart, smiled, then kissed again.

'Mr Kent!' the nurse shrieked. 'Stop! Stop this instant. Do you want to give your wife pleurisy as well? Put that mask back on.'

'You are such a martinet,' he said, 'such a dominatrix. Has anyone ever told you that? You'd have made a wonderful general, had things turned out differently for you.'

'It's my job to see you get better.' She whipped the curtains back. Lexie walked down the ward and waved from the end. Innes waved back. He was still arguing with the nurse.

When Lexie arrived the next day, he wasn't wearing the mask any more and was propped up on some pillows with some pages in his lap. He snatched off his glasses when he saw her and patted the bed beside him.

'Quick,' he said. 'Draw the curtains. Before the Gorgon sees you.'

Lexie pulled the curtains around the bed, then sat next to Innes. He immediately enveloped her in an enormous, crushing embrace. 'Wait,' she said. 'I want to look at you.'

'Too bad,' he mumbled in her ear. 'I want to touch you up.' His hands roved down her leg, searching for the hem of her dress, then, having found it, dived upwards.

'Innes,' she murmured, 'I really think this isn't the place for—'

He pulled back and gazed at her face. 'Oh, it's so good to see you. I passed a foul night. I don't know how anyone expects you to get well in hospital. You're kept awake for hours by all the old codgers spluttering and snoring, and the minute you do fall asleep the nurses wake you up again, wanting to shove thermometers into you. It's unbearable. I have to get out of here. Today. You have to help me persuade them.'

'I'll do no such thing.'

'Why not?'

'Innes, you're ill. Pleurisy's no joke. If they say you have to stay, you have to stay and—' She broke off to look at him, then laughed. 'Where did you get those?' He was wearing a pair of strange striped blue and grey pyjamas. He had never owned such things before and looked extremely peculiar in them, as if he had borrowed someone else's body.

'They,' he gestured towards the nurses' station, 'produced them from somewhere. I have to get out of here, Lex. I have to get back to work. The next issue's going to press on—'

'You don't. We'll manage. Somehow. You have to get well.'

He was about to protest when he was caught by a coughing fit. He hacked and spluttered, trying to draw breath. Lexie put her hands on his shoulders and held them as he struggled. The fit over, he lay back on the pillows, biting his lip. Lexie knew that look. It was one of fury, of thwartedness. He took her hand and folded it between both of his. 'I love you, Jezebel. You know that, don't you?'

She leant forward, kissed him, kissed him again. 'Of course. I love you too.'

He turned his neck back and forth, as if he was trying to get comfortable. 'We've been lucky, haven't we?'

'What do you mean?' His hands, around hers, were hot, she noticed, and damp.

'To find each other. Some people go their whole lives without finding what you and I have.'

Lexie frowned, then squeezed his hand. 'You're right. We are lucky.

And we're going to carry on being lucky.' She pushed her features into a smile.

'You haven't minded too much, have you, about the other thing?' He was staring at her, intently.

'What other thing?'

'The marriage thing.'

'No,' she said firmly. 'In all honesty, no.'

He smiled then. 'Good.' He fidgeted with the pillows. 'I was thinking, though . . .' He trailed away, reaching behind his head again to adjust the pillows.

She stood to help him. 'What were you thinking?'

'I'd like to talk to Clifford.'

'Clifford?' She had her back to him, pouring him a glass of water from the jug.

'My lawyer.'

She turned, amazed. 'Whatever for?'

He shook his head at the water. 'About you.'

'Me?'

'I worry, you see, about what would happen to you if I died.'

'Innes!' Lexie slammed down the glass of water. 'You are not going—'

He held a finger to her lips. 'Sssh,' he said, in a whisper. 'My little firecracker.' He smiled. 'Always going off without warning.' He pulled her to sit down next to him. 'I don't necessarily mean now. I just mean at some point. Being in here has made me think about it, that's all. I haven't even made a will. Never got round to it. And I should. Especially for you. Otherwise bloody Gloria will get the lot – not that there is much, as you know – and you'll be out on your ear.' He pinched her ear gently, then coiled a strand of her hair around his finger. 'And I couldn't bear that. I'd be unable to rest in peace. I'd be eternity's most unhappy ghost. You are my wife and my life. You know that, don't you?'

She caught his hand and kissed it crossly. 'You bloody fool,' she said. 'Why are you saying all this? You've gone and ruined my mascara.' She flopped down beside him, her body along his, and buried her face in his chest.

'Will you ring Clifford for me? The number's in my address book. Clifford Menks.'

She raised herself up on her elbow. 'Innes, listen to me. You have to stop talking about this. I don't like it one bit. You are not going to die. Or, at least, not any time soon.'

He smiled a lopsided smile. 'I know. But ring him anyway, for me, will you? There's a good girl.'

Innes died that night. His pleurisy developed into pneumonia. He died at around three a.m., of a fever and breathing difficulties. There was no one with him at the time. The nurse on duty had gone to fetch a doctor; when she returned with one, it was too late.

That Innes, the love of her life, had died alone: this, Lexie would never get over. That she had been sleeping, across the city, in their bed, at the time he drew his last breath, at the time his heart stopped its pulsing. That the doctor hadn't been where he was supposed to be but taking a nap in a different room down the corridor. That they had tried to resuscitate him but failed. That she wasn't there, that she didn't know, that she couldn't be with him and never would be again.

No one told her, of course. She was the illegal, unrecorded mistress in all this. She arrived at the hospital at two p.m. sharp, jaunty, with a bunch of violets, a newspaper, two magazines, his favourite cashmere scarf. Two nurses headed her off and took her into a room; one was the sister she'd met on the first night.

'I'm sorry to tell you, *Miss*,' she leant on that word, she wanted

Lexie to hear that she knew and perhaps had known all along, 'that Mr Kent died last night.'

Lexie thought that she was about to drop the magazines. She had to clutch at them, at their slippery covers. She said, 'He can't have.'

The sister looked at the ground between them. 'I'm afraid he did.'

She said, simply, 'No.' She said it again. 'No.' She put down the violets, very carefully, on a table. The magazines and newspaper she placed next to them. She was aware of thinking that she needed to behave well, that she ought to be polite. On the table, she noticed, there was a glass vial of some kind, a pair of tongs, a lid that didn't appear to fit the vial.

'Where is he?' she heard her voice say.

There was a silence behind her so she turned. Both nurses were looking vaguely embarrassed. 'His wife . . .' one of them began, then stopped.

She waited.

'His wife came,' the sister said, still avoiding her eye. 'She has made all the arrangements.'

'Arrangements?' Lexie repeated.

'For the body.'

Lexie could see this scene clearly in her head. Gloria arriving at the ward. Or would he have been moved to another room? Yes, they did that, didn't they, in hospitals, stripping the bed as soon as possible for the next person? Innes would have been taken, then, to a morgue, she supposed, or a room somewhere. She pictured Gloria arriving at the morgue – which in her mind Lexie placed in the basement – her heels tap-tapping across the floor, her hair swept up, rigid, her hands encased in gloves, her pallid child behind her. She would have examined the body – which was her body, Lexie's body, the body of her beloved, her darling – with those glacial eyes of hers. Lexie could see her doing this with a handkerchief pressed to her mouth, more for effect than anything else. Would she have worn a hat with a veil? Almost definitely. Would she have lifted the veil to look upon her husband for the last time? Almost definitely not. Would she have touched him, laid a hand upon him? Lexie doubted it. How long had she spent with him? Would she have spoken to him? Would the child? Then Lexie could see her leaving, moving into another room where she would request to use a telephone, where she could begin making her arrangements.

'May I see him?' Lexie asked the nurses. She was moving to gather her things, readying herself, when she became aware of their silence. She listened to it. She felt it. She tested its length, its breadth. She could have put out her tongue and tasted it. 'I want to see him,' she said, in case they had not understood, in case they had not heard her, in case it was not quite clear. She even said, 'Please.'

The sister made a movement with her head that was somewhere between a shake and a nod. And something seemed to break in her then because her voice was suddenly kind. 'I'm sorry,' she said. 'Family members only.'

Lexie had to swallow. Twice. 'Please,' she whispered this word, 'please.'

The nurse shook her head this time. 'I'm sorry.'

A noise came out of her then, something like a shout or a cry or a sob. Lexie clapped her hand over her mouth to stop it. She knew she had to stay in control because there were things she needed to know and if she cried as she wanted to she would never get to find out these things and somehow she knew this was her only chance. When she was sure the noise within her had been pressed down, for now, she spoke again. 'Can you tell me this?' she said. 'Just this. Is he still here or did she take him away?'

'I can't say,' the sister said, after glancing at the other nurse.

Lexie leant towards her, as if she was able to detect a lie just by smell. 'You can't say or you don't know?'

The other nurse made a slight movement. 'I believe . . .' she muttered, then stopped. The sister frowned at her. The nurse shrugged, glanced at Lexie, then drew breath and said, 'I believe Mr Kent's body was taken away earlier today. Around lunchtime.'

Lexie nodded. 'Thank you. I don't suppose you know where?'

'I don't.'

And Lexie believed her. And because there was nothing left for her in the building, she began to leave. She picked up the violets, she transferred them to the hand still holding Innes's scarf, and how incredible it was to see it still there; it was like an artefact from another age. It seemed impossible that it was only an hour or so ago that she had selected it from their cupboard for him to wear, impossible that there had been a time so recent that she did not know he had died.

He had died.

She looked at the nurses and already her vision was beginning to swim and melt with tears. 'Thank you,' she said, because she meant to remain composed, to hold herself together, until she was away from there, and she opened the door and stepped through. She could not look at the door to the ward, she could not look towards the bed where he had lain, where they had lain, only a few hours before, and where he had died, without her. She pushed herself through the hospital air into the corridor, she walked down it and out into the city, alone.

Part Two

Lexie sails along Piccadilly, bag slung over her arm. Felix finds himself weaving behind her, in her wake, dodging the crowds. Decked out in large sunglasses and a startlingly short coat, Lexie is attracting more than perhaps her fair share of admiring glances. As she reaches the gates to Green Park, Felix catches up with her and takes her by the arm, pulling her to a stop. 'Well?' he says.

'Well what?'

'Are you coming to Paris or not?'

She rearranges the collar of her coat – really it's too much, covered with black and white squiggles that make Felix's eyes ache; wherever does she find these things? – and tosses her hair over her shoulder. 'I haven't decided yet,' she says.

Felix takes a breath. She is, without doubt, the most infuriating woman he has ever known. 'Hasn't anything I've said made an impression on you?'

'I'll let you know,' she says, and her sunglasses flash as she turns her head away to look down the street.

He is seized with an urge to shake her, slap her. But she would no doubt slap back and his face is becoming more and more recognised: he can tell by the way people look at him, quickly, then away. He really could not be involved in a public brawl on Piccadilly.

'Darling,' he says, and he pulls her towards him, trying to ignore the fact that she immediately withdraws her arm, 'listen to me, the very last place I'd like you to be is in the middle of a riot. But if you came with me you'd be safe. And I could introduce you to people. The right kind of people. Maybe it's time.'

'Time for what?'

'To . . .' Felix circles his hand in the air, wondering where he is going with this '. . . to widen your scope a little. Professionally speaking.'

'I have no desire,' she snaps, 'to widen my scope. Whatever that may mean.'

He sighs. 'Look, the point is, you wouldn't have to come for work. You could just come.'

Her sunglasses flash again as she looks back at him. 'What do you mean?'

'You could come . . . with me.'

'In what capacity?'

'As my . . .' He realises he is on shaky ground now but something forces him on. 'Look, I can put you down as my secretary, there won't be a problem, a lot of people do it and—'

'*Your secretary?*' she repeats. More glances from around them. Do these people know who he is? It's impossible to tell. 'You seriously think I might agree to that, to drop everything and just—'

'All right, all right,' he says soothingly, but Lexie, as ever, is unsoothable. 'Not my secretary. That was a bad idea. How about as my—'

'Felix,' she says, 'I'm not coming to Paris as your anything. If I come it will be as a journalist. In my own right.'

'So you might come?'

'Perhaps.' She shrugs. 'Someone on the news desk this morning was asking me how good my French was. They want civilian stories. Interviews with the ordinary people of Paris. That kind of thing.' She narrows her eyes. 'The phrase "a female touch" was mentioned twice, of course.'

'Really?' Felix is at once excited and relieved but tries to show neither. 'So you wouldn't be out on the barricades?'

She removes her sunglasses with a flick of her wrist and regards him with narrowed lids. Felix, despite himself, despite their argument, which has now lasted an entire lunch, feels a stirring in his groin. 'I'll be wherever the ordinary people are. Which I believe, in a state of emergency such as this, is everywhere, barricades included.'

Felix considers his options. He could continue the argument – he and Lexie are practised at arguing with each other, after all – or he could forget their disagreement and ask her back to his flat. He places an arm on her sleeve, taking a surreptitious look at his watch. He then gives her a slow, deep smile. 'How much time do you have?' he says.

How to explain Felix? When Lexie first met him, in the mid sixties, he was a correspondent for the BBC. He was just graduating from radio to television. He had the exact looks for television then: good-looking but not distractingly so, tanned but not too much, blond but not too blond; he dressed well but not too well, his hair parted in the right way, in the right place. He specialised in war-zones, disasters, acts of God, the kind of bombastic reportage Lexie disliked. An army from a large, powerful nation drops bombs on a small Communist state: call for Felix. A sea rises up and engulfs a village: call for Felix. A dormant volcano rouses itself, a fleet of fishing boats is lost in the Atlantic, a fork of lightning strikes a medieval cathedral: Felix will be on the scene, usually in some dangerous spot, often in a bullet-proof vest. He liked to wear them. His voice was firm, serious, assured: 'This is Felix Roffe, for the BBC.' That line, delivered with an assertive nod, always concluded his reports. He pursued Lexie with all the determination, charm and focus with which he pursued natural disasters, political tyrants and a photogenic yet suffering populace. They were lovers, intermittently, for several years. They were in a constant state of flux, Felix and Lexie, separating, reuniting, parting, coming back together, over and over. She would leave, he would follow, he would draw her back, she would leave again. They were like clothes invested with static, adhering to each other but with an uncomfortable, aggravating friction.

They had met, some months prior to their argument on Piccadilly, with a single word, a single shout. His. *'Signora!'*

Lexie looked down from her vantage-point of a balcony, three floors up. The street was swirling with bubbling brown water, on which floated tree branches, chairs, cars, bicycles, street signs, strings of washing. The shops and apartments at street-level were engulfed, obliterated, the shop signs – FARMACIA, PANIFICIO, FERRAMENTA – just visible above the lapping scum of flood water.

It was November 1966. An entire season's rain had fallen in two days, the river Arno had burst its banks and now the city of Florence was drowning, awash, submerged: the river had spread itself everywhere. In the apartments, in the shops, in the Duomo, up staircases, into the Uffizi. It had claimed furniture, people, statues, plants, animals, plates, cups, paintings, books, maps. It had swept away all the jewels and necklaces and rings from the shops on the Ponte Vecchio: it had folded these things into its brown waters and taken them away, down into the silty mud of its bed.

'Sì?' she shouted back, to the two men in the boat, hands cupped around her mouth. She had just turned thirty – it was four years since she had walked out of the Middlesex Hospital with a bunch of violets, nine years since she had escaped Devon for London. She had been sent to Florence by her newspaper; she was meant to be cabling back stories about the untold losses from the city's art collections but instead she was bashing out accounts of the fifteen thousand people made homeless, the numerous dead, the farmers who had lost everything.

The fair-haired man put down his oars and stood up in the boat, somewhat unsteadily. 'Cathedral,' he shouted. 'Cath-e-dral!'

Gennaro, the photographer whose flat Lexie was in, appeared next to her on the balcony. He, too, looked down into the street. '*Inglese?*' he muttered.

She nodded.

'*Televisione?*' he said, indicating the other man's camera.

She shrugged.

Gennaro made a dismissive noise with his lips and went in to speak to his wife, who was trying to coax their small son into a high-chair.

Lexie watched as the man thought for a moment. '*Signora,*' he began again, 'cathedral? *Dov'è* cathedral?'

She stubbed out her cigarette on the balcony ledge. She considered giving him directions in Italian but thought perhaps her own language skills weren't up to it. 'First, the word is *duomo*,' she called down. '*Il duomo*. And it's that way. Don't you think you ought to have done a bit of homework before you came out here?'

'My God,' she heard him say to his cameraman, 'she's English.'

On Piccadilly, Felix is smiling at her in that way he has. Confident, intimate, unmistakably sexual, his lower body brushing hers. 'How much time do you have?' he asks.

He has been on at her all morning – is she coming out to Paris, she should come to Paris, she must stay at the St Jacques with him, she mustn't let the *Courier* put her up in some fleapit, she must let him take her to the Correspondents' Club there, he'll introduce her to useful people. He has ploughed his way through a lobster, pausing only to lecture her about Saigon, from where he has recently returned: the grenades, the explosions, the defoliating chemicals dropped by US planes, a city deluged by press and bombs and prostitutes and soldiers, how he could have got malaria, dengue fever, giardia and worse.

Lexie replaces her sunglasses, pushes back her coat cuff to check her watch. She is annoyed with herself for feeling a curdling, responsive desire. 'Precisely none,' she snaps.

'Dinner, then? Tonight? My plane doesn't leave until nine.'

She steps to the edge of the pavement. 'Perhaps,' she says. 'I'll phone you later.' She crosses the road at a sprint, or as much of a sprint as her boots will allow, and turns from the opposite pavement to wave to Felix. But he's gone, swallowed by the crowds.

She sets off, slinging her bag further up her shoulder. The world, even from behind her dark glasses, looks bright, the sun giving everyone walking down Piccadilly a fiery corona, as if they are all angels, as if they are all here in the afterlife, walking about London on a fine May afternoon. She is due to interview a theatre director in ten minutes at a restaurant in Charlotte Street. She quickens her pace, across Piccadilly Circus, up the curve of Shaftesbury Avenue, towards Cambridge Circus, where she will turn left up Charing Cross Road.

She will not take the direct route, through Soho. She never goes there, even now.

To flatten that thought, she reflects on the possibility of Paris, on Felix, on whether she should go. Felix had said, at their lunch, that it would also be good for her career. 'They must realise,' he said, twirling his wine glass, 'that you have more in you than pretty paragraphs about painting.'

She'd slammed down her fork. 'Pretty paragraphs about painting?' she'd repeated, the alliteration lending itself to fury. 'Is that how you view my work?' And then they were off. They were good at arguing. It was one of the things they did well together.

Elina is excited, charged. Everything seems to be coming together today. The baby bag is packed and ready by the door, the washing-machine is unloaded and rows of tiny vests and sleepsuits are leaping on the line, she's had breakfast, Jonah has fed, the sun is shining and she feels well. She actually feels well: Jonah woke only twice last night and she doesn't have the feeling that she might pass out at any moment. There is even a tinge of colour in her cheeks – just a tinge, but it's there – and earlier she found she didn't have to pause halfway up the stairs. She's well again! She feels almost crazed with excitement. She has it in her head that she will go for a walk and that she will make it up Parliament Hill for the first time since the birth. She will, she's determined. She will put Jonah in his pram and they will walk over the Heath, up the steep hill, along the avenue of trees. She has a clear picture of this: Jonah in his red hat and striped jacket, tucked neatly all around by his star blanket, her in sunglasses and a white shirt of Ted's, pushing the pram smartly, competently. She has forgotten nothing – muslin squares, nappies, wipes, the parasol. She will walk steadily and pleasantly. She will bend over her son in the sunshine; she will talk to him. Passers-by will smile to see them. She has had this image in her mind since early this morning, when she woke to see sunlight glowing around the edges of the blind: the two of them passing together under the dappled, refracting and re-forming light of the trees.

Except that she can't find her shoe. One of her sneakers is on the shoe rack by the front door but the other is – who knows where? Elina laces the one available shoe on to her foot, darting hurried glances around the hallway because she knows that this is a race against time, because she can feel the gap narrowing between the feed they've just finished and the next one. With one bare foot, she looks in the kitchen, she looks under the sofa, she goes upstairs to look in the bathroom, the bedroom. But there's no sign of it anywhere. For a moment, she is assailed by the wild idea that she could go out with only one shoe but then she rips off the partnerless sneaker and slips her feet into a pair of flip-flops she finds under the bed. They will have to do.

She races downstairs again, Jonah clutched to her shoulder. She must have moved in too jolting a way because he starts to fuss, just a little.

'Sssh,' she croons to him, 'sssh,' as she lowers him into the pram and tucks the blanket around him. But babies don't like a sense of urgency. Jonah looks up at her, anxiety gathering in his brow. 'Don't cry,' she tells him, 'don't cry.' She slings the bag around the pram handle, and this seems to upset Jonah even more. His face splinters into a cry. Elina jiggles the pram as she snatches her keys off the hook, as she bounces it over the step and down the path.

At the gate, Jonah is still crying. As she turns the corner of the street, he is crying louder, throwing off his blanket, twisting his head from side to side and, with a sinking heart, Elina recognises that particular cry. She has, she tells herself, learnt that much. He's hungry. He needs a feed.

Elina stops at the entrance to the Heath. She looks about her. She looks down at her son, who is crying real tears now, his fists clenched with need. How can he be hungry again? She only fed him – what?

– an hour ago. She brushes the hair out of her eyes. In the distance, she can see the trees on the Heath, bowing and tossing their branches, their leaves invitingly green. They are so close. She could keep going and feed him on a bench somewhere but what if it turns out to be one of his bad feeds, where he cries and struggles?

She grits her teeth, she tilts the pram, she wheels it around and back to the house.

They sit in a chair by the window and he feeds, concentratedly, for ten minutes. She lays him on his stomach across her knee, the way he seems to like after a feed, but instead of burping, he instantly falls asleep. She stares at him, hardly daring to believe it. Can he really be asleep? Is it possible? The lightly closed lids, the pouting mouth, thumb held near, at the ready. He is, she tells herself, asleep. Without doubt.

She looks about her, in the manner of a traveller who hasn't seen their home for a long time. She is light-headed with the possibilities open to her. She could read a book, phone a friend, send an email, write a letter, do a sketch, make some soup, sort out her clothes, wash her hair, go for that walk, turn on the television, check her diary, mop the floor, clean the windows, fiddle about on the Internet. She could do anything.

But should she risk moving him? She gazes at him speculatively. Is he far enough into sleep to accept a change of scenery? Will he wake if she were to lift him from her lap and put him in his cot or the pram?

Gently, gently, she slides her hands under his body, fingers under his ribs, thumbs under his head. He sighs and smacks his lips together but doesn't wake. With infinite care, she begins to lift. Instantly, his eyes flicker open and a hoarse, small sob escapes him. Elina puts him down. Jonah inserts his thumb and sucks it with a desperate, betrayed air. She sits motionless, barely breathing. He seems to drift back into sleep.

So, she thinks, no walk for you today. And she must sit here for however long he sleeps. Which isn't the worst thing in the world. Is it?

But for a moment it seems to Elina that it is. She has such an urge, such an ache to go out, to see something other than the interior walls of this house, to apprehend the world, to move about in it. Sometimes she finds herself eyeing Ted when he has come in from work, when the life of the city still seems to cling to him. She sometimes wants to stand near to him, to sniff him, to catch the scent of it, the sense of it. She wants, desperately, to be somewhere else – anywhere else.

She casts her eyes around restlessly, and catches sight of a folded piece of paper on the sofa next to her. She picks it up, smooths it out, and sees what she believes for a moment to be a shopping list, in Ted's handwriting. Then she realises it is not a shopping list at all:

unreliable
stones
the same man?
name possibly beginning with R
kite

There are two more words at the end, which Elina cannot decipher. One begins with *c* – it could be *cat* or *cot* or *cut* – and another that might be *lump* or *damp* or maybe *clump*. On the back is written *Ask E.* This has been crossed out.

Elina turns it over. She reads it again and then again. She reads it backwards, she reads it forwards, she tries to assemble it into a sentence or verse. What is this list? Why has he written it? Does he mean *unreliable stones* or *unreliable* space *stones*? And what's the difference? What *same man*? And why was he going to ask her but then changed his mind? Whose name begins with R? She turns it over and sees how the outer corners have turned blue: Ted must have been carrying it about in the pocket of his jeans. It must have fallen out as he sat on the sofa last night. She reads it and reads it until the loops and dashes of ink start to jitter before her eyes, until unreliable men with kites and stones are marching unchecked through her mind.

She is folding and unfolding it when she is struck by a thought. Or, rather, a sensation. She realises that she wants her mother. It is such a visceral, unbidden feeling that it makes her almost laugh. She wants to see her mother. How long is it since she felt that? Twenty years? Twenty-five? Since she started kindergarten? When she was pushed into a nettle patch by a big girl on the way home from school? Since that camping trip, aged about nine, when she forgot her sleeping-bag?

It will be midsummer in the archipelago now; high season at her mother's guesthouse. The children of Nauvo will be having swimming lessons in the sandy water of the bay; the hardware shop on the main street will be selling spades and buckets and fishing tackle to holidaymakers from Germany, families up for the weekend from Helsinki. Stalls will be lining the harbour edge, arrayed with knitted hats, deck shoes, T-shirts bearing the word 'Suomi'.

And her mother? Elina glances at the clock on the wall. It says eleven thirty, which means one thirty in Finland. Despite having been away so long, despite professing to loathe the guesthouse, its occupants, the archipelago, the small town, the whole country, despite having run away as soon as she could, as far as she could, as often as she could, Elina is still aware of the rhythms of the place. Her mother will be serving lunch to people outside in the garden, on mismatched plates with fluted edges. Drinks come in glasses of different colours, in varying sizes. If it's a rainy day, the guests will be lined up along the veranda. She can see her mother stepping from the door to the kitchen, with that rolling, unhurried gait of hers, bearing four plates, an apron over the inevitable cambric dress, those pink-lensed sunglasses hiding her eyes. If the tourists want to order, she will fish in her apron pocket for a pen, a pad, her half-moon glasses, all in the same meditative way. Then she will sway back to the kitchen, the pad in one hand, past the enormous beech tree, past the sculpture in chicken wire and stone and shell that Elina did at school and now cannot look at.

A longing to be there, fierce as a slug of whisky, passes through Elina. She wants to be sitting with her back against the beech tree, Jonah beside her, watching her mother come and go. She cannot, for the moment, imagine what she is doing here on her own in a house in London when she could be there. Why is she here? Why did she ever leave?

Elina reaches, carefully, carefully, without moving Jonah, for the phone, which is lying abandoned on the coffee-table. She dials the number, and as she listens to the pulsing rings, she imagines the phone sitting squat on the oak reception desk; she pictures her mother hearing it from the garden and walking through the sunroom, over the uneven boards and—

'Vilkuna,' an unfamiliar voice says, in an offhand tone.

Elina asks for her mother. The unfamiliar person goes away and then Elina hears unhurried steps coming towards the phone, along the passage, in shoes that flap free of the heels and the longing tightens like a scarf about her throat.

'*Aiti?*' Elina says, surprising herself by using a term she hasn't said for years. Since she was a teenager, she's always called her mother by her given name.

'Elina?' her mother says. 'Is that you?'

'Yes,' Elina says, switching to Swedish, like her mother.

'How are you? How is the little man?'

'He's fine. Growing, you know. He smiles now and he's just started to—' Elina breaks off because she realises that her mother is talking in a low tone to someone else, in Finnish this time.

'. . . into the garden. I'll be there in just a minute.'

Elina waits, holding the phone to her ear. She lays the list on Jonah's back. *Unreliable, kite, same man.*

'Sorry,' her mother says. 'What were you saying?'

'Are you busy? Should I call back?'

'No, no. It's OK. It's just that . . . it's OK. You were telling me about Jonah.'

'He's fine.'

There is a pause on the line. Is her mother talking to someone else again? Or gesturing to them?

'Thank you for the photos of him,' her mother says. 'We enjoyed them so much.' We? Elina thinks. 'We couldn't decide if he was like you or Ted.'

'Like neither of us, I think. Yet, anyway.'

'Yes.'

There is another pause. There is something in her mother's voice, a particular strain in tone, that makes Elina think someone is in the room with her again.

'I can call back if this is a bad time,' Elina says.

'It's not a bad time,' her mother says, with just a hint of annoyance. 'It's not a bad time at all. I'm always happy to talk to you, you know that. It's not often I get the chance. You're always so busy and—'

'I'm not busy,' Elina exclaims. 'I'm not busy at all. My life is . . . I spend all day at home and . . . and all night too. And I—' She breaks off. She wants to say, please, please, *Aiti,* I don't know what's happening, I don't know why Ted is drifting away from me, I don't know how to fix it, and please can I come home, can I come now?

Her mother is speaking again. '. . . Jussi was saying the other day that they had all of his sleeping through by four weeks. There's a book, apparently, that you can follow and . . .'

Jussi – Elina's brother. Elina sets her teeth as her mother talks on about the book and sleep training and about her four granddaughters and how they never wake up at night, even now, and how Jussi's wife, the bovine Hannele, wants another but Jussi isn't sure and neither is Elina's mother.

'Is Jussi with you, then?' Elina asks.

'Yes!' Her mother's voice lightens suddenly. 'They've come for the summer – all of them. Jussi has been painting the front room and he's about to start on the veranda. The girls and I have been swimming every morning – we've booked them in for the lessons, you remember the lessons, in the bay, and Jussi was saying he thinks the girls ought to go sailing today so I said that later I would . . .'

Elina holds the phone to her ear. She examines Jonah's fingernails, sees that they need trimming. She brushes some stray crumbs off the sofa. She discovers a stain on a cushion. She turns the cushion round so that the stain doesn't show. She takes the list off Jonah's back and holds it between her finger and thumb.

'I was wondering . . .' she interrupts a monologue about the second granddaughter's accomplishments on the flute '. . . I was wondering, was Dad . . . OK . . . after we were born?'

'Was he OK?'

'I mean, did he . . . go a bit funny?'

'Funny, how?'

'Sort of . . . I don't know . . . absent. Withdrawn.' Elina waits, holding the phone to her ear, as if anxious not to miss a sound.

'Why do you ask?' her mother says eventually.

Elina bites her lip, then sighs. 'No reason,' she says. 'Just wondered. Listen, *Aiti*, I was thinking I might . . . we might . . . come.'

'Come?'

'To Nauvo. To you. I . . . I thought that . . . you know, you haven't met Jonah yet and I'm . . . Well, a change of scene would do Ted good and . . . it's been ages since I was there.' There is a silence down the line. 'What do you think?' Elina says finally, desperately.

'Well, the thing is, Jussi is here for a month and then he's going back to Jyväskylä and the girls are staying here with me. I've got them all to myself for two weeks. And then I think Hannele is coming to collect them – I'll need to check – so I'm not sure when we might—'

'Right. Doesn't matter.'

'I mean, we'd love you to come. The girls would love to see Jonah. And so would I.'

'It's fine. Forget it. Another time.'

'Maybe in the autumn or—'

'I have to go.'

'September? The thing is it's not that—'

'Got to go. Jonah's crying. See you. 'Bye.'

Elina is pulled upwards from sleep. It feels as if she's been there for just minutes. The room is in pitch darkness, the two windows to her right casting only a very slight orange glow. Jonah is crying, calling to her. For half a second more, she lies on her back, unable to rise, like Gulliver with his hair tied down. Then she pushes herself from the mattress, lurches into the room towards the bars of the cot and lifts Jonah from it.

She changes his nappy, badly, clumsily, in the dark. Jonah is tense with hunger, his feet waving, she can't get them back into the poppered legs of his sleepsuit. She tries to push them in, tries to ease the fabric around his knees but he roars with outrage. 'OK,' she says, 'all right.' She scoops him up and carries him to the bed, settling herself on her side to feed him.

Jonah sucks, his fists gradually uncurling, his eyes becoming unfocused. Elina drifts in and out of consciousness: she sees the veranda on her mother's house in Nauvo, she sees the curve of Jonah's head in the dark, she sees the flat water of the archipelago on a windless day, she sees her brother walking away from her down a gravelled track, she sees a painting she was working on before Jonah was born, she sees the grain of the canvas beneath a thick layer of paint, she sees Jonah again, still sucking, she sees the pattern of intersecting tramlines on a Helsinki street corner, she sees—

Suddenly she is wide awake, back in the bedroom. She is cold, she thinks first. The duvet has gone.

Ted is sitting up in bed, his back straight, his hands cupped around his face.

'What's the matter?' she says.

He doesn't answer. She reaches out and touches his back. 'Ted? What's up?'

'Oh,' he says, turning round. His face is bewildered. 'Oh.'

'What is it?'

'I had this—' He stops, frowning, and looks around the room.

'It's very early,' she says, in an attempt to cover for him, 'one thirty.'

'Huh,' he says slowly. Then he lies back down, curving his body around Jonah's, putting his hand on her hip. She fits her knees to his, sliding her foot between his calves. 'God,' he whispers. 'I had this dream – a really horrible dream. That I was here in the house and I could hear someone, somewhere, talking. I was looking everywhere for you, all over the house, calling your name, but I couldn't find you. And then I came into our bedroom and you were sitting in the chair, with your back to me, with Jonah in your arms, and I put my hand on your shoulder and when you turned your head, it wasn't you at all, it was someone else, it was—' He rubs a hand over his face. 'It was horrible. I got such a fright that I woke up.'

Elina sits, raising Jonah to her shoulder. He feels slack in her hands, like a beanbag, and she knows by now that this is the feeling she needs, that this means more sleep, for him and for her. She rubs her palm against his back. 'That sounds awful,' she whispers to Ted. 'What a weird dream. I have dreams sometimes where I go to the cot and Jonah is gone. Or I'm pushing the buggy and I see he isn't in it. I think it's part of the bonding, you know, that—'

'Hmm,' Ted says, scowling up at the ceiling, 'but this was so real, as if—'

Jonah interrupts this with an enormous, resounding belch.

'Here,' Ted says, reaching for him, 'let me take him. You go back to sleep.'

Here is Lexie, on a humid spring night in Paris. She sits at a hotel dressing-table, her typewriter balanced in front of her. Her shoes are kicked off, her clothes sprawled on the narrow bed. She wears just a slip, her hair raised off her neck and secured with a pencil. The room is cramped, unbearably hot; she has left the windows to the tiny iron balcony open. The breeze inflates the thin curtains, then sucks them flat. The sounds of people running, shouts, police sirens, glass shattering reach her from the street below. She has been up all night, on the Boulevard St-Michel and around the Sorbonne, watching the students put up barricades, tear up the pavements, overturn cars and then the police attacking with clubs and tear gas.

She looks at what she has written. *Whether they were incited or provoked remains to be seen,* it reads, *but such a reaction from the authorities seems . . .* And there it stops. She has to finish this but, for now, she has no idea how.

She taps a full stop, pulls the carriage to a new paragraph, watching the woman in the dressing-table mirror do the same. The woman is thin in her slip, the bone of her clavicle stark, her eyes ringed by shadows. Lexie puts a hand to her brow, leaning in close to the mirror. She has fine, almost invisible lines now, around her mouth, at the corners of her eyes. She thinks of them as fault-lines, glimpses of the future, the signs where her face will fold in on itself, come away slack from the bone.

She doesn't know that this will never happen.

There is the sound of a knock at the door and her head snaps round.

'Lexie?' Felix's voice whispers loudly. 'Are you in there?'

She'd seen him earlier, positioned beside a blazing barricade, gesticulating for the camera, figures haring back and forth behind him.

She doesn't move from her seat. She bites the end of her pencil; she pleats and unpleats a section of her slip. Any man who isn't Innes would tonight be a travesty, a crime. She doesn't know why but she's felt him all day, hovering, slightly behind her, slightly to the left of her. She's kept turning her head, as if trying to catch him out. She finds she wants to say his name aloud, here in this hotel room with its peeling furniture and stained bedclothes. The word swells inside her throat, her mouth, like a balloon.

The knock comes again. 'Lexie!' Felix hisses. 'It's me.'

A moment longer and he gives up. She hears him shambling back along the corridor, yawning. She moves to the bed and lies down on her back. She stares up at the ceiling. She closes her eyes. Immediately she is presented with an image of Innes, sitting on the dressing-table stool she has just vacated, here, in the room with her. She opens her eyes again. The tears run sideways down her temples, soaking into her hair, finding their way into her ears. She shuts her eyes again. She sees: the view from the window of their flat on Haverstock Hill. She sees: Innes's hand and the way he held a pen, in a tilted, left-handed grip. She sees: him leaning against their bookshelves, searching for a book. She sees: him shaving at the kitchen sink, his face half lathered. She sees: herself, walking down a hospital corridor, dropping violets as she goes.

*

In London, a fortnight or so later, Lexie and Felix are walking together into the opening of Laurence's new gallery. Something about Felix's impeccable cuffs, his broad-shouldered blondness set against the crowd-pressed, wine-fuelled, frantic anxiety of the gallery makes Lexie want to laugh. But Felix, as ever, is striding into the room as if his place in it is assured, as if hordes of people are just waiting to make his acquaintance.

Which, annoyingly, they are. After the third person comes up to him with the words, 'Sorry, but aren't you . . .' Lexie steps out from his encircling arm and begins making her way through the crowded gallery to where Daphne is standing with Laurence, at the side of the room, their heads inclined to one another's. She knows they are talking about her, and they know she knows. They smile to see her approach.

'Excuse me,' she says, sliding sideways between a woman talking in a braying voice about Lichtenstein and a man knocking back a glass of wine.

'Here she comes,' Lexie hears Daphne say.

'Hello, gossips,' Lexie says, kissing first the cheek with which Daphne presents her, then Laurence's. 'Congratulations, Laurence. Good party. Good turn-out.'

'Yes, it's gone off rather well, hasn't it?' says Laurence, surveying the room. 'So far.'

'Don't say "so far",' Daphne scolds. 'It's good. People came. People are buying. Be happy. Enjoy it.'

'I can't, though,' Laurence mutters, running a finger around his collar. 'I won't be able to until it's over.'

Daphne turns to Lexie and looks her up and down. 'Anyway,' she says, 'we want to talk to you.'

'Do you?'

'Yes. Tell all.'

Lexie takes a swig of her cocktail. 'About what?'

Daphne lets out a small noise of exasperation at the same time as Laurence says, 'I like your get-up, Lex.'

'Never mind her get-up,' Daphne snaps, then seems to see Lexie's dress for the first time, 'although it is fab. Where did you get it?' Without waiting for an answer, she shakes Lexie by the elbow. 'We want to know all about it.' She jabs a finger towards the door.

Lexie looks over at where Felix is talking to two women who are leaning keenly towards him. 'Oh,' she waves her hand, 'that's just Felix.'

'We know who he is,' Laurence says. 'We've seen him on the box, braving the boulevards.'

'And,' Daphne cuts in, 'we've just been putting two and two together. You must have been in Paris with him. How dare you not tell us? I mean, we knew you'd had a bit of a thing but that was ages ago. We didn't know he was still present tense. Come on,' she jabs Lexie in the ribs, 'spill the beans. What's going on?'

'Nothing,' Lexie says.

'Nothing,' Laurence scoffs.

'It's . . . on and off.' Lexie shrugs and drains her glass. 'Nothing really.'

The three of them stand for a moment, gazing down into their glasses, until David, Laurence's lover, appears next to them. 'What are you three looking so serious about?' He puts a hand on Laurence's shoulder. 'And shouldn't you be mingling?'

'We were just grilling Lexie about her consort,' Daphne says.

'Her consort?' David enquires, and Laurence nods towards Felix, who is now regaling a rapt group with some story involving expansive gestures. 'Oh.' David raises his eyebrows. 'I see. You are a dark horse, Lexie.'

'It's nothing,' Lexie says again, and tugs at the hem of her dress to straighten it.

'It can't be nothing,' Daphne objects, 'if you're out and about with him like this.'

'I'm not out and about with him. I just mentioned I was coming and he said he'd come along.'

'Are you going to introduce us?' Laurence says. 'We promise to behave.'

'Not now,' David says. 'Can't you see the man's busy furthering his career?'

'I have one question,' says Daphne, in a serious voice, 'and then we'll leave you alone. Why him?'

Lexie turns to her. 'What do you mean?'

'I'm intrigued. Why him, rather than any of the others who've beaten a path to your door?'

'I can think of several reasons,' David murmurs, looking Felix over, and Laurence laughs softly.

'Because . . .' Lexie tries to think. 'Because he doesn't ask anything,' she says eventually.

'What did you say?' David says, leaning towards her. 'He doesn't ask anything?'

'Any questions,' Lexie says. 'He doesn't ask anyone anything. He's the most incurious person I've ever met. And that—'

'That suits you,' Laurence finishes for her.

Lexie half smiles at him. 'Yes.' She nods. 'It does.'

There is a pause. Then Daphne leans back and seizes a bottle of wine from the desk. 'A toast!' she cries. 'We haven't drunk to your gallery yet.' She slops wine into all their glasses. 'To Laurence and David and the Angle Gallery,' she says. 'May they live long, happy and prosperous lives.'

The middle of the night, the dead of night, and not much is stirring in Belsize Park. A car sped down Haverstock Hill a while back.

A squirrel – one of the rat-like, overfed grey ones – has just crossed the road, pausing in the middle to look around.

In front of the house is a small knot garden made of closely clipped box hedges. The children like to walk within its low spiral, turning and turning to its inevitable centre, although the mother prefers them not to. It weakens the roots, she says. Between this and the pavement is a low red-brick wall that was there in Lexie's day. There's a gatepost topped with a heavy white stone that glistens in frosty weather.

Lexie stood with her hand on this gatepost stone when she got back from the hospital after Innes died. It was early evening. Somehow she'd got herself to the flat, still holding the scarf and the magazines – the violets had gone by now – and just as she was about to go up the path, a man stood up from where he'd been sitting on the low wall.

'Miss Sinclair?' he said.

She swivelled towards him. Hand on gatepost.

'Miss Alexandra Sinclair?'

'Yes,' she said.

'I hereby serve you with these papers,' he said, and held out an envelope.

She took it. She looked at it. Plain, manila, unsealed. 'Papers?'

'Eviction papers, madam.'

She looked at him, at his moustache. She thought how odd it was that the moustache was brown yet his hair was grey. She looked at the gatepost under her hand. It felt grainy, rigid with frost. She took her hand away from it and felt for the doorkey in her pocket. 'I don't understand.'

'My client, Mrs Gloria Kent, requires you to vacate said property by tomorrow, taking with you only items expressly belonging to your own person. Should you remove anything belonging to the estate of her late hus—'

She heard no more. She ran up the path and into the house and slammed the door behind her.

Laurence appeared later. He'd been looking for her all over London, he said. He plucked the pink eviction papers from her hand and read through them. He swore several times, then said that Gloria was living up to her reputation. Lexie found out later that Gloria had already sent a lawyer's letter to the *Elsewhere* premises, informing them the magazine was to be sold. But Laurence didn't mention this at the time, or explain that this letter was how he and Daphne had learnt that Innes had died. He poured her a whisky, sat her in an armchair and wrapped an eiderdown around her. Then he set to work, dismantling the flat, her home, her life.

By the early morning, Laurence and Lexie were waiting outside the flat for a cab. Two suitcases stood next to them. Lexie was shivering or shaking or perhaps both, still clutching the eiderdown around her. 'Do you think,' she said, between her chattering teeth, indicating the eiderdown, 'that this belongs to the estate of Innes Kent?'

Laurence glanced at the eiderdown, then up at the lightening sky. Clouds were streaked with gold above them, the trees still, black cutouts. He let out a laugh but his eyes were brimming with tears. 'Jesus, Lex,' he murmured, 'what a thing to happen.'

When a cab came past, they hailed it and Laurence loaded Lexie and the suitcases into it. 'Wait here,' he said to the driver, 'won't be a sec,' and raced back into the house.

Lexie sat in the taxi, her belongings pressed together into two suitcases and a parcel or two, the eiderdown clasped around her. A long black car was pulling up and in it, at the wheel, was the unmistakable profile of Gloria. Lexie stared out at her. Those haughty lips, those arched brows. Gloria was snapping down the car mirror and checking her lipstick, saying something chattily, brightly to someone beside her. The daughter. There she was in the passenger seat, nodding, yes, Mother, no, Mother.

They were getting out. Gloria was settling her skirts clear of the car door, before slamming it smartly behind her. They were looking up at the house, at the flat at the top. Gloria suddenly frowned and shouted, 'You! You there!'

Lexie turned to see Laurence hurrying down the steps, lugging something large and bulky, which was wrapped in blankets. Instantly, she knew what they were – Innes's paintings. Laurence was saving the paintings.

'Stop! I demand that you stop!' Gloria shrilled. 'I must know what you've got there!'

Laurence leapt into the taxi. 'Go,' he said to the driver. 'Go, please!'

The driver let off the brake and then they were sweeping away from the house, down Haverstock Hill, and Gloria was running in her heels beside them, trying to see in, and the daughter was running the other side. She did a better job of keeping up. For several seconds, she ran alongside where Lexie was sitting, her face inches away on the other side of the window, her eyes never leaving Lexie's. Her stare was unbroken, fathomless, the dull eyes like those of a shark, fixed on Lexie's in – what? Accusation? Curiosity? Anger? Impossible to say. Lexie put up her hand to the glass to obliterate that terrible Medusa gaze. When she removed it, Margot had gone.

The time after Innes died was for Lexie an endless trail of days, blank hours, years that ticked by. In a sense, there is nothing to say about it. Because it was a time of nothingness, of lacking, a time marked by absence. When Innes died, existence as Lexie had come to know it ended and another began: she dropped, like Innes in his parachute, out of her life and into another. The magazine was gone, the flat had gone, Innes had gone. She didn't know it at the time but she would never return to the grid of streets that made up Soho, not even once.

If she thought back to the time just after her flight from the flat, she might claim she remembered nothing, that it was a long time before life and sentience re-emerged. But certain scenes would present themselves to her sometimes, like *tableaux vivants*. Her lugging her suitcases along Kingsway in Holborn; the hem of her coat has caught on a railing and is torn, hanging down at the back. Her looking around a basement bedsit, the landlady clutching a large tortoise-shell cat to her bosom. The room is narrow and smells of mice and damp, the window small, a peculiar oblong shape. 'What happened to the window?' Lexie is asking. 'Partitioned,' the landlady said. 'Cut in half.' Lexie staring at the cat and the cat staring back with wide, glossy pupils. Reflected in each of these pupils is the imprint of the partitioned window. Her trying to light the gas fire and failing. This causing her to burst into tears. The tears causing her to hurl a shoe at the wall opposite. Spent matches on the carpet around her. Stealing a handful of bluebells from Regent's Park. The stems weep into her palm, into her sleeve. She puts them in a jam-jar. They die. She throws them out of the window, jam-jar and all. Her standing beside her partitioned window, looking up at the pavement, at people's ankles, their shoes, the feet of dogs, the wheels of prams. With one hand she holds a cigarette she isn't smoking, with the other she tweaks hairs from her head, one by one, and lets them float to the floor.

She was standing like this when, without warning, the door was pushed open and a figure stepped through.

'There you are,' it said.

Lexie turned her head. She didn't recognise the person. It was a woman with hair cut short, above the ears, and she was wearing a swing coat and little flat shoes with buckles.

'Daph?' Lexie said.

'Good God.' Daphne advanced towards her. She shook her head and seemed unable to speak. 'Look at you,' she said eventually.

'What do you mean?'

'What's happened to your—?'

'My what?'

'Never mind.' Daphne let out a small tutting noise, then took a cigarette from the packet on the window-sill, lit it and unbuttoned her coat. She looked as if she was about to take it off, then cast her eyes around her and seemed to think better of it. She began to pace the room instead. Lexie watched as Daphne kicked the bed-end, twisted the tap, tugged at a piece of peeling wallpaper. 'Christ,' she said, 'it's a dungeon. And it stinks. How much are you paying for this?'

'None of your business.'

'Lex,' Daphne came to a stop in front of her and seized her by the shoulders, 'this has to stop. Do you hear me?'

'What has to stop?'

'This.' She gestured around her, at the room, at Lexie's head. 'And this.'

Lexie disengaged herself. 'I don't know what you mean.'

'You can't do this. To yourself. To Laurence and me. We've been going frantic over you, you know, and we keep thinking . . .'

'Sorry.' Lexie stubbed out her cigarette in an ashtray balanced on the sill.

Daphne moved towards the armchair, picked up the cashmere scarf left there and brandished it at Lexie. 'It's not going to bring him back, you know. And what do you think he would say? If he could see you now?'

'Put that down,' Lexie said and Daphne, as if realising she'd gone too far, did. She slumped into a chair and puffed away at her cigarette. Lexie turned back to the street and watched someone in brown shoes walk past.

'Do you remember Jimmy?' Daphne said, behind her.

'Jimmy?'

'Tall, ginger hair, works at the *Daily Courier.* Had a thing with Amelia, ages ago.'

'Um.' Lexie picked up the ashtray, then put it down again. 'Sort of.'

'I saw him last night at the French Pub. He's got a job for you.'

Lexie turned. 'A job?' she repeated.

'Yes, a job. You know. Work and pay and all that. Out in the world.' Daphne tapped her ash into the grate. 'It's all arranged. You start on Monday.'

Lexie frowned and tried to think of a reason she couldn't but was unable to come up with one. 'What is the job?' she asked.

'They need a person in Announcements.'

'Announcements?'

'Yes.' Daphne sighed impatiently. 'You know – births, deaths and marriages. It's hardly thrilling and you could do it in your sleep but it's better than this.'

'Births, death and marriages,' Lexie repeated.

'Yes. All the important things in life.'

'Why don't you want it?'

Daphne shrugged. 'I'm not sure it's very me – Fleet Street and all that.'

'Maybe it's not me either.'

Daphne stood up and brushed down her coat. 'It is,' she said. 'Or it might be. At any rate, it's better than going slowly mad among your blue roses. So. Monday, nine o'clock sharp. Don't be late.' She stood up and grabbed Lexie by the arm. 'Come on, get your coat.'

'Where are we going?'

'Out. You look like you need a square meal. I touched Jimmy for ten bob, so we're in luck. Let's go.'

*

On Lexie's first day at the *Daily Courier* she was shown to a desk squeezed in between a larger desk and a set of bookshelves. It was in a small room off a long corridor; the ceiling was low, the floor uneven and a murky window gave a view over a passageway that connected Nash Court with Fleet Street. The whole office had an air of hush, of stasis. There seemed to be hardly anybody about. Had she arrived too early?

She sat at her desk, placing her bag beneath it. The chair was covered with chipped green paint and had one unstable leg. On the desk were a typewriter, a blotting pad and a pair of rusted scissors. Lexie picked these up, opened them, shut them. The blades, at least, were operational. A heap of papers from the neighbouring desk had slumped on to hers. These, she pushed upright, tidying them into a neater pile. She picked up a mug off her desk and peered into its dark depths. A strong smell of coffee rose into her face. She put it down again. There was a note propped on her typewriter, which read, 'Ask Jones abt poss of 2 wks' worth copy.'

At noises in the passageway below, she stood up and went to the window. People were walking in off Fleet Street. She watched them from above and reflected that there was something about the angle that made the tops of their heads, the backs of their necks look vulnerable.

Just before lunch, a man rushed in through the office door. He had greying, wildish hair, an unbuckled raincoat, and he dumped a bursting briefcase on his desk, muttering to himself, then sat down in his chair, reaching for his telephone. 'GEO five six nine one,' he muttered under his breath, and began to dial. Only then did he notice Lexie. 'Oh,' he said, with a start, and let the receiver clatter back into place. 'Who are you?'

'I'm Lexie Sinclair. I'm the new Announcements person. I was told—'

But the man had his face buried in his hands, ranting, 'Oh God, oh God, oh *God*, will they ever listen to me? I told them, I specifically told them, not another—' He gestured towards Lexie. 'I mean no offence to you, my dear, but *really*. This won't do. I'll phone Carruthers now.' He snatched up the receiver. 'No, I won't.' He put it down again. 'What shall I do?' He seemed to be asking her. 'Carruthers won't be in yet. Simpson? He might help.'

Lexie stood up and smoothed the scarf covering her hair. 'I wasn't sure where to start,' she said, 'but a sub brought in some proofs earlier, for today's edition, so I marked them up. Here they are.' She handed them to him and he snatched them suspiciously. 'I wasn't entirely sure on the house style,' she continued, 'but I've put a question mark next to anything I wasn't a hundred per cent certain about.'

The man pushed his glasses to the top of his head and perused the proofs, the pages held close to his face. First one, then another, then the third. 'Hmm,' he said to himself. 'Umm.' When he finished the third, he let them fall to his desk. He sat for a moment with his head tipped back, his fingers laced together. 'The *Courier* doesn't italicise the titles of individual poems,' he said, addressing the ceiling.

'I see.'

'The titles of books, yes, but not individual poems or essays within a collection.'

'My mistake.'

'Where'd you learn to proof-read like that?'

'At . . . my last job.'

'Hmm,' he said again. 'Can you type?'

'Yes.'

'Can you cut copy to fit?'

'Yes.'

'Can you edit copy?'

'I can.'

'Where was this job of yours?'

'It was . . .' here Lexie has to pause '. . . at a magazine.'

'Hmm.' He flung the proofs at her desk. 'You need to initial them,' he said, 'or they'll never find their way back to us.' He fidgeted about with some papers on his desk. He withdrew a pencil from a pot and put it behind his ear. 'Well, don't just sit there, my dear,' he said, suddenly rather peeved, and flapped his hands at her. 'Take them back to the subs. Ring Jones. Find out when he's filing. Go and see if they've set the crossword yet. And your announcements need typing up. I like to have three days' worth at the very least under our belts. And the Country Reflections. Chop, chop, not a moment to lose.'

Lexie spent several months typing out lists of births, details of marriages, those of people's lifespans and descendants and survivors. The addresses of funeral parlours where flowers should be sent. She became adept at wheedling copy out of the recalcitrant Jones, at calming down her boss, Andrew Fuller, when he felt as though he was losing control, when the Country Reflections stockpile dipped below five, at relaying messages from Mrs Fuller about what time dinner would be served in Kennington. She also had to learn ways of sidestepping the attentions of the newspaper's various single men – and several of the unsingle ones. She quickly developed a few cast-iron methods of refusing an invitation to lunch, a request to share a pint, an outing to the theatre. Fuller wholeheartedly supported these refusals. He didn't like his assistant distracted. 'Don't come sniffing around here,' he'd shout at a man who'd appeared hopefully in the doorway, brandishing a pair of free tickets or a concert flyer. 'Let the woman work!' She acquired a reputation for being rather serious, distant, aloof. A 'blue stocking', one of her would-be suitors dubbed her, which was the one time she snapped, was ungracious. She would go to the pub at lunchtime with Fuller, or with the editor of the women's section, or with Jimmy. At one time a rumour circulated that she had a thing going with Jimmy, which Jimmy did nothing to quash; the rest of the office didn't know that during their lunches, Lexie counselled Jimmy as to what to do about the engaged girl with whom he was in love. She found the pace of a daily newspaper gratifyingly hectic, soothingly distracting, the way it was an insatiable machine that had to be fed and fed, that as soon as one day's work was done there was no break before you had to start on the next. There were no gaps, no crannies in which she could think or reflect: she simply had to work. The one photograph of her from her early years at the *Courier* is of a woman in a camel-coloured skirt, sitting on the edge of a desk, frowning at the camera, hair cut short, a particular cashmere scarf around her neck.

It might have continued like this for years had she not, as she thought of it later, given herself away. She was walking back from putting some crossword proofs on the subs' desk when she passed a group of three men talking in the corridor. The deputy editor, the assistant editor and the back-page editor.

'. . . profile possibility,' the back-page editor was saying, 'is Hans Hofmann—'

'Who?' Carruthers, the deputy editor, interrupted.

'Well, quite. To my mind—'

'Bavarian-born abstract impressionist,' Lexie heard herself say to them, 'emigrated to America in the early 1930s. Known not only for being a painter but also a teacher. Students include Lee Krasner, Helen Frankenthaler and Ray Eames.'

The three of them stared at her. The back-page editor went as if to speak but didn't.

'Excuse me,' Lexie muttered, and walked away, and as she did so, she heard Carruthers, whom she knew only by sight, say, 'Well, it looks as if you've found your expert.'

Ten minutes later the back-page editor came to find her. Fuller looked up from the contemplation of his crossword list but didn't yell at him to stop sniffing about.

'Look here,' the back-page editor said, 'you seem to know your stuff about Hofmann. The Tate have just bought two of his pictures. Can you let me have a thousand words by tomorrow? Don't worry too much about style – just the facts would be good. I can get one of my boys to rewrite it.'

It went into the next day's paper untouched. Next came a piece about David Hockney's interpretation of William Hogarth, and a profile of the new director of the National Theatre. Then the women's-section editor asked her to write about why more girls don't apply to art school. After this was printed, Carruthers called Lexie into his office. He had his long legs up on the desk, revealing burgundy socks, and a ruler balanced between his two index fingers. He indicated for her to take a chair. 'Tell me this,' he said, when she had settled herself opposite him, 'in what capacity are we currently employing you?'

'As Announcements assistant.'

'Announcements assistant,' Carruthers intoned. 'I had no idea there was such a position. You work for Andrew Fuller, yes?'

Lexie nodded.

'And your duties are what, exactly?'

'Editing births, deaths and marriages. Chasing copy for the crossword and Country Reflections. Proofing the Miscellany page, checking copy for—'

'Yes, yes,' he said, cutting her off with a flick of the ruler. 'It seems we may have been underestimating you.'

'Oh?'

'Where,' Carruthers swung his legs off the desk and fixed her with a narrow gaze, 'did you spring from, Miss Lexie Sinclair?'

'What do you mean?'

'I mean, one doesn't learn to write the way you can write being a desk assistant. One can't report in the manner that you can report in the natural course of life in Announcements. You must have learnt it somewhere and I want to know where.'

Lexie laced her fingers into each other. She met his gaze. 'Before I came here, I was working on a magazine.'

'Which magazine?'

'*Elsewhere.*' It occurred to her that this was the first time in a long time she had said the word. It felt strange in her mouth, after all these months, like a foreign term with an unfamiliar meaning.

'Under Innes Kent?' Carruthers demanded.

He and Lexie stared at each other. She inclined her head, once. He leant back in his chair and smiled a thin, quick smile.

'Well,' he said, 'it all makes sense now. If I'd known you were trained up by Kent I would have got you out of Announcements months ago. An editor of his calibre. A tragedy, what happened to him, of course, not to mention the magazine. I knew him a little. I would have gone to his funeral, had I known, but . . .' He continued to talk. Lexie laced her hands as tightly as they would possibly go and began to count the number of pencils in the jar on his desk. Three orange ones. Four red. Six blue, two shorter than the others.

She became aware that Carruthers was looking at her with a new, direct expression. 'I beg your pardon?' she said.

'You're not the one he . . . ?' he said, in a low voice, letting the end of the question dangle between them.

She allowed her chin to drop. If she kept looking at the fabric of her dress, if she followed the streams and eddies of the paisley to the places they tailed off into space, the moment would pass, she would be delivered from this.

'Forgive me,' she heard Carruthers murmur. He cleared his throat. He moved some pages from one side of his desk to the other.

'The point is,' he was using his booming, slightly nasal voice again, 'we want to move you away from whatever it is you're doing at the moment to a writing position. You'll be paid twice what you're earning now, you'll be working across a variety of pages, you may need to travel. You'll be the only woman in the reporters' room but I don't imagine that will be a problem for you. From what I gather, you're well able to look after yourself.' He waved his arm at her. 'Go and find yourself a desk with the rest of them. Good luck.'

Lexie was moved up to staff writer on the *Courier*. She was indeed the only woman in the job, and would continue to be so for several years. The invitations to pub lunches dwindled, as if her new status gave off a forcefield that no colleague dared penetrate. She took a two-roomed flat in Chalk Farm but she was rarely there. She lived, she worked, she travelled. She took up with Felix, indifferently, she dropped him, she took up with him again. Daphne went to Paris, to live with an artist, and was never heard of again; Laurence and Lexie mourned her loss. The Angle Gallery did so well that Laurence and David opened a second, the New Angle Gallery. *Elsewhere* reappeared as *London Lights*, with a new editor and new staff and a new office, and it sold at every newsstand. Lexie flew to New York, to Barcelona, to Berlin, to Florence. She interviewed artists, actors, writers, politicians, musicians. She wrote columns about radio stations, abortion laws, CND, teenagers and their motorbikes, the rights of prisoners, widows' pensions, divorce reform, the need for more women at Westminster. During this time, she would receive the occasional unsigned note via the *Courier*'s mailroom, written in a rounded, adolescent hand. *Does your employer know you steal paintings?* read one. *First you take my father, then you take my inheritance,* read another. Lexie ripped them to confetti and pushed them to the bottom of her wastepaper basket. She was thinner, she smoked more, her voice developed the slight huskiness of too many cigarettes. Her interviewees found her sympathetic, incisive, then suddenly ruthless; most of her male colleagues found her irksome and prickly. She knew this but didn't care. She rattled through life and through work, never stopping; she could be found at her desk in the office most weekends, most evenings. She wore the fashions of the time – the short hemlines, the long boots, the clashing colours – but with an effortlessness that bordered on disinterest. She never spoke of Innes to anyone. If Laurence mentioned him, Lexie would not reply. She hung the paintings around the walls of her tiny flat. She ate standing up, looking at them.

And just as she was sure that this was the way her life would be for ever, that this was her, finally and immutably, something changed, just as it always does.

Lexie makes her way along the corridor at the BBC, turns a corner and enters Felix's office without knocking. Felix is sitting with his feet on the desk, the phone cradled in his shoulder, saying, 'Quite, quite,' into the receiver. His eyebrows shoot up when he sees her. They haven't met for several weeks. They're having one of their off periods.

Felix puts down the phone and springs up, seizing her by the shoulders and kissing her on both cheeks. 'Darling,' he says, a touch too fervently, 'this is an unexpected surprise.'

'Don't be pompous, Felix.' Lexie sits in a chair and arranges her bag on the floor beside her. She realises, to her surprise, that she is rather nervous. She looks at Felix, who is lounging against the edge of his desk, then looks away.

Felix regards Lexie, arms folded. She has appeared unannounced in his office, as abrupt as ever but looking rather splendid in an emerald dress. She's had her hair cut, shorter at the back this time. He likes this very much, this whole scenario, this turning up like this, this looking like this. It's always been him who's had to do the running before. He'll take her out to lunch. Claridge's perhaps. He smiles. Lexie is back. Their last fight – whatever was it about, he forgets – seems to fade. What started as an ordinary day is now promising to be rather fun.

He is on the verge of saying, how about a spot of lunch, when Lexie says, 'I need to talk to you.'

Felix's face falls. 'Darling, if this is about the American girl, I assure you it's over and—'

'It's not about the American girl.'

'Oh.' Felix frowns, registers the urge to look at his watch but manages to resist it. 'Well, how about we talk over lunch? I thought Claridge's or—'

'Lunch would be nice.'

They get into a taxi. She permits him to put his hand on her thigh, which Felix takes as a good sign, a sign that all the unpleasantness about that other girl is forgotten, a sign that they'll be in bed together before the day is out. They zoom towards Claridge's, they go in through the revolving doors; the maître d' recognises Felix so they are seated swiftly and at a good table beneath the cupola. They are perusing their menus, when Lexie says, 'By the way . . .'

Felix is weighing up the grilled sole and the steak. What kind of mood is he in? Fish or meat? Steak or sole? 'Hmm?' he says, to show he's listening.

'I'm pregnant.'

He shuts the menu. He puts it down. He puts a hand over Lexie's. 'I see,' he says carefully. 'What do you think you will—'

'I'm keeping it,' she says, without looking up from her menu.

'Of course.' He wishes she'd put the damn menu down. He'd like to snatch it from her and hurl it to the floor. Then, all of a sudden, he is no longer angry. In fact, he wants to laugh. He has to put his hand over his mouth to stop it bursting out into Claridge's restaurant.

'Well, my darling,' he says, and she sees he is controlling laughter, the bastard, 'you are a one for surprises. I have to say I've never seen you as the maternal type.'

She removes her hand from under his. 'Time will tell, I suppose.'

He orders champagne and gets rather drunk. He seems pleased with himself and makes several references to his virility, all of which Lexie ignores. He brings up the subject of marriage again. Lexie refuses to discuss it. As the waiter serves their lunch, he is saying she has to marry him now. She snaps back that she has to do no such thing. He gets angry and says, why do you always say no? When there are girls queuing up to marry me? Marry one of them, Lexie says, pick whichever one you like. But I pick you, Felix says, frowning at her across his champagne glass.

They re-emerge on the pavement outside Claridge's, both in a temper.

'Shall I see you tonight?' Felix asks.

'I'll let you know.'

'Don't say that. I hate it when you say that.'

'Felix, you're plastered.'

He takes her by the arm and starts saying something about how it's time to stop all the arguing and accept the necessity of their marriage when, over his shoulder, Lexie sees someone.

For a moment, she can only register that she recognises this person. She cannot place her. She stares at the pale, wide face, the round eyes, the sinewy hands clutching the bag straps, the fine, wispy hair held back in a polka-dotted band, the way the mouth is held slightly open. Who is this person? And how does Lexie know her?

Then the clouds part. It's Margot Kent. But grown-up. Walking along Brook Street in high heels and a mini-skirt. The words *paintings* and *you'll be sorry* thread and weave through Lexie's mind. That uneven, rounded lettering in blue ink.

She comes closer and closer, her shoes scuffing against the pavement. They look at each other; Margot swivels her head as she passes. Then she stops. She stands on the pavement, staring at Lexie in that unwavering way she's always had.

Felix turns. He sees a young girl and, being Felix, assumes she has stopped to talk to him. 'Hello,' he nods, 'lovely day.'

'Yes,' Margot replies, 'isn't it?' She gives Felix a long, level look, then a smile creeps into her features. 'I know you,' she says, taking a step closer to him. 'You're on television.'

Felix treats her to one of his dazzling yet deprecating grins. 'Not, I believe, right at this moment.'

Margot laughs, an unbecoming snicker. She glances from one to the other of them, then turns and gives them a little wave as she walks backwards away from them. 'See you, then.'

'Goodbye,' Felix says, then puts his arms around Lexie. 'Now, listen,' he begins.

Lexie fights him off. Margot is still looking at them, over her shoulder, strands of her thin hair blowing over her face. 'Do you know her?' Lexie hisses.

'Who?'

'That girl.'

'What girl?'

'The one you just said hello to.'

'What? No.'

'Are you sure?'

'About what?'

'That you don't know her?'

'Who?'

'Felix,' Lexie thumps him in the chest, 'are you being deliberately obtuse? That girl. Do you know her?'

'No, I've just told you. I've never seen her before in my life.'

'But then why did you say—'

Felix catches her face between both of his hands. 'Why are we talking about this?'

'You must promise me,' Lexie says, then stops. She doesn't know what she wants him to promise but something is making her uneasy. She thinks of Margot and her mini-skirt and her slow smile and her fine, suddenly blonde hair. The way she looked at Felix, the snide delight in her features. *First you take my father.* 'You must promise me . . . I don't know. Promise me that if you see her again you won't say hello. Promise me that you'll stay away from her.'

'Lexie, what on earth—'

'Promise me!'

He smiles down at her. 'If you promise to marry me.'

'Felix, I'm serious. She's . . . she's . . . Just promise me, please.'

'All right, all right,' he concedes testily. 'I promise. Now, what about tonight?'

Lexie is sitting up in bed, cross-legged, her notes spread out on the counterpane around her. She is eight months pregnant and this is the only comfortable place she can work – the office is too much of a distance now. She has to finish this piece on Italian cinema before she can go to sleep.

She removes the pencil from behind her ear and reaches for a piece of paper to her left; the pencil slips from her fingers, rolls over the counterpane and drops to the floor. Lexie curses. For a moment she contemplates leaving it there but she doesn't have another to hand. She slides the typewriter off her knees, manoeuvres herself through her notes and down on to her hands and knees to look under the bed. No pencil. She crawls towards the bedside table and peers under that and, as she does so, there is a strange down-dragging sensation in the pit of her stomach. Lexie straightens up, the pencil forgotten. The pain disappears as quickly as it had come. She gets back on to the bed; she reads through what she has written and, towards the end of the article, the sensation comes again. Lexie looks down at her stomach and frowns. It cannot be, it simply cannot. It's much too early. She has an interview tomorrow – with an activist she's been pursuing for months – and a leader to write before the end of the week. The sensation comes again, stronger this time. Lexie swears and slams down the pages. This cannot be happening. She stamps into the kitchen to make a cup of tea and feels the clench of another contraction as she fills the kettle – a small surge, like driving too fast over a hump-backed bridge, like swimming through a wave in the ocean.

'Listen,' she says aloud, 'this is not on. You have to wait. It's not time to come out yet. Do you hear me?'

While she drinks the tea, she looks at the paintings – the Bacon, the Pollock, the Hepworth, the Freud. She brushes her hair, still looking. She scrubs her teeth and, as she spits, the surges are turning into clenches, like a fist tightening, like a drawstring bag pulled too tight.

She picks up the phone and calls a cab. 'To the Royal Free Hosp—' The word is torn off because instead she says, 'Ow.'

She presents herself at the labour ward just as dusk is falling.

'Look,' she says, to the nurse behind the desk, 'this is happening much too early. I've got a pile of work to do this week. Can't you do something to stop it?'

'Stop what?' the nurse says, nonplussed.

'This.' Lexie points at her belly. Is the woman particularly stupid? 'It's too early. It can't come now.'

The nurse looks at her over her spectacles. 'Mrs Sinclair—'

'Miss.'

Several more midwives gather round her, shocked. 'Where is your husband?' one of them says, looking around. 'You're not alone, are you?'

'I am,' says Lexie, leaning on the desk. She can feel another of those pains approaching, can sense it on the horizon.

'Where is your husband?'

'Don't have one.'

'But, Mrs Sinclair, it—'

'Miss,' she corrects them again. 'And another thing—' Again, her words are strangled by a surge of pain. She clings to the edge of the desk. 'Damn and hell,' she hears herself shout.

'Gracious me,' the nurse tuts. Then Lexie hears her say to someone else, 'Would you telephone the father? His telephone number is down here and—'

'Don't you bloody dare,' Lexie roars. 'I don't want him here.'

Several hours later she is clinging to the leg of a hospital bed, a sailor in a storm holding on to a mast, and she is still saying it's too early, that she has work to do, and she is still swearing. She is swearing like she's never sworn before.

'Get up off that floor, Mrs Sinclair, this minute,' the midwife says.

'I will not,' Lexie gets out from between her teeth, 'and it's Miss not Mrs. How many times do I have to tell you?'

'Mrs Sinclair, get off the floor and on to the bed.'

'Shan't,' she says, and then she lets out a howl, a scream, followed by a string of invective.

'Such language,' the midwife tuts. They keeps saying that to her. That or 'Get on the bed.' She is still crouched on the floor when she gives birth. They have to catch the baby in a towel. The doctor says he's never seen the like. Like a savage, he says, or an animal.

Such language. These were the first words Lexie's son ever heard.

Later, at visiting time, the ward began to fill with husbands in hats and raincoats, bearing flowers. Lexie watched them, looked at their nervous fingers gripping ribboned boxes of chocolates, their tight collars, their overshaven chins. The squeak of their shoes, the rain on their hats, the redness of their hands as they leant on the cots of their new children. Lexie smiled. She looked down at her son, who was swaddled in a yellow blanket, staring up at her with an expression that said: At last, there you are.

'Hi,' Lexie whispered, and put her finger into his hand's grip.

A nurse appeared beside her. 'You shouldn't be holding that child unless it's feeding time. You'll make a rod for your own back. You should put him in his cot.'

'But I don't want to,' Lexie said, without taking her gaze away from him.

The nurse sighed. 'Shall I draw the curtains for you?'

Lexie looked up sharply. 'No.' She settled the baby so that he was closer to her. 'No,' she said again.

Towards the end of visiting time, there was the sound of regular, assertive footsteps in the ward. Lexie knew those footsteps. She raised her head to watch Felix take his walk of honour past all the beds, where the women looked up at him, their eyes wide, their mouths breaking into smiles. He was on television every night, these days. He nodded and smiled back at them. His coat was loose, as if he'd run here in a rush, and he was carrying an enormous spray of orchids in one hand and a basket of fruit in the other. Lexie rolled her eyes.

'Darling,' he boomed, as he neared her, 'I just got the call. I would have come sooner.'

'Really?' Lexie said, glancing at the clock. 'Haven't you just finished tonight's programme?'

He laid the flowers on the bed, on top of Lexie's feet. He said: 'A boy. How marvellous. How are you?'

Lexie said, 'We're fine.'

She saw him smile, lean towards her. 'Congratulations, sweetie, very well done,' he said, and kissed her cheek. Then he sank into a chair. 'Although I'm a tiny bit cross,' he said, 'that you didn't call me straight away. You poor darling, coming in here on your own. Very naughty of you.' He treated her to one of his deep, intimate smiles. 'I sent a telegram to my mother. She'll be delighted. She'll be looking out the family christening robe as we speak.'

'Christ,' Lexie muttered. 'Tell her not to bother. Felix, haven't you forgotten something?'

'What?'

'Have you forgotten why you came?'

'To see you, of course.'

'And the baby, perhaps? Your son? Whom you don't seem to have glanced at yet.'

Felix sprang to his feet and peered at the baby. His face, fleetingly, showed a mixture of distaste and fear before he retreated back to his chair. 'Wonderful,' he declared. 'Perfect. What name are we going to give him?'

'Theo.'

'Oh.'

'As in Theodore.'

'Isn't that rather a . . . ?' He stopped. Smiled at her again. 'Why Theodore?'

'I like it. And it suits him. Maybe because it contains the sound "adore".'

He put his hand over hers. 'My darling,' he began, in a low voice, 'I spoke to the nurses on the way in and they think – and, of course,

I agree with them – that you can't possibly go home alone to your flat. I really think that—'

'Felix, don't start on this again.'

'Won't you come and live in Gilliland Street with me?'

'No.'

'I'm not talking about marriage, I promise. Just think about it. The two of us under one roof—'

'Three.'

'Sorry?'

'The baby, Felix.'

'I meant three, of course. Slip of the tongue. The three of us under one roof. It is for the best. The nurses think so too and—'

'Please stop!' Lexie shrieked, making several of the bedjacketed mothers look over. 'And how dare you speak to the nurses about me behind my back? Who do you think you are? There's no way I'd live with you. Ever.'

But Felix was impervious. 'We'll see,' he says, covering her hand with his own.

Lexie checks herself out early – she cannot stand the intimate camaraderie of the ward, the public life of it – and takes her baby home. They get a cab together. It seems a very simple equation: she went to the hospital as one person and she comes back as two. Theo sleeps in the bottom drawer of a chest. Lexie takes him out for walks in a big squeaking silver pram, given to her by a neighbour. She is awake for a great deal of the night. This is not a surprise but no less a trial. She stands at the window with her baby, in her dressing-gown, looking down into the street; she listens for the whirr-stop-whirr of the milk float and wonders if she is the only person awake in the city. The warm weight of Theo's head balanced in the crook of her left arm, always her left, his ear pressed to her heart. His body slack with sleep. The room shimmers with the metallic white light of dawn. Around the bed are strewn the spoils of the long night they have lived through together: several soiled nappies, two crumpled muslin squares, an empty water glass, a jar of zinc ointment. Lexie scuffs her bare foot against the rug, then stops to look down at her son. His features cloud briefly in his sleep, then relax. His hand rises up, flails through the air, in search of something – texture, purchase, reassurance – finds a fold of her dressing-gown and clenches decisively around it.

The shock of motherhood, for Lexie, is not the sleeplessness, the troughs of exhaustion, the shrinkage of life, how your existence becomes limited to the streets around where you live, but the onslaught of domestic tasks: the washing and the folding and the drying. Performing these makes her almost weep with furious boredom and she more than once hurls an armful of laundry at the wall. She eyes other mothers when she passes them in the street and they look so poised, so together, with their handbags hooked over the pram handles and their neatly embroidered sheets tucked in around their babies with hospital corners. But what about the *washing,* she wants to say, don't you loathe the *drying* and the *folding*?

Theo grows out of the drawer. He grows out of the matinée jackets people knitted for him. Again, this is not a surprise but it happens faster than she'd expected. She rings the *Courier.* She writes a piece about the Anthony Caro exhibition at the Hayward Gallery and she is able to buy a cot. Theo grows until his feet touch the bottom of the pram. She rings the *Courier* again and she goes for a meeting, taking Theo with her. Carruthers seems horrified at first and then intrigued. Lexie jiggles Theo up and down on her knee as they talk. She gets a commission for an interview with an actress. She takes Theo along with her to the house. The actress is charmed and Theo crawls under the sofa, chasing the actress's cat. Then he appears with a shoe of the actress, the strap of which he has chewed. The actress is suddenly less charmed. Lexie gets paid and she buys a pushchair. It has red and white stripes. Theo sits forward in it, hands gripping his knees, leaning sideways to take the corners. She finds a neighbour, Mrs Gallo from a few doors down, who is willing to mind Theo for a few days a week. She is from Liguria and has reared eight children. She sets Theo on her knee, calls him 'Angelino', pinches his cheeks and says, 'May God protect him.' And then Lexie goes back to the office, back to the reporters' room, to earn a wage, to commune with her old life. Her colleagues know why she's been away but very few of them mention the baby, as if he's something not to be spoken of in the noisy, concentrated atmosphere of the newspaper. When she leaves the house on these mornings, she senses a thread that runs between her and her son, and as she walks away through the streets she is aware of it unspooling, bit by bit. By the end of the day, she feels utterly unravelled, almost mad with desire to be back with him, and she urges the Tube train to rattle faster through the tunnels, to speed over the rails, to get her back to her child as quickly as possible. It takes her a while, once she's there again with him, to wind herself back to rightness, to get the thread back to where it ought to be – a length of no more than a couple of feet or so feels best, Lexie decides. When Theo sleeps at night she goes to her desk to finish whatever she hasn't managed to get through that day. She sometimes thinks that the sound of typewriter keys must be, to Theo, a kind of lullaby, wreathing like smoke into his dreams.

When Theo begins to pull himself up on chair legs, when he begins to walk, when he begins to drag things off tables, when he very nearly kills himself by pulling the typewriter down on himself, Lexie realises something.

*

'I need to move,' she said to Laurence.

Laurence was watching Theo noisily emptying a kitchen cupboard on to the floor. 'Amazing,' he said, 'that something so simple can be such fun. It makes one want to be a baby again.' He turned to look at her. 'You need to move? Why? Is the landlord turfing you out?'

'No.' Lexie cast her eyes around the room. It was a large room, admittedly, but it contained her bed, Theo's cot, the sofa, a playpen, a desk where she worked at night.

Laurence was following her gaze. 'I see what you mean,' he said. 'But where will you go?'

Theo dropped a metal sieve on the floor, which produced a resonant clang. 'Ha,' he said. 'Ha.' He bent to lift it again. Laurence leant forward to cut himself another slice of cake. Lexie watched her son hurl the sieve to the floor again. She found a particular pleasure in his green towelling romper-suit, the way his hair was growing in a V over his brow, in his fingers gripping the handle of a pan.

'I thought . . . I was thinking . . .' she began '. . . that maybe I should . . . buy somewhere.'

Laurence's head snapped round. 'Have you won the pools?'

'If only.'

'Is whatshisface paying?'

'Certainly not. I wouldn't accept money like that from whatshisface.'

Laurence frowned. 'Well, more fool you. How are you going to—' He put down his cake plate. 'Ah,' he said, in a different tone and, if circumstances had been different, Lexie might have smiled. It was one of the things she liked best about Laurence – the speed of his intuition.

He and Lexie looked at each other for a moment and then they turned to the wall opposite. The Pollock, the Bacon, the Freud, the Klein, the Giacometti. Lexie put her hands over her face and slumped down into the sofa. 'I don't think I can,' she said, from behind her fingers.

'Lex, I don't see that you have a choice. You either ask whatshisface for a slice of his fortune—'

'Not an option.'

'Or you sell Theo to slave traders.'

'Also not an option.'

'Or you sell one of these.'

'But I don't want to,' she moaned. 'I can't.'

Laurence got up, walked over to the pictures and looked at them, one by one. 'If it's any consolation,' he said, as he stopped in front of the Lucian Freud portrait, 'I think he would have told you to do exactly this. You know that. He wouldn't have hesitated for a moment. Remember how he sold that Hepworth lithograph so that you could come and work with us?'

Lexie said nothing but took her hands away from her face.

Laurence moved on, past the Minton and the Colquhoun and the Bacon and came to a stop in front of the Pollock. He tapped the frame with his fingernails. 'This'll get you and Theo a palace somewhere. Dying is such a clever commercial move for an artist.'

'Not that one,' Lexie muttered, picking cake crumbs from the folds of her dress.

Laurence turned to look at her questioningly.

'His favourite,' Lexie said.

Theo, from the kitchenette, suddenly let out a mournful howl. Lexie went through and lifted him out of the mess of pans, baking trays, biscuit cutters. He immediately leant into her shoulder, exhausted, putting in his thumb, twirling his spare hand in her hair.

'The Giacometti sketch might fetch you something. It's signed,' Laurence said. 'They've gone up in recent years. David and I can sell it for you, if you like.'

'Thank you,' Lexie murmured.

'We'll do it anonymously. No one will ever know.'

'OK,' she said, turning away from the wall. 'Take it now, will you?'

She bought the third place she saw – the bottom half of a house in Dartmouth Park. Two rooms upstairs, two rooms downstairs, a passage running right through it from front door to back. A patch of garden at the back, with a snaggle-branched apple tree that yielded sweet-fleshed yellow fruit in autumn. Lexie hung a swing from its branches, and the first weeks in which she and Theo lived there, he would sit in the swing, fists resting on the wooden spars, watching in amazement as she scaled the branches, feet bare, collecting apples in her knotted skirt. She peeled up the rotten carpets and old, damp lino, scrubbed the boards and varnished them. She whitewashed the back of the house. She rubbed the windows with newspaper and vinegar until sunshine glowed through, Theo coursing back and forth across the garden with a watering-can. It seemed astonishing to her to own a patch of land, an arrangement of bricks, mortar and glass. It seemed an impossible swap: some money for a life like this. In the evenings, after Theo was asleep, she would often walk from room to room, around the perimeter of the garden, unable to believe her luck.

The lost Giacometti sketch haunted her, though. She hung and rehung the paintings over and over again, trying to find an arrangement that didn't show its absence. You had no choice, she kept telling herself, you had no choice. And: he wouldn't have minded; under the circumstances, he'd have suggested it himself. But she was still gnawed by guilt, by regret, in the small hours of the night, as she lifted the paintings off the walls, to try another new combination.

To distract herself, as ever, she worked. *The women we become after children*, she typed, then stopped to adjust the angle of the paper. She glanced at the paintings, almost without seeing them, then cocked her head to listen for Theo. Nothing. Silence; the freighted silence of sleep. She turned back to the typewriter, to the sentence she had written.

We change shape, she continued, we buy low-heeled shoes, we cut off our long hair. We begin to carry in our bags half-eaten rusks, a small tractor, a shred of beloved fabric, a plastic doll. We lose muscle tone, sleep, reason, perspective. Our hearts begin to live outside our bodies. They breathe, they eat, they crawl and – look! – they walk, they begin to speak to us. We learn that we must sometimes walk an inch at a time, to stop and examine every stick, every stone, every squashed tin along the way. We get used to not getting where we were going. We learn to darn, perhaps to cook, to patch the knees of dungarees. We get used to living with a love that suffuses us, suffocates us, blinds us, controls us. We live. We contemplate our bodies, our stretched skin, those threads of silver around our brows, our strangely enlarged feet. We learn to look less in the mirror. We put our dry-clean-only clothes to the back of the wardrobe. Eventually, we throw them away. We school ourselves to stop saying 'shit' and 'damn' and learn to say 'my goodness' and 'heavens above'. We give up smoking, we colour our hair, we search the vistas of parks, swimming-pools, libraries, cafés for others of our kind. We know each other by our pushchairs, our sleepless gazes, the beakers we carry. We learn how to cool a fever, ease a cough, the four indicators of meningitis, that one must sometimes push a swing for two hours. We buy biscuit cutters, washable paints, aprons, plastic bowls. We no longer tolerate delayed buses, fighting in the street, smoking in restaurants, sex after midnight, inconsistency, laziness, being cold. We contemplate younger women as they pass us in the street, with their cigarettes, their makeup, their tight-seamed dresses, their tiny handbags, their smooth, washed hair, and we turn away, we put down our heads, we keep on pushing the pram up the hill.

Felix would come, between his stints in Malaysia, Vietnam, Northern Ireland, Suez. He stayed sometimes for an afternoon, sometimes for a day, sometimes for weeks at a time. Lexie made sure he kept his own flat. He proved to be a fond, if semi-detached, parent. He would bounce Theo up and down on his knee for a few minutes, then put him down and pick up a newspaper, or lie on a rug in the garden while Theo pottered around him. Lexie once came out into the garden to find Felix asleep, covered with sand – and Theo industriously heading from sandpit to prone father, trowel in hand, burying him bit by bit.

It's hard to say what Theo thought of Felix, of this man who appeared in the house after long gaps, bearing expensive yet inappropriate gifts (Meccano for a one-year-old, a cricket bat for a child who couldn't yet walk). Theo didn't call him 'Daddy' or 'Dad' ('Rather silly names, don't you think?' said Felix) but 'Felix'. Felix called him 'old chap', which never failed to irritate Lexie.

Ted stands in his back garden, contemplating the flowerbed. Perhaps 'flowerbed' isn't quite the right word. Bindweed-and-dock-bed. Tangled thicket of weeds. Complete bloody mess.

He sighs, leans forward to pull at a particularly voracious plant with a fronded top but it refuses to leave the soil, breaking off in his hand. He sighs again and tosses it aside.

Elina is behind him somewhere, in the house. He can hear her talking to Jonah, on and on, in Finnish. Sometimes, she's told him, she switches to Swedish, just for a change. Ted can't tell the difference. As a language, it defeats him utterly. He knows a total of two words in Finnish: 'thank you' and 'condom'. He's never heard Elina talk Finnish much before – occasionally when she's on the phone to her family, and sometimes if she met up with a Finnish friend. But now she seems to speak it all the time.

Ted picks a pair of shears and kneels on the grass. They open with a clean *sssshkk* sound, the blades moving across each other. Surprisingly, they are unrusted inside. He positions the V of the steel near the earth, then slices. The weeds topple, then fall. He does this again, then again. Weeds lie stranded all about him.

Yesterday he'd caught Elina staring out of the back windows of the house. Jonah was propped against her shoulder, eyes facing the door, so that it was the baby's sudden jerk of head that had alerted her to his presence.

'What you looking at?' he'd asked, coming to put his arms around her, to pull faces at Jonah, who stared at him in astonishment.

'My studio,' she'd said, without looking away. 'I was just standing here, thinking that . . .'

'What?'

'It looks like Sleeping Beauty's castle.'

Ted had racked his brain to remember this story. Was this the one about the glass shoe? No. Or the one with the woman and her long plait of hair? 'In what way?' he asked, deciding to play for time.

'Look at it!' she said, suddenly angry. 'You can barely see it any more for all the weeds. Another few weeks and it will have completely disappeared. When I finally do have the chance to work I won't be able to get in there.'

So here he was, on his hands and knees, saving her studio from being engulfed by the garden. He wants to give her a surprise. He wants her to be happy. He wants the baby to sleep for more than three hours at a stretch. He wants to have if not his old life then some kind of life, not this constant lurching from one day to the next. He wants Elina not to have huge dark circles under her eyes all the time, for her not to have that tense, bitten-lip look she's developed recently. He wants the house to stop smelling of shit. He wants there to be a time when the washing-machine isn't on. He wants her to stop getting upset with him when it slips his mind to take the laundry out of the machine, to hang the laundry, to fold the laundry, to buy more nappies, to make the dinner, to clear away the dinner.

Ted slices and slices at the weeds and when he's cleared the area outside the studio door, he begins to push the fallen plants into a plastic sack.

It is a simple movement: scrape-scrape-gather with one hand, then shovel into the bag held by the other hand. There is something hypnotic in it, in the noise, in the movement. Ted watches his hands, engaged, seemingly without his input, in this straightforward act. Here he is, he thinks, a man, a father, weeding a garden on a Saturday afternoon. There is the sound of a helicopter somewhere in the sky above him, the *saarh* sound of his breath as it enters his body, the *haarh* as it leaves, the sense of his lungs as a pair of bellows, powering his system, his hands in their rhythmic movement, the noise of some children on the other side of the wall, heading on bikes towards the Heath, the weeds' reproachful rustle as they enter the sack, and perhaps there is something familiar in this act, this movement, or perhaps it is some confluence of elements causing a new connection because it is suddenly as if he has fallen through a trapdoor or down a rabbit hole. Ted can see himself as a small boy, he is himself as a small boy, and he is crouched at the end of a lawn and he has in his hand a small green plastic rake.

Ted blinks. He straightens up, turns his head from left to right.

Here he is, back in his life. The weeds, the shears, the garden, Elina and Jonah somewhere behind him. But at the same time he is also a little boy, crouching at a lawn edge with a green plastic rake in his hand and people behind him. His father, sitting in a deck-chair, and someone else, just out of sight: the hem of a long red dress and a bare foot, the nails painted purple, shoes lying discarded in the grass. His father is lighting a cigarette and he is speaking, his lips clenched around it. *I never said anything of the sort.* There is a sudden movement and the other person has got out of their deck-chair. Ted sees the red of her dress as it swirls about her ankles. The red hem, the purple toenails, the green grass. *It's out of the question,* she says.

And then she leaves.

The dress swoops behind her as she walks away from them towards the house – and what house is this, what place is this, with plant pots lined along a patio, with a narrow door? Ted sees her back as she strides over the lawn; he sees long, smooth hair tied in a scarf. It's out of the question. He sees the ties of a red dress fluttering, the white soles of feet flashing at him in turn. Ted looks down at the rake he's holding. He looks at his father. He looks at the empty shoes lying on the grass. He looks as the woman with the long red dress and long smooth hair disappears into the dark oblong of the back door.

Elina steps out of the kitchen into the garden, Jonah in one arm, a blanket over the other. She tries to spread out the blanket on the lawn but it's hard with one hand so she says, 'Ted, could you help me?'

He is standing with his back to her. He doesn't turn round.

'Ted?' she calls again, more loudly.

Ted is rubbing and rubbing his forehead. Elina lets the blanket slide to the decking. She nestles Jonah inside it and walks over to Ted. She touches his shoulder. 'You all right?'

She feels him start beneath her touch. 'Yes,' he snaps. 'Of course. Why wouldn't I be?'

'I was only asking,' Elina snaps back. 'There's no need to shout.'

He stops rubbing his forehead, puts his hand into his pocket, then takes it out. 'Well, I'm fine,' he says.

'Good. I won't make the mistake of asking next time.'

Ted mutters something inaudible and turns away, back to the flowerbed. Elina looks at the ground, which is littered with fallen flowers.

'What are you doing, anyway?'

He mutters again.

'What?' she says.

He turns his head towards her and says, 'Weeding.'

'Weeding?'

'Yeah. What's it look like?'

'I'm not sure,' she says. 'Aren't you supposed to pull weeds out by the roots, not just cut them? They grow again if you leave the roots in, don't they?'

Ted picks up some shears, opens the blades. The light glances off the steel, sending sparks all over the garden. And they launch with something close to relief into the argument, as if they had both been waiting unconsciously for this release. He is saying you have to cut weeds before you can clear them and that plants can't grow without their leaves.

He's losing his temper. He's flinging away the shears, point down, so that they stab into the grass and stay there, like Excalibur. She's using this as more fuel for her anger, pointing at the shears and at the proximity of her foot, meanwhile telling him he's an idiot. He's shouting that he can't do anything right.

Jonah lies on the blanket on the decking. He has his thumb deeply inserted in his mouth and is sucking it with alert, concentrated intent. His eyes are round, unblinking. He is listening to his mother's voice, raised in anger, in distress, and the four-month-old neurones in his brain are trying to decode what this might mean, for her, for him. A tiny, momentary frown dips his brow and it is the perfect simulacrum of an adult frown.

He pauses in his sucking, doubt crossing his features, and he is trying to twist now, raising his legs in the air, trying to see his mother, trying to alert her to his worry. But he's not quite there yet, not quite old enough. He lets out a cry of frustration – small, barely audible – and tries again to roll on to his side. No luck. He thrashes and wriggles like a hooked fish. Then the full horror of his situation suddenly strikes him. His thumb falls from his lips, his face crumples inwards and he screams.

In a flash, Elina is there, lifting him away from the blanket, and hurrying into the house.

Ted stays in the garden. He picks up a stick and lashes at some weeds. He pulls up the shears from out of the lawn, then drops them again. He stands for a moment, leaning with one hand against Elina's studio.

Half an hour later, everyone is in different clothes and in the car. Elina and Ted haven't spoken a word to each other beyond, 'Did you call a cab?' 'Yes.' And they are off to Ted's parents for lunch.

'And I'd only left the thing switched on all day!' Ted's cousin, Clara, finishes her story and everyone bursts into laughter, except Ted's mother, who murmurs about how it's dangerous to leave electrical items on, and Elina, who hasn't entirely followed the story. Something about a boyfriend and hair-straighteners – Elina had missed the beginning, but she smiles and lets out a little laugh, in case anyone notices.

They are sitting at the table. They have eaten fish, which was grilled and smothered in a strange, slightly gritty sauce, and a crumble, 'made with gooseberries from the garden', as Ted's mother told them. Ted's other cousin, Harriet, has made coffee and everyone is talking about Clara's recent trip to LA, about a film Ted edited that has just appeared in cinemas, about the actor who lives down the street. Ted's grandmother is mumbling to herself about how she asked for cream with her coffee, not milk, and doesn't anybody drink coffee properly any more? And Elina is looking and yet trying not to look at Harriet, who is holding Jonah. Holding Jonah in the crook of her tanned elbow. Holding him as if she's forgotten she's holding him. Holding him so that his body is slumped across her lap and his head is alarmingly close to the table edge. Harriet is gesturing, talking, the silver bangles up her arm clattering and tinkling, and Jonah's head bumps up and down with every emphatic bounce Harriet gives. His expression is one of perplexity. He looks lost, he looks confused.

Elina has been sending silent signals to Ted, who is sitting next to Harriet: rescue your son, rescue your son. But Ted is apparently absorbed in the back garden. He has been staring through the window for the past five minutes, not listening to a word Harriet is saying. In a moment, Elina tells herself, you'll get up and take Jonah, casually, very casually. You could say, lightly, as if it doesn't matter at all, as if he's not your child that you love beyond knowing, as if—

'She looks like that other one, doesn't she?' Ted's grandmother mumbles this across all the noise. She is pointing at Jonah.

Clara leans towards her. 'It's a boy,' she says loudly. 'Jonah. Remember?'

The grandmother shakes her head, as if trying to rid herself of an aggravating fly. 'A boy?' she snaps. 'Well, he looks like that other one. Don't you think?' At this, she turns to her daughter.

But Ted's mother is busying herself across the room in the kitchen, unloading plates from a tray. She is speaking to Ted's father, who is puffing cigarette smoke out of the back door, saying something about port glasses.

'What?' Ted says. 'Who do you mean? What other one?'

His grandmother appears to think for a long time, frowning. She whirls a hand in the air, then places it back on the arm of her wheelchair. 'You know,' she says.

Ted twists round in his chair. 'Mum!' he says. 'Who does she mean?'

'. . . and put that out, for goodness' sake,' his mother is saying, as she returns from the kitchen with an empty tray in her hands, 'with the baby here.'

'Who does she mean?' Ted asks again.

His mother is collecting wine glasses, crumpled napkins. 'Who does who mean?' she says.

'Grandma says Jonah looks like "the other one".'

Ted's mother snatches a napkin off the table and the movement upsets a glass. The liquid spreads, dark and smooth, over the cloth, coursing between plates, cutlery, and forming a small waterfall off the edge to the lap of Elina's skirt. Elina jumps up, wine falling to her shoes, and tries to dab it with her own napkin. Clara wheels the grandmother's chair back, away from the table and the spilt wine. Everyone is standing suddenly, with cloths, advice, admonishments, and Ted is still saying, 'Who does she mean?' and his mother is saying, 'I haven't the faintest idea, darling,' and his father is passing behind Elina, she can smell the acrid cigarette smoke off him, and as she turns to him, he says, 'A flutter in the hen-coop, eh?' and winks at her.

Elina escapes to the loo and when she gets back, the table, the whole room, is empty. For a moment or two she has an uneasy, sickish feeling in her stomach, like a child who discovers it has been left out of a game. Then she sees them all, arranged on various deckchairs and rugs, in the garden. As she comes out, she hears Ted's mother say, 'Now, give me that baby, quick, before—' She swallows the rest of the sentence as Elina crosses the patio. Elina takes a place on a rug beside Ted's father without meeting anyone's eye.

Harriet gets up and gives Jonah to Ted's mother. She makes a small, unintelligible noise as she takes the baby and Elina catches sight of long, sharpened nails next to Jonah's cheek before she looks away. Ted's mother will, she knows, be rearranging Jonah to her liking. His hair, which always stands on end, will be smoothed flat. She will button his jacket to the top; she will pull his socks higher or comment that he's not wearing any; she will tug his sleeves down over his fists.

Elina doesn't look at this; she looks about her. Harriet is reclining on a rug, her head in Clara's lap. Together they are looking at a bracelet Clara is wearing. The grandmother has been parked under a tree, where she has fallen asleep, slippered feet propped up on a stool. Ted is sitting hunched in a deck-chair, legs crossed, arms folded. Is he watching his mother with Jonah? It's hard to tell. He could be or he could be staring into space.

Elina finds Ted's parents' house strange. It's tall, with floors stacked on top of each other, the staircase curling up through the middle of it like a helix. Its front faces out over a square lined with duplicate houses – iron balconies, evenly spaced sash windows, black railings around the basement windows. At the back, though, there is a garden that seems too small, too inadequate for the house's height. Elina doesn't like looking up at the house from the back. It is as if it might topple at any moment.

'How are you, Miss Elina?'

She turns to Ted's father. He is putting a cigarette to his mouth and patting his pockets for a lighter.

'I'm well, thank you.'

'How are you finding the whole . . .' he sparks the lighter and holds it to the cigarette until the end glows '. . . baby thing?'

'Well.' She considers what to say. Should she mention the nights spent awake, the number of times she must wash her hands in a day, the endless drying and folding of tiny clothes, the packing and unpacking of bags containing clothes, nappies, wipes, the scar across her abdomen, crooked and leering, the utter loneliness of it all, the hours she spends kneeling on the floor, a rattle or a bell or a fabric block in her hands, that she sometimes gets the urge to stop older women in the street and say, how did you do it, how did you live through it? Or she could mention that she had been unprepared for this fierce spring in her, this feeling that isn't covered by the word 'love', which is far too small for it, that sometimes she thinks she might faint with the urgency of her feeling for him, that sometimes she misses him desperately even when he is right there, that it's like a form of madness, of possession, that often she has to creep into the room when he has fallen asleep just to look at him, to check, to whisper to him. But instead, she says, 'Fine. Good, thanks.'

Ted's father flicks ash to the ground, then looks Elina all over, from her sandalled feet, up her legs, over her torso, to her face. 'It suits you,' he says finally, with a smile.

She recalls, not for the first time, that Ted once described his father as 'a randy old goat' and she pictures him fleetingly with a white beard, tethered to a stake, straining at his chain. She feels her face twitching with amusement. 'What does?' she says, and with the effort of not laughing, the words come out louder than she intended.

He takes another drag of his cigarette, regarding her with narrowed eyes. She can see that, in his day, he would have been handsome. The blue eyes, the curled upper lip, the once-blond hair. Odd how the beautiful can't ever quite let go of that expectation, that assurance of admiration.

'Motherhood,' he says.

She tugs her skirt further down, over her knees. 'Do you think?'

'And how about my son?'

Elina glances at Ted and sees that he is alternately screwing his eyes shut and opening them again. 'What about him?' she asks, distracted.

'How is he acquitting himself as a father?'

'Um.' She watches as Ted sits forward in his deck-chair, putting a hand over first one eye then the other. 'Well,' she murmurs, 'fine, I think.'

Ted's father stubs out his cigarette in a saucer. 'It was easier in my time,' he says.

'Was it? How?'

He shrugs. 'Nothing was expected of us – no nappies, no cooking, nothing. We had it easy. Just turn up at bathtime every now and again, a trip to the park on Saturday mornings, that kind of thing, the zoo on birthdays. And that was it. It's hard for them.' He nods in Ted's direction.

She swallows. 'But how about—'

From across the garden, she hears someone say, 'Oh dear.' Elina is on her feet before she's even aware of moving. Ted's mother is holding out Jonah at arm's length, her nose wrinkled. 'I think he needs a bit of attention.'

'Of course.' Elina takes him, carries him against her shoulder into the house. Jonah twines his fingers into her hair and says, 'Ur-blur-mg,' into her ear, as if imparting a secret.

'Ur-blur-mg to you too,' she is whispering, as she picks up the bag from the hall, as she carries him into the bathroom. It is a small bathroom – Ted's mother calls it 'the cloakroom', and Elina had initially expected it to be filled with cloaks. She unpacks the wipes, the clean nappy, the tissues, and lays them out beside the sink. She then seats herself on the closed toilet seat and places Jonah across her lap.

'Eeeeeuuuuuurrrrrkkkkkk!' he shrieks gleefully, at the top of his voice, grabbing for his toes, for her hair, for her sleeve as she bends over him, and the noise bounces around the walls of the tiny bathroom.

'Ow,' she murmurs, as she disentangles her hair from his fingers, unpopping his suit. 'That's a very loud noise. Some would say it's a very—' Then she stops. Then she says: 'Oh.'

The shit has gone down Jonah's legs and up his back. It has soaked through his vest, his Babygro, his jacket and, now she thinks about it, it is soaking into her skirt as she sits there. He hasn't done one of these overflowing ones for ages and it would have to be here, it would have to be now.

'Damn,' she mutters, 'damn, damn.' She unpops the rest of the Babygro and eases Jonah's hands out of the sleeves, taking care to avoid smearing him. Jonah suddenly decides that the undressing is a step too far. His face looks unsure and then his lower lip goes stiff.

'No, no, no, no,' Elina says. 'It's OK, it's OK. Nearly done.' She whips the Babygro away, trying to hurry through the last bits. As she pulls the vest over his head, she must have caught his ear by mistake because he lets out a roar. His body goes stiff with outrage and he takes in a shuddering breath, ready for the next cry.

Elina balls up the shitty clothes and drops them on to the floor. She turns Jonah over very quickly, he screams and struggles, and she cleans the shit off his back as quickly as she can. It feels incredibly hot in here. Sweat is pricking at her upper lip, under her arms, in a trail down her back. Jonah is naked now, and furious, slippery with cleaning wipes, and she is scared she might drop him. She is just reaching for the clean nappy – get the nappy on, then everything will be all right – when she feels his body strain. She has the nappy in her hand, it's almost there, she is so close, when she looks down and Jonah is letting out another stream of shit.

It is an incredibly large amount. And it comes out with remarkable force. She will reflect on this later. It spatters the wall, the floor, her skirt, her shoes. She hears her own voice say, 'Oh, God,' and it sounds very far away. She is frozen for a moment, unable to move, unable to see what she should do next. She is holding the nappy under her chin, and as she starts scrabbling for the wipes, he lets out another. She can only think: There is shit all over Ted's mother's cloakroom. All over her. All over Jonah. Tears spring painfully into her eyes. She doesn't know, she can't see, what to clean first. The baby? The wall? The skirting-board? The impossibly white hand-towel? Her skirt? Her shoes? She can feel shit between her toes, squelching and sticky. She can feel it soaking through her skirt into her underwear. The smell is indescribable. And Jonah screams and screams.

Elina leans forward and unlatches the door. 'Ted!' she yells. 'TED!'

Clara swishes into the hall, one brow arched. Elina sees her pleated silk dress, the gold shoes that lace up her calves. 'Hi,' Elina says, in what she hopes is a normal voice, through a crack in the door. 'Could you ask Ted to come here?'

Minutes later, Ted is slipping into the cloakroom. Elina thinks she has never been so pleased to see him.

'Jesus Christ,' he says, surveying the room. 'What happened?'

'What does it look like?' she says wearily. 'Can you take Jonah?'

She sees him hesitate, glance down at his clothes.

'You can either take Jonah or clean the poo off the floor,' she says, over the noise. 'It's your choice.'

Ted takes his screaming, writhing son and holds him at arm's length. Elina wipes him again then straps a clean nappy on to him. 'Right, the clean clothes are there. You get him dressed and I'll clear this up.'

Ted squeezes past her to the basin and Elina gets on her hands and knees to mop the shit off the walls, the skirting-board, the floor. When she's finished, she steps past Ted, who is putting on Jonah's vest inside out.

She stands for a moment in the hallway, her back against the wall, her eyes shut. Jonah's screams are settling into hoarse, shuddering sobs. After an interval, she hears Ted step out of the cloakroom. She opens her eyes and there before her is her son, face wet with tears, his thumb jammed tight in his mouth.

'You need some clean clothes,' Ted says.

Elina sighs and brings her hands up to cover her face. 'Can we go home now?' she says through them.

Ted hesitates. 'My mum's just made a pot of tea. Do you mind if we stay for that? Then we'll go.'

She lets her hands drop; he avoids her eyes. She feels the possibility, the temptation of arguing over this, but then she remembers something. 'Is everything OK, by the way?'

He looks at her. 'What do you mean?'

'You were doing that thing again.'

'What thing?'

She mimes the blinking. 'That thing.'

'When?'

'In the garden. Just now. And you seem a bit . . . I don't know . . . out of it.'

'No, I don't.'

'Yes, you do. What's the matter? Did you have one of those things again? Did you—'

'It's fine. I'm fine.' Ted hefts Jonah to his shoulder. 'I'll ask my mum about some clothes,' he says, and disappears.

Elina follows Ted's mother up the stairs, up and up the winding centre, past door after shut door. She has never been in this part of the house. She doesn't think she's ever been further up than the big drawing room on the first floor. Ted's mother leads her two floors above this, to a bedroom thick with beige carpeting, with draped curtains held back with swags of tasselled material.

'Well,' Ted's mother says, opening her wardrobe, 'I don't know what I'll have that will fit you. You're so much bigger than me.' She pushes a hanger to one side, then another. 'Taller, I mean.'

Elina stands by the window, looking down into the street, into the square, into the gardens there, the trees swaying in the breeze. The leaves, she notices, are edged with orange-brown. Can autumn really be coming?

'How about this?'

Elina turns and sees that Ted's mother is holding out a dress in fawn jersey material. 'Great,' Elina says. 'Thanks.'

'Why don't you get changed in here?' Ted's mother says, opening a door, and Elina darts through.

She finds herself in a dressing room. The walls are papered with large yellow chrysanthemums and winding stems. There is a dressing-table by the window, covered with a surprising number of bottles, pots, tubs. Elina goes closer as she unfastens her skirt. As it drops to the floor, she tilts her head to read: 'anti-ageing formula', says one, 'for neck and décolletage', says another. She is smirking – who'd have suspected Ted's mother of such indulgences? – when she catches sight of herself, skirtless, in a shit-stained blouse, hair standing on end, grinning lopsidedly, in the mirror. She drops her gaze, rips off her blouse and pulls on the unpleasant dress. Just as she is struggling with the zip, she sees something else.

It is the right-angled corner of a canvas. Peeping out from its hiding-place behind the dressing-table. Here, in Ted's mother's dressing room. The incongruity of it makes her want to laugh.

At first she registers only this: its existence, the strangeness of its position between the furniture and the wall. She sees the thickness of the paint, the colours: grey, muted blue, black. At this point she lets go of the zip. She crouches beside it. She goes to touch it, to feel the grain of the paint, but stops herself at the last second.

Elina gets closer and closer to the canvas, then pulls back. She can see perhaps a ten-centimetre strip of the painting. She looks at the swirled colours, dripped thick to the canvas; she sees hairs from the brush, set deep into the paint. There is no doubt in her mind whose work this is but incredulity, disbelief, makes her crawl into the space under the dressing-table to see as much of the painting as she can. She crouches at skirting-board level, edging along the rim of the canvas, until she finds the artist's signature, unmistakable, in black paint, slightly smeared, at the bottom right-hand corner.

The knock at the door gives her such a fright that she thwacks her head on the underside of the dressing-table.

'Auts,' she whimpers. *'Kirota.'*

'Are you all right?' Ted's mother's voice comes from the other side of the door.

'Yes.' Elina shuffles backwards, rubbing her head. 'I'm fine. Sorry.' She opens the door, pushing hair away from her face. 'I . . . er . . . I . . .'

Ted's mother comes into the room. They regard each other for a moment, wary, unsure, like cats who have just met. It is not often they are alone together. Ted's mother looks about the room, in the manner of someone who thinks she may have been burgled.

'I dropped something,' Elina mumbles, 'and, er . . .'

'Do you need a hand with your zip?'

'Yes,' Elina says, relieved. 'Please.' She turns round. As Ted's mother's hands land on the small of her back, she sees the corner of the canvas again, the swirls and drips of paint. 'You've got a Jackson Pollock behind your dressing-table!' she blurts out.

Ted's mother's hands pause halfway up her back. 'Is that right?' The voice is cool, calm.

'Yes. Do you have any idea how much it's . . . I mean, that's not the point. But . . . it's incredibly valuable. And incredibly rare. I mean, how come . . . how did you . . . where did it—'

'It's been in the family for years.' The hand continues up to the nape of Elina's neck. Then Ted's mother walks towards the dressing-table. She looks down at the edge of the canvas. She touches the bottles and pots, as if counting them, straightens a hand mirror. 'There are others—'

'Other Pollocks?'

'No. I don't think so. Other paintings from the same era, I believe. It's not something I know much about, I'm afraid.'

'Where are they?'

She waves a hand through the air, dismissively. 'Around. I'll have to let you look at them one day.'

Elina swallows. She cannot quite catch up with the strangeness of this situation. She is here, in Ted's mother's dressing room, zipped into Ted's mother's dress, in the same room as a Jackson Pollock, which has been shoved behind some furniture like a piece of car-boot-sale tat, talking about a possibly priceless art collection as if it's an array of homemade doilies. 'Yes,' she manages to say, 'that would be good.'

Ted's mother gives a gracious smile, indicating the subject is now closed. 'How is your own work going? Are you managing to get anything done at present?'

'Er . . .' Elina has to think. Her own work? She can't even remember what that is. 'No. Not at the moment.' She scratches her head. She is unable to look away from the strip of that painting.

'Shall we go down?'

'Yes. Sure.' Elina turns towards the door, then back to the painting. 'Um, listen, Mrs R—'

'Oh, for heaven's sake,' Ted's mother interrupts, sweeping out of the dressing room, holding the door open for Elina. 'Call me Margot, please.'

Lexie sits at her desk in the *Courier* office, tapping her pen against the phone. Then she snatches up the receiver and dials. 'Felix?' she says. 'It's me.'

'My darling,' he says, down the phone, 'I was just thinking about you. Am I going to see you tonight?'

'No. I've got a deadline.'

'I'll come over. Later on.'

'No. Didn't you hear what I said? I've got a deadline. I need to work as soon as Theo goes down.'

'Ah.'

'You could always come and make him his dinner. Then I could start earlier.'

There is a short silence. 'Well,' Felix begins, 'I could, I suppose. The problem is—'

'Forget it,' Lexie says impatiently. 'Listen, I need a favour.'

'Anything.'

'The paper has asked me to go to Ireland to interview Eugene Fitzgerald.'

'Who?'

'Sculptor. Greatest living. It's extremely rare for him to agree to an interview—'

'I see.'

'So obviously' – Lexie ignores the interruption: she has to say this quickly or she'll never get it out – 'I have to go and I was wondering if you could come and look after Theo for me while I'm away.'

Another silence. This time stunned. 'Theo?' Felix says.

'Our son,' she clarifies.

'Yes, but . . . What about the Italian woman?'

'Mrs Gallo? She can't do it. I've already asked her. She has family visiting.'

'I see. Well, I'd love to. Obviously. The thing is—'

'OK,' Lexie snaps. 'Forget it. I had serious misgivings about even asking you, but if you can't be bothered to even contemplate looking after him for three days, then just forget it.'

Felix sighs. 'Did I say that? Did I say no?'

'You didn't need to.'

'Three days, you say?'

'I said forget it. I've changed my mind. I'll find someone else.'

'Darling, of course I'll have him for you. I'd love to.'

Lexie is silent this time, trying to sense if there's a catch in this, if he's lying.

'I'm sure my mother will come down from Suffolk,' he continues. 'She'd be delighted. You know how she dotes on the boy.'

Lexie sniffs, considering this. Felix's mother has taken everyone by surprise and put aside her initial horror at Felix and Lexie not being married and become a devoted grandmother, abandoning her WI meetings and jam-making at the drop of a hat to come to London to see Theo and to take him out for the day if Lexie needs to work. This is, if Lexie is honest, the outcome she'd been hoping for. She'd never leave Theo in the sole care of Felix. God only knows what would happen to him. But Felix's mother, Geraldine – there is something comforting and utterly dependable about her muddied wellies and silk headscarves. And Theo adores her. But Lexie is still annoyed that Felix sounded so reluctant at first. 'I'll see,' she says.

'Very well,' Felix replies, and she can hear the amusement in his voice. 'I'll speak to my mother about it, shall I? See if the old girl's willing?'

'If you like,' Lexie says, and hangs up the phone.

In the event, Geraldine Roffe is tied up. She is sorry but she cannot get out of whatever church activity she's committed to. It's something to do with the altar cloths and their need to be laundered – the precise details are unclear to Lexie. She has, then, no option but to take Theo with her. It is early February. England is shrouded in misty sleet; dirty snow is piled up at the sides of the pavements. She takes a train to Swansea and then catches the night ferry to Cork. She clings to the rails as the boat rides the steel-grey waves of the Irish Sea. She pulls Theo's knitted hat far down over his ears, tucking a blanket around him. The boat docks in a blue, drizzling dawn at Cork. Lexie changes a nappy on the floor of a toilet in the port. Theo screams and kicks out at this indignity and several women come to stand and watch. She catches a train towards the ragged dog-legged coastline. Theo presses his face to the window, letting out a stream of surprised nouns: horse, gate, tractor, tree. They arrive on the Dingle peninsula around lunchtime and Theo's vocabulary runs dry. Sea, Lexie tells him, beach, sand.

When the train slows and she sees a green sign with SKIBBERLOUGH flash past, she jumps to her feet, puts Theo in his carrier, hauls it to her shoulders and pulls her suitcase down from the rack. SKIBBERLOUGH – SKIBBERLOUGH – SKIBBERLOUGH, the window tells her, SKIBB— She swings open the door and has to step back: below her there is no platform, just a large drop to a muddy path beside the train tracks. Lexie peers out of the door, looks up and down. The station, if you can call it that, is deserted. There is a small wooden shelter, the green sign, the single set of rails – and nothing else.

She hurls the suitcase to the ground with a thud and climbs down after it. The train begins to clank and groan as it gathers itself into movement. Theo chatters and exclaims at the sight, the noise of it. Lexie hauls her suitcase up out of the mud and, as she reaches the wooden shelter, a man appears from around it.

'Excuse me,' Lexie says. 'I wonder if you can help me—'

'Miss Sinclair, I assume, of the *Daily Courier*,' the man says, in a clipped English accent. Not Fitzgerald, then. He is unsmiling, slightly dishevelled, his collar crooked, his jacket undone. He takes her in with an expression of naked shock – her muddy shoes, the child on her back, her disarrayed hair – but refrains from comment. Wisely, Lexie feels. 'This way.' He reaches out for her suitcase, closes his fingers around the handle.

Lexie doesn't let go. 'I can manage,' she says, 'thank you.'

The man shrugs and relinquishes the handle.

Beside the road there is an open-backed truck that, beneath the filth and rust, would once have been red. The man climbs into the driver's seat and fires the engine while Lexie tries to find a place for her suitcase in the back, which is mainly occupied with dog baskets and rolls of chicken wire.

When she has sat herself in the passenger seat, with Theo on her knee, when they have swung out on to the road, Lexie turns to examine her driver. She clocks the glasses, folded and stuck into the breast pocket of his tweed jacket, the stain of blue ink on the index finger of his right hand; she clocks the book pushed between the car seats, the week-old copy of an English newspaper – not hers, the *Courier*'s direct competitor – beside it, the hair pushed back off the brow, greying a little at the temples.

'So,' she begins, 'you work with Fitzgerald?'

The man frowns, just as she had known he would. 'No.'

They continue along a narrow road for some minutes in silence.

'Brrm, brrm,' Theo comments.

Lexie smiles at him, then turns to look at a church as it flashes past, the woman coming out of its wooden doors. 'You're a friend of his?'

He doesn't frown this time. Just says, 'No,' out of the corner of his mouth.

'A neighbour?'

'No.'

'A relative?'

'No.'

'His valet?'

'No.'

'His dealer? His doctor? His priest?'

'None of the above.'

'Do you always answer questions with one-word answers?'

The man glances in the rear-view mirror, removes a hand from the wheel to scratch his chin. The road rolls past. Twisted, blackened branches of thorn trees, a donkey tethered to a stake. 'Technically,' he says, 'they were not questions.'

'They were.'

'No.' The man shakes his head. 'They were statements. You said, "You work with Fitzgerald. You are a relative." I merely refuted what you said.'

Lexie turns to look at this trespasser on her field of expertise. 'Questions can be formed from statements.'

'They can't.'

'Grammatically speaking, they can.'

'No, they can't. It wouldn't be allowed in a court of law.'

'We're not in a court of law,' Lexie points out. 'We are, I believe, in your truck.'

'Truck!' Theo shouts.

'Not my truck,' says the man. 'Fitzgerald's truck. One of.'

'So is that what you are? A lawyer?'

The man seems to consider this for a moment. Then he says, 'No.'

'A barrister?' she suggests.

He shakes his head.

'A judge?'

'Wrong again.'

'A spy? A secret agent?'

He laughs for the first time and it is a surprisingly nice laugh – deep, resonant. Hearing it, Theo breaks into laughter too.

'I can't see any other reason for your secrecy. Go on, you can tell me. I won't breathe a word to anyone.'

He swings the car round a hairpin bend. 'You expect me to believe that, coming from a journalist?' They hit a pothole and the car jounces violently, the three of them jolting in their seats. Theo finds this very funny too. 'I don't want to tell you the truth now,' he admits, 'because it would seem so dull. I feel honour bound to protract the fantasy life you've constructed for me.'

'Go on. Put me out of my misery.'

'I'm a biographer.'

Lexie considers this. She glances again at the inked finger, the folded glasses. Then she smiles. 'I see,' she says.

'What do you see?'

She shrugs, looking out of the windscreen. 'I see everything now.'

'What, precisely?'

'You. Why you're being quite so . . . prickly. You don't want me here. You're busy beavering away on a biography of Fitzgerald and the last thing you need is a bit of competition turning up.'

'Competition?' The car ascends a steep bit of hill and suddenly they are out of the trees and pulling up next to a large, crumbling house built on the bluff. 'My dear woman, if you think your interview, or whatever you're doing with Fitzgerald, poses any kind of threat to my work, I have to tell you that you're labouring under a grave delusion.'

Lexie pushes open her door, settling Theo on her hip, and reaches for her suitcase. 'Tell me, do you write the way you talk?' she says.

He heaves himself out of the truck and regards her over the roof. 'What do you mean?'

'I just wondered whether it was a general principle of yours to use twenty words where ten might do.'

He laughs again and strides across the gravel towards the door of the house. When he reaches it, he half turns. 'At least I know the difference between a question and a statement.'

Lexie slams the car door and follows him into the house.

There is no sign of Fitzgerald anywhere. And by the time she and Theo have climbed the steps, the man has disappeared. Lexie stands in the hallway. Several threadbare rugs cover the stone-flagged floor. A large, wide staircase sweeps up to the floor above. On the walls, spotted old hunting scenes are mixed with charcoal sketches of abstract shapes. There's a coat-stand heaped with moth-eaten jackets and several umbrellas without fabric. A striped cat sleeps half in and half out of an upturned straw hat. A heap of dirty dishes lies abandoned on a wicker chair. The ceiling above them is domed and Theo, tipping his head back, shouts, 'Echo! Echo!' The ceiling sends back his voice, smaller, distorted, and he and Lexie laugh.

A woman in an apron appears out of a door, frowning at the noise. She leads Lexie and Theo through another door, muttering to herself about how no one does any work around here except herself, along a dark passageway and up some narrow steps at the back of the house.

She bangs open the door of a whitewashed room with sloping ceilings and an unnaturally high bed, and gestures Lexie to go in. Lexie asks her the name of the man who drove the car and receives the reply: 'Mr Lowe.'

Lexie thinks for a moment. 'Robert Lowe?'

The housekeeper shrugs. 'I wouldn't know.'

Lexie asks how long he's been here and the housekeeper rolls her eyes and says, 'Too long.' Lexie lets out a laugh. The housekeeper is suddenly content to play with Theo as Lexie unpacks. Robert Lowe works all day, she tells Lexie, clapping her hands at Theo, who claps back. His room is a mess of notes and papers and books. An impossible mess. He doesn't say much to anyone, but his wife sends him a telegram every week. The woman seems shocked by the expense of this. Mr Lowe writes to her every day. He walks into the village to post the letter. The wife is an invalid. The woman whispers this last word. In a wheelchair, God love her. I see, Lexie says. And does Mr Lowe spend much time with Mr Fitzgerald? The woman grins and shakes her head. No. Himself, as she refers to Fitzgerald, is working on something, something big, and doesn't want to be disturbed. Every day Mr Lowe goes knocking on the studio door and every day Himself is telling him, no, not today.

When the housekeeper leaves, Theo falls asleep almost instantly. Lexie lays out her notebooks and pens on the dressing-table. She changes into a warmer sweater, peers out of the tiny square window, set deep into the thick stone walls. She can see a small patio below, gilded with moss, an abandoned wooden table, chairs leaning against it. A long-legged black dog wanders across the patio, stops to sniff at the ground, then skitters off in the opposite direction.

Lexie is, she realises, famished. Carefully, carefully, so that he doesn't wake, she eases Theo into his carrier and hefts his sleeping weight to her back. The narrow landing along which she'd walked is empty, lined with vacant chairs. She opens a door off it at random and finds a library filled with the smell of mould; she opens another into a bathroom, the paint peeling off the walls, the tub stained green by a dripping tap. She goes down the back stairs and finds the kitchen and, after hesitating a few moments, opens a cupboard. It's filled with plates and cups and fishing tackle, stacked haphazardly together. She falls then upon an earthenware pot with a lid and finds a half-loaf of bread. She tears off a piece and pushes it into her mouth.

She wanders around the patio, the gardens, the lawns choked with dock and clover. Theo sleeps on and on, his head a warm pressure on her neck. She finds a swimming-pool, filled only with leaves and a puddle of dirty water. She walks out on to the diving-board and stands there, a woman and a child suspended in space, for a moment. She circles an outhouse or barn with high, yellow-lit windows and the sounds of scraping and clattering coming from within. It must be Fitzgerald's studio. She circles it again but can't see anything other than the barn ceiling, studded with lights. She returns to her room, lays Theo carefully on the bed and lies next to him. Within about five seconds she is asleep.

A loud crashing sound wakes her. She sits up, shocked, still in the depths of a dream about Innes, about the *Elsewhere* office. The room is dark and shadowed, icy cold. Theo lies beside her, feet in the air, thumb in mouth, humming to himself.

'Mama,' he says, seizing her around the windpipe, 'Mama sleeping.'

'That's right,' she says. 'But I'm awake now.'

She scrambles from the bed. The sound comes again and this time she realises what it is. A gong. It must be dinner-time. She flicks on the light, ransacks her clothes to find a cardigan and yanks it on over her sweater; she pulls a brush through her hair; she applies a swift slick of lipstick, then lifts Theo off the bed and they make their way downstairs.

The dining room is deserted. Three places are laid at the table, with three steaming bowls of soup. But there is no one to eat them. Feeling like Goldilocks in the wrong house, Lexie sits in front of one and eats it, feeding every second spoonful to Theo, who stands at her side.

'Where is everyone?' she says to him, and he looks at her face, straining to understand.

'Everyone,' he says back.

She drinks a glass of wine. She is tempted to start on a second bowl of soup, but restrains herself. She breaks a roll into pieces and eats those. Theo finds a basket of pine cones and begins taking them out, one by one, and putting them back, one by one. The housekeeper stumps in with a dish of roast potatoes and cold cuts of meat, which she thumps down on the table with bad grace, muttering about the empty chairs. Lexie helps herself. She eats, looking around the room, feeding some to Theo when he can be distracted from the pine cones.

She leaves the table and wanders to the fireplace – which is enormous and piled with blazing logs – warming her back and watching Theo, who is balancing pine cones along the hearth. She is chewing a piece of bread from the basket on the table. Empty sofas and chairs are arranged around her, as if she is a hostess expecting a large party of people. Around the walls are numerous framed pictures. Lexie moves over to look. A sketch of Fitzgerald's, a watercolour, a pencil study of a naked woman; she moves on, shifting from one foot to the next. She pushes the last crust between her teeth as she studies an Yves Klein.

'That's not his,' a voice behind her says.

Lexie doesn't turn round. 'I know that,' she says. She hears him sit heavily in one of the chairs at the dining-table. She hears him spooning potatoes on to his plate. She moves on to the next picture – a sketch by Dalí.

'Hello,' Theo shouts, sprinting towards him over the carpet, evidently delighted by the appearance of someone else.

Lexie hears him murmur, 'Hello,' back, and then: 'What have you got there?'

'Hello!' Theo shouts again.

'I've read one of your books,' Lexie says.

'Oh, really.' He's trying to sound casual but she's not convinced. 'Which one?'

'The Picasso.'

'Ah.'

'I thought it was good.'

'Thank you.'

'Although you were rather hard on Dora Maar.'

'Do you think?'

Lexie turns to look at him. He has changed his clothes. A white shirt, open-necked, a different jacket. 'Yes. You depicted her as a groupie, a hanger-on. But she was a talented artist in her own right.'

Robert Lowe raises an eyebrow. 'Have you seen any of her work?'

'No,' Lexie says. 'I'm basing my opinion on no knowledge whatsoever.' She comes and sits opposite him at the table. Theo climbs into her lap, a pine cone clutched in each fist.

'Careful,' he says to Robert. 'Soup hot.'

Robert smiles at him. 'Thank you. I'll be very careful, I promise.'

'Where is Fitzgerald, anyway?' Lexie says.

'Careful, careful,' Theo warns again.

Robert shrugs, opens his hands, then closes them again. 'Where indeed?'

'Is that his studio in the barn out there?'

Robert nods. 'He could be in there or he could be out hunting for pheasant. Or he could well be in the pub in the village, on the prowl for young girls. He might be out tracking foxes. Or he could have driven to Dublin. No one knows. Fitzgerald keeps to his own schedule.'

'Hot,' Theo exclaims, and Robert nods, makes a show of blowing on the surface of his soup.

Lexie folds her napkin. 'Well, maybe I should just go and knock on the door and tell him—'

'He won't answer. Even if he's there.'

Lexie looks at him. It's impossible to know if he's telling the truth. 'But he might not know that it's dinner-time.'

'Believe me, he'll know. He'll just have chosen not to come. We're at his mercy. We have to wait for him to come to us.'

'Really?' She reaches for an apple from the fruit bowl. 'How very . . . nineteenth century.'

'Nineteenth century?'

'Yes. As if we're young maidens, meekly awaiting our suitor.'

Robert harrumphs into his soup. 'I don't feel like a young maiden.'

She laughs. 'You don't look like one either.'

Robert places his cutlery on his plate and pushes it to one side. 'Thank you. I think.' He takes a long time selecting a piece of fruit for himself. He picks up an apple, puts it down; he toys with a plum, then discards it before settling finally on a pear. 'You're married to that war-reporter chap, aren't you?' he says, as he slices it lengthways.

'Pear!' Theo shouts in delight. 'Pear!'

Lexie twists the stalk off her apple with a snap. 'Not married.'

'Oh. Well. I merely meant that you're . . .' He circles his knife in the air, waiting for her to fill the gap.

She refuses to help him out. 'I'm what?'

'With him. Together. An item. A couple. Lovers. Partners. However you want to put it.' He hands Theo a slice of the pear.

'Hmm,' Lexie says, sinking her teeth into her apple. 'How did you know?'

'Know what?'

'About Felix. And me.'

'That's a rather paranoid question,' he says.

'Is it?'

'I saw you with him once, at a book launch. A year or two ago. You were pregnant at the time.'

'Was I? Which book launch?'

'That biography of Hitler.'

Lexie thinks. 'I don't remember meeting you.'

'You didn't.' He smiles. 'Television folk tend not to mix with men of letters.'

She is riled now. 'I'm not television folk.'

'You're married to one.'

'No, I'm not.'

'Married, attached. Let's not split hairs.' He cuts Theo another slice of pear. 'I met you before that, though.'

Lexie looks at him. 'When?'

'A long time ago.' He's concentrating on his plate, on a piece of pear, which he is peeling, defrocking. 'You came to my house once.'

'Did I?'

'With Innes Kent.'

Lexie puts down her apple, straightens her fork. She smooths the hair off Theo's brow, pulls his bib straight.

'My wife is quite a collector of art,' Robert says. 'She bought a few things from Innes. We always trusted his judgement – he knew what he was about.'

She clears her throat. 'He did.'

'You came with a Barbara Hepworth lithograph, I think it was. We still have it. He had it propped up in the back of his car. You stood in our hall and talked to our daughter about fire engines while Innes brought it in.'

She takes up her fork, a slim, silver thing. It feels peculiarly unbalanced, top heavy, as if it might pitch forward out of her hand if she doesn't cling to it. 'I remember,' she says. 'It was . . .'

He shoots her a glance from under his brow, then looks away. 'It was a long time ago,' he finishes for her.

'Yes.'

They eat in silence.

The next day Theo wakes up early and so, therefore, does Lexie. She manages to persuade him to stay in the room until seven. Then she bathes in astonishingly cold water and they are out in the courtyard after breakfast. She needs to do the interview with Fitzgerald today; she has to see the work; and then she has to get back to London.

She asks the housekeeper if she would mind Theo for her and the housekeeper is very happy to do so. Lexie watches them wander off together towards the orchard, with a basket of washing and some pegs. The housekeeper is talking and Theo is exclaiming lots of words back to her: peg, flower, foot, shoe, grass.

The doors of the studio are shut but the padlock that was on them last night hangs unlocked from a chain. Lexie stands next to it, staring at it. She puts a hand around it. It is, she thinks, the size of a human heart.

'He won't be in there,' Robert says, from behind her, 'not at this time of the day.'

She whirls round. 'Do you make a habit of creeping up on people?'

'Not always.'

She sighs, her breath exploding white into her face. 'I've got to get back to London. I was hoping to get to the ferry tonight.'

He frowns, kicks at a stone. 'Are you going all that way on your own?'

'No,' she says. 'I'll have Theo with me.'

'That's not what I meant,' he murmurs. 'I meant that it's not . . . it's hardly ideal, is it?'

'What?'

'A woman alone, travelling about with a young child.'

'It's fine,' she says, a touch impatiently. 'And it's not as if I have any choice.' She takes two steps away from the studio door, then stops. 'I don't know what to do,' she says, almost to herself. 'I can't hang around indefinitely like this.'

A loud hammering sounds behind her. Robert Lowe is banging on the barn door with a closed fist. Almost immediately, it opens a crack.

'Fitzgerald,' Robert says, 'may I introduce you to Lexie Sinclair, from the *Daily Courier* in London? You agreed to an interview with her, I believe. She has to hot-foot it back to London tonight. Would you be able to see her now? Here she is.'

The interview goes rather well. Fitzgerald shows her a nude he's working on. He is forthcoming and lucid, which she's heard is not always the case. Maybe she got to him early enough in the day. She asks him about his childhood and he gives her several quotable stories about his violent father. He is garrulous on the subject of his inspiration, on the history of his house, his views on the Anglo-Irish in Ireland. At the end of the interview Lexie makes a show of putting down her shorthand pad, just as she always does, because an interviewee will always say the most interesting, most revealing things if they are under the illusion that they are no longer on record. Innes taught Lexie this and she thinks of him every time she puts down her pad. Make them think you're their friend, Lex, he'd told her, and they'll tell you anything, show you everything.

Fitzgerald shows her his tools, the rows and rows of chisels, the type of hammer he prefers. He shows her the blocks of marble he is yet to start on. He starts to talk about his wives, counting them off on his fingers. He becomes graphic on the subject of sex. Lexie nods distantly, her head on one side. She is sure to keep the bench between them. But as she's thanking him and turning to leave, he catches her arm and presses her up against the hard edge of a sink, his old-man breath in her face, his arthritic fingers clutching at her waist.

Lexie clears her throat. 'I'm flattered, really I am,' she says, beginning the words of the speech she always delivers at a time like this, 'but I'm afraid—' She immediately forgets the rest of her speech because she sees that Robert Lowe is standing in the room with them.

Fitzgerald turns. 'Yes?' he snaps, at his biographer. 'What can we do for you?'

'Miss Sinclair is wanted on the telephone,' Robert says, his eyes averted.

Lexie slides herself out from between the basin and Fitzgerald's pelvis and walks towards the door with as much nonchalance as she can muster.

In the hallway, she picks up the receiver. 'Lexie Sinclair,' she says. She waits a moment, then replaces it and goes into the kitchen. Robert is sitting in an armchair by the range, a book in his lap. 'There's no one there,' she says.

He doesn't look up. 'I know.'

'Well, then, what . . . ?' She gazes at him, perplexed. 'Why would you do that?'

He coughs and mumbles something that sounds like '. . . of course.'

'I beg your pardon?'

'I said,' he glances up now, 'I thought perhaps the interview had run its course.'

Lexie is silent.

'But I'm sorry if I interrupted.'

'No.' She looks away into the garden. 'You didn't. It was . . . The interview was finished. I should . . . I thought . . . Well, thank you.'

'It was my pleasure,' he says quietly. They look at each other for a moment and then she turns and leaves the room, heading up the stairs to pack her case.

On a Saturday afternoon Lexie is standing in her bedroom. Theo is in the room next door, asleep, tired out by a long walk across the Heath. She is sorting through a pile of toys that has collected around her chest of drawers. A dog on a string, a tin drum, a rubber ball, which slips through her fingers and bounces away over the boards, vanishing under the bed.

She bends to find it, lifting the edge of the counterpane and looking under the bed. She sees the ball, just out of reach; she sees a shoe lying on its side; she sees something else, further in. Lexie peers closer. She reaches in and gets hold of it. It is a hairband. One of those rigid plastic ones that grip your head. Polka dots, white on navy blue. Lined with rows of small, sharp teeth.

Lexie sits back on her heels. She holds the hairband at arm's length, between thumb and finger. There is a long, lightish hair attached to it, like the sticky thread of a spider. She tweaks the hair off it, holds it up to the light. In her other hand, she turns the hairband over. She examines every plane, every surface of it, every tiny tooth. Then she drops it and the hair to the bedside table.

She stands. She walks to the window. She looks down into the street, her arms folded. A man and a woman are getting out of a car below; the woman tugs at the hemline of her skirt as she steps to the pavement; the man is bouncing a tennis ball as he stands waiting for her, bounce, catch, bounce, catch; the woman is laughing at him, tossing her hair in the bright sun.

Lexie turns. She goes downstairs, into the kitchen, where she pours herself a glass of wine. She walks about drinking it. She goes to her paintings and seems to count them: the Pollock, the Hepworth, the Klein. They are all here. She touches each one, as if to reassure herself. Back up the stairs, into Theo's room to check on him, into her own where she avoids looking at the hairband. She tidies her notes on the desk, reads through a line or two of her current piece. She straightens a lamp. She lifts a hairbrush from the dresser, puts it down. Then she opens the window. She picks up a shirt of Felix's, a grey one with a long collar, from where he left it last night on a chair and flings it out into the warm, afternoon air. It floats, arms stretched out, down to the front garden where it comes to rest near a bank of tulips. She takes a few sips of her wine. Then she picks up a pair of his socks, drops them out of the window. She follows this with some cufflinks from the dresser, a belt, a fistful of ties, which writhe and snake as they fall to the ground.

As Felix is paying the taxi driver, he sees a number of people grouped on the pavement. They are all looking up at something, pointing. Felix shifts his wallet to his other hand. At this point it occurs to him that the group of people are near Lexie's flat – but nothing more.

Then he sees it is Lexie's flat they are pointing at. He crosses the road, shoving his wallet into his jacket. He sees Lexie, or her head and shoulders, appear from her window. In her hands is a suitcase. Which she drops. It falls with a crash to the front step. She reappears a second later with an armful of what look like clothes. These, she also empties into the garden.

Felix breaks into a sprint. 'Lexie!' he shouts, as he rounds the gate. 'What the hell's going on?'

She leans against the window-frame. She tosses a silk handkerchief out into the air, then a tie, then a pair of underpants, like a croupier dealing cards. Felix moves forward in an attempt to catch them but stumbles on the suitcase, then slides on a stack of records.

'Nothing,' she says. 'Or, rather, nothing out of the ordinary.'

'Christ almighty, Lexie.' Felix is furious now. 'What in God's name do you think you're doing?'

'Giving you a hand clearing your stuff out of my flat.' She says this with a flick of her wrist and a toothbrush comes hurtling towards him.

Felix darts to catch it but misses. Two people in the crowd behind him say, 'Ooooh.'

Felix draws himself up to his not inconsiderable height. 'May I ask what this is all about?'

Lexie disappears from the window for a moment, then reappears, holding something out to him. 'This,' she says, and drops it.

It is horseshoe-shaped, flimsy, and it twists in the air before it falls to the steps, bouncing towards him. Felix picks it up. It is blue with white spots. A hairband. For a moment he can't place it, but there's one thing he knows for sure – it's not Lexie's. He experiences, for the first time, a slight tremor of foreboding. 'My darling,' he says, stepping forward, 'I have no idea where this came from. I don't think I've ever seen it before and—'

'It was under the bed.'

'Well, isn't it entirely possible that the charlady left it there? I mean . . . Look,' he says, 'we can't talk about it like this. I'm coming in.'

'You can't,' she says, pushing her hair off her brow. 'I've bolted the door. You're not coming in here ever again, Felix, and that's final.'

'Lexie, I'll say it again. I have no idea where this came from. It's nothing to do with me, I assure you.'

'I'll tell you where it came from,' Lexie says, leaning menacingly out of the window. 'It came from the head of Margot Kent.'

'It can't possibly . . .' He falters to a stop. There is a fatal pause before he continues, 'I'm not sure I even . . .'

Lexie folds her arms, looking down at him. 'I told you,' she says quietly. 'I warned you. I said, not her. And you have the gall,' her voice rises to a shout, 'to do it with her, here, in my flat. In my bed. You're a shit, Felix Roffe. How bloody dare you?'

He has no idea what she's talking about. He doesn't even remember the girl. Unless it's that pallid wisp of a creature who made a play for him that time and has been phoning him up ever since. Could it be that one? Felix feels a weakening in his chest. He did have her here, come to think about it, while Lex was away in Ireland. His flat was having plumbing work done. But he hadn't meant to. And, frankly, it's unlike Lexie to be threatened by a girl like that.

'Sweetie,' he attempts to speak soothingly, his usual tone with Lexie, 'don't you think you're getting this a little out of proportion? Whatever it was, it was nothing. You know me. Nothing at all. Why don't you let me in and we can talk about it properly?'

Lexie shakes her head. 'No. I knew she'd do this. I knew it. I warned you, Felix, I warned you and I always mean what I say.'

'What do you mean,' he says, 'you warned me? Warned me about what?'

'About her. About Margot Kent.'

'When?'

'After that lunch at Claridge's.'

'What lunch at Claridge's?'

'We saw her outside and I said, stay away from her, and you promised me you would.'

'I didn't.'

'You did.'

'Lexie, I have no memory whatsoever of this conversation. But I can see you're upset. Why don't you let me in and we can—'

'No. That's it, I'm afraid. Everything should be there.' She gestures at the garden. 'Goodbye, Felix. Good luck with getting it back to your place.' She slams the window shut.

It is one of their more dramatic splits. And, as things turn out, their last.

A week or so later, Lexie was having a bad day. She had been late for an appointment with someone at the Arts Council, the Tube train having sat in a tunnel for half an hour. She was supposed to be writing a piece on a production of *Accidental Death of an Anarchist* but the director she'd been hoping to speak to had come down with shingles so Lexie had to push the piece back a week and come up with something else at short notice. Felix had called three times this morning, in contrite, pleading mode. Lexie hung up on him every time. Theo had looked this morning as if he was coming down with a cold, and at the back of Lexie's mind all day was the hope that it was only a cold. She still hadn't got used to the constant undertow of maternal anxiety, the pull he exuded from their house in Dartmouth Park, as she went about her business in central London. He was her magnetic north and her needle swung always in his direction.

'Thank you so much . . .' Lexie was saying into her telephone, already halfway out of her seat and scrabbling with her spare hand for her bag under the desk. 'Please tell her I really appreciate it . . . Yes, absolutely . . . I'll be there in half an hour at the latest.'

She yanked on her coat, hauled her bag on to the desk and threw in a pad and pencil. 'Off to Westminster,' she said to her colleagues, 'if anyone asks. Back soon.'

She hurried into the corridor, belting her coat, going over in her mind what she needed to establish in the interview, when someone touched her elbow. She jumped and whirled round. There, next to her, was a man. The corduroy jacket, the open-necked white shirt were instantly familiar but it took her a moment to place him.

Robert Lowe. It was such an incongruous, such an unexpected sight – Robert Lowe in the dingy corridor of the *Courier* – that she laughed. 'Robert,' she said. 'It's you.'

He shrugged. 'It's me.'

'What are you doing here?'

'Actually,' he began, and then he stopped. 'I . . . I was seeing a friend who works at the *Telegraph* and . . . I thought, seeing as I'm on Fleet Street, that I'd come and look you up. But,' he gestured at her coat and her bag, 'you look as if you aren't in a position to be looked up.'

'Oh,' she said, 'I'm not. I'm having a rather disastrous day. I've got to go over to Westminster.'

'I see.' He nodded, pushed his hands into his pockets. 'Well . . .'

'You could walk me down to the street . . . if you like . . .'

'The street?'

'I have to find a taxi.'

'Ah.'

'Only if you have time.'

'I do,' he said. 'I will.'

Lexie walked ahead of him on the stairs. 'How are you?'

'I'm fine. And you?'

'Fine. As well. When did you get back from Ireland?'

'Yesterday.'

'Did you get much out of Fitzgerald?'

'Not a great deal.' He smiled. 'He's not an easy subject, as you know.'

'Yes.'

'I'll have to go back. In a month or so. Sometimes you can catch him on a talkative day. As you did. He was rather disappointed when you left.' He held open the door for her and as she passed through she thought she heard him add, 'As were we all,' but she wasn't sure.

Outside, the sky was flat and white above them. Lexie stood at the kerb, looking up and down Fleet Street. 'No taxis,' she said, 'of course.'

'There never are, when you want one.' He cleared his throat, folded his arms, then unfolded them. 'How's Theo?'

'He's fine. Got a bit of a cold.'

Robert came to stand next to her at the kerb. 'It means "God's gift",' he said.

'What does?' Lexie was distracted, straining her eyes into the traffic, searching for an orange light.

'His name. Theodore.'

She looked at him, amazed. 'Does it?'

'Yes. From the Greek *theos,* meaning God, and *doron,* meaning gift.'

'I had no idea. God's gift. You're the only person in the world who'd know that.'

There was a pause. They were two people standing on a pavement in the watery London sunshine, waiting for a taxi. It was a simple scenario but it seemed suddenly fraught with significance and Lexie wasn't sure why. She had to swallow and glance down at the ground to clear her head of the thought. 'It's nice to see you,' she said because it was and she couldn't for the life of her work out why he was here, on a Wednesday morning, in Fleet Street.

'Is it?' He passed a hand through his hair. Then he stretched his arm up in the air. 'There you are,' he said. 'Look.' A taxi slowed, swerved and arrived at the kerb.

'Thank God,' Lexie said, and climbed in. Robert shut the door for her. 'Goodbye,' she said, and put her hand out of the window. 'I'm sorry I had to dash.'

He took it and held it. 'I'm sorry too.'

'It was lovely to see you.'

'It was lovely to see you too.' They were talking like caricatures or people in a bad play. It was unbearable. He released her hand and she watched out of the window as the figure on the pavement got smaller and smaller.

A few days later she was coming into the reporters' room when her colleague Daniel waved the telephone receiver at her. 'For you, Lexie.'

'Lexie Sinclair,' she said.

'It's Robert Lowe,' came the familiar voice. 'Tell me, are you dashing about again today?'

'No. Not today. I'm . . . What am I doing? I'm lounging. By comparison.'

'I see. I'm not sure what lounging constitutes but does it allow for lunch?'

'It does.'

'Good. I'll be outside at one.'

In the event, they came straight to the point. There was no hedging, no pursuit, no uncertainty, no seduction. Lexie walked up to where he stood on the pavement. Neither of them said hello or made any greeting. She drew a cigarette out of the packet, put it into her mouth.

'You strike me,' he said, after a moment, 'as someone who is good with secrets.'

'Good in what way?' she said, searching her bag for matches.

'In that you keep them.'

'Oh, yes,' she said, and held the flare of a match to her mouth. 'Yes, of course.'

'You know that I'm married?'

'I do.'

'And so are you,' he held his hands up to ward off her interjection, 'or whatever you want to call it. I have no desire to leave my wife. And yet . . .'

Lexie exhaled her smoke. 'And yet,' she agreed.

'What shall we do?'

She thought for a moment. It occurred to her afterwards that he might have been talking about where to eat lunch. But at the time, she said, 'A hotel?'

Such deals can be struck so easily sometimes.

They went to a street near the British Museum where there were several hotels that accepted people during the day. Lexie didn't ask how Robert knew this. The room had velvet curtains of a faded blue, a potted fern, a washbasin with a chipped mirror. There was an electricity meter that wouldn't accept any of their shillings. The pillows were hard, the sharp ends of feathers prickling from the cotton cases. They were both nervous. They made love quickly, more from a desire to get it done, to gain that sense of having embarked. Then they talked. Robert tried again to feed shillings into the meter, with no success. They made love again, with more leisure and more skill this time. As she dressed, Lexie watched the clouds piled up beyond the narrow window.

The arrangement they devised was simple, straightforward, perfect, you might say, worked out in moments. They would meet twice a year, no more, and never in London. An exchange of telegrams was to be their method. THE GRAND HOTEL, SCARBOROUGH, they might read, THURSDAY 9 MARCH. And nothing more. No one was ever to know. They never spoke of Robert's family, of his wife Marie. Lexie never enlightened him as to what had happened with her and Felix.

Robert never asked, never questioned why Theo always came with her to their assignations. Perhaps he guessed the truth of the situation, perhaps not.

It was hard to know whether Theo remembered Robert, from one time to the next. He was always pleased to see him, always took him by the hand and dragged him away to show him something – a crab in a bucket, a shell from the beach, a stone with a hole worn through it.

Mrs Gallo and Lexie were in the kitchen, fiddling with the cooker dials and arguing amiably about whether or not it was right for Mrs Gallo to cook Lexie a chicken pie. Mrs Gallo had just commandeered the oven when the doorbell rang.

'I'll go,' said Lexie, backing away from the oven and touching Theo's head as she passed. He was piling cushions into a soft, towering heap.

'Darling,' Felix said, when she opened the door, stepping forward to envelop her in a rather lingering embrace, 'how are you?'

'Fine.' Lexie disentangled herself from him. 'I didn't know you were coming. You should have phoned.'

'Don't be anti-social. Can't I drop in on my son and heir if I want to?'

'Of course. But you should phone first.' They glared at each other in the close confines of the hallway.

'Why?' he said, without moving his eyes from her face. 'Who have you got here?'

She sighed. 'Paul Newman, of course. And Robert Redford. Come and meet them.'

'Going away, are you?' he said, pointing at the bags in the hall. Lexie and Theo had just returned from seeing Robert in Eastbourne.

'Just got back, actually,' she threw over her shoulder, as she walked into the sitting room, where Mrs Gallo was watching Theo leap off the sofa and on to the cushions.

Felix stood at the edge of the rug, like a man hesitating before deep water. 'Hello, young man,' he boomed down at Theo, before nodding at Mrs Gallo. 'Mrs Gallo, how are you? You're looking terribly well.'

Mrs Gallo, who did not entertain a high opinion of Felix, based on the view that any man worth his salt would have made an honest woman of Lexie long ago, gave a sound between a tut and a cough.

Theo looked up at his father and said, with devastating clarity, 'Robert.'

Lexie almost laughed but managed to stop herself. 'Not Robert, sweetheart, it's Felix. Felix. Remember?'

'Who's Robert?' Felix was saying, as Lexie went into the kitchen.

She ignored him. 'Would you like tea, Felix? Coffee?'

He followed her into the kitchen, just as she had known he would. She got out three mugs from the cupboard, milk from the fridge, eyeing Felix as she did so. He read the notes pinned to her fridge; he picked up a beaker of Theo's, looked at it, put it down again; he took an apple from the fruit bowl, then put it back.

'How's work?' he said abruptly.

Lexie filled the kettle at the tap. 'Fine. Rushed. You know.'

'I saw your piece on Louise Bourgeois.'

'Oh.'

'It was very good.'

'Thank you.'

'I . . .' he began, then stopped. He leant on the counter and buried his head in his hands. Lexie replaced the lid on the kettle, then put it on the hob, striking a match and holding the flame to the gas, all the time watching Felix or, rather, the top of his head.

'I've got myself into a bit of a tight spot,' he said, his voice muffled behind his hands.

'Oh?' Lexie opened the caddy and spooned tea leaves into the pot. 'What kind of tight spot?'

'There's a girl.' Felix straightened up.

'Ah. And?'

'She . . . she tells me she's got a bun in the oven. Claims it's mine.'

'And is it?'

'Is it what?'

'Yours.'

'I don't know! I mean . . . it could be, I suppose . . . but how does one ever know?' He glanced at Lexie, then said hastily: 'I don't mean you, darling, I mean her. It's not that often we've . . . that she and I . . . I mean, I've hardly . . . you know.'

'I see. Well, you'll have to take her word for it, I suppose.' She gives him a sideways look. 'What does she want to do about it?'

'That's just it,' Felix says despairingly. 'She says we have to get married. Married!' He pushed himself away from the kitchen cupboard and roamed to the window and back. 'The idea makes me sick. And now,' he muttered, 'I've got her damn mother breathing down my neck as well. And a right battleaxe she is.'

The kettle started to shudder and tremble, letting out a jet of steam. Just as the whistle shrilled in the kitchen, Lexie seized it and lifted it off the heat. She put it down next to the sink. She placed her hands on the edge of the cupboard. She didn't look at Felix. She could see the backs of his trouser turn-ups, his heels, as he stood at the window. 'Are we,' she said, 'talking about Margot Kent?'

His silence was enough. She saw his feet move as if he was about to come towards her. Then he must have changed his mind because he headed for the table. She heard him pull out a chair, sink into it. 'It's damned bad luck,' he murmured. 'That's what it is.'

When she didn't answer, he fidgeted in his chair, twisting round and twisting back. 'I don't want to marry her,' he said, a trifle petulantly. 'I think it's all her bloody mother, pushing her from behind.'

Lexie let out a short bark of a laugh. 'I'll bet,' she said.

Felix stood up and came towards her. 'You know her mother as well?' he asked.

'I do,' she said, 'have that particular pleasure, yes.'

She saw a flicker of interest in Felix's eyes. 'What is your connection with them again?' he said.

'None of your business,' Lexie said, and her throat felt raw and scraped. 'That's what it is.' She thought for a moment. 'Has Margot never said?'

Felix pulled a grape from a bunch in the fruit bowl and tossed it fretfully into his mouth. 'I don't believe she has. Look, Lex,' he said, still chewing the grape, 'only you can help me.'

She looked at Felix. 'Sorry?'

'Only you,' he said urgently. 'If I . . . if we say that we are . . . you know . . . married, then I can't marry her. They can't pressure me into it. Do you see? I mean, they know about you and me. And Theodore. God knows how. But if I could tell them we'd got married, which isn't totally out of the question, is it, then that would be that. Problem solved.' He beamed at her with a mixture of hope and lust. He placed a hand on her shoulder, applying a little pressure, to draw her towards him.

Lexie put a hand against his chest. 'I find it hard,' she began, very slowly, 'to say which part of that speech is more odious to me. Maybe it's just the idea of being married to you. Or is it that you want to marry me to save yourself from being forced into marrying someone else? No. Perhaps it's that, in your mind, our getting married isn't – how did you put it? – totally out of the question. Perhaps it's the thought of my having any connection whatsoever to those evil, manipulative, devilish . . .' she searched for the right word, before she remembered '. . . maenads that strikes such sheer horror into my soul. But, like I said, it's hard to say.' She knocked Felix's hand off her shoulder. 'Get out of my house,' she said. 'Now.'

Midnight in the Blue Lagoon Café Bar. The baristas have gone for the night, having swept the floor, wiped the tables, bagged up the rubbish and locked the door behind them.

In the dark, shut café, the cappuccino machine cools, unplugged at the socket. The chrome of its casing will give a loud click every few minutes. Cups and glasses stand inverted on the draining-board; tepid water slides off them to pool in circles around their rims.

The floor has been swept, but not very well. There is a focaccia crust under Table Four, dropped by a tourist from Maine; the floor around the door is littered with fragments of leaves that have fallen from the plane trees of Soho Square.

Far above in the building, a door slams, muffled voices are heard and there is the sound of feet rapidly descending a staircase. The café seems to listen attentively. The dried glasses on the shelves vibrate against each other, in sympathy with the crashing footsteps. The contracting metal of the cappuccino machine clicks. A drop of water falls from the tap, spreads over the bowl of the sink, then trickles towards the plughole. The footsteps are thudding along the passageway beside the wall of the café, the front door slams and out on to the pavement comes the girl who works nights upstairs.

She stalks the pavement outside the shut door of the Blue Lagoon;

back and forth, back and forth, she goes, in her red ankle boots with dagger heels. She crosses and recrosses the paving slab where Innes first embraced Lexie in 1957; she passes the kerbstone where Lexie stood, trying and trying to hail a cab to take her to the hospital; she leans for a moment against the piece of wall against which Lexie and Innes posed for John Deakin on an overcast Wednesday in 1959. And right where the girl from upstairs is grinding out her cigarette is where, in wet weather, it is possible to see the ghost-outline of letters spelling 'e l s e w h e r e', and probably no one notices this and if they did they wouldn't know why.

The girl flicks the butt into the gutter, wrenches open the door and disappears. Her footsteps judder the glasses on the shelves, the salt cellars on the tables, even that chair by the window with one leg shorter than the others.

After this the café is quiet, the cappuccino machine cooled, the cups standing in wet circular pools, the focaccia crust lolling on its side. A magazine on a table lies opened at a page with the headline *How to Become Someone Else.* A sack of coffee beans slumps, exhausted, against the counter. A bicycle skims past the window, the beam of its light veering over the dark street. The sky outside is mineshaft black, washed with orange. As if sensing the night-time calm, the refrigerator obligingly shudders into silence.

A light wind outside pushes a drink can off the top of a bin on to the pavement, where it rolls into the gutter. A police car glides along Bayton Street, its radio crackling and spitting. *Two males . . . heading south . . .* it sputters brokenly . . . *disturbance in Marble Arch.*

The earth continues to turn. The sky is no longer mineshaft black but five-fathom blue, and this drains slowly into a milky grey, as if the street, the whole of Soho, is rising upwards, towards the surface of the sea. The girl from upstairs leaves, replacing her red boots with trainers, locking the door behind her, buttoning her coat. She looks both ways, up and down the pavement, then sets off towards Tottenham Court Road.

At six in the morning, an elderly man in a suit comes walking down the middle of the street, with an uneven, limping stride. He has a little dog at the end of a purple leather lead. He pauses outside the Blue Lagoon. The dog looks up at him, puzzled, then strains forward on the lead. But the man continues to peer at the café. Perhaps he comes here during the day. Or perhaps he is one of the few who remembers it as the *Elsewhere* offices; perhaps he used to drink with Innes in one of the places around here. Or perhaps not. Perhaps it just reminds him of another place. He walks on and in a few moments he and his dog disappear around the corner.

At eight o'clock, the morning baristas arrive: first a woman, who unlocks the door, turns on the lights, plugs in the cappuccino machine, opens the fridge to check the milk, repins a fallen poster to the wall. She is followed by a male barista, who fills a bucket with water and pushes a mop around the floor. He, too, fails to find the focaccia crust.

And, at precisely a quarter to nine, as the first customer of the day, in comes Ted.

Ted orders a latte to go and waits at the counter. He is early today. The waiter is still mopping, dipping the strings of the mop into the grey, greasy water, then slopping their tangled mess out on the floor. Ted watches the mop strings as they swish back and forth, like hair caught in a current. And without warning he is suffused with the feeling he keeps getting – that something he's never seen before is oddly, closely familiar. Importantly familiar. A mop swishing back and forth on a bare, wooden floor. Why should this sight fill him with such a sense of significance, of meaning? As if he believes it could tell him something. Isn't that the first sign of madness, seeing signs in everything, believing mundane things and acts are imbued with messages? He finds he wants to put out a hand to the man and say, please. Please stop that.

He blinks and forces himself to look away. At the rows and rows of glasses on the shelves behind the counter. At the waitress who is pulling levers on the cappuccino machine. At the nimbus of steam wisping from the machine's side.

It is, he decides, like putting on a diving mask and peering beneath the surface of water and seeing another world that has, apparently, existed there all along, beneath a flat, inscrutable surface, without you being aware of it. A world teeming with life and creatures and meaning.

'Here you go.'

The words startle him and he turns quickly. The waitress is holding a cup towards him.

'Oh,' he says, 'thank you,' and he hands her some coins.

Outside on the pavement, he stops. He is remembering or seeing or recognising something. What exactly? Almost nothing. The kind of thing everyone must remember. Being held up at a window, the sill of which is painted green. Someone's arms are around him, beneath him. 'Look,' this person is saying, 'do you see?' The bodice and cuffs of her dress are embroidered with threads of many different colours and sewn into these threads are hundreds of tiny mirrors. 'Look,' she says again, and he looks and sees that the garden has disappeared under blankets of heavy white. Such an ordinary recollection, but why does none of it fit with the childhood he knows as his own? And why does it imbue him with this sense of panic?

Ted looks up at the colourless, empty sky above Bayton Street. He leans against the wall. He allows himself to form these words inside his head: here it comes again. His head seeming to fill with mist, his heart speeding up, as if it knows of some enemy, some danger of which he is as yet unaware. Points of light begin to puncture his vision. They jig and glitter in the flat, depthless sky, in the windows of the shops opposite, in the tarmac of the road. Look, this person had said, do you see. The tiny mirrors in her dress that caught the light, that set constellations in the walls around her. He can recall exactly the sensation of hooking his fingers into the warm dip of her clavicle, the end of her hair against his cheek. And the face. The face was—

'You all right, mate?'

Ted sees a pair of tan leather brogues, the bottom portion of blue jeans. It is a sartorial combination for which he has a particular dislike. He realises he is bending over, his hands on his knees. He raises his head to look at the person with the tan shoes. A man, older than him, is looking down at him with concern. 'Yes,' he says, 'I'm OK. Thank you.'

The man claps him on the shoulder. 'You sure?'

'Uh-huh.'

The man laughs. 'Rough night, was it?' And he walks away.

Ted straightens up. The street is the same; the café behind him is the same; Soho is still here, going about its early-morning business. He bends to pick up his coffee. He takes a sip and tries to ignore the fact that his hand is shaking. He needs to – what? He needs to think straight. He needs to sort this out. He needs to get a grip, that's what he needs.

He is telling himself this, over and over, as he rounds the corner to the street where he works, as he pushes through the glass doors, as he presses the button for the lift. But as he steps into the lift, he thinks of something else: sitting on a rug, pushing chocolate buttons into his mouth, one by one. The feel of the chocolate buttons against his tongue, their domed tops, their latticed bases, which melt into smoothness as he sucks. He is watching his father, who is standing beside a fireplace, his hand on a woman's sleeve, the woman turning away.

Felix corners her at the mantelpiece as she is handing out slices of cake. She's been aware of him since he entered the room – someone, not her, must have opened the door to him. She's skirted round him throughout the opening of presents, through the playing of games, as Theo and the other children waited, tense with longing, to pass the parcel from one to the other, as she served tea and wine and black olives in brine to the grown-ups and crisps and orange squash to the children. As Felix presented Theo with a wooden push-along train. As they sang happy birthday, dear Theo, and she gave Theo the star-shaped cake that the previous night she'd been up with past midnight, studding it with chocolate buttons. Theo had had to gaze at it for a moment, immobile, the points of the star before him, the three lit candles, leaking red wax tears, the chocolate buttons bending and softening in the heat. 'Blow out your candles, sweetheart,' she'd had to whisper into his hair before he came to, recalled himself and bent over his cake. 'Make a wish,' she'd added, possibly too late.

And now here was Felix, standing between her and the room. 'Well, and how are you, Alexandra?' he says jovially.

But she recoils. 'Don't call me that.'

'Sorry.' And he looks it. For a moment, they stare down into their drinks. They haven't seen each other for a while. When he comes to visit Theo, she arranges for Mrs Gallo to be in the flat while she works upstairs. 'You're looking well,' he says.

'Thank you.' She edges round him, scanning the room, pretending to be engaged with her duties as hostess. She sees Laurence, across the room, pull a face at her, and she smiles wryly back.

'I like your dress.' He leans forward, propping himself up with an elbow on the mantelpiece. 'Wherever do you find these things?'

Lexie glances down at her dress. It is quite her most favourite thing to wear at the moment – long and scarlet, it flows from the deep-cut neckline all the way to her ankles. 'It's an Ossie,' she says.

'A what?'

'An Ossie. Ossie Clark.'

'Never heard of her.'

'Him. And that doesn't surprise me.'

'Really?' He takes a swig of his wine and, despite herself, she watches his lips fitting around the rim of the glass, the constriction in his throat. 'Why?'

'I don't see him as Margot's style. Tell me, how is married life?'

'A living hell,' he says cheerfully, draining his glass. 'My wife occupies this godawful mausoleum of a house her mother gave us. The mother, by the way, lives in the basement. Or, at least, that's the official line. She spends far too much bloody time above ground for my liking. I, as a consequence, take every trip abroad going and spend as little time as possible in Myddleton Square. And that, since you ask, is my married life.'

Lexie raises an eyebrow. 'I see. Well, don't say I didn't warn you.'

'Thank you,' he says, leaning even closer. 'I'm overwhelmed by your sympathy.'

'And how many children do you have by now in the Myddleton mausoleum?'

Abruptly, he draws himself upright. 'Ah,' he says, in a different, tight voice. 'None, actually.'

Lexie frowns. 'But—'

'Our son,' he nods towards the rug where Theo is methodically picking all the chocolate buttons off the icing of the cake, 'is my sole issue.' Felix sighs, puts down his glass, thrusts a hand through his hair. 'She keeps . . .' he makes an indecipherable flicking gesture with his hand '. . . having miscarriages.' He says the word in a low tone. 'Over and over again. Can't seem to get the blasted things to stick.'

'I'm so sorry,' she begins, 'I should never have asked. I don't—'

'No, no,' he waves a hand at her, 'don't start all that apologising and sympathising.' He inhales deeply. 'It's a dreadful thing to say but perhaps it's for the best.'

'Felix—'

But he cuts off her objection. 'I mean because I'm not planning to stick around. Saw a lawyer the other day, in fact. This is strictly entre nous, of course.'

'Of course.'

'There being no children makes it less complicated.'

'I see.'

'Although,' he seems to slide closer again, his hand moving along the rim of the mantelpiece, 'we've managed pretty well, haven't we?'

'Managed what?'

'The children thing.'

Is it her imagination or is his hand in close, hot proximity to her waist? 'Do you think so?'

He smiles at her. 'Seeing anyone at the moment, Lex?' he murmurs in the same, intimate tone.

She clears her throat. 'That's really none of your business.'

'Why don't we have lunch?'

'I don't think so.'

'Next week.'

'I can't. I'm working. And I have Theo.'

'Dinner, then. Next week. Or next weekend?'

Next weekend she will be in Lyme Regis with Robert, for the first time in eight months. She got a telegram today. She wonders what Felix would say if she told him she had a clandestine arrangement with Robert Lowe and she has to suppress a smile. 'No,' she says.

'We can talk about our son.' He lays his hand on her sleeve.

'What about our son?'

'Anything. Schools. You know.'

Lexie lets out a short laugh. 'You want to talk about Theo's schooling? Since when?'

'Since now.'

'You're unbelievable.' She shakes his hand off her sleeve.

'So is it a date? Dinner next week?'

She slips away, across the room, towards Theo. 'I'll let you know,' she says, over her shoulder, before she reaches her son, before he clutches at a fistful of her dress, before she sweeps him up into her arms, settling the familiar, smooth weight of his body on her hip.

The day is not what they had hoped for. When they had set out from London, the sky had been a bolt of blue cloth thrown over the city and the sun had been glowing off every surface. They had zoomed through the streets with the windows down and the sun-roof rolled back. But the further west they got, the more the clouds gathered, like a frown, on the horizon and Elina could feel the wind buffeting the side of the car. Needles of rain were falling now, pulled by the wind into streaks along the window beside her.

They are going to Simmy's parents' house for the weekend; the parents are away and, Simmy says, they'll have the run of the place. Elina has never been to a – what was it Ted called it last night? – a country seat. Will there be servants, she'd asked Ted, and he'd shaken his head. It's not that posh, he'd said.

Jonah is asleep in his car seat, both fists gripped out in front of him, as if in his dreams he's tightrope-walking with a pole in his hands. Ted and Simmy sit in the front. They're listening to an improvised comedy programme on the radio and every now and again will erupt into laughter, but the jokes are too rapid, too idiomatic, for Elina to follow.

She has the beginnings of what might be a headache, a tightness or tenderness at her jaw hinges, at the muscles running from her shoulders to her neck. But nothing serious. She is glad to be getting out of London, glad for the flashes of trees and fields she can see from the car. She thinks of the journey out to Nauvo, to her mother's house, along the chain of islands, the road that unwinds the length of the archipelago, the bridges over the gullies, then the yellow ferry, the flat expanses of green, the red and white wooden buildings, the sense that you are travelling as far as the land lasts, until soil and rock run out on you, give way to water, lapping, restless water, and only then will you stop, pulling up on the gravel beside the veranda, beside the silver-trunked trees.

She must have fallen asleep because she dreams she is in Nauvo with Jonah and she can't seem to get him out of his car seat – the straps won't come off, the buckle won't undo. And then she's aware of her head pressed up against a car window and she wakes to find they are no longer on the main road but winding down a narrow street with high hedges, towards the sea, into a town.

'Are we there?' she asks.

'Not yet,' Simmy says, over his shoulder. 'We thought we'd stop here for lunch.'

The streets of the town are cramped and steep, the pavements filled with people. They park in a car park behind a public toilet. The sky sags low above them as they walk. Elina has wound Jonah into his sling and the weight of him pulls at the tender muscles in her neck. Simmy and Ted walk fast up the hill of the main street, Elina trying to keep up, her arms wrapped around the shape of Jonah. They survey one café, reject it; they stop in the doorway of another, decide the menu is too 'measly', walk on. A third has a good menu but there are no tables; another has a reasonable menu but they decide they want to sit outside. They walk up, then down the street. They walk along the promenade, the whole length of the town. They stop outside a pub near the harbour to debate the merits of line-caught fish. Jonah wakes, finds himself in the sling, decides he hates it and starts to yell and struggle. Elina unwinds him and carries him on her shoulder, where he carries on yelling.

'A pork pie,' Simmy is saying. 'Is that too much to ask?'

Ted is peering at another menu inside a restaurant window adorned with fishing nets. 'What is it with scampi,' he mutters, 'and seaside resorts? It's not as if they catch scampi here, is it?'

Elina hefts Jonah to her other shoulder, dropping the length of purple material, and has to lower herself to her knees to pick it up. A mother with two children of varying ages in a twin-buggy of pink and sparkling chrome gives her a look of incomprehension, of distaste. Elina looks down at herself. She is wearing striped tights that she has cut the feet off, scuffed plimsolls, a dress made by a friend. It has a looped hem, asymmetric sleeves and a slashed neckline. Elina loves it.

'I'm going to sit over there to feed Jonah,' she says to the other two. 'Come and find me when you've decided.'

Elina walks off towards a bench in the lee of the harbour wall, out of the breeze. She settles herself in her looped-hem dress with Jonah held in one arm. Jonah is ravenous, tense with rage, as she fiddles with her clothes, unclips her bra. As he feeds, going at the milk like a Tudor despot at a feast, she looks out to sea. The harbour wall is curved, she sees, enormous, reaching into the water like a huge, protective arm. Elina frowns. She feels sure she recognises it. Has she been to this town before? She doesn't think so.

Jonah feeds, first one side, then the other. The sea rises and falls, retreating down the sides of the wall, shrinking into itself. Just as she feels she might faint from hunger, Simmy appears. 'Sorry it took so long,' he is saying. 'Everywhere is packed to the gills. We got sandwiches in the end.' He holds out a brown-paper package towards her. 'Cheese and pickle all right?'

She nods. 'Anything.' She tries to open it with one hand, before Simmy takes it from her, saying, 'Sorry, should have thought of that.' He unwraps her sandwiches and balances them on her knee, all scrupulously without looking in the direction of her exposed breast. As she bites into it, she looks round for Ted.

He's not on the bench, he's not on the harbour wall. She twists round to look behind her. 'Where's Ted?' she says.

Simmy shrugs, taking a bite of his sandwich. 'Probably gone for a slash,' he mumbles.

Elina eats half of her lunch, straps herself back into her dress, burps Jonah, cleans a thin line of regurgitated milk from her front, drinks some water.

'Here, let me take him for a bit,' Simmy says.

Elina hands him the baby and watches as Simmy sits him on his knee. 'Hello,' Simmy says solemnly. 'Did you have a good lunch? Milk again, was it?' Jonah stares at him, entranced.

Elina stands, swings her arms up and above her head. She glances down the harbour. No Ted. She glances back at the bench, where she sees a waiting package of sandwiches. Ted's. Elina steps away from the bench to look up the harbour towards the curve. Nothing. Where can he have got to? Elina runs up the narrow, jutting steps to the top of the wall and finds herself on a higher level, a sloping stone surface that tilts sickeningly towards the sea. She holds her hair out of her eyes and looks about her.

'Can you see him?' Simmy says from below.

'No.'

And then suddenly she can. He is coming around the curve of the grey wall. He must have been out to the end. Something about the way he is moving alerts her. The left arm clutched in the other. The bowed head. The stumbling, uneven walk. Elina moves forward on the tilting stones. She raises her hand to wave. But Ted turns away from her.

He looks down into the sea, which swells and recedes just below him, and the thought crosses her mind that he is about to jump in, but then Ted never swims, she doesn't even know if he can – he hates the idea, he always says, why would anyone want to do that? She sees him rear back from the water and then he falls. Or stumbles. Or perhaps collapses. She isn't sure which.

Elina shouts his name but the wind snatches away the sound. She breaks into a run but she is a whole level above him and she can't find a way down and when she does find another stone staircase it is worn and vertiginous and she must be careful not to trip and fall. When she gets to Ted, there is a crowd of people already around him. Simmy is there, with Jonah held in his arms – Elina can see his back in its striped shirt. He is crouched over, with his ear to Ted's chest. People in the crowd must see her significance or her panic because they stand aside to let her through, and when she reaches him, she kneels on the wet stone beside him and takes his hand; she strokes his hair, she talks to him in Finnish and then in English, and when the ambulance comes, she gets in beside him, still holding his hand.

There follows a great deal of waiting. There are forms to fill in. They are asked to move from corridor to corridor. And a number of people ask Elina the same questions, over and over again. What's Ted's age? Where does he live? What's his full name? Has he taken anything? Does he use drugs? Is there a history in his family of heart problems, diabetes, low blood pressure? Has this ever happened before? No, Elina says, and no, no drugs, no medication, Roffe, Ted Roffe, Theodore Roffe. Someone brings her a cup of tea and, later, someone gets her some spare nappies for Jonah. Thank you, Elina finds she keeps saying, thank you, thanks.

She and Simmy wait in a corridor. Jonah fidgets and cries and feeds again. He is sick, copiously yet matter-of-factly, all over the next chair. He grabs handfuls of Elina's hair, sucks it crossly, then investigates the fastenings of Simmy's jacket. He seems baffled, impatient about this unusual turn of events, as if he can't understand why they have taken him away from the seaside to sit in these featureless beige corridors. Elina bounces him up and down rhythmically on her knee; Jonah holds his legs stiff and Elina imagines all the small black bruises that will cover her thighs tomorrow.

Then there is a flurry of doctors and student doctors and nurses coming to talk to them and the news, they say, is good. It's good! Simmy is leaping up and he is smiling. It wasn't a heart-attack after all! They are all striding along the corridor now and several people are talking at once. The word 'eeceegee' is mentioned and Elina has no idea what it means but Simmy is nodding and still smiling, and the words 'clear' and 'tested negative'. As they enter a room, the doctor is saying 'a form of panic-attack' but Elina isn't listening because Ted is there on the bed and he is dressed and he looks normal again.

Elina rushes over to him, puts her hand on his arm, kisses his cheek and, as she does so, Jonah gives a painful yank to her hair so that she cries out, 'Ow,' just as her lips touch his skin.

Ted's face is filled with alarm. 'What's the matter?' he says, cringing away from her.

'Nothing. Sorry.'

'Why did you say that, then?'

'Jonah just pulled my hair. It's nothing. How are you feeling?'

Ted continues to stare at her. And Elina sees that his face is white, his pupils wide and black. He moves his gaze and stares at Jonah. Then back to her. Elina glances at Simmy, who is looking carefully at Ted.

'Umm,' she says. 'Do you feel OK now? Ted?'

Ted looks at his son again. Then he lies back on the pillows behind him and stares up at the ceiling. He puts both hands over his face. 'Do I feel OK?' he repeats, inside the tent of his hands, very slowly. 'Do I feel OK?'

Simmy clears his throat. 'The doctor said you can go but if you think—'

'I don't know,' Ted intones. 'Is the answer.'

Simmy and Elina exchange a glance over Ted's body. Jonah huffs on the skin of her neck, sucks briefly on her collarbone, drags up a fistful of her dress to taste, arches back in her arms to examine the ceiling, kicks his legs against her abdomen.

'I'm just going to find a loo,' Simmy says. 'Be back in a sec.'

And then they are alone, Elina, her man and her baby. It seems incredible to her that Ted has been delivered back to her, after she had seen him fall on the harbour, after his body was crumpled like that on the ground, crumpled and horribly twitching. It seems nothing short of a miracle that they should have come through such a thing and found themselves here, in an empty hospital room with striped sheets. Elina stares at the stripes, which seem, like everything else at this precise moment, magical. The way they alternate, white, blue, white, blue, the weft and warp of the cotton meshing together to make this. A sheet. For Ted to lie upon.

Elina sits herself on the bed next to him, her hip pressed against his. 'You scared me so much,' she murmurs. Jonah leaps and writhes like a fish in her arms and she has to hold tight to his ribcage. 'The doctor said you must go and see the GP as soon as we get back h—'

'The thing is,' Ted interrupts, still staring at the ceiling, 'none of it adds up. I just know that everyone's been lying. About everything. I see that now. And I don't know where to turn, who to ask because everything is deception, and I can't trust anyone. Do you see?' He looks at her or near her or through her. 'Do you see that?'

Jonah twists in her hands, stamping his feet on her legs. Elina can feel her arms trembling, her whole body trembling. She has no idea what to say, no idea what to do. She wonders if she should call a doctor, but what will happen then? What is happening to them?

'Ted,' she gets out, and her voice cracks, as if she might cry, 'what are you talking ab—'

'Right.' Simmy has re-entered the room, rubbing his hands together. 'The doctor says we can go. Shall we make a move?'

'Sim,' Elina says, but Ted is leaping from the bed.

'Come on,' he says, seizing Elina by the elbow and dragging her towards the door. 'Let's go.'

'I think we should wait and see if—'

'We have to go,' Ted says, shoving his way out. 'We have to get back to London.'

This is where the story ends.

Lexie became what she is today during a swim off the Dorset coast in late August. She and Theo are with Robert in Lyme Regis. They have eaten fish and chips, they have talked about the hotel they stayed in when they last met, they have argued about an article of Lexie's that Robert read recently, Theo has filled a bucket with stones, he has found a dead crab, and Lexie has stripped off her clothes and swum. Robert has watched her, holding the towel for her, waiting. Like the husband of a selkie, Lexie thinks. She watches them both from the water, Robert sitting on the steep shingle, the buggy parked next to him, in which Theo sleeps, knitted cat clutched in his hand.

When Lexie gets out of the sea, walking carefully because the beach is pebbled and sharp, and Robert puts the towel around her, she knows that she has to be in bed with him in the next few minutes. It is a necessity to her and life itself. He is rubbing her under the towel, his palms moving up and down her back, her arms, her hips.

'The hotel,' Lexie says, her lips rubbery and strange with cold, 'let's go.'

And Robert just says: 'Yes.'

She loves him for that yes, for the way he turns to pick up their bags, for the way he strings her discarded clothes over his arm, one by one, the way he bends to unlace the shoes she'd kicked off in her impatience to be in the water, and helps her on with them so that she can dash, with him carrying the buggy and the napping Theo, up the concrete steps to the promenade, up the hotel steps, past the shocked face of the manager, up the four flights of stairs, and her in only a bikini and towel.

The way he turns the buggy towards the wall. The way he rips off, first the bedcovers, then his shirt, then her towel. She likes the ordering of that. The way his skin seems scalding hot against the chill of her own. The way he struggles to unwind her from the clinging, winding straps and catches of her wet bikini, swearing with impatience, until she does it for him. The way he seizes the damp bundle from her and hurls it at the wall. A shadow on the plaster will be there afterwards and for the rest of their stay, in the shape of a jellyfish, and later guests will look at it and ask themselves what could have made such a strange stain.

She loves him for all these things, and for the paradox of his body – the hardness of it under the softness of the skin – and for the line of hair that runs down his stomach, which she had forgotten was there. For the intent, concentrated way he encounters her, for the expression of utmost seriousness on his face, for the feel of him inside her, at last, and after such a long time.

Afterwards, he falls asleep. Lexie does not. She stretches, yawns, gets out of bed. She picks up her dress and pulls it on. She goes over to Theo, still slumped in his buggy, eyes moving beneath the lids, lips pouting in sleep. She watches him for a while. She watches him and touches his hair. One of his hands is loosely uncurled on his lap and she spends a while looking at the hundreds of tiny lines criss-crossing his palm.

She wanders to the open window. On the promenade below, people are eating ice-cream, leaning on the railings, walking up and down. The tide has come in since they were on the beach: its frothed waves lap and lick at the promenade wall. An old man is letting his dog pee against a statue. A small child skips out of a shop with an armful of oranges. It amuses Lexie that everyone is going about their business while she, a woman in a dress at a window, can secretly look down on them.

She is thinking about where they might eat later, about when Theo might wake up, about whether he might like to fly a kite – she's seen a red one with a yellow tail in a shop she might get him. She is looking at the great grey Cobb, lying like a sleeping serpent, half out of the sea.

A movement from the buggy makes her turn. She crosses the room. Theo is waking up, twisting his head from side to side. She turns the buggy around and crouches in front of him. 'Hi,' she whispers.

He yawns and then says, quite precisely, with his eyes still shut, 'I said I didn't want it.'

'Did you?'

'Yes.' Then he frowns and blinks and looks around him. 'This isn't home.'

'No. We're in Lyme Regis, remember? In a hotel. You've had a little nap.'

'Regis,' Theo repeats, then his face seems to tense with a thought. 'A . . . a bucket with stones.'

'That's right. It's over there, look.'

He stretches and then pushes himself out of the buggy, tucking his knitted cat up under his arm. 'Alfie doesn't like Regis,' he states, as he goes towards the bucket, which Lexie has left beside the door.

'Doesn't he?'

Theo leans over the bucket and examines it carefully. 'No,' he says.

'Why not?'

Theo has to think for a moment. 'He says it's too damp.'

Lexie, sitting on the edge of the bed, tries not to smile. 'Well, he is a cat. Cats hate the wet.'

'No, not wet. Damp.'

'Damp is wet, darling.'

'No, it's not!'

'OK.' She bites her lip. 'Would you like a drink?'

Theo is lining up the stones in a row, taking them one by one out of the bucket. The grey ones, she notices, he discards.

'Theo?' she tries again. 'A drink?'

He places a smooth white stone next to an orange one. 'Yes,' he says, distant but firm. 'In fact, I would.'

Later, they go out again. Lexie buys the red kite with a yellow tail and they go to the beach beyond the town, beyond the Cobb. Theo holds the string in his hand and Lexie puts her hand around his. Robert watches them from a rock where he is searching for fossils.

'That's it,' she murmurs to Theo. 'You've got it.'

The kite floats directly above them, an inverted plumbline, its tail swirling and snapping. Theo gazes up at it, rapt, unable to believe that when he jerks his hand this ethereal thing above them will dance in response.

'It's like . . .' he struggles to find what he wants to say '. . . a dog.'

'A dog?'

'A . . . a floating dog.'

'Oh, like on a lead, you mean?'

He turns his blue eyes to hers, in joy, in delight at being understood. 'Yes!'

She laughs and hugs his body to her and the kite above them dips and sways.

After a while they join Robert and sit together on a rock. Robert finds an ammonite, a ridged creature, curled into itself, petrified into rock. He puts it in Lexie's hand and she feels it begin to warm in her palm. Theo is lining up stones again, this time in diminishing size order.

Lexie stands. 'I might go for another quick swim. And then we'll find something to eat.'

Robert looks at the sky, at the sea, which is flecked with white horses. 'Are you sure?' he says. 'It's getting cold.'

'It's fine.' She slips the ammonite into her dress pocket.

'We haven't got a towel.'

'I'll dry,' she says, laughing. 'I'm waterproof. I'll run around until I'm warm.' When she's down to her underwear, she crouches to kiss Theo on top of his head. 'I won't be long, sweetheart.' And then she's off, down the shingle, on to the sand, into the water. Robert watches as more and more of her disappears into the sea – it claims her quickly. Her ankles, her knees, her thighs, her waist. Then she's in, with a small cry. He watches as she does a few strokes of crawl, the water churning in her wake; he watches her dive under, sees her slick head break the surface, further out now, and then she glides into an even breaststroke.

Robert looks back to Theo. He is pushing the stones, one by one, into the sand, saying, 'There you go,' with each one. 'There you go, there you go.'

It will be unclear to Robert, later, how much time passes here. He knows that he started looking again, idly, for fossils. He knows he took a few stones and hammered them against rocks, to crack them open like eggs, to see if their innards revealed anything. He knows he looked out to sea at least once and saw her head, near the curve of the Cobb. He knows he listened to Theo, saying, there you go and, occasionally, she'll run around until she's warm.

After cracking open the third stone, he hears Theo say something else. Robert looks up. Theo is no longer crouched over his stones.

He is standing up, his sandy hands held away from his body, fingers splayed, staring out to sea.

'What did you say, Theo?'

'Where's Mama?' the child asks, in his clear, high voice.

Robert is weighing a fourth stone in his hand, considering it, examining it – will it yield another perfect ammonite, like the one he gave Lexie? 'She's gone for a swim,' he says. 'She'll be back soon.'

'Where's Mama?' he says again.

Robert looks out to sea. He looks left, towards the Cobb, he looks right. He straightens up. He follows the charcoal line of the horizon. Nothing. He shades his eyes against the dull glare of the setting sun. 'She's . . .' he begins. Then he walks towards the shore. Waves rise and collapse against the sand. He scans the sea stretched before him.

He sprints back up the beach towards the child, who is still standing, fixed to the spot, his hands covered with sand. Robert picks him up and hurries over the shingle. 'We'll go up to the Cobb and look from there, shall we?' he says, and the words come out not as he'd hoped, reassuring and calm, but ragged and panicked. 'She might have swum round the end and be coming down the other side.'

Robert climbs the steps on to the Cobb's high wall. He races along the sloped stones, Theo clutched in his arms. Halfway along, he comes to a stop.

'Where's Mama?' Theo says again.

'She's . . .' Robert looks. He looks and looks. His eyes ache with looking. He cannot remember ever seeing anything other than sea, endless, puckered water, unbroken. Every few seconds, his heart leaps at something – a buoy, a particularly peaked wave. But there is nothing. She is nowhere.

He scrambles down off the wall, to the lower part of the Cobb, and runs towards its end. The water here is deep, sinister green, dipping and snatching at the wall. Theo begins to cry. 'I don't like it,' he says. 'That sea is too close. That sea there.' He points at it, in case Robert hasn't understood.

Robert turns, rushes back along the wet Cobb as carefully as he can, to where several fishing-boats are moored. In one of them a man is standing, his arms full of knotted nets.

'Please,' Robert calls down to him. 'Please. We need help.'

Then there is a long stretch of time when Robert is sitting on a bench on the Cobb, with Theo in his arms. Beams from the lights of trawlers, the lifeboats, the coastguard sweep over them from time to time. He has wrapped the child in his coat. Only his hair is visible. Theo shivers rhythmically, gently, like an engine in low gear. Robert rocks him back and forth, sings a song he used to sing to his own children a long time ago, his voice cracked and hoarse. Someone – he doesn't see who, one of the policemen, perhaps – brings a woven bag and places it next to him. He doesn't recognise it for a moment. At the top of the bag is a loosely folded piece of fabric. Then he sees that it is Lexie's dress, Lexie's bag, that someone has collected them from where they were sitting on the beach. Without letting go of Theo, he picks up the dress. It unfolds in his fingers like something sentient, like something alive. He almost drops it but doesn't, and then he is puzzled by the weight of it. How can something of thin cotton be so heavy? It swings back and forth like a pendulum in the stiff breeze. Then he remembers the ammonite. She put it into her pocket just before—

He puts the dress down quickly, stuffs it back into the bag. And then he sees the toy Theo loves, the stuffed cat, among a tangle of beakers, spare shorts, buckets and spades, a green rake. He lifts it out, places its nonplussed face at the gap in the top of his coat, where Theo's bright, golden hair can be seen. For a moment nothing happens. Then fingers appear, clutch at the cat and pull it down inside the cave of the coat.

And then two policemen are running down the brow of the Cobb towards the dock. The other police, seeing them, start moving too. Robert stands, hoisting Theo up. He hears someone mutter, 'They've got her.'

And he is moving forward. A boat is rounding the tip of the Cobb, a small trawler, its lights blazing, a man at the helm and another standing at the stern with a rope. Robert strains his eyes and sees, unbelievably, a shape crumpled at the bottom of the boat, half covered with tarpaulin and he finds he wants to shout, to cry out to her, but then a policeman is standing between him and the docking boat and he is saying, stand back, sir, please, get back, take the child, take him away.

This is how it ends. Those words were running through her head. *So this is how it ends.* She knew what was coming. There was a stretch of time, out there beyond the reach of the Cobb, several minutes long, where she was flailing against the cold, muscular clutch of the current. And she saw. She saw what was coming. She knew the struggle had begun and she knew that she was losing.

She didn't think in that moment of herself, of her parents, her siblings, of Innes, the life she left behind when she stepped into the waves, the moment when she could have changed everything, when she could have stayed on the beach, turned her back on the sea. She didn't even think of Robert, who was sitting there with her clothes, who would soon be calling her name into the restless wind.

As the waves thrust her under, she could think only of Theo.

They heaved her up and heaved her under, and every now and again she could struggle to the surface, she could make the waters part so she could take a breath, but she knew, she knew it couldn't be long, and she wanted to say, please. She wanted to say, no. She wanted to say, I have a son, there is a child, this cannot happen.

Because you know that no one will ever love them like you do. You know that no one will look after them like you do. You know that it's an impossibility, it's unthinkable that you could be taken away, that you will have to leave them behind.

She knew, though, that she would not see him again. She would not be helping him cut up his dinner tonight. She would not be folding the kite or airing his damp clothes or running him a bath at bedtime or taking his pyjamas out from under the pillow. She would not be rescuing his cat from the floor in the middle of the night. She would not be able to wait for him at the gate at the end of his first day at school. Or guide his hand as he learnt to shape the letters of his name, the name she'd given him. Or hold the seat of his bicycle as he did without stabilisers. She would not be nursing him through chicken pox and measles; it would not be her measuring out the medicine, or shaking down the themometer. She would not be there to show him how to look left, then right, then left again, or to tie his own shoelaces or brush his teeth or manage the zip on his cagoule, or to pair his socks after a wash or to use a telephone or to spread butter on bread, or what to do if he got lost in a shop, or how to pour milk into a cup or catch a bus home. She would not see him grow as tall as her and then taller. She would not be there when someone first broke his heart or when he first drove a car or when he went alone out into the world or when he saw, for the first time, what he would do, how he would live and with whom and where. She would not be there to knock the sand out of his shoes when he came off the beach. She would not see him again.

She fought like a crazed thing. She fought to live, she fought to come back. She has always wanted to tell him this, in some way. She tried. She would like to say to him, Theo, I tried. I fought because I didn't see how I could leave you. But I lost.

What she would have given to win? She could not say.

It's nightfall by the time they reach London. Elina sits in the back, her hands squeezed between her knees. Jonah sleeps in his car seat. Ted has stared straight out of the windscreen for the entire journey. On the Westway, he says, 'Take me to Myddleton Square.'

Simmy glances at Ted, then his eyes meet Elina's in the rear-view mirror. 'Ted,' he begins, 'don't you think you ought to—'

'Take me to Myddleton Square, Sim, I mean it.'

Elina leans forward. 'Why do you want to go there, Ted?'

'Why?' he snaps. 'To talk to my parents, of course.'

'It's quite late,' Elina ventures. 'Won't they be asleep? Why don't we wait until—'

'Either take me,' Ted says, and his voice sounds near tears, 'or let me out of the car and I'll go by Tube.'

'OK,' Simmy says soothingly. 'OK. Whatever you want. Why don't I drop Elina and Jonah off at home first and then—'

'I'll go with Ted,' Elina cuts in. 'It's fine. Jonah's asleep. I'll go with you,' she says, and lays a hand on Ted's shoulder.

When Simmy pulls up in Myddleton Square, Ted is out of the car and running up to his parents' front door before either Elina or Simmy have taken off their seatbelts. Elina releases the catch on Jonah's seat and opens the door.

'Are you coming?' she says to Simmy.

Simmy turns round and they look at each other. 'What do you think?' he says, in a low voice.

'Maybe you'd better,' she says quickly.

Simmy takes the car seat from her and they go towards the door, which is now opening, a slice of light appearing and falling over the pavement, and there is Ted's father, whisky glass in hand, saying, 'Good grief. Hello, old chap. Didn't know you were coming.'

'I need to talk to you,' Ted says, and pushes past him.

In the kitchen downstairs, Elina sits at the table with Simmy and Ted's father. Ted strides to the back door, to the window, to the table, to the cooker.

'What's going on?' Ted's father says, looking at them all one by one.

Elina clears her throat, wondering what she should say. 'Well,' she begins, 'we were in Ly—'

'Answer me this,' Ted shouts, from across the room, and Elina whirls round to look at him. He has his wallet in his hands and is struggling to pull something – money? A credit card? – from it. She stares at him, appalled, as he bears down on them. He hurls something, something white, a piece of paper or card, on the table in front of his father. 'Who is that?'

There is a long silence. Ted's father glances at the piece of paper, then glances quickly away. He reaches into his shirt pocket for his packet of cigarettes. He extracts one, puts it to his mouth and leans sideways to get a lighter from his back pocket. His hands, Elina notices, are shaking. He gets the lighter and then places it square on the table. Instead of picking it up and lighting his cigarette with it, he picks up the piece of card, the postcard, again and holds it near his face. Elina leans over and looks at it too. It is a black and white shot of a man and a woman, leaning against a wall. She thinks she has never seen it before and then she thinks that maybe she has, and then she realises it's one of the John Deakin photos from that exhibition they went to see. It is bent and creased from being folded inside Ted's wallet. She opens her mouth to speak, then shuts it again.

Ted's father puts it down. He props it with great care against a salt cellar. Only then does he light his cigarette. He inhales, blows out the smoke, inhales again.

And then he utters the following incredible words: 'She's your mother.'

'My mother?'

'Your real mother. Lexie Sinclair,' he rubs his brow with an index finger, 'was her name.'

Ted leans both hands, curled into fists, on the table edge. He has bowed his head, like a supplicant, like a man about to receive communion. 'Then would you mind telling me,' he says, his voice muffled, 'who that is asleep upstairs?'

Felix takes a deep draw on his cigarette. 'The woman who brought you up. From the age of three.'

'And you?' Ted says. 'Are you my father?'

'I am. Without doubt.'

'And something happened to her. My mother. In Lyme Regis.'

Felix nods. 'She drowned.' He circles his cigarette around his head. 'A swimming accident. You were there. It was a week or so after your third birthday.'

'Was it . . . ? Were you there?'

'No. There was a . . . friend of hers with you both. I came to collect you that night. I brought you back here and . . . and Margot looked after you.'

Ted picks up the postcard. He looks at his father, whose face is wet. He looks at Elina. Or, rather, his eyes pass over her as he turns away, towards the windows to the garden.

'Now, old chap,' Felix says, getting to his feet, 'I'm sorry, of course I am. Perhaps we were wrong – to hide it from you, I mean – but we—'

'You're sorry?' Ted repeats, turning to his father. 'You're sorry? For lying to me my entire life? For passing off someone else as my mother? For pretending this never happened? It's – it's inhumane,' he gets out, in a hoarse whisper. 'You realise that? I mean, how did you manage it? I was three, for God's sake. How did you do it?'

'We . . .' Felix's shoulders slump. 'The thing is, you sort of . . . forgot.'

'I forgot?' Ted hisses. 'What do you mean, I forgot? It's not something you forget – seeing your mother drown. What are you talking about?'

'It sounds odd, I know. But you came back here and—'

'What's going on?' a voice trills from the doorway. Everyone turns to see Margot, her hair flattened on one side, a dressing-gown tied tight around her middle. A confused smile lighting up her face. 'Ted, I had no idea you were here. And Simmy and darling Jonah! What are you all . . .' Her voice trails away. She looks from face to face. Her expression fades into uncertainty, then mistrust. 'What's the matter? Why is everybody . . . ?' She sidles into the room. 'Felix?'

Felix reaches out and takes the postcard from Ted's fingers. He hands it to Margot. 'He knows,' he says, and comes to stand beside her or, rather, alongside her, puffing at his cigarette, as if he is in a queue with her, waiting for a bus, perhaps, as if she is no more to him than a stranger who just happens to be travelling in the same direction.

Felix and Margot and Gloria sit at the table in the kitchen of Myddleton Square. Opposite them sits the boy. He is perfectly still, his hands resting, upturned, one on each knee, his head slightly bowed. He has a ragged cat toy tucked into one armpit. He doesn't even seem to blink. He stares at the plate of sausages in front of him. Or perhaps he is staring past it, at something he sees in the tablecloth. He is like the wax model of a boy, an effigy, a sculpture. *Boy, At Table.*

'Aren't you hungry?' Margot says, in a bright voice.

He doesn't reply.

'You need to eat up,' Gloria joins in. 'Then you'll grow big and strong.'

The sausages have cooled and are set in gelid puddles of grease. The boiled potatoes next to them have a floury, dry appearance. Margot puts up a nervous hand to fluff out the hair at the sides of her head: her mother's always told her that flat hair makes her face look thin.

'Listen, old chap,' Felix says, 'I'm going to go into the garden in a minute and do you know what I'm going to do?' He pauses to see if the boy will reply. When he doesn't, Felix presses on: 'I'm going to light a bonfire. You'd like to come and help with that, wouldn't you? A big bonfire? Eh?'

Margot hasn't spoken to Felix directly this morning. She hasn't forgiven him for putting the boy to sleep in the nursery last night. The nursery that had once been hers and which she had decorated two years ago with a frieze of rocking horses and jack-in-the-boxes and a matching coverlet in primrose yellow.

'Well, where else should I have put him?' Felix had said, when she'd objected.

'I don't know!' she'd cried. 'The spare room!'

'The spare room?' He'd gazed at her as if he didn't recognise her. He was slumped against the landing wall, still in his raincoat, still wearing his driving gloves, and his face was ashen and hooded in the dim light. Something told her she should curtail this conversation; she ought to take him down to the drawing room, give him a whisky, take his coat for him. But she couldn't. He'd put that boy to sleep in there, under her primrose coverlet.

'It's my nursery,' she'd tried to explain but she heard the bleat in her voice, and saw the flare of anger in his eyes. He'd pushed himself away from the wall and stepped up very close to her. For a moment she thought he might strike her.

'That child,' he began, in a quiet, frightening voice, 'has just lost his mother. Do you understand that? He's seen his mother drown. And all you can think about is yourself. You . . .' he hesitated, choosing his words, as he sometimes did when she watched him on television, when he was faced with something moving, a flood perhaps, a famine of vast proportions, the collapse of a valued building '. . . you disgust me.'

Then he'd turned and walked down the stairs. And she'd known she should leave it, she'd known she should say nothing more but she somehow couldn't stop herself and she'd shouted after him, 'You're upset because it's her, aren't you? You can't bear that she's dead. You love her. You love her and you – you despise me. You think I don't know it but I do. I do!'

At the bottom of the stairs, he turned and looked back at her. In the light coming from the hall lamp, she saw suddenly that he'd been weeping. 'You're right,' he said softly. 'On all counts.' And then he went into the study and shut the door.

In the kitchen, Felix gets up and goes to the sink. He drinks a glass of water; he leaves the glass on the side; he comes over to his son. He places a hand on top of his head. 'Shall we make a start, old chap?'

The child still doesn't move. Margot isn't sure that he even knows Felix is there. She hears her mother, next to her, let out a sigh.

'On the bonfire?' Felix prompts. 'What do you say?'

He says nothing. Felix stands there, clearly at a loss to know what to do.

Margot clears her throat. 'Why doesn't Daddy go and start' – she addresses the child in the high, brittle voice in which she seems to have been talking all this long morning – 'and when you're ready you can go and join Daddy? How about that?'

He blinks, once, and Margot and Felix strain forward, ready to catch whatever sounds he's prepared to send their way. But nothing comes.

'Well,' Felix says, and he is using Margot's bright voice – it seems to be catching, 'I'll go and do that. You be sure to watch out of the window.' He heads off into the garden, putting on his boots at the back door, then retreating down the path. Gloria murmurs something about needing a lie-down and disappears into her rooms.

And so Margot finds herself alone with the boy. The hair gleaming in the sunshine. The small shoulders beneath the shirt, which, she notices, has been patched on the collar. He has the same set jaw as his mother, she sees, the line of her nose, the slight overbite. Margot looks away. She crosses her legs, she picks a bit of lint off her sweater, she fluffs her hair again. When she looks back, the boy is staring straight at her and the dark, frank eyes are so unsettling, so disconcerting she almost jumps.

'Oh.' She lets out a little laugh and rises from her seat. She has to get away from that gaze, so like his bloody mother's. To cover herself, she reaches for the plate of sausages. 'Let's take these away, shall we?' She carries them to the kitchen, where she busies herself with scraping the food into the bin and putting the plate in the sink for the char to wash later. Then she thinks of something.

She walks to the table, where she bends down. 'Theodore,' she says, trying to swallow, to suppress the fact that she now knows his middle name is Innes – how dare she? Damn that woman to hell, she catches herself thinking, and feels ashamed, 'how would you like some ice-cream? Hmm? We've got vanilla or—'

'I'm not Theodore,' he says, quite clearly, and his voice is a surprise. Huskier than she would have thought, lower. He says f instead of th: Feodore.

'You're not?'

'No.' He swings his head from side to side.

'Then who are you?'

'I'm a very sharp pair of scissors.'

Margot blinks. She thinks about this. She gives the idea very serious consideration but still feels unable to come up with a suitable response. A pair of scissors, did he say? 'Well,' she comes out with eventually, 'well I never.' She gives a chuckle. 'Now how about this ice-cream?'

'I don't like ice-cream.'

'You don't like ice-cream? Of course you do! All children like ice-cream!'

'I don't.'

'I'm sure you do.'

'In fact, I don't.'

Margot straightens up. She is no good at this. She doesn't know much about children. She clenches her hands together over her apron. She is not going to cry, she is not, she is not. But she cannot stop herself recalling the feel of that ominous hot slide, down low, in the place that it's not nice to name, the startling jewel-red of it, and how much there always is, so much of it, an unbelievable amount, more than she would ever have thought her body could contain.

She walks to the window and looks to the bottom of the garden, where Felix is piling leaves on to a sullenly smouldering bonfire. You're right, he'd said, on all counts. You're right. The tears feel hot on her cheeks. They follow the line of her neck and then disappear into the collar of her sweater.

She sees something passing in the air near her, something low-down, something golden-yellow, and she gives a start. It's the boy. Unbelievably, she'd forgotten about him for a moment. He's come to stand next to her at the french windows. She sweeps her palms quickly over her face and smiles down at him. But he is examining the garden.

'Look,' she tries again, 'there's Daddy. He's got that bonfire going, hasn't he? Just like he said he would.' She hears the hollowness of her words. She'll never be any good at this. Maybe that's why it keeps happening. She hasn't got it. She hasn't got the children thing – gift, aptitude, whatever you want to call it. She sounds like an actress pretending to be a parent.

'Is that my daddy?' the boy asks.

'Yes, sweetie-pie, of course,' Margot says, with a bright peal of laughter, brushing away another tear, fluffing up the right side of her head.

The boy frowns. He puts up his hand and presses his palm to the glass. 'Is this . . .' he begins, then stops.

Margot waits.

'Is this my garden?' he asks, and he turns to her, touches her hand with his, and she almost gasps.

'Yes, Theodore, it is your garden. You can play in it whenever you want and—'

'I'm not Theodore,' he says again. Feodore.

'I see,' Margot says. She crouches, steadying herself on the door, so that she is on a level with him. 'It is rather a mouthful, isn't it? I used to know someone named Theodore but everyone called him Ted.'

'Ted,' the boy repeats, still staring into the garden. 'Where's the swing?'

'Do you want a swing? We can get you a swing.'

'The orange one.'

'Of course. An orange one. Whatever you want.'

And then, without looking at her, he says, 'Are you my mother?'

The word has an extraordinary effect on Margot. It seems to fall all the way through her, like a coin in a slot-machine. It seems to unpick the threads of something that has been knotted at the very core of her for a long time now. She looks at this child standing next to her, then she looks over her shoulder. She straightens up, licking her lips, which feel suddenly dry. The room is empty. Rosebuds stand in a china vase, their mouths puckered shut. The clock on the mantelpiece ticks away, oblivious, surrounded by wooden cherubs with lacquered limbs. The porcelain shepherdesses in the alcove bend solicitously towards each other, their tiny ears stoppered with glaze. There is a noise from the kitchen, which could have been something falling from a shelf or two plates shifting position in the sink. Margot looks back at the boy. His face is tipped up towards hers and it is uncertain, troubled, cocked to one side, as if he is straining to hear something. The curtain next to him trembles, a draught knifing in from the garden.

Margot swallows. She licks her lips again. She takes his hand in hers. 'Yes,' she says quickly. 'I am.'

Elina hurries down the stairs and opens the front door. Simmy stands on the doorstep under a huge red umbrella.

'Hi,' he says, 'how are you?'

'Very pleased to see you,' she manages to say. 'That's how I am.'

He steps into the hall, shaking his umbrella. Water flies off him and Elina is reminded of a dog emerging from a lake. 'Filthy day,' he says. Then he reaches out and pulls her into an embrace.

'Thank you so much for coming,' she mutters, clutching at his elbow. 'I don't know . . . I didn't know what else to . . . I mean, I don't want to leave him . . . you know . . . on his own . . . I couldn't just go out and . . .'

Simmy nods and pats her back soothingly. 'Of course, of course. I'm more than happy to come. Whenever. I mean it.'

There is a high-pitched squeal from the sitting room. Elina brushes a tear roughly from her cheek. 'I've just got to—'

'Go ahead,' Simmy says.

Jonah is on his playmat on the sitting-room floor. He rolls on to his stomach, then back again. He raises his legs in the air and lets them fall sideways, then wriggles round on to his front. Then on to his back. The process repeats itself. He pants and grunts with concentration.

'Fascinating,' Simmy murmurs, as he watches him. 'The effort of it.'

'I know,' Elina says. 'He did it all day yesterday and all day today. He's this close,' she holds up her finger and thumb, 'to crawling. But not quite.'

'It's quite painful to watch,' Simmy says. 'You just want to help him.' He puts his head on one side. 'It's rather like the knight's move, isn't it? In chess. Sideways then up, sideways then up.' Then he slaps his hands together and looks at Elina. 'So, tell me, what's been going on?'

Elina sighs again. She sits down. Then she slides to the floor and comes to kneel next to Jonah. 'He won't get out of bed,' she says in a low voice. 'He won't speak, doesn't say anything at all. He won't eat. I can just about get him to drink, but only just. He's not asleep the whole time but he seems to be sleeping most of the day and most of the night as well. I don't know what to do, Sim.' She cannot look up at him so she picks up a toy of Jonah's, a rattle with a bell, and shakes it. 'I don't know whether to call a doctor or . . . or . . . but I don't know what I'd say.'

'Hmm. And have Felix and— Has Felix been in touch at all?'

'He's been round. He rings every day. Sometimes twice.'

'And Ted won't talk to him?'

Elina shakes her head. 'She came round too,' she whispers. 'That was when Ted . . .'

'Smashed the window?'

She nods, swallowing hard. 'It was awful, Sim. I thought he was going to – that he would . . .'

Simmy shakes his head. 'Poor Little My,' he murmurs.

'No, not at all,' she returns. 'It's poor Ted.'

'Well, poor all of you, I suppose.'

Elina lifts Jonah on to her hip. 'We should go up,' she says.

As they climb the stairs, she turns to Simmy. 'I won't be away long,' she whispers. 'No more than an hour, I should think. I don't even know if I'm doing the right thing. But if it's going to help . . . you know . . .'

'Of course,' Simmy says. 'Even just the slightest possibility is worth it.' He fumbles in his pocket and hands her something. 'Listen, take this. Take my car.'

She sees Simmy's car keys lying in her hand. 'Sim, it's fine – I can catch a cab.'

'No. It's parked outside.' He curls her fingers around the keys. 'Take it.'

She nods and slides them into her pocket. 'Thank you,' she says.

'Don't mention it.'

They arrive at the landing.

'Ted?' Elina says. She hesitates at the open door to their bedroom. A trapezoid of light lies on the carpet, a single blue sock at its centre, like an actor in a spotlight.

'Ted?' she says again.

He is lying in bed, the duvet draped over his body. He is curled up, facing the wall.

'Ted, Simmy's here.'

The hunched shape in the bed does not move.

'Did you hear me?' Elina says. 'Simmy's come to see you. Ted? How are you feeling?' She glances back at Simmy.

He steps forward. 'Ted,' he says, 'it's me. Listen, Elina's popping out so I've come to keep you company. I've got magazines, I've got newspapers, I've got snacks, I've even got a six-hundred-page novel about convicts up my sleeve, so we're not going to be bored.' He lowers his bulk into a chair. 'Shall we start with the convicts? Or would you prefer a little light reading on the state of the economy?' Without waiting for an answer, he opens the novel and begins to read aloud, in a sonorous, fake-Australian accent.

Elina waits a moment longer, then leans over Ted and kisses him. His eyes are closed and the stubble on his face feels sharp against her lips. ''Bye,' she whispers. 'Won't be long.'

The floor in the hall of the house in Myddleton Square is tiled with blue and white octagons. They spread from the door, from the mat, all the way past the stairs, a geometric expanse, a Cubist impression of light on water.

Several of the tiles near the bottom of the stairs are cracked, in a wavering line. This often makes Margot frown. She has talked about replacing them but has never got around to it. They were repaired, under the auspices of Gloria, in the late sixties, with glue and polish. But these fixings have since worked themselves loose and they rattle slightly if stepped on.

It was on them – or at least near them – that Innes was standing when he returned home from his internment in Germany and looked up the stairs to see a man in his father's dressing-gown. The man demanded, 'Who the hell are you?' and as Innes stood there on the loose, cracked tiles, he realised his marriage was over, that his life was about to take another unexpected turn.

It was Innes who damaged the tiles, although none of the current residents of the house know this. On a wet day in the late 1920s, a seven-year-old Innes stole a metal tray from the kitchen and carried it all the way up to the top of the stairs and proceeded to toboggan down, skidding over the carpet, from landing to landing, riding the swells and troughs of the stairs, until he arrived with a resounding crash in the hallway. The impact of the edge of the tray with the Victorian tiles caused a long, snaking crack; Innes hurtled forward to collide with the sharp corner of a coat rack. His screams brought Consuela running from the kitchen, brought his mother down from the drawing room above. There was a lot of blood on the tiles that day, red among the blue and white. He had to have two stitches in his forehead and there would be a small, vertical scar there for the rest of his life.

The octagonal tiles go past the cloakroom, in which Elina had her recent problems with Jonah, and end at the door to the basement. The steps here are twisting, narrow and dim – one of the bulbs blew last week and Felix, in true Felix fashion, has not yet got around to replacing it or, indeed, even noticing it.

Down in the kitchen, a tap is dripping, beads of water falling into the porcelain sink with a quiet *plic* sound. *Plic,* it says, insistent, steady, *plic.* The noise is enough to distract the person in the room.

Gloria has been parked in her wheelchair at the patio doors. A carer from the council comes in every morning to get her up and give her breakfast; after this she wheels her here to 'get some sun'. Gloria sits with her head bent, her eyes directed towards the bright metal of her chair armrests. She sits in the place where her daughter stood with Theo on a morning a long time ago, watching Felix set alight a bonfire at the bottom of the garden. The carer brushed Gloria's hair this morning and her scalp still tingles with the sensation of the bristles, and the noise of the tap is confusing her, setting her thoughts off their tracks: she is thinking about a telegram arriving, the boy coming to the door and saying, a telegram for you, missis – *PLIC* – she is thinking about a teapot her mother gave her, beautiful it was, with gilt around its rim; the gilt wore off, of course, because the daily would insist on washing it with a scourer – *PLIC* – she is thinking about a day trip they took to Clacton, before he went off to war, the sky looking as though it threatened rain and he said, as he held her hand, what was it, a chiaroscuro sky, she'd had to look it up later—

Gloria has been down here for a long time on her own. Not that she has much concept of time, these days. But where are the other inhabitants of the house today? The garden is empty. The swing seat sways to and fro vacantly. The surface of the pond holds a section of sky. The trees extend their branches stiffly and at their ends the leaves are crisp and curling.

A clock upstairs strikes midday; seconds later another answers it, at a higher pitch.

In the drawing room, Margot is sitting in a chair near the window. She doesn't know this but it is the chair Ferdinanda used to favour for doing her embroidery: a Georgian nursing chair, armless, with a low seat and dainty, fluted legs. It has since been re-covered, by Gloria, in a rather unbecoming tomato-red velvet. It sits, by chance, very close to the place Ferdinanda used to have it – angled towards the window, towards the light.

Margot has been crying, on and off, all morning, in different locations about the house. She sits now, surrounded by a litter of tissues, her head leaning on her arm. She is still crying and has assumed the shuddering, swollen-faced aspect of someone worn out by grief.

Two floors above her, past the bedrooms, and up into the attic, is the noise of someone moving heavy boxes around, shifting furniture. Someone is conducting a search. A crash, a thud, the sound of someone swearing, a pause, then another thud.

Margot sobs, tweaks another tissue from the box, blows her nose, sobs again, then stops, drawing in a sharp breath. Felix is standing in the doorway. He is holding an ancient, dusty typewriter in his hands.

'Felix,' Margot says unsteadily, 'that's mine.'

'No, it's not.'

'It belonged to my father. Mother said so and—'

'It was Lexie's. I know it was.'

'Yes, but, you see—'

'What about everything else?' Felix says, in a voice so quiet she has to strain to hear him, and Margot knows that voice. It's the one he used to employ in interviews with particularly slippery politicians – icily calm, insidiously polite. It's the voice that said to them, and the nation: I've got you and you're not going to get away. It's the voice that made him famous, all those years ago.

And now he's using it to her. Margot swallows, tears rising in her eyes again. 'What do you mean?' she says, trying to rally herself.

'You know what I mean,' he says, still in tones of Arctic courtesy. 'Lexie's stuff. Where is it?'

'What stuff?' she blusters, but she knows he's got her and she knows he knows.

'Her clothes, her books, her things from the flat. The letters Laurence wrote to Ted, before he died.' He lists these things with infinite patience. 'All the stuff I cleared out of her flat and put in the attic.'

Margot shrugs and shakes her head at the same time. She reaches for another tissue.

Felix puts down the typewriter. He advances towards her. 'Are you telling me,' he murmurs, 'that it's gone?'

Margot holds the tissue to her face. 'I . . . I don't know.'

'This is unbelievable,' he says, and his tone has moved up a notch or two in volume. She'd forgotten that this is where the voice goes next – strident, domineering, in for the kill. 'Unbelievable. It's gone, hasn't it? You and your bitch of a mother got rid of it all. Behind my back.'

'Don't shout,' she whimpers, even though she knows he isn't shouting, that Felix never shouts, never needs to.

'Tell me,' he says, standing above her. 'Did you throw everything out?'

'Felix, I really—'

'Just give me a simple answer. Yes or no. Did you throw it out?'

'I will not be bullied like this—'

'Yes or no, Margot.'

'Please stop.'

'Come on. If you're brave enough to do it, you're brave enough to say it. Say, "Yes, I threw it out. All of it."'

There is silence in the room. Margot picks at the skin around her nails, discards a tissue on the floor.

Felix turns and walks to the window. 'You realise,' he says to the glass, 'that Elina is coming? That I asked her to come. I told her we had all Lexie's things up in the attic. That we'd give them to Ted and he could look through them. The least we could do, I said. You realise she's coming here to collect it and you,' he turns to her, 'have gone and thrown it out.'

Margot begins a fresh bout of sobbing. 'I'm sorry,' she wails, 'I didn't mean to . . . I . . .'

'You're sorry. You didn't mean to,' Felix repeats. 'I'll tell Ted that, shall I? Margot didn't mean to throw out all your dead mother's things but she did anyway. Dear God,' he spits, 'Elina will be here any minute. You'll have to tell her that all we've got is an old typewriter and some dusty paintings, and you can tell her why as well—'

Margot half rises from the chair. 'Those paintings are mine, Felix,' she begins. 'They were never Lexie's. They were mine all along. I took what belonged to me and—'

'Spare me your petty, avaricious—' Felix stops. The doorbell is ringing downstairs.

Felix opens the door to the street. Elina stands on the step. She is, as ever, dressed in an ensemble of extraordinary clothes: a long, loose cloth thing with hems that are ripped and fraying. Purple tights. Paint-stained sneakers on her feet. Jonah is in a sling on her front, like a small marsupial. He is awake, his eyes wide with astonishment, and when he sees Felix his face breaks into a delighted smile. Which is more than can be said for his mother.

'Elina,' Felix says, standing back to allow her to step inside, 'how are you, my darling?'

'I'm . . .' She shrugs, avoiding his eyes. 'You know.'

'Thank you so much for coming.'

She shrugs again. 'I don't have much time. I have to get back.'

Felix realises at this point that he usually greets Ted's girlfriend, the mother of his grandchild, with a kiss on the cheek. But it seems too late to give it now.

'Yes, of course.' Felix clenches and unclenches his hands. He finds it often helps him think. 'So, how is he?'

'Not good.'

'Still in bed, is he?'

'Yes.'

Felix swears, very softly, then says, 'Sorry.'

'It's OK.'

'Would you . . . would you give him a message for me?'

'Of course.'

'Tell him . . .' He hesitates. He is acutely aware of the presence of Margot, a floor above him, and that of Gloria, a floor below. 'Tell him I'm sorry,' he says. 'I'm truly sorry. For all of it. Tell him . . . tell him it wasn't my idea. And that I never agreed with it.' He sighs. 'They cooked it up between them and I . . . It sounds pathetic, I know. I should have made a stand at the time, but I didn't and I must take responsibility for that. It was a terrible, terrible mistake. And . . . and tell him I'd like to see him. Whenever he's ready. Tell him to call me. Please.'

She inclines her head. 'I will.'

Felix carries on. He finds he cannot stop speaking now that he has started. He finds himself saying things about Lexie, about how they met, about the night he picked up Theo in Lyme Regis, about how he got into an argument with Robert Lowe at the police station and a policeman had to come tell them to keep it down, to think of the boy, please, gents. At one point, he is clutching Elina's arm and telling her that he loved Lexie, like no one else, that he made mistakes, yes, but that she was the love of his life, does she hear him, does she understand? Elina listens with a kind of doubtful intensity. She looks down at the tiled floor of the hallway. She runs the toe of her sneaker, stained red with paint, over the cracks. And then Felix tells her that the things have gone. Been thrown out. That there's nothing. Nothing for Ted.

Elina looks straight at Felix, shaking her fringe out of her eyes. Then she says, 'Nothing?'

Jonah chooses this moment to start to yell. He struggles and shouts in his sling, arching his back, his face reddening. Elina jigs up and down. She makes soothing, clicking noises at him. She unstraps him from the sling and hoists him to her shoulder.

'There's a typewriter. And some pictures.'

Elina is rubbing her hand up and down Jonah's back. She is turned away from him, still jigging up and down in the way that women with babies have. Jonah's cries are subsiding. He looks at Felix over his mother's shoulder with an expression of injured outrage. Sorry, Felix wants to say, I'm sorry. He is filled with an urge to apologise to all of them, one by one.

'I can show you,' he says instead. 'Come up.'

He and Elina and Jonah go up the first flight of stairs. There on the landing sits the typewriter. It is clogged with dust, the ribbon dried and flimsy. Looking at it gives Felix a feeling close to vertigo. He realises he can replicate in his head the exact sound it used to make. The clac-clac-a-clac of the metal letters hitting the paper, the ribbon raising itself each time to make the impression. The machine-gun fire of it, when the work was going well. The stops and pauses when it wasn't, to allow for a sigh, a draw on a cigarette. The ding every time the carriage reached its limit. The whirr as the page was snatched out, then the rolling ratcheting as a new one was wound in.

He looks away from it. He clears his throat. 'And these are the pictures. I think I found all of them. There might be a couple more around but I can always—'

Elina astonishes him by handing him the baby.

'Oh,' Felix says. Jonah dangles there, hoisted by his armpits in Felix's hands. His feet circle each other, as if he's riding an imaginary bike. He looks at a point above Felix's hair, at Felix's ear, down at the ground; he tips back his head to check the ceiling.

'Jubba jubba whee,' Jonah says.

'Right,' Felix says, 'old chap.'

Elina is wiping her hands on her cloth dress. She is crouching beside the pictures stacked up against the wall. She looks at the outermost one – a jumble of triangles in murky colours, Felix has never liked it much – eases it forward and looks at the next, then the next, then the next. She is frowning the whole time, as if displeased. Perhaps, Felix thinks, she doesn't much want these dusty old things in her house, but then he'd have thought that she might have shown a bit of interest, painting being her thing, after all, and—

She astonishes him again by saying: 'I can't take these.'

'But, my darling, you must.' Felix is firm. 'They are rightfully Ted's. They belonged to Lexie. They hung in the flat where, you know, he lived when—'

'No,' Elina interrupts. 'I mean I can't take them.'

Felix looks at her, perplexed. She has, he's always thought, unusually large eyes, set into that pale, pierrot face of hers. They look larger than ever in the dim light of the landing. 'Sweetie, I'm afraid

I don't follow you. They were Lexie's pictures. They are now Ted's. He may want them.'

'Do you have any idea . . .' She stops. She puts a hand to her forehead. 'Felix, these paintings are extremely valuable.'

'Are they?'

'Beyond valuable. I have no real idea what they're worth but they ought to be . . . I don't know . . . somewhere. In the Tate. In a gallery.'

'No,' Felix says. 'I want Ted to have them. They're his.'

She rubs her hand over her face, seems to think. 'I understand,' she says. 'I understand why you want that. But . . . the thing is . . . it's not as if we can . . .' For a few seconds, she lapses into a foreign language, Finnish, he supposes, muttering something under her breath, turning towards the pictures, then away. 'I can't take them now, anyway,' she says again.

'But—'

'Felix, I can't just sling them into the boot of Simmy's car. Please understand. These are . . . They need proper crates and packaging. Insurance. We need a qualified art transporter.'

'We do?'

'Yes. I can get you the number of someone, if you like. I just don't know . . .' she leans out and takes the baby from him '. . . I don't know what Ted will think about this.' She looks at her son. She straightens his hat. 'I should go,' she murmurs.

Felix walks with her down the stairs, out of the front door and into the sharp sunshine of the street. As she buckles the baby into his carrier, Felix places the typewriter on the passenger seat.

They face each other on the pavement.

'Tell him,' Felix says, 'tell him . . .'

She nods. 'I will.'

'And you'll get me the number of a transporter person?'

She nods again.

Felix reaches forward and kisses her first on one cheek and then the other. 'Thank you,' he mutters.

She responds by putting her arms around his neck and giving him a hug of surprising intensity. He is so taken aback by this that he feels sudden tears rising in his throat. He has to hang on to the thin frame of his son's girlfriend as they stand there in the early-autumn sun; he has to close his eyes to the glare.

He carries the impression of her touch at the back of his neck, around his shoulders, long after she has got into the car and after she has driven away around the corner. Felix stands on the pavement, staring at the spot at which her tail-lights disappeared, as if waiting for her to return, as if not wanting to break the spell.

Elina sits in traffic on Pentonville Road. The cars ahead of her stretch out like a glacier of chrome and glass. Tributaries of traffic wait at crossroads to join the line. She glances back at Jonah, who has fallen asleep, his thumb held slackly in his mouth. She switches on the radio but the only sound that comes out is the lonely blizzarding of static. She twiddles various knobs for a while and occasionally she finds the blip and peep of a voice, struggling to make itself heard through the storm. But nothing more. She turns it off. She glances across the car at the typewriter. She takes her hand off the wheel and touches its metal casing. She runs her fingertips over the keys, along the roller, into the dip where the letter struts wait for instruction. She looks back at the road, at the traffic-lights turning pointlessly from red to amber to green and back again. She looks again at the typewriter; she glances back at Jonah; she watches the branches of a plane tree caught in the wind, the leaves released, showering down on top of the cars. One falls to her windscreen, right in front of her face, and as she stares at it, its webbed veins, its waxy greenness, its stiff stem, an idea comes to her.

Elina checks her watch. She rummages in her bag and brings out her mobile phone. She rings Simmy. 'How is he?' she asks. 'Can you stay for a bit longer?' Then she indicates, wheels the car around and drives into an empty road.

She is away for several hours. She has been so absorbed in what she's been doing that she's got a parking ticket, which she crams into her bag. When she gets back, the house is silent. It feels as if she's been away for days, weeks, instead of hours. With her bag still slung across her body and Jonah on her hip, she climbs the stairs. 'Hello?' she calls. 'I'm back.'

Simmy is waiting at the top.

'How is everything?' she whispers to him.

'Fine. He's been asleep but I think he's awake now. I was just about to go down and make a cup of tea. You go in.'

Elina comes into the bedroom. Ted is lying in bed, much as he was when she left him, the duvet draped over his body. He is curled up, facing the wall.

'Ted?' she says. 'Sorry – I was longer than I thought. How have you been? It's a beautiful day out there.'

She sits down on the bed. She puts Jonah on the floor with his favourite wooden rattle.

'Ted,' she says. She knows he's not asleep. She can tell by the shallowness of his breathing. But he doesn't move.

She climbs further on to the bed, dragging the bag with her.

'You know what?' she says, laying a hand on his side. 'I've found out that's not really your name. She called you something different.'

She waits. He doesn't answer but she can tell he's listening. She delves into her bag and brings out a sheaf of paper. 'I've been to the newspaper archives. It was amazing – they were so helpful. I found out all sorts of things,' she spreads the papers out on the bed and shuffles through them. 'Lexie was an art critic. She wrote articles about Picasso, Hopper, Jasper Johns, Giacometti. She knew Francis Bacon and Lucian Freud. And John Deakin – that whole group. She interviewed Yves Klein and Eugene Fitzgerald and Salvador Dalí. She had dinner with Andy Warhol in New York. Did you hear that? Andy Warhol. And . . .' Elina shuffles though the papers, looking for a certain article '. . . she was out in Vietnam at one point. Can you believe that? There's one here about life in Saigon during the war. Somewhere. I can't find it now. Maybe that's how she knew your dad. You could ask him, I suppose. Anyway, she wrote hundreds and hundreds of articles. And I've got some of them here. For you. Ted? Do you want to see them? Look.' She picks up a sheaf and, leaning over his prone form, places them next to his face. His eyes, she sees, are shut. His lips look dry and cracked, as if it's been a long time since he drank anything. From downstairs, there comes the noise of Simmy moving about in the kitchen, a kettle being filled, water rushing through pipes.

'Ted?' she says again and she hears in her voice that she might cry so has to take a deep breath. 'This one has a photo of her, on a balcony. Do you see? In Florence, it says. Look. She's older there than in that other photo. Ted, please look.' Elina lays her cheek on his arm. 'Please.'

She sits up and riffles through the papers again. 'You know what else?' Tears are falling now, to make dark, transparent circles on the photocopies. She dashes them from her face, scrubs at her cheeks with her sleeve. 'She wrote about you.'

Elina finds the pages she wants – she remembers now that she pinned them together specially at the archive place. 'She did a column called "From the Frontline of Motherhood".' She takes a deep breath. 'It's about you. Do you want to hear?'

She sees his arm twitch and she watches, breath held. Will he move? Will he speak? The hand reaches up and scratches the back of his head. But he says nothing.

'This is the first one,' Elina says. 'I put them in order. Listen. "As I write, my son lies sleeping across the room. He has been alive two hundred and fifteen days. He and I live together in one room. He has three teeth and two names: Theodore, which is what health visitors call him, and Theo, which is what I call him."

'Did you hear that?' Elina lowers the papers. She takes his hand. 'She called you Theo.'

His body stirs beneath the sheets. He twists his head from one side to the other. His eyes, she sees, are open. Then she feels a pressure on her hand and he speaks his first words for a week. 'Keep going, El,' he says, 'keep going.'

And so she does.

Acknowledgements

I could not have written this book without the help and encouragement of several people. My heartfelt thanks to:

William Sutcliffe
Victoria Hobbs
Mary-Anne Harrington
Jenna Johnson
Françoise Triffaux
Susan O'Farrell
Daisy Donovan
Bridget O'Farrell
Ruth Metzstein

I am also indebted to the following books: *Soho in the Fifties and Sixties* by Jonathan Fryer (National Portrait Gallery Publications, 1998); *Never Had It So Good: A History of Britain from Suez to the Beatles* by Dominic Sandbrook (Abacus, 2005).